BRING ME BACK

KAREN BOOTH

BRING ME BACK

Copyright © 2013 by Karen Booth

All rights reserved.

Cover image licensed from Deposit Photos.

❀ Created with Vellum

For Steve, Emily, and Ryan.
With you, my world is a beautiful place.

FOREWORD

March 7ᵗʰ, 1986

    Dear Diary,

    Scott from next door gave me a ride home from school today because I missed the bus again. (I know, I know. Big surprise.) I was kind of excited since he has his own car, but he was such a creep when we got home. He asked me about Banks Forest, which he knows I love because everybody knows they're my favorite band. I told him how I can't wait to see Banks Forest in concert and he put his hand on my boob. I told him he was gross and he got all mad and said I shouldn't dress like Madonna if I don't want boys to grab my boobs. He's such an idiot. I haven't dressed like Madonna since 9ᵗʰ grade.

    Speaking of Banks Forest, (when am I not?), I rearranged my BF posters after school. I figured out that if I put the best poster of Christopher Penman (the medium sized one, without his shirt) on the wall next to my closet, it looks like he's lying next to me in bed if I'm on my side and squint my left eye. What a babe. I look at him and I just want to die. Why can't he go to my school? Wouldn't that be amazing? If he was a senior, but still a super famous rock star and he was my boyfriend. The mean girls would hate me even more than they already do. My life would be perfect. I wonder if there's any way I will ever meet Christopher. There has to be some reason that he and I are both on planet earth at the same time. It just doesn't seem like that would be totally random.

XO

Claire

P.S. Only 27 days until Banks Forest live and I get to see Christopher Penman in the flesh! We will be in the same place, breathing the same air.

CHAPTER ONE

Twenty-two years later

AFTER AN EXTRA-LONG MORNING RUN, also known as procrastination, I plopped down at my creaky desk and picked up the phone to call my dad. It was a task I'd put off for two days, even when I knew that every minute I delayed was only ammunition for him to guilt me about not staying in touch. The voicemail tone buzzed in my ear and I cursed myself for waiting so long. *Crap. He beat me to it.*

There were two messages, fewer than ten minutes apart, both from Patrick Collins, senior music editor at *Rolling Stone*. I'd long had the nagging suspicion that Patrick was humoring me, which made the desperation in his voice seem more like a practical joke than a plea for help. He'd never, in all my years of pushing for more than a token assignment, wanted a call back ASAP.

"Claire," he answered, before I'd heard a single ring. "I've been trying you for an hour."

"I went for a run. What's up?"

"Another writer pulled out of an interview that's scheduled

for Monday. Are you available? I'd need you here in New York."

I flipped through my planner, hoping the sound of rustling paper would make it seem as if I was impossibly busy and therefore, in demand. "I'd have to find someone to stay with my daughter for the night. Who's the interview with?"

"Christopher Penman, from Banks Forest."

I nearly choked on my own breath. "He agreed to an interview?" A long-forgotten hum surged through me, dotting my arms with goose bumps. "You've got to be kidding. He hates writers." Everything I'd ever thought or read or seen of Christopher Penman brewed a frothy chaos in my head. "Really, really hates writers."

Patrick cleared his throat. "I think he's hoping for some good publicity. He's got a new record coming out."

I knew there had to be a catch—a new solo album. His first outing without his band had been an unlistenable flop, panned by everyone, even me.

"It'll be the cover if you can get him to talk," Patrick continued.

"The cover?" I'd been dying for Patrick to give me a real assignment, but a cover? The adage about things that are too good to be true didn't merely spring to mind, it set off sirens in my head.

"Yes, the cover, but I need an answer now." He clicked a pen at his usual neurotic pace. "You know, you're always begging me for something meaty."

Meaty? You have no idea. "Let me think." *Would I be able to form coherent sentences? Would I remember how to put one foot in front of the other without making an ass of myself?*

"Don't take this the wrong way, but I need someone with your experience. We both know that you'll have to ask some uncomfortable questions. I don't see him trusting one of the younger writers."

"Oh, okay." *I'm thirty-nine. When did I become one of the older writers?*

"I could really use you."

This will never work. "Yes, of course. I'll do it."

"Great." He blew out a breath. "I trust that you know this is a big deal, Claire."

Thank you for the understatement of the millennium. "Yes. I'm well aware of what I'm up against." *The question is whether I will survive it. Or him.*

"And you understand that I need you to ask those difficult questions, right? We need the whole story. Every last sensitive subject."

"Yes. Got it." *Every last unbelievable drop.*

"Okay, then. Christopher Penman is all yours."

I hung up to silence, or perhaps I hadn't noticed in all of the confusion that my brain had swelled and plugged up my ears.

Oh. My. God. Christopher. Penman.

I was seventeen when I fell ass over teakettle for Mr. Penman—madly, deeply in love. He was the dreamiest guy in the world—tall and handsome in a skinny boyish way, although there'd been no question that he was a grown man. He had a scrubby head of copper-brown hair, perfect for digging fingers into, and his bright white smile came as a flash, potent enough to melt me into a puddle, quivering and eager to surrender. I squandered embarrassing amounts of time gazing at pictures of him, captivated by his freakishly green eyes.

I'd been a devoted fan of his band, Banks Forest, and spent hours every day in my bedroom, high on ditz and hormones, listening to their music. My preoccupation coincided with a few sub-par report cards, but I'd felt that homework time was better spent writing my married name, Claire Louise Penman, in my best cursive. My dad had made no effort to understand me at all. My argument that he should encourage my appreciation of the arts never seemed to get me anywhere.

Christopher was my respite at a time when boys were a constant disappointment. He was the ultimate imaginary boyfriend, fiery and intense during the dreamy liaisons I concocted in my head, with an uncanny ability to satisfy my every need, emotional and physical. Although I had far less real-life experience than I would have liked, Christopher taught me everything I needed to know and I was a quick study under his skilled tutelage. He was always tender afterward, making me laugh and telling me that I was the most incredible girl in the world. Everything about our illusory love story had been perfect; no-birth-control-necessary sex on a puffy cloud.

Of course, Monday would be anything but a day-dreamy frolic through cumulonimbus. Agreeing to interview Christopher Penman was the professional equivalent of jumping out of an airplane with a second-hand chute. He was notorious for his secrecy and he hated the media, writers and photographers at the top of the list. You couldn't blame the guy. He'd suffered through years of rumors and innuendo about his private life, drugs, and his nightmare of an ex-wife. I wasn't being sent in to help his situation at all. Despite what Christopher's agenda might be, nobody would care about the new solo record. People would only want to know if the filthy personal stuff was true.

———

My cranky Volvo station wagon wasn't a grand statement about individuality, it was more a product of my finances, but it had helped me stubbornly dodge the modern definition of suburban mom for years. Granted, I would have needed a husband to fully participate in that stereotype. Lining up behind the minivans at school, at least I could take comfort in the fact that I had resisted the temptation to assimilate.

My darling Sam, flanked by her best friend Leah, sauntered through the double doors, Sam's buoyant blonde curls responding in time to every step. The pair was a flurry of conversation, but came to a halt the instant a pack of boys crossed their path. A seemingly undernourished boy in baggy-butt jeans stopped to talk and the girls smiled in gleaming white, long enough for their lips to stick to their teeth.

Sam was a junior, recently seventeen. Knowing we had only two more summers together before she went off to college was more than a thorn in my side—it made me queasy. I'd felt too young to become a mom at twenty-two and now I was unquestionably too young to live out my days in a nest for one.

"Hey, Mom," Sam said as she climbed into the passenger seat. "Can I sleep over at Leah's tonight?"

Leah waited at the curb, cheeks turning red from the blustery March day. She granted me half of a wave as she checked her cell phone.

"Sure, honey." Another Friday night alone, but at least I could work on my Christopher Penman interview without the motherly guilt.

Sam gave Leah thumbs up and slammed her door.

"How'd the English test go?" I asked. A mom in an Escalade, yelling at her brood to get in the damn car, blocked my escape from the car circle. I considered laying on the horn, but decided I didn't dare risk my already tenuous social status with the PTA.

"It was fine," Sam said. She took a piece of gum from her backpack and crumpled the wrapper before dropping it in the cup holder. "I think I did okay, but I won't find out until next week."

"How was the rest of your day?" I asked, turning out of the

school parking lot. Whenever I could convince Sam to take a ride home after school, that ten-minutes was a gift, a veritable parental goldmine. She found my thirst for knowledge less menacing when it was acceptable to avoid eye contact and I, happily, deflected the title of grand inquisitor.

"Okay." Her deep blue eyes found mine for an instant. "Remember Andrew Mills? He hung out with Leah and me at lunch for a while. I forgot how funny he is."

"Gotta love a funny guy." I regretted my choice of words as soon as they left my mouth. Any enthusiasm on my part might sour her opinion of the unsuspecting Andrew.

"He's cuter since he got his braces off. He started a band with some guys from school. They're practicing this weekend."

I was a predictable sucker for any guy in a band when I was Sam's age, which made me assume that Andrew would be a shoe-in, but I didn't push the subject once we got to the house— our cute and tidy, albeit tired, nod to a normal life—white with faded black shutters.

I'd purchased the house when I moved to North Carolina and Sam was a baby. The down payment had come as an uncharacteristically lavish birthday gift from my dad. I'd feigned refusal, but he insisted that my mom, if she'd been alive, would've wanted it that way.

Once inside our Fifties-era kitchen that I'd decided long ago was retro and not run-down, Sam rummaged through the fridge. Her cell phone buzzed and I caught her fighting a smile.

"Change in plans?" I flipped through the mail and set aside several letters for her from far-off schools.

"No. It's, um..." She beamed at her phone. "It's Andrew. He wants me to watch his band practice tomorrow."

"Sounds like fun. I'll drive you. I haven't talked to his mom since our book club imploded." I hadn't laid eyes on Andrew in two years. A reconnaissance mission was in order.

"Mom, please. Can't I take the car by myself?"

"No way. I'm still recovering from the trip to the grocery store last weekend." I caught her reaction and reminded myself that the eye roll was nothing personal. "I'll be in my office. Let me know when we need to leave."

I had an hour until Sam would need a ride to her sleepover, so I tucked one leg under the other, typed "Christopher Penman" in my browser's search box, and settled in for the start of what would likely be a sedentary weekend. The official Banks Forest website had what I'd expected, a discography and a time-line, details I'd memorized long ago. There were hundreds of old photos too, including the quintessential shot of the band, Christopher with his shirt blown open by a tropical breeze to reveal what made a perfunctory appearance in every video Banks Forest made—his smooth, broad chest.

That image in particular was as familiar as my own family photos, the shots of my sister Julie and me at the Grand Canyon, both of us wearing striped orange and brown tank tops and khaki safari shorts. Julie had her lustrous golden hair in braids, but Mom made me wear my dishwater blonde in pigtails. She'd spared us the tube socks, but otherwise dressed us like boys, a hippie theory of hers about not forcing gender rules.

The Christopher Penman website was next, complete with a scheme of smoke and mirrors to prop up his first solo outing. In the interest of journalistic thoroughness, I carefully studied every image of him in the photo gallery. I'd forgotten how sublimely his well-made jaw paired with the mole on his left cheek.

The search results that followed were an ocean of muck: fan pages, gossipy entertainment sites and links to tabloid articles. I was already at a disadvantage; I'd only sporadically witnessed the more dubious years of Christopher's public life. Banks Forest had released the first of their two "Best of" albums well after I was out of college and they were no longer legitimate in my burgeoning music writer brain. He seemed to embrace every Rock 'n' Roll cliché during that time, much of it captured quite poignantly by the paparazzi. He and his then wife even made a couple's trip to rehab.

"Mom?" Sam popped her head into my office with a bulging purple duffel bag over her shoulder. "Come on, let's go. We decided to catch a movie. Leah hates it if we miss the previews."

Sam and I ducked through icy rain, tiny pellets hitting the back of my neck as we dashed to the car. The Volvo's heat refused to kick in and I was forced to steer with my knee while warming my hands in my jacket pockets.

"Mom, please drive like a normal person," Sam begged, as if she had any business criticizing someone else's driving.

"Oh, sorry." I shook my head to clear it, placing my hands on the wheel. "So, honey, I need to fly to New York on Monday morning to do an interview. Do you think you can stay with Leah?"

She clucked her tongue on the roof of her mouth. "I'm old enough to stay by myself."

"But I'll be so far away. What if you need me?" I glanced over and wondered if she'd gotten taller since that morning.

She wagged her cell phone in the air. "I know how to order a pizza. I'll be fine. I won't get any homework done if I stay with Leah." Sam was much more responsible than I'd ever been. Her guidance counselor had said she'd likely have her pick of schools. The trick would be whether I'd ever find a way to pay for any of them.

"Okay. If you say so."

"Who are you interviewing?"

A stupid smile crossed my face, not my usual reaction to most work assignments. "Um, Christopher Penman. He was the guitarist in a British band called Banks Forest. They were my favorite band when I was your age."

"I know Banks Forest! Leah made me an '80s mix CD with some of their songs on it. Is he, like, really old now?"

"No," I huffed. "He's only five years older than me. I think he's even better looking now than when he was younger."

"So, that's who you were drooling over on the computer."

"I wasn't drooling." I crinkled my lips. "It's called research."

She pretended to stick her finger down her throat. "You're such a bad liar."

———

AFTER HOURS at the computer that night, leftovers seemed appropriate while I suffered through the last half of a mindless romantic comedy on cable, all about a scatterbrained woman finding true love with the bookish, yet ruggedly handsome, guy working in the next cubicle.

It had been six months since the end of my most recent romantic comedy, with Kevin, a fellow music writer who lived in LA. I should have recognized that we were doomed from the start. I'd never been able to make the long-distance thing work, especially not with a daughter at home.

I hated myself for being drawn to him at all—he was hopelessly cocky about his writing ability, which he tempered by falsely dismissing his good looks. My only excuse was that he'd had a soft spot for me and that had been hard to resist. There were even times when I wondered if being with Kevin was what being in love felt like. Not that it mattered. Love or not, I fell out of it after learning he had a soft spot for several other women, too.

I'd tried and failed at love so many times that I'd often wondered if I was too picky, but my boyfriend wish-list was only designed to weed out the really bad ones. I didn't need the world. All I ever wanted was funny, smart, tall, employed, patient, non-judgmental, good kisser, able dishwasher, music fan, reader, and a healthy libido. Maybe I would never find a man who could send flowers and be monogamous, but I had to keep trying.

The movie credits rolled and I stretched and turned off the TV. I stalked up the stairs to my room, still reeling from the idea of what was going to happen on Monday. Of course, meeting Christopher Penman wasn't going to play out as I'd once imagined. We were not being brought together by some magical, romantic set of events. This assignment was more about dumb luck, even if I'd worked my butt off for years for a cover story this big.

Perhaps my luck wouldn't end up being dumb—maybe I'd nail the interview and still manage to nab a stolen moment with Christopher. I'd dreamt of the latter countless times—a laugh or a smile, a blissful instant of flirtation—it wouldn't need to be much to last me a lifetime. Although, no matter what happened on Monday, I'd surely be left wanting more.

CHAPTER TWO

PATRICK'S ASSISTANT had arranged for a car to pick me up at LaGuardia airport and the driver greeted me with a funny brush of a moustache and a dry-erase sign with my name on it. I focused on the one positive thing I could come up with to keep my mind from settling on the idiotic enormity of what I was about to do. At least I was on the ground.

I'd planned to use the time in the car to go over my notes but found myself hopelessly distracted by the city—the commotion, a busy tempo unlike any other place. I used to say that I wished I lived in New York, but that seemed like an empty statement now. I'd never really wished it; I'd only thought it sounded like something a music writer should do.

Forcing myself to return to interview preparation, all I could do was agonize over the sequence of my questions. Three hours was a very small window in which to earn Christopher's trust and get him to do the improbable—betray his biggest secrets, on the record. I had to ease him into things carefully, but quickly.

The car arrived at The Hotel Rivington on the Lower East Side before I could complete my last minute cramming. It was a bizarre looking building—a modern grid of steel and glass, a colorless Mondrian skirted by Brownstones, the site of the inter-view and my home for the next twenty-four hours.

The driver held my door open and I slipped him a five. "Thank you, Ms. Abby," he said, as I nearly tripped over the curb.

Bitter cold whipped between the buildings, gripping my shoulders and sending a chill through me as the doorman rushed to let me in. There was no time for my eyes to adjust from late morning on the street to the softly lit lobby before my surroundings faded and my vision focused on a point. The image ahead left me considering an abrupt turn on my heel and a swift escape.

There he sat, no more than ten yards away, reading the *New York Times* while wearing silvery sunglasses. I decided he must be napping because he didn't strike me as the type to read the *Times*.

He wore an artfully distressed pair of jeans and a black t-shirt under a tan canvas jacket, much too light for such a cold day. His short, chestnut brown hair was arranged into a tousled mess.

I mulled over my best approach and then he confounded me a second time by looking up and making eye contact, through the sunglasses no less, folding his paper and striding toward me. I looked behind me assuming he must recognize someone else.

"You must be Ms. Abby." He held out his hand. "Chris Penman."

Countless thoughts and questions erupted in my head. *Wow. I'm glad I wore heels. He's tall. His accent is different in person. It's like butter. British butter. Did I remember perfume this morning? Oh crap. My breath. I should have had a piece of gum in the car. Are my hands clammy? Why do they always get that way when I'm nervous?*

"Yes. Oh, Claire." I offered my sweaty hand. "Please. Thank

you. Hi." Cotton candy had graciously stepped in to take over for my saddled brain.

"Oh great, uh, it's Claire then." He cocked his head to the side. "Please, call me Chris. I Googled you this morning and found a photo. I like to know what I'm up against." He chuckled, removed his sunglasses and shook my hand in one seamless movement.

I caught a glimpse of his eyes and everything turned syrupy. I began searching for words, an intelligent response, and it happened—I became tangled up in his eyes, drawn into them because my mind was convinced there was nowhere else to go. The color was so astounding it deserved its own name. Calling them "green" would have been flat-out dismissive. It couldn't begin to capture the hypnotic nature of the hue. Apple, forest, grass, jade, emerald, moss, clover—somewhere, there had to be a name for his green.

Christopher duly noted my disorientation and nudged the day ahead. "Shall we?" he asked, motioning for the lobby door.

"I'm sorry. I thought we were doing the interview in the hotel," I pleaded as I shuffled along with him.

"If it's all the same to you, I was hoping to skip that. A bit contrived, isn't it?"

"Uh, sure." I stopped. "I need to check my bag..." My voice feathered away.

"Here." He plucked my overnight bag from my hand and marched it to the front desk. "Please hold this for Ms. Abby. She'll be checking in later." He returned in a flash. "Better?" He towered over me, seeming annoyed.

"Yes. Thank you. Where are we going?"

He didn't bother with an answer, but instead sent a profusion of warmth over me by hovering his hand near the small of my back as the doorman held the door.

"As planned, Mr. Penman?" the driver asked, as we climbed into his idling town car.

"Yes, Lou. Thank you."

I did my best to get situated without fidgeting, but my long, black wool coat was bunched up under my butt. Like an idiot, I popped up from the seat over and over, trying to yank it out from under me. The instant I felt settled, he went and did it again, removing the damn sunglasses and looking at me as if it was the most innocent thing in the world. He had to know the effect he had on women. It had to be intentional.

"Now, don't worry," he said. "This won't cut into your three hours. We're just doing a bit of multi-tasking. I have to run by a friend's shop. She's ordered some trousers from England and I need to try them on in case they need to go to the tailor."

It was difficult to imagine a world in which a garment wouldn't fall in line with Christopher Penman's every wish. I dared to look him in the eye again and he began slathering on the charm with deliberate bats of his lashes, like basting a turkey with butter, priming me to toss out every good manner my mother had taught me. I knew then that if I wanted to make it to the end of the day, I should focus on breathing when possible.

I righted my brain and dug my digital recorder and notes from my bag. "We should probably get started," I said, determined to play a meaningful role in the situation. I was on the clock, after all.

"Down to business." He wagged an eyebrow.

You have got to stop doing that, buddy. I shuddered and focused on the floor mat, employing a new strategy: avoid eye contact.

"Are you cold? Lou, can we have a bit more heat back here?" he asked.

Right. Cold. That's the problem. "Okay, then." I smiled,

forcing an air of relaxation with a flip of my hair, as if this sort of thing happened to me every day. "You have a new record coming out in a few months. How was it getting back into the studio?"

"It was great. I love being in the studio." He smiled narrowly.

I waited, wondering if that was my sign that he'd concluded his answer. "You chose New Orleans this time. What was it like to work there?"

"It was brilliant. The city has a great atmosphere." There was another twinkly, yet diminutive smile. Perhaps he thought he could hypnotize me.

"Anything else you liked about recording there?"

"The people, I suppose. I felt a connection with them. They're re-building their city. I'm re-building my career."

He paused and searched my face as if he was waiting for a response. There was no question I was on a two second delay, which undoubtedly made me seem like a ditz, but it was only because I was juggling too much in my head.

He continued, "Anyway, New Orleans was brilliant. Great studio. Wonderful people."

My eyes darted back to my notes and I tugged on my lower lip. "Tell me about the musicians who played on the new record. You worked with friends on this one, but you used studio players on your first solo record. Why the new approach?"

"Well..." He turned toward me as if he was switching to a more serious interview mode. "This project is much more personal. I wanted to surround myself with people I know, people I could trust. And I was looking for collaboration. That's something I miss about being in a band. The first solo record was made in a vacuum for all intents and purposes." He glanced out the window. A delivery truck was blocking traffic in both directions and a chorus of car horns blared. "I'd show up and tell the hired guns what to do or even worse, I wouldn't show up at all and the engineer would tell everyone what to do. It wasn't a good idea for me to have free reign at that time." He inched his eyes back to me. "This project has more meaning, so working with my friends made sense. Plus, New Orleans is too much fun to be there by yourself."

He unleashed a knowing smile and I swallowed, hard. I gauged his words. He was being cooperative. His answers were stilted, but I was already getting more than I'd expected and he hadn't been anything other than pleasant. Mostly, I was impressed with my ability to notice anything at all because his lips were tormenting me with words beginning with "p".

"What do you mean when you say the new record is more personal?" I looked up to catch Chris and Lou exchanging secret signals.

"Sorry, dear. You'll have to hold onto that thought. We're here."

CHAPTER THREE

THE SHOP his friend owned was a posh boutique in SoHo. Chris again put his hand close to the small of my back and gestured toward the entrance. I felt a tingle, which caused me to gawk at him as he opened the door for me.

The late morning sun beamed through tall windows onto wide plank wood floors and there was perfume in the air, as if someone had been primping. Music played and although I knew the song, I blanked on the title and artist.

The boutique had perfect stacks of sweaters and jeans perched atop long, clear acrylic tables. There were racks of expensive looking clothing, men's on one side and women's on the other, a few of each style or color, hanging on precisely spaced wood and chrome hangers.

From the staircase that led to the second floor, a statuesque woman floated over, squealing and smiling at Chris. Her wavy, auburn mane swished behind her and she just so happened to be at the perfect height for Chris in her sky-high shoes.

"Christopher, love," she purred. The two embraced with noisy kisses on each cheek. She stepped back with her enviable legs, bathed in chocolate brown tights beneath a short navy blue dress. The woman eyed him in a way that made me wonder if I should excuse myself.

Chris introduced me to Francesca and I knew at once that she was appraising both my clothes and me. She may have been stunning, but I doubted she could keep up with me intellectually and she had a bony butt. Mine might be better described as perky, thanks to a lot of hard work, but still, I was glad to be wearing good shoes.

"Your things are upstairs, darling," Francesca said to Chris. I trailed behind after he made sure I knew to join them, the beautiful Amazon pair.

The second floor expanded into a loft-like space with white-curtained dressing rooms and a seating area outfitted with modern white leather sofas and chairs. A bottle on ice and a pair of champagne flutes sat at the ready, confirming my status as third wheel.

"Christopher, these are the pants I ordered and the others are just a few goodies I knew would look fabulous on you." She lingered after he thanked her, before raising her chin and throwing back her shoulders. "I'll leave you two alone." She winked at me, a look that said she knew I was in over my head.

"Champagne?" Christopher asked, handing me the glass of pale gold bubbles. His warm fingers brushed my hand and I craved champagne like I never had before. He wore a light-hearted smile, which took me by surprise. I hadn't expected any and I'd already had several. "I'll try these on straight away. I know we're on a tight schedule. Go back to your questions. I can do two things at once."

I had no doubt about that.

He removed a few items from the rack while I settled in the chair closest to his dressing room and took the moment of relative privacy to compose myself. I patted my forehead with my fingers and took several deep breaths.

"Uh, so, back to what we were talking about earlier. Why was it important to make a personal record?" I asked, raising my voice even though there was only a fabric curtain separating us.

"Um, well..." He was quiet for a moment and I worried I'd touched a nerve already. He pulled back the curtain and strode out in unmistakably well-made black dress pants and his black leather shoes, untied. "What do you think?"

It took painful amounts of self-control to refrain from dropping my jaw to the floor or simply fainting. "Great. They look really, really great." I stared. "Perfect length," I added, so as not to dwell on how great they were or reveal what part of him I'd been ogling.

He checked out his butt in the mirror. "These don't give me a square bottom, do they?" He wagged his hips and smiled at me again. "No, I think they'll work bloody well." He stepped back into the dressing room and zipped the curtain closed.

I considered re-phrasing my question, but he surprised me by returning to the topic.

"As you probably know, I've had some rough patches over the last few years. I really needed to clear my head, especially after my divorce. Writing music is my way of working through these things. I'm not the bloke who goes to a therapist." He stopped and the quiet made me wonder what was happening behind the curtain. "I didn't know that sorting through my personal issues would turn into a record. I didn't plan it."

"At what point did you realize that you had enough material to record?" The question was immediate and natural. It was such a relief to feel like I was getting into a groove. Although I loved to look at him, it was much easier when he was hidden from view, when his physical presence wasn't pulling me in seven different directions.

"It happened quickly. Once I reached the point where I was writing good music and exploring things on a personal level, I couldn't stop. It was complete catharsis. It was only a few weeks before I had eight or nine songs."

He emerged from behind the curtain again and turned to face me in a marine blue dress-shirt with a texture like superfine embroidery. He hadn't bothered with most of the buttons and I could see more than a conciliatory patch of his chest. The light-weight gray wool pants he was wearing looked as if they'd already been to the tailor—the fit couldn't have been better.

"How many songs did you actually record?" I had to glance away after the first few words. Talking to him while looking at him was a talent I didn't possess.

"Let me think." He stared at the ceiling, flaunting his jaw and rubbing his neck while his irresistible smell washed over me. "I went into the studio with easily twenty songs. We recorded fifteen and I believe twelve will end up on the record." He eased into the chair next to me and finished off the final drops in his glass, setting it on the table between us.

This was all a brand new kind of weird, talking to Christopher Penman while he tried on clothes. I was even getting comfortable with his appearance, but it was more difficult when he'd been out of sight for a minute and reappeared. Then he knocked the breath right out of me.

"So, if many of the songs were about dealing with your divorce, what were the other songs about?"

"The other side of it was dealing with what was my fault. That was more difficult, because it felt horrible to think about what a prat I'd been, but it was ultimately the most rewarding part."

I nodded, feeling better about my decision to focus on his record at the beginning. It was leading to the other topics and I felt sure it had helped me earn his confidence. The answers seemed to be coming easily now.

"Aside from lyrics, was there anything about the process of writing that contributed to the personal nature of the record?"

He scratched his head. "I had a lot of 'aha' moments. They weren't always thoughts that went into lyrics, but they were part of my state of mind. You can say it any way you want, but the record is the documentary of my mid-life crisis, in feeling and in substance." He stood and headed back into the dressing room. "This is the last one. Thanks for being such a good sport."

"Of course," I called. "Thanks for the private fashion show," I mumbled under my breath, disbelieving the words.

Mr. Perfect exited his dressing room, remarkable in his own black t-shirt and a mind-blowing pair of jeans. He peered down at me and swept his floppy hair from his forehead. The only thing that could've kept me from holding an impolite stare was his question about the pants, "What about these?"

I sat, dumbfounded. If it was all a distraction technique, it was working.

"Are you hungry?" he asked. "I'm starving. I know a great place."

CHAPTER FOUR

TO SAY the interview had diverged from what I'd anticipated was like saying it's fun to drink beer. I'd imagined us sitting in a generic hotel meeting room with a pitcher of ice water and wallpaper as far as the eye could see. I would've asked my questions, he likely would have skirted many of them, and I would have flown home, the recipient of three antiseptic hours with the captivating Christopher Penman. There wasn't a single reason to expect anything more.

The subject of my interview was what had really shattered my preconceptions. Sure, he was charming. That was to be expected. What I hadn't counted on was his seeming candor. I was supposed to be the enemy. The media had made much of his unhappiness a public matter and although I still didn't know what had been exaggerated, several missteps had been made to look as bad as possible.

More than a year ago, I'd seen tabloid photos of Chris and his then wife in front of an LA restaurant, looking as if they'd had the spat of the century. The pictures were unflattering at best, splotchy faces, scowls and wrinkled foreheads. I hadn't bothered to open the magazine and read the article. I did what most people do—I paid for my groceries and went about my day, with a horrible image of two people I didn't know burned into my brain.

Now I wondered where the real Chris was. I found it difficult to believe he was on the cover of that magazine, but I'd only known him for an hour. Maybe that was the way he used to be, when he was married and unhappy. I glanced at him, trying to stay under the radar. He grinned, making a motion with his hand to suggest he had a big talker on the line. I smirked and rolled my eyes in sympathy, thinking that he was such a lethal package.

A mass of faces crossed the street, likely rushing off to lunch. You could still see their breath—even with the sun at its highest point, the day hadn't warmed at all. Lou slowed through the intersection, eventually forced to stop for pedestrians crossing against the signal on the other side. We were headed to a place in Little Italy and we could've walked there faster, but I was thankful to have the time away from the cold.

Lou pulled up to the curb and Chris was at the restaurant door before me, raising his face to the glow of the mid-day sun. "I hope you're hungry." Now his lips were distracting me with all words, not just the ones that started with particular letters.

Twenty or so tables and booths filled the dining room, covered with red and white-checkered tablecloths, all of them empty. A round, gray-haired man materialized and he and Chris exchanged hugs and handshakes.

"Claire, please meet Marco. This is his restaurant."

"Ah, Miss Claire. Happy to meet you." He looked at Chris and then at me. "Christopher always brings the pretty ladies with him. Such beautiful blue eyes and blonde hair. If we went to Italy, you would have to beat the men with a big stick."

"Thank you." I blushed, taken aback by the newly planted image of Marco and me in Italy with a man-beating stick. "Did we miss the lunch rush?"

"Oh, no," he chuckled. "We opened for Christopher. Our favorite customer."

Marco saw us to our table, a half-round booth with red leather upholstery on a raised platform, providing a view of the street through the requisite white lace café curtains.

I took a sip of water and discovered how thirsty I was, finishing in as lady-like a gulp as possible before the ice collapsed against my upper lip. I wiped away the watery moustache with the white linen napkin, only to see Chris watching me.

"Thirsty?"

"I guess so." I smiled, sheepishly.

"Stay hydrated. Wouldn't want a dead writer on my hands," he said, laughing to himself.

Funny. Dead writer—I get it.

Marco brought a bottle of red wine and Chris checked the label. All I could think was that it must be nice to have someone open his restaurant for you. It was probably a normal Monday for Chris.

"Ah, so Christopher, how did you meet the lovely Claire?" Marco uncorked the bottle and poured a splash of wine in Chris's glass.

"Excellent question. How *did* I meet the lovely Claire?" Chris grinned at me and took a sip. "This is perfect, Marco. Thank you."

I tried to shake the image of Chris's lips on the wine glass. "I'm a writer. We're doing an interview for his new album." I placed my recorder and notes on the table.

"Fantastic. He's a wonderful man, you know," Marco said as

he filled my glass. "Make sure you say how wonderful he is." He smiled playfully, which made my cheeks flush again.

"We'll have to see how the rest of the interview goes," I said, without thinking.

Chris shifted his weight, then sat back and took a lengthy drink of his wine. He straightened his knife and fork, drawing to light the beauty of his hands for the first time.

I started my recorder. "So, you said that the record is a documentation of your mid-life crisis. Can you tell me more about that?" As soon as I'd asked, I was sure that was what he hated about writers—having your own words thrown back at you in the form of a question.

He took another sip of his wine, never taking his eyes off me. I sensed he was making a careful assessment of me, possibly a final decision on how much information to share. "Claire, do you have anything else you need to do today? Any other appointments or meetings?"

I wrinkled my brow. "No. I planned to go back to the hotel and start on the story, maybe get in a workout. I was hoping to meet with my editor at *Rolling Stone,* but his schedule was full. I fly home tomorrow morning."

"Perfect. What do you say we finish the interview later and enjoy our lunch, like normal people? We won't talk about me at all."

I was more than a little deflated since I'd been hoping for a good answer to my question. "I guess that would be all right," I said, shutting off the recorder. It all seemed very convenient for him. "When you say finish later, do you mean this afternoon or tonight?"

"Don't worry. You'll get your interview."

I tried to imagine a scenario in which our lunch was a good idea because I felt as though I was allowing him to put me off like a stupid girl.

My mom weighed in on the situation from inside my head, as she was apt to do whenever I was confused. She and I had been exceptionally close when she was alive and somehow our running conversation never ended when she was no longer among the living. She told me to stop being stupid, smile, and eat my lunch. She also thought I should show some leg, but I reminded her that I was wearing pants.

Marco and a waiter brought plates and platters of wonderful looking and smelling food—steaming bowls of home-made ravioli with tomato sauce, veal cutlets, seafood risotto.

"I'm definitely going to need that workout after this," I said, reaching for the ravioli.

"Please don't tell me you're one of those women who doesn't eat. I can't stand that."

"I didn't say I wasn't going to eat. I'm just going to pay for it later." I dished the pasta onto my plate.

There was pleasant conversation during our marathon lunch, but all of it was about me so I found that aspect of things to be quite dull. Chris asked me all sorts of questions, about where I lived, my career and family. He even asked if there was a Mr. Abby. Sometimes I didn't hear the answers come out of my own mouth because everything he did was so enthralling.

Over the course of the meal, I think we both sensed that it didn't have to be controversial if we enjoyed each other's company—we seemed to naturally warm to each other and we had fun, laughing more now that we were on our second bottle of wine. It even felt as if we could end up being friends, but perhaps that was the Merlot talking.

When we finished, Chris went to the kitchen to thank the chef and I scrolled through my messages, finding a text from Sam. She'd worn me down the night before and I'd spilled the story of my adolescent crush on Chris. Now that she was on her way home from school, she was dying to know what'd happened.

There was no sign of a bill and when I asked about it, Chris said, "It's taken care of." He seemed to catch the look on my face. "You're my guest, Claire. Relax."

Right. Relax.

Marco gave me a bear hug and a kiss on the cheek when we said our goodbyes.

"He likes you," Chris said, outside the restaurant.

"Good. I like him too." I'd definitely had one too many glasses of wine. "Where's your car?" I asked, scanning the street.

"I called Lou and told him he could head back to the hotel." He popped a mint from the restaurant in his mouth. "I thought we could do as New Yorkers do and walk."

Several paces ahead, Chris strolled backwards, motioning me to catch up with him. It was still chilly, especially now that the sun was starting to duck behind the buildings.

"Aren't you freezing?" I asked, certain he was about to turn into an ice cube in his thin canvas jacket.

"No, but if you're concerned, you can keep me warm when it gets to be too much," he replied, with another of his devastating grins.

My cheeks burned from the wind, but I lasted for several blocks without caring at all. The notion of a stroll down a busy Manhattan street with him was enough to warm me. But then the wind picked up and I tucked my chin inside my coat and shuddered, which he seemed to find funny.

"Look at you. I'm the one who doesn't know how to dress himself and you're shivering." He was still laughing when he put his arm around my shoulders. "Come here. I can't bear to see a damsel in distress."

"I'm not in distress, nor am I a damsel. I'm cold." I added in my defense, "I'm very temperature sensitive." I looked up at him and he returned the look as we continued to walk, except he had his sunglasses on and the glare made it impossible to see his eyes.

Damn those glasses. I wasn't sure how many more times I'd get to see that particular view, if ever.

CHAPTER FIVE

THE TEN-BLOCK WALK may have been the best in my life, but the lobby was a merciful escape from the cold. The tops of my thighs and tips of my fingers stung like sunburn.

We stepped to the front desk and I checked in while Chris spoke with the concierge about dinner plans for tomorrow night. I wondered with whom he'd be dining. The young blonde helping him was radiant, openly flirting with him as he recipro-cated. I fought a scowl, guessing that was how he was with all women.

Having finished his planning and flirting, Chris waited while I got my room key. "Share an elevator?" he asked.

"Sure." We made our way with a sudden stiffness to every-thing. The air, our conversation, my whole body felt rigid. "When can you finish the interview?" I asked. I had to pin him down or he'd continue to delay. We'd already discussed the new record. He'd probably said everything he wanted to say.

He stared at the numbers above the elevator doors as we made a slow climb.

"How about five-thirty? Will that give you enough time?"

"That depends on how long you let me stay."

"We'll have to play it by ear, but in theory you can stay as long as you like." He gave me an indecipherable look and held the elevator door when we reached the sixth floor. "I'm in 912."

"Sounds good," I said, doing my best to ignore his sudden troublesome mood.

Alone in my room, I tossed my bag onto the chair. It tipped over and tumbled to the floor, but I left it, too tired and preoccupied to care. I flopped back on to the bed and sank in the comforter as if I was preparing to make snow angels. I would've enjoyed the luxury of it if my brain hadn't been in overdrive, going over the details of the day and to my detriment, dwelling on the change in his disposition. Surely he would've preferred a date with a firing squad rather than finish the interview.

A headache sprouted behind my eyes and I rolled out of bed and trudged to the bathroom to take something to soften the pain. I scrutinized my face in the fluorescent light while pouring a glass of water. I looked like I felt, tired and confused. I slugged down two Tylenol as my phone rang, an unfortunately familiar number on the caller ID.

Great. Just what I need. "Kevin. What do you want?"

"Hey, Claire Bear, are you in New York?"

My stomach instinctively lurched at Kevin's voice; every utterance was so grating. It was hard to believe I'd ever enjoyed listening to him talk. "Please don't call me that ridiculous nickname. And how did you know I was in New York?"

"I just got off the phone with Patrick Collins. Have you done your interview with Chris Penman?"

"Part of it. We're finishing tonight. Why?" I rubbed my temple and plopped back down on the bed.

"Patrick asked me not to say anything, but this whole thing sounds fishy. I'm pretty sure Penman demanded a woman writer at the last minute."

"I don't understand."

"Claire, come on. Think about it. He's a good-looking guy. He wants to rehab his image. He probably got panicky and figured he wouldn't have much sway with a guy."

"But Patrick said he wanted someone experienced, someone who Chris could trust and talk to."

"Exactly why you had to be the person to write the story. I'm sure Patrick is thinking you're woman enough to keep Penman on his toes and a good enough interviewer to drag the story out of him."

My head sputtered, putting facts together until I realized that had to be exactly why Patrick had been so anxious for me to accept the assignment. And Chris had likely organized every detail on his end—the restaurant, the private fashion show, the wine and champagne, even the walk back to the hotel. He'd probably paid Marco to say that stuff about fending off men with a stick.

"I can't talk about this." I closed my eyes, understanding what a girl I'd been all day. The fact that the message was delivered my ex-boyfriend in no way softened the blow.

"What are you going to do? You can't say anything, to anyone. It's just my guess."

"There's nothing to do. You told me your stupid theory and now I'm going to finish the interview." I couldn't bear to tell him how I'd been so gullible.

"Be careful, Claire Bear. You know, everybody says he's a dog."

I hung up the phone and knew one thing. I was not going down in a fiery crash. I'd put my story and my future, Sam's future, at risk by allowing myself to be swayed by Mr. Perfect. I had to take control of the situation. It was my only hope to finish the interview and get out with what I needed—a story worthy of a cover, and that meant dirt.

A shower seemed like the remedy for many of my problems —the headache, the residual cold, and the sting of the truth. Chris Penman wasn't being nice to me. He'd used his charming exterior to make the best of a situation he'd avoided for more than a dozen years.

The hot water lapped at my muscles and my body bubbled back to life when I dropped my head forward, rolling it from side to side as the scalding water beat on my neck. Time to start fresh. If Chris Penman wanted a woman, I was going to give him one. If I did it right, I could distract him exactly as he'd distracted me.

Always prepared for a last-minute dinner invitation or a disastrous coffee spill, I'd packed a snug black skirt and a killer pair of black pumps in my suitcase. I chose the slim-fitting sapphire blue cardigan I'd planned to wear home minus a t-shirt underneath. An extra button left undone did the trick—the sweater made my eyes look an exceptional shade of blue, not that they were the intended focus, with the help of a well-engineered bra.

I turned in the mirror, confident that with the way I filled out the back of the skirt and a waft of perfume as my starting point, persuading him to spill his handsome guts would be much easier.

In final preparation, I flipped through my notes to the most indelicate questions, reading them aloud. I couldn't run the risk of tripping over my words or being surprised by the sound of my own voice.

When five-thirty came, I slipped into my pumps, quickly recalling the effort it took to walk in them. Alas, they were an essential part of the package. I teetered my way to the elevator and down the hall to his room.

Chris answered the door, his reaction to my appearance

transparent. He blinked several times, his mouth agape. "Don't you look smashing?"

I breezed past him and the door clicked shut, followed by the sound of the latch. My heart skipped a beat, but I took a deep breath and kept it together. "I had to take a long, hot shower after our walk. I was freezing." I gracefully bent over to place my bag in a chair and felt his eyes on me.

He was wearing the same clothes from earlier, but was barefoot with splendidly disheveled hair. He looked sleepy and gorgeous, as if he'd just climbed out of bed, and my doltish mind drifted over the image.

His suite was several times bigger than my room and huge by New York standards. The windows were astounding, floor to ceiling, and lining one entire wall. We stood in a spacious living area with the bedroom beyond, featuring a King-size bed and the same sumptuous white linens I had in my room. I considered it for a minute—if I'd wanted to, I could screw the whole music-journalism gig and make my greatest adolescent dream come true. A bounce on the edge of the bed and a welcoming pat on the mattress was probably all it would take.

But no. I had work to do. I focused on exactly that while the perfect words popped from my mouth. "Where do you want to do this? On the couch?"

A smirk spread across his face. He was enjoying himself. Good. He could have fun while I held him over the coals. "Sure, the couch, the floor, the bathroom. Whatever you like," he shot back. "Can I get you a drink? Beer? Wine?"

"I'd love a bottle of water."

"You sure? I've got plenty of the good stuff." He cast me another of his enticing looks.

"Thank you. I'm sure."

He ambled to the couch, beer in hand, spreading his gangly

arms over the back and stretching out his remaining lovely limbs. "Shall we?" He patted the spot next to him.

The couch seemed to shrink the instant I sat down. I crossed my leg and eased my skirt up over my knee, intentionally putting my shoe dangerously close to his leg. He studied every movement, but I wasn't sure if I should feel flattered or scared. I glanced up to see that it was getting dark outside, the windows turning steely.

I started my digital recorder. "Let's get back to where we were this afternoon. You said you had a mid-life crisis after your divorce and that influenced the record. Tell me about that."

He sucked a deep breath through his nose and rolled his head toward me, conducting a thorough search of my face. He held his stare without blinking for what felt like an eon.

"It wasn't anything special. A guy turns forty and he wonders what he's done with his bloody life."

"But you're several years beyond forty and this was last year. I'm not sure I follow what you're saying."

His stare narrowed. "Cute. I'm forty-four and I was forty-two or forty-three when it happened, it's not a big difference. May I continue?"

I nodded and retreated to my notes.

"My marriage didn't end. It disintegrated." He drew out his words as if it would help me grasp how awful the experience had been. "Elise had been the center of my life and that was over. We hurt each other a great deal." He continued to look at me, never glancing away. "At that point, my friends were tired of me. I'd been too wrapped up in Elise's drama to be a good friend. I'd spent all of my time dealing with her."

"When you say you were dealing with her, you're referring to her drug use?" The question was irksome even to me, and the look in his eyes said that he recognized my new tack.

"Is this where we're going with this? Because I don't have to keep talking."

"This is background on your divorce and how that played into the writing of the record." I didn't dare look at him, so I focused on my notes.

"I'm telling you now, I don't plan to share all of that with you. I'll tell you the basics, as it pertains to our divorce and the record." He cleared his throat and shifted in his seat. "I'll give you that much. It's no secret that Elise has a drug problem. That caused our marriage to fail. All she wanted to do was party every night and sleep all day. There's a reason it's a cliché. It gets old, fast."

I stole a breath as encouragement for the question that had to be asked. "What about your own drug use? It was widely reported that your problem was as bad as hers."

"No, I was never as bad as Elise."

"Isn't that all relative though? If you weren't quite as bad, you could still be in rough shape."

"As I said, I never had a problem as bad as Elise."

"Then how do you explain your stint in rehab together?"

His jaw tensed and it made me hold my breath. His eyes darted back and forth as he seemed to be grappling with what I'd provoked.

"I don't see how this relates to my new record. We were discussing Elise, not me." He jerked forward and clunked his empty beer bottle on the table and stood. "I believe I told you that this is off limits." He trudged back to the mini fridge.

Another moment without eye contact bolstered my confidence. "I understand that you may not want to talk about some of these things, but this is what people want to know about you. Surely, you had to know that I would ask you about this. You don't get to be on the cover of *Rolling Stone* by telling people only what you want them to hear."

He popped the top off another beer and returned to his place at the opposite end of the couch. The wheels were busy churning behind those exquisite green eyes of his. At times, it felt as if I could see the years of secrets bottled up inside. If he was weighing his options, throwing me out of his hotel room was likely first on the list.

"Are you saying they might take away the cover?"

"They very well might. I only know you'll guarantee it if you answer my questions."

He gave me another of his intense penetrating stares.

"Think about it this way," I continued. "This might be your one chance to tell your story on your terms, to a huge audience."

"I don't know."

"You control the story this way. No more speculation. No more rumors. Just the truth."

He pursed his lips. "If I talk to you about all of this, you can't twist my words to fit your idea of what the story should be. You have to promise me you won't screw me over."

"I would never screw you over."

"Good, because it'd kill me if you did." He took a slow, full breath and closed his eyes. He seemed to be regaining his composure. "That's why I never do interviews. Writers love to take you out of context and make you look like a bloody jerk. No offense."

"I have no interest in doing that. I want to know the truth, so I can put it in a story that portrays you accurately. You're going to have to tell somebody these things, some day. It may as well be me." I smiled, as if I could win over one of the most secretive and handsome men in the world with a show of my teeth.

"If I do this, it's only because I trust you," he again searched my face. "For some reason."

Was that really true? Had I earned his trust? "You can trust me. I promise." It felt as if he left me waiting for an eternity.

"I'm going to hold you to that."

Goose bumps blanketed me from head to toe. I wasn't even sure of what I'd heard. My sense of accomplishment was quickly tempered by the fear of what would come next. Most likely he was about to tell me things that would destroy my adolescent fantasy, forever.

CHAPTER SIX

"THIS WILL TAKE SOME TIME, you know. If I'm going to spill my guts, we could be here until two or three in the morning. I hope you're ready."

"I should use the bathroom before we start."

"Good idea." Chris seemed to relax again, much more this time. "Have you eaten?" he asked as I stepped past the previously beckoning bed into his immense bathroom.

"No. I'm still full from lunch," I called.

"I ordered room service before you got here. It should be here any minute. We can share."

I wriggled my hips back and forth, hiking up my skirt to pee, my outfit now seeming beyond harebrained. I washed my hands in the white porcelain vessel sink and smoothed back my hair.

He sat on the bed waiting when I opened the door. He smiled, which generated a stabbing sensation in my chest, but I returned the gesture politely. "My turn," he quipped as he stood.

Even with my shoes on, he kept an advantage of three or four inches. I tingled when he passed me, a subtle rush of air between our bodies. I shied away to keep the reverberation to myself, but recognized one indisputable fact—the world was different around him. I didn't possess all of my faculties in his world, I couldn't breathe most of the time, but I couldn't bring myself to leave. There was something new at every turn and I didn't care that I had no idea how to survive.

Chris yelled to me from the bathroom. "Why don't you take off those ridiculous shoes? They've got to be killing your feet."

"How do you know that?" I grumbled under my breath. Men were supposed to think my shoes were hot.

He emerged from the bathroom, having changed into black track pants. He fetched another beer and offered me one again, but I stuck with water. "I thought I'd get comfortable since we're hunkering down for the night."

"Good idea. Comfortable is good."

"Do you want to change?" He pointed at me with his beer bottle. "You look smashing, don't get me wrong, but that outfit should be worn for very short amounts of time." He winked at me, telling me he'd known exactly what I was up to when I arrived. Of course. He'd probably seen every trick a woman could have in her arsenal.

"No, I'm fine."

"Don't be silly. That skirt can't be comfortable. It's like a second skin. I'll wait while you run downstairs."

"Really, it's fine. We should focus on the interview."

A knock came at the door and Chris answered it quickly. The room service guy wheeled the cart into the room, looking quizzically at us and taking full survey of the situation. I felt goofy and self-conscious, dolled up when Chris was practically in his pajamas. Chris signed for the food and loudly announced as the room service guy was leaving, "Is it five hundred for the whole night or do I have to pay extra for that?"

"I suppose you think that's funny," I said.

He laughed. "I know it's funny."

"It's not *that* funny." I looked over the food he'd ordered, a cheeseburger with onion rings, fish and chips, and cheesecake. "Healthy. God forbid you should order a salad."

He downed an onion ring. "The burger comes with lettuce."

"Are you ready to launch into this?" It wasn't an actual question, but I had to steer us back to the task at hand.

"You're all business, aren't you?" He arched one of his very talented eyebrows, again, and carried the plates of food to the coffee table in front of the couch.

"Yes. I guess I am," I said, joining him. "There's one common thread I found in my research, that you and Elise both had a serious drug problem. So, why don't you tell me what the truth is?"

Chris peered at me while he finished a bite of his burger. "Thank you for asking me to tell you the story, rather than asking a leading question that makes me sound like a bloody tosser." He wiped his hand on the napkin. "Mmm. Good burger." He nodded eagerly. "I'm not going to say that I never did drugs, because I did. Much of it was on the road with Banks Forest, normal backstage partying. I smoked pot and did coke when it was around, but I never got into the more serious stuff." He took another bite.

"Tell me more about Elise. Was she an addict when you met her?"

"I didn't realize she had a problem when I met her. We met backstage at a show in Montreal. She was with this guy, a dealer, who was tight with one of our roadies. He was her boyfriend too, but she latched on to me right away."

He described their first few months together; she'd seemed different from the typical groupie and he was intrigued when she'd called herself an artist although that later turned out to be a lie. The beginning of their relationship seemed to hinge on three things: his fame, her beauty, and drugs.

"When did her addiction become an issue?"

"I suppose it was always an issue, but I dealt with it. We had years of an on-again, off-again relationship. She'd get pissed at me for something and leave for a few weeks, but she always came back. After we were married, I started to see just how bloody barmy she was." He took a drink of beer. "Banks was still together and our last tour before we took our hiatus was massive. We had paparazzi following us everywhere and she loved the attention."

He continued after several more bites of his burger. "Elise got really wrapped up in it, especially because her friends treated her like royalty. They were parasites. They only wanted to be backstage or go to parties and they were always wasted." He leaned back on the couch now that most of the food had disappeared. "Much better. I was starving."

He turned in my direction and pulled his leg up on to the couch, resting his knee against the back. He smiled as he settled in and I felt a spark, a verifiable jolt. Honestly, there was one every time he looked at me, but some were stronger than others.

He continued with his story. "During the hiatus, I hoped it'd be a chance to be normal. I tried to insulate her from her friends, but that didn't work at all. They always found a way to be around and I'd eventually give up because she'd take it out on me if she couldn't be with them."

"What do you mean by normal?"

"I really wanted to have children, but Elise refused. We argued about it constantly. She said she didn't want to be tied down and she didn't want it to ruin her body. She even suggested that I get a vasectomy, which I refused to do. That wasn't a fun conversation."

His voice wobbled on this topic. It made me sad to hear that tone in his voice, so out of step with his generally upbeat demeanor.

Now that he was talking, it seemed like it might be hard to get him to stop. He continued for at least two more hours, telling stories about his tumultuous marriage, her drug use, and his desire to become a dad. Things got worse when the band reunited.

"The reunion tour gave me something to do, and I needed a distraction if Elise wasn't going to give in on the baby. It was literally driving me crazy."

"What made you want to be a father so badly?"

He shrugged his shoulders. "I thought it would be great to be a dad. Having a little one running around and being able to show them the world, that seems like the greatest experience a person could have."

I knew, firsthand, that he was right.

"And I lost my dad when I was eight," he continued. "Heart attack. He went to bed one night and never woke up. I was so young I don't remember much about him, not like my sisters do. After he died, I used to pretend he was around, that he was there to do things with me like play in the yard. It seemed so normal at the time. He reappeared in my mind as easily as he disappeared from the real world." His voice trembled again. "I still want the chance to do those things with my own child."

I cleared my throat to keep the tears at bay. I'd known his dad has passed away, but hearing him tell the story made it much more than a fact about someone I was interviewing. "I'm sorry," I said, softly. I couldn't bear to look at him, fearing my own reaction.

"It's okay, Claire."

"I lost my mom. I know how hard it is." I stared at my notes, not seeing the words, and swallowed back my emotions. "Please, go on. You were talking about the reunion tour."

"Right. Well, Elise was excited about the tour because it meant partying every night, but we fought all the time. We'd go out on our days off and if I said or did something she didn't like, she would act up in front of the paparazzi to get back at me. It was usually harmless, but you can't give those vultures any ammunition."

He paused. "I don't know if you know about this, but there was a pretty infamous shot of us outside of a restaurant in LA. Photographers had been following us everywhere the whole day. Elise got drunk at dinner and accused me of flirting with the waitress. When we went outside to wait for the valet, she blew her top, a bloody temper tantrum. The photos were all over the Internet within an hour and in the tabloids after that. People ate it up."

It made me sick to think about the photos now, knowing the truth behind the images. It was all too easy to tell a lie with a photograph.

"After the tour," he continued, "I prayed things would calm down. That's when everything changed." He was struggling, looking at me, then away and back again. "You know, I don't think I want to go any further." He pleaded with his eyes.

Seeing that look on his face, I felt torn between being a writer and being human, knowing that some things should remain private. Whatever he was about to talk about seemed to weigh on him even more than the subject of losing his dad.

"All right. I understand. You've said a lot." We shared a moment of crystal-clear eye contact where I felt the entire universe shift, as if it was making room for something. "I hope you know that you really can trust me. I don't have a single reason to do anything other than treat you and your story with respect."

"I don't know that you really want to hear this."

"If you're willing to tell me, then I do." I braced myself for the answer. The silence nearly shook the room.

He closed his eyes and his forehead wrinkled. "Elise got pregnant. I had no idea until she was nearly three months along, but she'd known for weeks. She was on the pill, but I'm sure she forgot to take it. Funny, since she seemed to take everything else." A pained rush of air escaped him. "I was excited, but I was also at sixes and sevens, freaking out. She'd been using and drinking and she'd lied to me about the pregnancy. I was worried. I begged her to go into rehab so they could watch her twenty-four hours a day. I knew she had to quit everything right then and there."

He continued. "She agreed to it, but only if I went with her. I wasn't even drinking at the time, but I was desperate to get her there and I didn't trust her to do what she needed to do. We checked ourselves in very early the next morning. The paparazzi caught wind of it, probably from one of Elise's friends. They would sell tips to the photographers. Anything to make some money." He shook his head in disgust. "The photos of us walking into rehab were everywhere in less than twenty-four hours. It was awful. I knew my mom and sisters had to be in a state. I'd go to support meetings, lying through the sessions so it seemed as if I belonged there."

The corners of his mouth drew down. "She lost the baby four days after we checked in." He sat up and settled his head in his hands, and I had to battle my inclination to comfort him. "I suppose it was a blessing because the baby probably would've had all kinds of problems. It's not like she would've made a good mother."

I didn't move, to take in every piece of sad and delicate information as he intended. No wonder he'd never wanted this to be public, then or now.

"Our marriage was completely irreparable by that point. We

stayed together for a few weeks, but that was all I could take. I finally just told her to leave. I couldn't save her and we were never going to have a family. I had to accept that and grieve for the child we'd lost because I knew she never would."

CHAPTER SEVEN

WE SAT IN SILENCE. He had to be exhausted and I was still processing everything he'd said, everything the world supposedly needed to know. I excused myself and patted cold water on my cheeks in the bathroom, avoiding my eyes and the mascara that would run. He was still on the couch when I opened the door, his forearm over his eyes. I tiptoed my way over, thinking he might be asleep.

"You're back," he said softly, once I'd interrupted his solitude by taking my seat.

Sitting all alone with him was too much to take. I wrestled with my infatuation. It kept creeping into the feelings I had about everything he'd told me. "I should let you get some sleep," I said. "You've had a long day."

"We've both had a long day. You're probably just as knackered as I am." He spoke in a sleepy voice that made me feel as though I might melt into a puddle on the sofa. "When does your flight leave?"

"Nine-thirty. I need to head to the airport in a few hours."

"Let me take you. We can talk. Off the record."

I swallowed and cleared my throat. "Oh, thanks, but the magazine is sending a car."

"Don't worry about that. I'll take care of it."

"It's three in the morning. I don't even know who you're supposed to call."

"Don't make things so complicated. I insist." He sat up and I was quite conscious of our new proximity, but it didn't seem to faze him at all. Our legs touched and he clapped me on the back.

"Are you really taking me to the airport?" I asked, as I got up to collect my things. I was concerned about wearing out my welcome, transparently making idle comments to steal his time.

"Yes, I'll send Lou a text right now. I'm sure he's dying to get up early."

When I got to my room, I let the door slam behind me. I collapsed on the bed and curled into a ball. I found the pillow by feel and buried my face, unconcerned about falling asleep and missing my flight or more importantly, my final sliver of time with Chris. My brain would need days to shut down. I couldn't believe that I'd convinced him to talk, that I'd actually done what I set out to do.

I was dreading having to say goodbye. It would be the end of my dream, a fantasy I'd held near and dear for more than half of my life. Even when it'd been set aside or forgotten, it was still there in the back of my head, waiting. There was no going back or undoing any of it. The Chris that once only existed in my head would never compare to the real thing.

I arrived downstairs early, wearing the blue sweater with a white t-shirt. I was exalted when he emerged from the elevator five minutes ahead of schedule and flashed his giant smile at me before granting me a kiss on the cheek. It felt as if we were old friends.

"Good morning. Don't we look lovely?" he asked.

He knew exactly the right thing to say to a woman and, yes, *we* did look lovely. He wore the spellbinding jeans he'd just bought and a light gray sweater. Like the coziest blanket ever made, he was ideal for wrapping up my entire body, very tightly.

"That's sweet of you, considering you kept me up all night."

"I believe it was you who kept me up, madam. You need to check your facts," he replied, exaggerating his accent.

"Careful. I haven't written the article yet."

"Oh, right. Power of the media. Bloody racket."

A man in telltale driver's garb entered the lobby and Chris didn't hesitate to seize control. He strode over and the driver was soon laughing, Chris patting him on the shoulder as he slapped some money into his hand.

"That was nice of you," I said, when he returned.

Chris's cell phone rang and it was apparently Lou because he said, "That's us." He then placed his hand very low on my back. I felt his palm and fingers, pressure and warmth, through the thickness of my sweater. Wonderfully, it felt like more than a gesture to steer me somewhere.

Once in the car, he made my lightheaded by removing his sunglasses. "You should call me. If you have any follow up questions. Hand me your phone. I'll give you my number."

I reminded myself to stay cool. "That'd be great." I couldn't hand him my phone fast enough. "Now I won't have to bother your publicist if something comes up when I'm writing the story."

"The label handles that, but the publicity department hates me. I prefer to deal with most things myself." He finished with my phone and then pulled out his own. "I'm going to take your number. So we're even." He winked at me while I impolitely stared. "Call me if you need anything. You know all of my deep dark secrets. We may as well be friends." He returned my phone. "Here. I put it under Chris P."

I looked down as though the item in my hand was a mystery. "Wow."

"Wow?" He crinkled his forehead. "Don't say wow. I like talking to you. You're different from most women I meet." He scanned my face, resting his eyes on mine more than once. "I find you, uh, refreshing." He looked satisfied with his word choice, but I could've suggested a few alternates.

"Refreshing?"

"It's a compliment. I enjoy your company. Most women I meet are rather one dimensional."

"Maybe you're hanging out with the wrong women."

"You know I've been hanging out with the wrong women. I believe we touched on that last night."

I considered the topic—I didn't want to cross a line, but this was a chance to ask something I'd always wondered about men like him. I looked at him while searching for the right words. "Why do men like you only end up with women who are beautiful, but lacking in other qualities like intelligence or sanity?"

He smiled wide at me, letting me squirm in my seat. "We're having a normal conversation as friends, right?"

"Right." *Except that nothing about this conversation is normal.*

"Honestly, those are the only women I meet. Most women wouldn't have the confidence to approach me in that way. They assume I wouldn't be interested. They might ask for an autograph or take a picture. When I was younger, they'd scream and cry. It's hard to ask someone out after that. Not that I didn't like being screamed at, because I did." He continued, "I suppose it's because of what I do."

"Interesting."

"Please don't say that. What are you thinking?"

"I'd never thought of it like that. Even though it'd be more fun to call you a jerk, you have a tiny speck of a valid point."

"A speck. That's all I get?"

"Sorry." I squinted and pinched my thumb and index finger together for him. "And it's a teeny tiny speck. I don't exactly feel sorry for you."

"I don't understand the question coming from you anyway. You're just as capable of dating a rock star as any other woman I might meet."

"Yeah, right." I looked down for a moment, feeling embarrassed that we were discussing me in this light. I did better when he was our focus.

"That's false modesty."

"No, I'm pretty sure it's not false. I'm certainly not a model or an actress."

"That's probably why I like you so much. I may have to add writer to the list of women it's okay to date." He tilted his head, jutting out his lower lip. "It's not a bad idea, really. It might help my career."

"I know some very unattractive writers, frumpy, poorly dressed. You might want to reconsider that."

"Excellent point." He looked at me in a way that was unbelievably flirtatious, driving every atom in my body frantic. "Then I'll merely add you to my list. Everyone else will have to be on a case by case basis."

My face became white hot. "That's one way to do it."

I glanced out the window and saw that we were getting close to the airport, nearing the end of our time together. I put on a good face, I smiled, but I was about to crack wide open on the inside.

CHAPTER EIGHT

I STOOD on the curb outside the terminal building as if what was transpiring was no big deal.

"It was great, Claire. I'm glad I agreed to the interview." Chris put his sunglasses on, obscuring the green that I would never become accustomed to. "Just think, we never would've met."

I swallowed at the thought of fate, my fantasy partially fulfilled. "Thank you for everything. I'll call you if I have any follow-up questions." I felt a sinking in my heart, as if I could fold up into my own body and vanish.

"Yes, do that. If I don't hear from you, I'll ring you." He placed his hand on my shoulder and pecked me on the top of my head with a half-hug to follow, the extent of my physical contact with him, forever.

I wandered into the terminal, trying to put the right spin on what had happened, yearning for a way to keep myself from plummeting into the pits of self-doubt, desperate to prevent my inevitable over-analysis of the last twenty-four hours.

The flight home was bumpy and I grabbed the armrests when the plane dipped, surely driving the man next to me nuts.

He was young and good-looking. I would've put effort into being charming or friendly if I could have, but I was too tired to think straight. Instead I worried about falling asleep at the wheel on the way home and gracefully gliding into a guardrail, never to be heard from again.

I made it to the house late morning, barely identifiable as a human being. The effects of saying goodbye to Chris hung heavily on my shoulders as I trudged upstairs and sank into my bed, pulling the quilt over my head.

My eyelids drooped with sleep, but just as I began to drift, a scent hit my nose. I took several deep breaths. The fragrance seemed to be his, but I wasn't sure so I buried my face in my arm and inhaled. Without a doubt, my sweater was perfumed with his heady smell. I curled into a ball, taking in a whiff as I floated off to sleep.

I woke up in a panic, forgetting where I was, what day it was, and what I was doing. I frantically looked at the alarm clock. Two-thirty—I'd managed a few hours of sleep, enough to be ridiculously groggy.

My first thought was coffee, although my stomach quickly begged for attention since I hadn't had a thing to eat since room service. As the coffee dripped into the carafe, I noticed what a lovely day we were having, splendid and full of promise. The sun shined brilliantly, birds chirped and flitted as they visited my next-door neighbor Rosie's bird feeder. It was all so sickeningly pleasant.

I reached into the cupboard for a mug and noticed a note from Sam on the fridge.

Mom,

Grandpa called. He's "very disappointed" you didn't ask him to stay with me for the night while you were gone. He wants you to call him. See you at school.

I closed my eyes, praying for strength.

The caffeine finally kicked in while I sat in line at school waiting for Sam, sipping my second cup from a travel mug. My phone rattled and jumped in the cup holder, taking me by surprise. A text, from Chris P. My pulse thumped, urging me to hurry and read.

Home OK?

I smiled as if he'd just sent me a lengthy love letter. I'd certainly never expected this.

Yes, thanks, tired.

As soon as I hit send, my phone rang.

I groaned, quietly, but answered. "Dad, hi."

"Did you get my message?"

"Yes, I did, but—"

"I can't believe you wouldn't ask me to drive down and stay with her for the night. Why in the world would you be so irresponsible?"

I sighed, watching Sam file down the sidewalk.

"Dad, she's seventeen. She's fine. She can take care of herself." I hesitated to say more. Arguing would get me nowhere. "I'm sorry. You're right. I should've called. Look, Dad, I'm picking Sam up at school and there's a long line. I'll call you later. Love you." I hung up before he said goodbye.

Sam opened the car door and plopped down in her seat with enough force to make the car bounce. "What happened? Your text basically said nothing." She slammed the door and glared at me. "Tell me everything."

I kissed her on the cheek and pulled out of the school parking lot. "Hello to you, too. Why do you always assume I'm going to leave something out?"

She groaned with frustration.

"Okay, I get it," I said. "It went great. We had some rocky moments, but overall the interview went well and I guess we became friends. He gave me a ride this morning."

"He drove you to the airport?"

"His driver did. Chris came along. It was nice. We could talk without worrying about the interview anymore. He's such an amazing guy."

"You totally like him," she accused, pointing her finger. Her eyes blazed, pleased with her conclusion. "You have a crush on him. Again."

"Of course I like him." I fought the goofy grin on my face. "He's charming and you never completely get over teenage crushes." I sighed, thinking about that morning. "It's nothing. It was a fun day I can tell my girlfriends about."

"Mom. You don't have any girlfriends. You're a total hermit. You write all day and talk to Aunt Julie only if she calls you. I'm practically your entire social circle."

"That's not true."

"Oh yeah? How many numbers do you have saved in your phone?" She plucked it from the cup holder and pushed a button.

"Hey, that's private."

"Mom!" she gasped. "You have a text and it's not from me."

Here it comes.

"Oh. My. God. Is Chris P. who I think it is?"

"What if it is?"

"He wants you to call him tonight."

"What? You're lying. Give me my phone." I lunged for it, but she was having none of that and I had to make a sharp swerve to avoid a trashcan.

"No way. Not yet. Are you telling me everything?" She held the phone to her chest, staring with bug-eyes.

"Yes, I swear. That's everything."

For the remainder of the afternoon, I became consumed with the question of when "tonight" was. It could be eight or eleven; either time would still be post meridian. I didn't want to seem too eager, like the poster child for poor impulse control, so I decided on nine o'clock.

Until then, I worked. I made dinner. I paid a few bills, but that did nothing in terms of settling my nerves. I glanced at the clock on my laptop for the fiftieth time—fifteen minutes until nine. *Now what?* I got a drink of water in the kitchen and flipped through a magazine, but eventually became preoccupied with the pink and gray speckled boomerang pattern of the counter top.

Eight forty-eight came. *This is stupid.* I dialed, the phone rang, and my heart pulsed in my chest.

"Claire, hello."

My heart raced even faster as I realized I hadn't planned out what to say. I should have made notes, written myself some snappy dialogue. "Hi. What's up?" I almost sounded comfortable, not at all like I felt.

"I just got off the phone with the engineer. We start mixing the record tomorrow."

"Oh, great," I said, happy with my immediate and logical participation in the back-and-forth.

"Definitely. It puts me one step closer to the finish line. That feels good."

"Great." My mind turned frantic as I struggled for vocabulary. It felt as though it was still my turn to talk. "Is there something you wanted to talk about?"

"I thought we could chat. It gets dreadfully boring in a hotel room."

"Didn't you have big dinner plans tonight?" I asked. "Am I keeping you from something?"

"I cancelled those." He hesitated. "So, no, you're not keeping me from anything."

There was a lull and I began to fear the worst, but he surprised me by launching into the personal.

"I was wondering something today. I know we discussed your job at lunch, but I'm curious which came first? Music or writing?" he asked.

It was hard to believe there was anything more to know after he'd grilled me at Marco's, but I indulged him because it wasn't my inclination to do anything less. "Oh, uh, music. I love to write, but that didn't start to come together until high school. I've always loved music."

"Any particular bands that you really liked?"

I panicked, realizing what band was at the top of the list at that time. "Just the normal stuff. I loved The Beatles when I was in middle school. My parents had a bunch of their old 45s. Then, I got into punk and new wave when I was a teenager. I liked a lot of local bands from Minnesota." I walked upstairs with the phone and crept past Sam's room, ducking into my bedroom to be alone with his voice. "What about you?" I stretched out on the bed and shut my eyes.

"You aren't interviewing me again, are you?"

"Oh, no. It's just a question. Unless it's something you want me to put in the story." I sat up, struck by the enormity of the gray area we were entering.

"I'm kidding. We're chatting, right?"

"Of course." I relaxed and dropped back against the pillows.

"My dad loved music. He used to play Wilson Pickett and Marvin Gaye for me. He showed me some chords on the guitar when I was five or six." The idea of the five-year-old version of Christopher learning to play guitar was adorable, little uncoordinated fingers on the fret board. "When I was in school, Graham from Banks Forest and I idolized The Jam and The Clash. Funny, those guys weren't much older than us."

We spent more than an hour on subjects from first loves to my favorite flower, but I was drifting, even though I couldn't bear to get off the phone. What I longed for, more than anything, was to talk to him until I fell asleep. I wondered if that would be okay with him.

"Claire, you sound tired. Get some sleep. We can talk tomorrow."

"Are you sure?" The whole scenario was so strange. It seemed impossible that Christopher Penman would want to talk to me on the phone even once, let alone two days in a row.

"Yes, go to bed. I'll ring you tomorrow."

"Okay. Thanks."

"Goodnight, Claire."

I floated off to sleep in exhausted bliss, the sound of his voice my only fading thought.

CHAPTER NINE

I WAS up with the sun to see Sam off to school, just like my mom used to do for my sister and me. My mom also served us homemade granola and did Tai Chi in the kitchen until the bus honked at the end of the driveway, so I wasn't mirroring the family tradition in every way.

After Sam left, I cranked the shower and let the water run. I tossed my overnight bag onto the shabby chair in the corner, finding my blue sweater slung over the back. The steam began to escape the bathroom, but I was overcome by a flaky compulsion to smell the sweater again. I knew it was crazy. There was court-ordered therapy for this sort of behavior. *One more time.* Sadly, his scent was nothing more than a shadow.

I worked through lunch, making little progress with transcribing the interview tape. The welcome interruption of text messages from Chris all afternoon made it impossible to focus.

Just got to studio. What r u doing?

Fun. I'm writing.

About what?

Ha. You know.

Engineer has big hairy mole.

Where?

Wouldn't you like to know?

Ewww.

I think he likes me.

Ewww.

You're just jealous.

The phone rang and my heart leapt when I saw that it was Patrick from *Rolling Stone* returning my call. Even though I'd only called him that morning, it felt like I'd been waiting forever to do my victory dance.

"Claire. I'm glad I caught you." Patrick's voice was cold. "I need to ask you a question."

"Of course," I replied, irked that he wasn't allowing me to launch into my account of what I hoped would prove to be the pinnacle of my journalistic career.

"Did something happen between you and Chris Penman on Monday?"

My heart wormed its way into my throat. "I'm not sure I understand." My voice came out in an anxious flutter.

"Let me send you something. Are you at your computer?"

Seconds later, Patrick's message appeared in my in-box. I didn't recognize the web site, but I clicked on the link and waves of nausea struck me as I watched the image load. I'd seen similar photos before, candid shots of someone at a restaurant or outside of Starbucks. It was so disorienting; it was hard to believe I was one of the people in the picture.

Chris's arm was slung around my shoulder as he wore a smug grin, his silver aviators magnifying every facial asset. I was only in profile, gazing at him with my mouth agape, looking as if I'd been struck in the butt by cupid's arrow. The caption read: "Former Banks Forest guitarist Chris Penman out for a romantic mid-day stroll on the streets of New York with a mystery woman."

"That's you in the picture, isn't it?"

My stomach churned. "Uh, yes, it's me. We were walking back to the hotel from lunch. We were on our way to finish the interview."

"You two look awfully chummy."

Now I wondered if Kevin was on to something. Maybe Chris had requested a female writer and Patrick had agreed. "I don't know what to tell you. Nothing happened."

He stuck me with the ominous clicking of his pen. "I'll have to take your word for it. I hope it's understood that anything like that is unacceptable in my book. That's a great way to keep yourself out of the magazine."

I swallowed. "Of course. It's not an issue."

"How did the interview go?"

"It was amazing," I answered, feeling deflated. "I think you'll have everything you wanted."

"Good. One more thing. I want you to review Penman's new record and we'll run it as a sidebar with the story. I don't want to waste space with a stand-alone review if his new record is as bad as the last one."

———

THAT NIGHT, Sam and I had pasta for dinner with what was left of last summer's pesto. The fragrance and taste of basil only made me crave the warmer days ahead. It was probably odd to most people that I had such a hatred for the cold since I'd grown up in Minnesota—common sense suggests that it would feel familiar. Although the winters in North Carolina were a vast improvement from endless months of snow, even a mild winter was still winter to me. There's no pretending it's something else.

I moved to North Carolina, to Chapel Hill, to be closer to my dad after my mom passed away. He'd told my sister and me that he was moving to Asheville, in the mountains, because he'd always wanted to live there. In truth, it felt as though he'd closed his eyes and dropped a finger on the map. I knew the real reason he chose a place as different as could be was because he needed to get as far away as he could. He couldn't survive in that house any more—the three-bedroom with a porch swing and crooked front steps that my parents had occupied since they were married in 1965. They'd brought home two daughters to that house and raised them, and my mom took her final breaths there, skinny and frail in a bed full of pillows and plastic tubes. He couldn't spend every day knee-deep in memories with the ghost of his wife, my mother, in attendance. It was too much.

Sam and I were finishing the dishes when there was a knock at the door—the arrival of Andrew, for their first homework date. She was off in a flash, leaving me no time to do anything about my t-shirt, wet with dishwater.

Andrew had been like a baby giraffe the last time I'd seen him, with an abundance of knobby limbs, but all six feet of him had evened out since then. His light brown hair was messy, an accurate portrayal of a skater boy along with his clothes, worrisome for many moms, but not me. I suspected that Andrew was a good kid behind the skinny black jeans and studded belt and most likely refrained from murdering squirrels in his spare time.

"Hey, Ms. Abby." Andrew waved, staring at his shoes.

"Thanks for bailing me out on the Physics homework. I'm sure Sam will enjoy your help much more than mine."

Sam shot me a look and was quick to end my interaction with Andrew. "We're going to go study."

Andrew followed Sam and I smiled when I caught sight of him reaching for her hand at the top of the stairs. I waited for the recognizable click of the bedroom door latch, but it never came and I decided to give Sam the trust she'd earned.

Listening for the door brought me back to Monday night—

the lump Chris put in my throat when he'd locked his hotel room door. I had an irrational longing for a different memory of that night. The adolescent parts of my brain had since concocted several alternate endings to our evening, none of them G-rated.

I decided to be bold. I decided to send Chris a text.

Going to bed soon. R u busy?

My pulse raced for nearly an hour as I checked email and waited for my phone to do something. I tried again.

R u there? U must be busy.

Thirty minutes and there was nothing. I put my laptop to sleep and laid my head on my desk. My expectations needed an overhaul and I knew it—it was staring me in the face. He was probably only calling and sending texts so he could make sure I didn't screw him over with my story. He'd probably been nothing more than bored last night. He'd probably sent those text messages to charm me. It was foolish to believe it could be anything more.

CHAPTER TEN

I WOKE the next morning full of disappointment from what hadn't happened—no phone call from Chris, no returned text message. I rolled out of bed and sought coffee, resenting everything that dared not cooperate with me. The coffee grinder was acting up and I came close to chucking it in the trash, but that would've meant no coffee and that would've been a disaster.

I ignored my email and went straight to work, but quickly remembered how atrocious my writing could become when I was pissed off. I'd write a line or two, become disgusted with myself, and then delete. I did that non-stop until my cell phone rang after ten. I looked at the Caller ID and it was as if the bluebird of happiness had landed on my windowsill.

"Morning, Claire," Chris said, with a sleepy velvet tone to his voice.

My shoulders dropped in relief. "Good morning," I replied, hearing my own voice dip toward his octave.

"I'm sorry I didn't call yesterday. Things got incredibly busy. We had a long day mixing and I didn't want to wake you last night."

His voice made me appreciate why I'd been so annoyed when I woke up—I'd already learned to miss him.

"So, how does it feel to be the mystery woman?" he asked.

I gulped. "You saw that."

"A friend sent it to me. He's very curious about you."

"My editor called about it. He was sure something had happened between us."

"Did you tell him it was just sparks?"

"What? Huh?" My left eyelid twitched like crazy. "Oh, you're joking."

He chuckled. "Come on, Claire. You can't tell me you didn't feel something between us on Monday. That picture is compelling evidence. We look great together. We're clearly enjoying each other's company."

The corners of my mouth popped up and I felt my face turn into a moon. "I figured you have that with every woman."

"Sure, with most women, but not to that degree very often. Maybe it was because you were flirting so mercilessly with me."

"I was not. You were flirting with me."

"The skirt you wore to my hotel room. That wasn't flirtation? What about the shoes? Those were some sexy shoes, Claire."

My heart squirmed at the subject. "Don't you need to get to the studio or something?"

"Oh, I see. We're going to live in denial. Okay. I won't give you a hard time." He laughed again, under his breath. "You know, my label called this morning. They wanted to make sure I get them a CD for Claire Abby as soon as possible. She's very important."

"That's funny," I said, realizing it wasn't the slightest bit humorous.

"I told them I'd take care of it personally since we're friends now. I'll make sure you get one late next week."

"You told the people at your record label that we're friends?" Things were becoming more tangled at every turn. We could be caught doing this, whatever it was, and that would mean I was screwed, royally.

"Sure. It's the truth, right?"

I sighed, uneasy. "Of course."

———

Everything blew up in my face the next morning. Patrick called, roaring with anger.

"Claire, I can't ignore the rumor mill. Even the interns are talking about it. You two have become friends? Seriously? How are you supposed to write an unbiased piece if you're in his back pocket?"

"Well, you know, that's not really fair—"

"And after that photo ran. Was that not enough to convince you that people will talk and always assume the worst?"

"I, uh..."

"Look, don't even bother. I don't know what's going on and frankly, I don't think I want to know. I just want to make sure you've got your priorities straight. This is your shot. This could open a lot of doors for you." The pen clicking began—never a good sign. "It's your choice. Either you're known as the one writer on the planet who could convince him to talk or people think of you as one of Penman's dingbat bimbos."

My heart pounded when I hung up. It felt as if the universe was sending me an unsubtle hint to put an end to childish flirtation. I was so close to reaching a turning point in my writing career and I couldn't squander it for a few minutes on the phone with a man, even if the man was Christopher Penman.

I pushed his number on the speed dial, my finger twitching,

but not out of my usual capricious anticipation. This was cold, dark dread.

"Hiya," he answered. "This is a nice surprise."

His voice dug into me, and I sighed, feeling sick and already regretful. "Uh, hey. Listen, we need to talk. We can't do this anymore." All I could hear was his breathing, making me feel as if I might drown in the quiet.

"And what are we doing?"

I groaned. "This. We can't keep talking on the phone. Everyone at your record label is gossiping about us."

"They are? I wasn't aware we were engaging in any nefarious activity. Aren't we entitled to be friends?"

"No. Everyone assumes that if you're friends with a woman there's something else going on. I can't risk this professionally."

"Are you asking me to stop calling you?"

That sucked the air right out of me, like a hot, gnarled rusty nail through the arch of my foot. I was asking Christopher Penman of all people, to stop calling me, to stop flirting, and to stop making me feel amazing. "I think it's for the best."

"That's too bad. I thought we were having fun." The moment of silence on his end of the phone was agonizing. "Best of luck with everything. Bye." And then he hung up.

CHAPTER ELEVEN

I STARED at my phone for two days. I did some other stuff too, but I was going through the motions. *What did I do?* I'd rejected one of the most amazing men on the planet, certainly the best one I'd ever met. He just wanted to be friends. I couldn't begin to think of a time when I'd been a bigger idiot.

I threw myself into my writing because I had to, my deadline moving in like a dark menace, but that only reminded me of what was wrong. My mom wouldn't stop stomping around in my thoughts. She was disappointed—I hated it when she used that word because there was no defense against it, it was daughterly kryptonite. She thought I should follow my heart, insisted that everything else would take care of itself but my heart needed help, it needed encouragement and constant bolstering.

On the third day, I couldn't take it. Mom was talking to me inside my head all day, every day, sometimes when I was sleeping, wearing me down like a woodpecker with great attention to detail. I decided to send a text to see what would happen; knowing the embarrassment of a snub could be enough to last a lifetime.

Hi. Do u hate me?

My message went unanswered for several hours, each minute an excruciating lesson in humility. I imagined him reading the text and deleting it, perhaps commenting to someone nearby that I must be patently unbalanced.

Then, finally, there was a glint of hope.

I don't hate u, waiting for u to call.

I couldn't help it; the giddiness worked through me, it wouldn't stay out of my veins.

How long have u been waiting?

Since u dumped me.

I didn't dump u.

Call me. My thumbs r tired.

I dialed, exponentially more anxious than the first time I'd called him. "Hi," was all that came out of me when he answered.

"Who is this?" he asked.

I held my breath, feeling as if I'd called the most popular boy in school only to discover he didn't know I existed. "Uh, it's Claire."

He laughed heartily. "You're too easy. How are you? It's nice to hear your voice."

I melted into my office chair and began spinning, propelling myself with a kick of my foot. "It's nice to hear your voice, too. What are you doing?"

"I just got to the studio so I only have a few minutes. Does this mean you've reconsidered?"

I smiled; continuing to spin, embracing lightheadedness and watching my office go by in a blur. "Yes, I've reconsidered. But we have to keep this a secret. That's my only condition."

"Keep what a secret? Our entirely innocent phone friendship with a thinly veiled attempt at flirtation?"

"If that's what you want to call it, yes."

"Whatever you want. Mum's the word."

Chris and I exchanged dozens of text messages that night and then slipped into a routine effortlessly, talking every morning and texting when he was in the studio mixing.

Things had to stay top secret, especially since we usually only talked about personal things—pet peeves, grade school crushes, and drinking stories. We nudged the boundaries every day and Chris seemed to be quite comfortable as chief of nudging. I was his sidekick, the adoring follower, and I mostly did whatever he wanted me to do.

He told Banks Forest stories one day, still unaware of my love for the band. That information could stay under wraps forever, but I closed my eyes and sighed when he told me about the night he and the drummer, Nigel, smuggled a live goat into lead singer Graham's hotel room. I didn't even think to ask where they got a goat; I simply soaked up every tasty piece of backstage shenanigans.

Everything took a turn the next day.

"So, Claire," he started. "I want to know if you're ready to take our relationship to the next level."

I giggled. "The next level, huh? What did you have in mind? Web cam?" I flopped down on the couch and cradled the phone in my neck.

"Now, why didn't I think of that? You're such a clever girl. No, I was thinking good old-fashioned phone sex. We've been on dozens of phone dates and there's been nothing. I'm beginning to think you're a tease."

I could see his devilish smile in my head. I knew I should be strong and resist, but I didn't really want to. "It's the middle of the day."

"Why should that stop us?"

"I'm not a phone slut. You're going to have to romance me if you want phone sex." The embarrassment of admitting that I was incapable of talking dirty on the phone would be more than I could take.

"Now I'm confused because I know you're a text slut. You said some very naughty things last night."

My eyes clamped shut. I'd known that was dumb when I did it. "That's not the same thing."

He laughed. "So I was right, you are a tease."

———

I MADE coffee Thursday morning and got right to work after Sam was off to school. I was in the home stretch with the article —I needed to listen to the record once Chris got me the CD, write the review, and then the final polish. The phone rang and I took the pencil out of my mouth, a bit dismayed by the number of teeth marks in it.

"Chris, hi," I answered, saving my work on my laptop.

"Hello, yourself. What are you doing?"

"I'm writing a magazine article about some musician from England. He's a real ass."

"They all are, and yet you make it sound fascinating." He cleared his throat. "So, my dear, I'm calling to extend an invitation and just tell me if you want me to bugger off. Would you like to come up to the city for the weekend? We could spend some time together and I could deliver your CD in person."

The question sent my mind racing. "You know that's not a good idea. I would be in serious trouble with *Rolling Stone* if anyone saw us together."

"Of course." He hesitated for a moment. "I could come to see you."

Now it was full-on panic. "Oh, wow, you know, that sounds great, but I'm not sure that would be very smart either."

"Nobody will find out about it if I come down there. You

live in North Carolina for God's sake." It was going to be tough to break it to him that we didn't have tumbleweeds rolling down the street in front of the General Store. "Seriously, Claire, it's been two weeks and our phone calls aren't cutting it anymore."

I didn't have enough time to think let alone come up with a good excuse. It was a huge risk. But my mom was there in my head. She'd conveniently decided that she now had a vote on anything related to Chris. She thought I should say, "yes" and worry about everything else later.

"I guess it would be okay."

"Wonderful. Where should I stay?"

The thought of him booking a hotel made me even more nervous—registering names, using credit cards, being in a public place.

"It might be best if you stay here, in my guest room. But this is just as friends. Can you live with that?" My heart thumped like it couldn't find the right gear—speeding up and slowing down, sometimes stopping altogether and then racing back to life.

"Of course, just as friends."

CHAPTER TWELVE

I WAS FRANTIC, with a disaster for a guest room, including a closet full of wrapping paper and the hideous crystal bowl my sister gave me for Christmas. Finding the good sheets meant some lengthy exploration of the linen closet, but I wanted Chris to be as comfortable as possible.

The doorbell rang when I got out of the shower. I rushed to answer it in my robe, dripping water on the floor. I greeted the deliveryman with the twisted towel on my head flopping to the side and prayed I wasn't giving him a free peek as I signed for the flowers, several dozen purple tulips.

Sam yelled for me from upstairs.

"Yeah. I got it," I answered, but she was already standing on the stairs.

"Who are those from?"

I shook my head as I plucked the envelope from the arrangement. The card read: *In anticipation of a wonderful weekend, Christopher.* I blew out an exhalation, appreciating the striking color of the tulips.

"Well?"

"Um, they're from Chris."

She slid her hand down the banister and jumped the final steps. "Oh, boy." She was fine with Chris coming for the weekend, but openly suspicious of him and his motives, which was normal for her. She questioned any man that came into our life.

When I pulled up to the airport terminal, I was horrified by the semi-disgusting state of my backseat. I crumpled the greasy fast food wrappers that Sam and Leah had left behind, dashing to a trashcan on the sidewalk.

"Destroying evidence?"

I turned to glimpse an implausible sight—the source of that heavenly voice, dressed in jeans, a gray t-shirt and a beautifully beat-up caramel brown leather jacket. He dug his hand into his hair and smiled a smile that crumbled my insides, leaving fragments of me scattered on the sidewalk. I'd forgotten the full scope of how tempting he was in person.

"No. I mean, just some trash from the car." He had me flustered from the word go—it was so much easier to speak in sentences on the phone.

He curled me into a hug with one arm and kissed the top of my head. "Your hair smells good."

Goose bumps started at my shoulders and made a slow outward crawl. I'd never survive an entire weekend of him. Every nerve in my body would be shot by the time it was over.

"Thanks. I just took a shower." I looked down, feeling shy. "Thank you for the flowers. They're beautiful."

The airport security guy with the Day-Glo yellow jacket blew his whistle sharply, eyeing my car. I hurried Chris and sped away before I got the lecture about leaving my car unattended at the curb.

I felt more at ease once I could busy myself with driving. "How was your flight?" I glanced over to see his profile and the seductive mole on his left cheek. *Drive the car, Claire.*

"Boring, but short. I can never read or sleep on the plane so I end up pestering the poor soul next to me or ogling the flight attendants. Uh, there's someone in that lane." He pointed out the other car with an anxious jab.

"Yeah, I see him. Are you hungry? I thought we could pick up Thai food. It's Sam's favorite."

"Sounds perfect. I look forward to meeting Samantha. It'll be interesting to see how much she's like her mother."

"What do you mean by that?"

"Well, I'm guessing she's as much of a handful as you are."

"Who says I'm a handful?" I changed lanes to pass an annoyingly slow driver and I noticed Chris watching over me, grinning at my huffy response.

"Oh now, don't start this. You're so defensive. You need to loosen up." He put his hand on the back of my neck and began kneading, creating a most pleasant friction. "You assume I'm going to say something bad."

Sam was waiting for us in the kitchen when we got to the house. She'd showered and changed into her UNC sweatshirt, her blonde spirals back to their usual springiness. I only hoped her mood would match her happy hair.

"Hi, honey." I set my things on the kitchen table and took the take-out bags from Chris, who'd insisted on carrying everything. "Chris, this is my daughter, Samantha."

He extended his hand and gave hers a quick kiss. "Your mum was right. You're quite a beautiful young lady."

I watched, anxious to see her reaction. Nothing could crack open a woman's tough exterior faster than a compliment.

"Yeah, she says that stuff. Last night, she was going on and on about how handsome you are and, what was the word you used, Mom?" Sam narrowed her focus. "Oh yeah, hot."

Chris grinned, looked at the floor, and then up at me. An instant of quiet played out and I felt the need to fill the embarrassing void.

"We picked up Thai food. I got the red curry you like."

"Awesome. That should totally clean out my sinuses," she replied, still sizing up Chris.

"Let me show Chris up to his room and we'll back down in a minute. You can get started if you're hungry."

The guest room was at the end of the hall, with a queen bed that I hoped would accommodate his limbs, and my mom's antique dresser she'd had when she was a girl. One door down from my room, the proximity was foolish, not that I could do anything about it. I already knew I would have a difficult time sleeping with him breathing nearby.

"You have your own bath. I know it's not The Rivington."

"It's perfect. Thank you."

The appreciative look on his face had me feeling as though a lumbering oaf was clog dancing on my chest. "Hungry?" I asked.

"You know it."

Sam had set the table while we were upstairs—two place settings and candles while conspicuously dimming the lights. She was sticking it to me, hard.

"Aren't you joining us?" I asked her.

"Nah. I want to check my e-mail. I'm sure you two want to be alone anyway."

We sat down to eat, the candlelight casting an irresistible glow on Chris's face. He raised his wine glass to clink with mine and his green eyes, which were almost black in the low light, deepened the channel he'd begun digging through my psyche at the airport.

Our dinner was so intoxicating that I felt hammered after one glass of wine. We talked about our week, which meant we talked about him, but that was perfect as far as I was concerned. He said astonishingly clever things and I giggled like a little girl and used every excuse I had to stare at him.

After dinner, I washed the dishes while Chris explored my CD and record collection. "Very impressive," he commented when I joined him, an unfamiliar grin on his face.

"Uh, thanks," I replied, wondering why he was so smiley.

"I discovered something quite interesting. You own every Banks Forest record on both vinyl and CD. You have some singles that are quite difficult to find."

My heart froze in my chest. I hadn't thought to hide my Banks Forest collection. Dumb, dumb, dumb.

He pulled out a rare Japanese import 12" single—white vinyl. I'd paid too much money for it, spending two solid weekends babysitting to earn the money. I'd called the record store every day after school to see if they still had it, their only copy, hanging in a plastic sleeve on the wall behind the register.

"I don't even have this one," he said.

The back cover had a photo of the band that still electrified me—Chris looked unbelievably dreamy, glowing tan with streaks of blonde in his coppery brown hair. His feet were bare and his shirt was, of course, open wide. They were in St. Barts, in the Caribbean, where the band had shot several videos. Even now, the image sent waves of fiery tingles down my spine.

"Why didn't you tell me about this?" he asked.

"Uh, I was a fan in high school. That was a long time ago." I stumbled over my words, playing it off as a triviality. "I didn't say anything because I didn't think it was important. I'm doing a story about you, not Banks Forest."

"True." He seemed to be enjoying every moment of our exchange. "Let's do the math, Claire. How old were you when you bought this?"

"I don't know, seventeen or so." I had an inkling of what was coming and I scoured my brain for a way out of it, but came up with nothing.

"I see." He looked at the single again and returned it to the shelf. "It's been a long time, but I seem to remember that most of the Banks Forest fans were girls about that age, sixteen or seventeen." He stepped closer, ramping up my nervousness. "I don't want to make sweeping generalizations, but most of our fans had romantic feelings toward one of the band members."

I tried to send him psychic messages. *You already know the answer. Please don't make me say it.*

"I'm curious, just for my own personal information of course, which member of the band you had an affinity for."

CHAPTER THIRTEEN

"HMMM, Claire? Was it Graham? The girls just loved Graham." He stepped closer and narrowed his stare. "Maybe Nigel?" He inched toward me again. "Surely, you must remember who your favorite member was."

I twisted my mouth in an attempt to disguise my embarrassment, but that look of British smugness told me I'd never get out of it. I glanced down at my bare feet and then around the room, studying the red and blue Oriental rug and my dinged up coffee table. I searched for a place to rest my eyes, ultimately landing on a plant in need of water.

"You were my favorite," I confessed in a whisper.

"I knew it." He winked at me. "Now things are getting interesting."

"No, nothing is interesting. That was a long time ago." My defense was pathetic, but I persisted. "What was I supposed to say to you the day we met? Hi, I'm Claire." I mocked myself, staring at the ceiling, knocking my head from side to side. "I was totally in love with you and your band when I was a teenager."

He interrupted. "Hold on. When you say you were in love—"

"You know what I mean." I squinted, beyond annoyed. "I was in love with the idea of you, let's put it that way. You don't honestly think I should've told you that before the interview. I would've had zero credibility. Would you still have told me everything?"

"No. I would've seduced you and sent you on your way. After lunch, of course."

"Very funny. You know, I totally figured out that you planned the trip to Francesca's and our lunch, that you were trying to butter me up." It seemed like the perfect time to bust him and it happily deflected things from me.

"You're right. I did plan all of it. I thought it'd be more fun." I was perturbed by his ready disclosure of the facts because it felt as if I hadn't caught him in a thing.

"Oh, and the whole trying on clothes thing, that didn't have anything to do with your good looks and the fact that I'm a woman."

"Just like your change of clothes that night had everything to do with me being a man."

I pursed my lips, confronted again with my attempt at matching his manipulation.

He lowered his voice, "I never planned for it to go beyond lunch." Now he seemed unsure of himself—vaguely unsure, but I would take what I could get. "You're a mystery to me, quite fascinating actually. You're the first woman I've met in a very long time, possibly ever, who didn't seem the slightest bit impressed by me. You're definitely the first woman I've ever met who didn't want anything from me."

He passed along a piercing gaze that left me needing air and took my hand. He wound up with only a few fingers, but it didn't matter. I was too wrapped up in words like fascinating.

"I wanted to spend more time with you. That's why I put things off when we got to the restaurant." Anyone else would've had a hard time with it, but he looked me right in the eye, unafraid. "Let's sit," he suggested, with brand new optimism in his voice.

I followed, but left a polite distance between us. "It's not true that I didn't want anything from you. I wanted you to tell me things that you didn't want to. That's something."

"That's not what I mean, Claire." It was heaven to hear him say my name. Claire, Claire, Claire. "A lot of women would've been fawning over me, especially with the events of that day, and you didn't seem to care at all."

"I was working. Even if I was impressed, which I was, it wouldn't have been professional for me to let on to that."

"You'd be surprised what some women will do. Most women flaunt their feelings so they can get a piece of me."

"I was too busy being pissed at you."

He laughed, smiling softly and reaching his arm over the back of the couch, bridging the divide between us. "You're so far away. Come here."

I scooted across the seat cushion a millimeter at a time. I was one weak moment away from pushing him back on the pillows and unleashing twenty-two years of pent-up teenage desire. My eyes remained on alert, my shoulders scrunching around my ears as if I was a turtle unsure of the world outside her shell.

He put his arm around me and cupped my shoulder with his exquisitely tingly hand. "This is better." He kicked off his enormous black leather shoes and stretched out his long legs beneath the coffee table, making himself at home. "Why were you so angry?"

"Because I felt like you tricked me and I felt stupid for not seeing it while it was happening. I never should've let things get so far off track. I could've screwed myself out of a very important interview."

He shifted his body weight toward mine and that made my entire body teeter on the edge, his presence creeping over me.

"Is that why you came to my room distracting me with perfume and cleavage while you asked me those awful questions?" he asked, further softening his voice.

My own voice squeaked in my throat. "I wouldn't exactly call it cleavage. And I had to do something..."

He reached over and his hand touched mine, putting an end to my train of thought. His thumb rode across my knuckles while his remaining fingers tucked underneath to touch my palm. I sat mesmerized by his hand on mine—so innocent and sweet, and such a dangerous boundary to cross.

My heart ached and struggled. I could've written a surprisingly detailed inventory of the reasons I shouldn't do this. My career, my future, Sam's future; all tied to one moment, one act that would mean I'd crossed the line, and for what? My heart would undoubtedly get broken. Chris Penman didn't fall for women like me.

He spread his hand over the top of mine, obscuring it beneath his fingers, strong from years of guitar playing. I tried to stop, but I couldn't help but turn toward him as he lowered his head to mine. My eyes closed and I became painfully aware of every uncertain move my body made.

The heat radiated from him as he drew closer, time moving at a crawl, my mind moving at record speed. I desperately wanted the kiss, despite my miles-long list of doubts. I could feel it in my head before it happened—the protracted version of my teenage daydream.

He gently pulled me closer, locking his hand around my waist. His face brushed against my hair and he moved his mouth to my ear, leaving my cheek white hot and me flustered. "May I kiss you, Claire?"

Just do it already. "We shouldn't," I murmured, finding my face nestled in his magnificent neck, the stubble gently poking at the bridge of my nose as I recognized his smell, pure and pleasing.

He eased my hair away from my neck and his lips wandered closer to my skin. "Because we're just friends?"

I'd have to be an idiot to be just friends with you. "I guess so." I was ready to give in after nanoseconds of superficial protest—right when our glorious moment dove sharply and went down in flames.

"Mom? Are you in here?" Sam flipped on the overhead light. "Oh! Sorry!" She jumped and flapped her hands, averting her eyes from what was probably a horrific scene to her. "I didn't know you were...I'm sorry."

I sat up straight and blinked from the sudden brightness, distancing myself from Chris. "It's okay, honey. We were just talking."

Chris cleared his throat, which only made us look guiltier. He rubbed my back as I leaned forward and craned my neck to see Sam.

"What do you need?" I asked.

"Is it okay if Andrew comes over? I know it's kind of late, but he won't stay long."

"Is this okay with his mom?"

"Yes. Can he?"

"I guess so," I said. "But he needs to be out of here by eleven-thirty."

"Thanks, Mom." Phone in hand, she flitted away.

"You'd better clean up your room," I yelled after her. I slumped back on the couch while every molecule in my body reminded me it was furious. "I guess I'm on teenager duty. Sorry."

Chris raked his fingers across my shoulder. "That's all right. I understand." He followed me to the kitchen, rubbing my shoulders and making me mental in the process. "I need to use the men's room. I swear I won't dirty the guest towels." He laughed.

I wondered how he managed to shrug off every little thing. "It's the door at the bottom of the stairs."

I opened the refrigerator, staring because I couldn't remember what I'd opened it for. The light was unpleasantly bright, cutting a wide swath in the dark across the gray and black checkerboard linoleum.

"Mom, I'm so sorry." Sam walked in and glanced out the window. "You should've warned me."

"Honey, really, it's fine. Don't worry about it." I closed the fridge and smiled, riddled with guilt at putting her in the situation. "I had no idea I'd need to warn you," I whispered.

Sam lowered her voice, "You really like him, don't you?"

I shut my eyes before stretching them wide. "It's that obvious, isn't it?"

CHAPTER FOURTEEN

THE SMELL of bacon woke me the next morning and I bolted out of bed, thinking I'd overslept. Downstairs, an unlikely pair of grins greeted me—Samantha and Chris, in their pajamas, making breakfast.

"Aren't you two cute?" I chirped. The sun rushed through the kitchen windows as specks slowed in the beams.

"Morning, Mom," Sam said, tending the bacon on the stove.

I poured myself a cup of coffee as Chris abandoned his post at the toaster and came up behind me, softly tucking my hair back behind my ear and whispering, "Good morning." He subtly pressed his body against mine, conveying everything I'd ever wished for in a nearly imperceptible show of force.

I turned in the sliver of space between him and the counter and looked into his gleaming face. "Be good," I mouthed, just as Sam turned to catch us standing too close. I ducked and stepped away. "Smells great. What are we having?"

"Eggs and bacon," Sam said.

"Thank goodness," Chris said. "I was wondering when I'd get a decent meal around here. I'm starving."

"You're always starving," I said.

Sam's eyes darted to me, seeming to take note of the familiarity my comment suggested.

We sat at the kitchen table and I was overcome with an unexpected contentedness, eating breakfast with the two of them. "What time did Andrew leave last night?" I asked, well aware of the answer. I'd been lying in my bed, alone, listening for kissing and the sound of jeans dropping to the floor.

"It was after eleven-thirty. Sorry it got so late."

"You must've been pretty engrossed in whatever you were doing." I eyed Chris and he appreciated my motherly torture with a grin.

"We were talking." She smirked. "Just like you and Chris."

Chris finished his breakfast in record time and sat back in his chair, lacing his fingers and stretching his arms above his head. He focused on me with his undeniable green eyes, at a slow burn this morning. His rumpled black t-shirt revealed a peek of the stomach I'd spent so much time pining over as a teenager. I hoped like hell that I'd live long enough to see the rest of it.

I dismissed Sam from clean-up duty after breakfast. Chris had offered to help, but I insisted he'd already done enough by burning the toast.

"What shall we do for an entire day together?" He sat at the kitchen table with his lanky legs crossed, the question dripping with ulterior motives.

"We should listen to your record. That's why you came to visit, isn't it?"

"Oh, no. I only promised to deliver the CD. I never said we'd listen to it together. I'll need a stiff drink before I subject myself to that."

He stood and crept up behind me. I grinned, watching his superb reflection in the kitchen window while my hands stayed submerged in hot, soapy water, leaving me conveniently defenseless.

"You know that's not the real reason. I came to see you." He placed his hands on my shoulders and leaned down, kissing my neck, the lowest spot where it curved into my shoulder. The kiss was subtle, evaporating quickly, but leaving behind a lasting tingle.

I closed my eyes as the dishwater steamed, swirls of suds, and my body warmed from his touch. "We agreed this weekend was just as friends," I croaked. The sun beating through the window, my hands in scalding dishwater—none of it left me as hot as he did.

"I'm sorry." He kept hold of my shoulders, murmuring with his face at the back of my head. "I had the feeling you were re-thinking that last night."

I dried my hands and turned, a grave error on my part. It was impossible to form coherent thoughts with his face so close. "I was, I mean I am, but not now. I don't know if this is a good idea and it's hard when you do things like that because it makes me want to give in."

A satisfied smirk washed over his face. "Well, now that I know that you might give in, I can try to behave." He played with my fingers, hot and chapped from the dishwater.

"Good. I appreciate that," I said, happy I'd established order.

With that, he bundled me in his arms and pushed his hand into my hair, creating chaos, kissing me exactly as I'd wanted him to last night. It was fluid and more exceptional than I'd ever imagined, his lips moving perfectly with mine as he tugged me closer. I rose on to my tiptoes, no longer bothering with the charade of resistance, arching my back while grasping at his. It surpassed the proverbial opening of floodgates, my entire being at his mercy, which he seemed to sense as he softened our connection, torturing me with a delicate brush of his mouth against mine.

I didn't dare open my eyes. Good or bad, I was terrified by what might happen next.

His breath, gentle and hot, grazed my lips. "I was hoping that might help you decide if this is a good idea."

————

I WAS unrecognizable after my shower. The woman in the mirror had a flush in her cheeks and her eyes were a vivid blue, nearly violet. I hadn't felt so good and frustrated in a very long time.

Chris was waiting for me downstairs in another devastating pairs of jeans and a white shirt, frayed at the cuffs and collar. On any other man, I would've thought the shirt was a sign he was in need of a wardrobe overhaul. He sat in my favorite chair, reading a magazine with hair that was damp from his shower. That alone demanded restraint. I imagined myself slinking over and running my fingers through his glorious mop—he probably would've loved it.

"There you are," he said, tossing the magazine on the table. "I was about to send a search party."

"I must require more maintenance than you do." I perched on the arm of the chair but kept my hair-messing hands to myself. My role in his bad behavior became evident when his arm curled around my hip and he tried to pull me onto his lap. "You're not holding up your end of the deal," I said, grinning.

"I said that I would try. I will sporadically slip up. You can hardly blame me."

Sam came downstairs, engrossed in a novel, wearing a lavender flea market cardigan with a short black skirt and grungy Converse high tops. She'd done her own thing with clothes as soon as she'd learned to dress herself. I'd encouraged her no matter how loony the outfit, even when it meant sending her to school looking like a box of Froot Loops.

"I'm going to do homework at Leah's. Then we're going over to Andrew's house to watch his band practice."

"Ah, Andrew is in a band," Chris interjected.

"It's part of his appeal," I said.

"Mom. Please." She wedged the book into her backpack and the zipper strained when she closed it. "I'll be home by four. Okay?"

A car horn made a muffled honk and Sam was gone like a lavender streak. I locked the door after her, out of habit, and my stomach lurched when I realized we were alone, nothing but privacy and a colossal lack of willpower between us.

I strayed to the kitchen for water, hoping that would calm everything brewing inside me, but Chris followed and his physical presence, the way he took up space, made me woozy.

"Now what?" He placed a hand on my hip, hooking his thumb into one of the belt loops on my jeans.

"This would be a good time to listen to your CD."

"I'm not ashamed to admit I'm afraid of your opinion." He playfully tugged at my waist.

"I thought you were happy with the way the record turned out."

"I'm still gun-shy." His face was so distracting. A girl could spend days going from one captivating feature to the next—the green, the impossibly square jaw, those perfect pinkish brown lips. "Once you hear it, you and I will be the only people on the planet who know both the music and the story behind the songs. It's like I'm baring my soul to you. Again."

For the first time since the interview, I saw the vulnerability he hid so well. He'd clearly learned to use his many assets—good looks, fame, sense of humor, to deflect the bad things. I knew then that there were parts of him that were fragile, broken even, despite the capable and commanding persona he showed the rest of the world.

"I promise to be fair."

"What if you don't like it? That will certainly kill the mood." He pulled me closer, searing me with a dreamy gaze.

"Please, Chris. You're killing me."

"Oh, right. Sorry." He kissed me on the forehead and raised his hands in surrender. It was meant to look as if he was relenting when I suspected he was building things he could set aside for later.

I shook my head to erase the fuzziness. "Let's do this. You'll feel much better when it's over."

"Hey, that's my line." He walked away and swiped the CD from my desk. "Remember, only half of these songs are the final mixes and nothing has been mastered yet." He was locked and loaded with qualifiers, reasons why it might not be perfect.

"Got it. Now play it. Enough build-up."

Chris put in the CD, pushed play and quickly traveled to the other side of the room, distracting himself with book spines.

"Don't you want to sit?" I asked, finding my spot on the living room couch and tucking my legs under my butt.

"I would love to sit with you, but I can't bear to watch your reaction."

I couldn't blame him. It was never easy to listen to music with the musician or band in the room and it had to be much more difficult the other way around. Still, I felt as if I owed him my honest assessment in person, even if he thought he didn't want it.

He seemed to relax after the first two songs, but could never bring himself to look at me. The record was surprising—soulful, genuine—the opposite of his last attempt. Many of the songs were nothing more than his voice and guitar and sometimes drums or piano, but that let the lyrics, everything he needed to express, float to the surface.

I was relieved and truly happy for him when we finished listening. I didn't love all of it, but he had every reason to be proud. The look on his face was awful when I approached him. He preemptively recoiled as if I was about to throw a punch.

"It's amazing. Your voice sounds incredible and the lyrics are so poetic, they're heartbreaking."

He stared at me for a moment, holding my arms at my side. I had no idea what he was searching for—a fissure that would give away what he feared was my true opinion.

"How do I know you aren't lying?"

"I didn't like two of the songs."

"Okay..." He nodded, but his eyes narrowed as if unconvinced.

"And I hated your first solo record. I thought it was one of the worst things I'd ever heard."

He blinked. "Uh, thank you, I guess. I mean, you're right. The first one was awful. It's good to know you'd tell me if it was bollocks. Which ones didn't you like on the new one?"

"The third one and the second-to-last one," I replied, hoping I wouldn't hurt his feelings. "They aren't bad, I just didn't like them that much."

"Was it my singing?"

I tilted my head to the side. "Don't torture yourself. You did a great job. I probably just need to listen to it again." I snapped up my keys from the coffee table and looped a fluffy gray scarf around my neck. "Let's get out of here and find some lunch."

Chris studied me with a peculiar look. "I have to stop you from doing this."

"What?"

"You know what. Give me the keys." He snatched them from my hand. "There's no way I'm letting you drive. You are the bloody worst driver I've ever seen." He'd crushed me with the insult but then he had the nerve to continue, "Including my mum, who has very poor vision and babbles to herself constantly."

"I'm not a bad driver. This town is full of bad drivers. I drive defensively."

He held open the kitchen door, making a point of keeping the keys out of my reach. "Listen to yourself. Does it make sense that you'd be the one good driver and everyone else is barmy?"

With any other man, this would have prompted true indignation from me. "You know, you're the first person who has ever criticized my driving."

"I'm not surprised. Everyone has been living in fear. The intervention is long overdue."

Chris stepped ahead of me and opened my car door. I couldn't recall any man opening a car door for me, other than one who'd been paid to perform the task. It made me feel overly lucky as he rounded the front of the car. He drew me in so easily when it was just the two of us, when my worries about what I was doing were frolicking in the outer reaches of my mind, near the spot where my mom hangs out until I need her.

"Where to?" he asked.

I didn't want to go anywhere. What I really wanted was to take him back inside and get past the build-up, but I held fast and directed him to a pizza place uptown. Afterward, we walked among small packs of students, out for a Saturday study group or ice cream. I wrestled with my paranoia about anyone seeing us together, but decided to set that aside for the day. I even let him take my hand.

We returned to the house before Sam was expected and I put on some Coltrane and a pot of coffee. The caffeine was supposed to get us through the rest of the day, but Chris sprawled out and fell asleep on the couch. He was bewitching, his chest rising and falling with every breath, an arm tucked under his head, and his mouth agape in complete relaxation.

I folded myself into the chair across from the couch with a magazine and my second cup of coffee. The idea of reading anything was a ruse, I could only sit and pore over him. While he was asleep, I could look at him without my pulse racing.

Hours later, there were signs of life. "Hey, sleepyhead," I said.

He smiled and stretched. "That felt great. Couldn't tell you the last time I had a kip."

"You must've needed it." It was dorky, but I felt a pride at the fact that he'd taken a nap at my house. Drawn to him, I slinked to the end of the couch, at his feet.

"What time is it?"

"Around five." Without thinking, I placed my hand his leg. I had to touch him.

"I slept for a long time. What've you been doing?"

"I read a magazine. Sam came home and packed up for a sleepover."

He propped himself up on his elbow and ran his hand through his unbelievable, sleepy hair, turning to give me one of his looks. I didn't have a name for it or know exactly what it meant, but I had an idea.

"A sleepover," he said. "So, it's just us. For the night."

"Yep."

"That's an interesting development." His matchless eyes flickered. He moved his legs and sat up next to me.

Had it occurred to Chris that I'd dreamt of a moment like this off and on since I was seventeen years old? Because I had. My hand impulsively moved to his thigh, but then I froze. I couldn't even look at him.

He graciously put his arm around me and pulled me closer. He did it without any sense of urgency, not the way I would've done it at all. My whole body was boiling over with anticipation; I couldn't see how he could be so nonchalant once we were touching.

He gave me what was best described as a hug, holding the side of my head flat against his chest. His heart beat quickly, but at an even pace, while mine rattled around in my body. He kissed the top of my head. "Your hair is so soft, Claire."

The instant he said my name I'd had enough. I wrangled my head from his grip and grappled with the resulting look of surprise on his face. "I'm going to explode if you don't kiss me." My only thought was that I couldn't risk falling prey to a rare tropical disease tomorrow or accidentally drinking drain cleaner.

He smiled at my impatience and leaned down to give me a kiss, delicate, but longer than the one in the kitchen. He pursued things slowly, being too gentle—it annoyed me at first, even though we were doing exactly what I wanted to be doing. He soon intensified things, showing more passion, his tongue deftly finding the most sensitive part of my lips.

I shifted to my knees to get closer to him, but it wasn't enough so I swung my leg to the other side of his hips, straddling his lap and wrapping my arms around his neck.

He laughed quietly between our lips. "Easy, tiger."

His shirt—his crisp, white shirt with what seemed like fifty buttons had to go. I fumbled while he sweetly kissed my neck, and I pushed the white fabric back over his shoulders and pulled it down his arms to be rid of it. His chest and stomach were even better than I'd imagined, mostly smooth with a medium patch of reddish-brown hair in the middle and lower, the most amazing bit of hair around his belly button.

I shied away at first, about to touch territory that had once held endless mystery. I extended my hand with caution, but things changed once I'd done it, once my fingers rolled over his

shoulder. Then I became an ill behaved child in the candy aisle
—I wanted everything so beautifully displayed before me and
my hands were everywhere.

He pressed his gaping lips against the base of my throat and
slid both hands under my sweater. His warm palms inched up
my back, causing a sensation that made me shudder, stirring up
every desire held tightly in my head. He carefully peeled away
the sweater. The feeling of the skin of his stomach against mine
was unspeakable, sweet relief.

He sat back and eyed me. I'd been quite judicious with my
choice of bra that morning, striking a balance between sweet
and seductive, ivory and lacy. He poked a finger under the strap
while he smiled at me with bedroom eyes. He sought my throat
again and mumbled, "Claire, you're so beautiful," against
my skin.

I was amazed when I didn't black out at his devastating
choice of words.

He traveled down my chest with his mouth until he reached
the center point of my bra, then along the edge that cupped my
breast. I was desperate for him to take it off and I arched my
back. I was about to give orders—to remind him that the hook
was right where his capable hands were, but he took his sweet
time, torturing me with every movement, driving me crazy with
his exquisite lips, and I kept quiet.

Then I worried about the practical. If things continued the
way I hoped, we would need a condom. He was unbelievable, a
dream come true, but his penis was probably a Petri dish.
There'd been a mess of women before me.

My brain then escalated its rude intrusion, attempting to
take over when I wanted it to be all about my body. I tried to
push the thoughts aside, but they fought to return, they
screamed for my attention. *What about the story? What about
my career?* I was being nothing but reckless. This would make it

very hard to write an unbiased piece and I'd arguably already crossed that line. Why couldn't I control myself?

"Is something wrong?" he asked, still kissing my chest. He stopped and peered at me with his otherworldly green, and I couldn't help it.

"We can't do this." I shut my eyes and pinched the bridge of my nose.

"What's wrong? Are you okay?" He closed his arms around my lower back.

I almost wanted him to be mad—shut me off completely. I swallowed, searching for the words to explain my stupid problem. "I want to do this, I really do. I've thought about you constantly since the day we met. But this doesn't feel right."

"You've thought about me since the day we met?" He smiled and traced his finger along my collarbone, totally putting me off track.

"Of course I have." I hated that he was acting dense about how much I obviously liked him. "I'm worried about what this will do to each of us and our careers, if we do this." I stared at the ceiling, afraid to read his reaction and ashamed of my crooked logic.

He held me tighter and rested his lips on my shoulder.

I could tell he was thinking, but I was too scared to know the specifics. I continued my rambling, seemingly endless justification. "The piece I'm writing is so important to both of us and I don't want it to be overshadowed by something else. You know how people love to talk."

"Shhh. It's okay, Claire. Really."

CHAPTER FIFTEEN

MOST MEN WOULD'VE BEEN INCREDIBLY PISSED. I would've been, if it had happened to me. Instead, he held me in his warm embrace.

"I'm so sorry," I muttered. "You probably think I'm a nut job. I wouldn't blame you if you wanted me to take you to the airport right now." I whispered, my voice cracking.

"Don't be ridiculous. You're so hard on yourself." He grasped my shoulders and eased me back. "I like you. It doesn't have to happen this weekend. We can have other weekends."

"We can?"

"Of course."

"Oh." I smiled, shyly. "I didn't know."

That, he found laughable. "Have I not given you enough hints? The kiss in the kitchen wasn't enough? What about just now?"

I felt thickheaded. "I didn't think there was any way this could be real. That you could be real." My words floated away as I set a finger to his shoulder, distracted by the appeal of his bare skin. Sometimes, it all felt so impossible.

He smirked. "Please don't put me on a pedestal. Someday

I'll show you how deeply flawed I am as a human being." He gave me a quick kiss. "Now, you need to put your clothes back on or I might have to rescind my promise to be understanding."

I climbed off his lap and forced my hands through the arms of my sweater, watching him stand and turn his shirtsleeves right side out, eyeing that spot around his belly button before it disappeared as he fastened the buttons.

"Now what?" I asked.

"Now we enjoy a quiet evening together, alone." Chris pulled my hand. "We'll need to avoid horizontal surfaces."

I decided we should start drinking, a bottle of wine or at least a few beers—Chris opted for beer and I agreed. It was far less romantic than wine. I sifted through the fridge, searching for something to make for dinner. "You must be hungry."

"Of course."

"I have some steaks. We could throw them on the grill."

"Sounds perfect."

Well after dinner, by nine-thirty, I was yawning.

"Looks like somebody's zonked," Chris said.

"I didn't sleep well last night."

"You won't hurt my feelings if you want to get some sleep."

My heart sank. He'd been so sweet to me all day. "I don't want to waste our time together."

His eyes softened. Anyone else would've been nothing but frustrated by my erratic behavior. There seemed to be contemplation before a grin spread across his face. "We could sleep together in your room. Your rules. No funny business."

I groaned inside at the thought of my rules. "That would be so nice, but are you sure?"

"I can't wait to sleep in the same bed with you and have absolutely no sex, whatsoever," he replied, in a rebuilt version of his accent. "I trust you have something suitably frumpy to wear." He started to laugh. "I'm thinking flannel."

I skipped up the stairs after he'd made his suggestion. The sex could wait. I hoped he was serious when he'd said we'd have other chances.

He was nuts if he thought I was going to wear something frumpy to sleep with him the first time, even if we were going to be on our best behavior. I changed into light blue pajama pants and a tank top and finished getting ready for bed. When I flipped my bathroom light off, Chris was waiting for me on the bed in a gray t-shirt and navy blue striped pajama pants, unfairly handsome. My willpower wavered. I knew I'd done the responsible thing, but my body wasn't on board with the decision at all.

"Where do you want me?" he asked, clearly inquiring on which side of the bed he should sleep.

"Oh, uh, it doesn't really matter. How about the left?"

"Do you mean the left when you're in the bed or when you're looking at the bed?"

"Why do you have to be so difficult?" I asked, smirking as I climbed over him to the other side of the bed.

"Is that how it's going to be then?" He flattened me on top of the covers and then hopped up and threw back his side of the comforter. "Come here."

"No way. I don't trust you," I answered, breathless.

"I want to conduct an experiment. You're going to have to trust me at some point." He had that look in his eye—the one that prompted me to force the issue on the couch. "Give me your hands. Both of them."

"Why?"

"I can't tell you or it won't be scientific. You might try to throw off the results." He fought a smile.

I decided to give in, mostly confident that he was too much of a gentleman to renege on his promise. "Okay, but this is against my better judgment."

He took my hands and pressed them together with palms facing. I relaxed and settled the side of my face on the cool pillow, watching. He gathered my wrists in his one hand, leaving the other free.

"Now, this won't hurt a bit."

He began tickling me, mercilessly, all over my stomach, on my sides, in my armpits, and in the crook of my neck. It was likely only twenty seconds of complete bodily chaos, but it felt like an hour. I was dying, in pain from laughing so hard and jerking all over the place—I could barely breathe by the time he was finished. I hadn't yet seen him laugh that hard.

"Don't," I gasped, "ever do that again." I huffed and laughed. "What in the hell would make you do that?"

"Curiosity," he said, flatly. "I don't know why, but I enjoy doing that to people."

"And by people, you mean women."

He grinned. "Yes, I suppose I do mean women."

The gross disparity between our love lives was something I'd thought about more than once. I didn't want to know the specifics and he'd probably lost count years ago. There had to have been at least one girl in every city before Elise came along, and Banks Forest circled the globe countless times. Since his divorce, he was a tabloid regular, always with a new companion on his arm.

I, on the other hand, was still in the single digits. None of them was spectacular, although Kevin had had his moments.

We settled in, now that tickling torture time was over and I turned off the bedside lamp, leaving us in darkness. I thought I'd feel great about the decision to hold off on anything physical if I didn't have to look at him, but his pull on me was still considerable in the dark.

"Claire, I've been wanting to ask you. What's the story with Sam's father?"

I felt no hesitation at telling the story, however painful. Chris had shared his secrets with me. "His name is Brian. We met in college. We both worked at the campus radio station. We liked a lot of the same bands." This was dredging up things I hadn't thought about in a long time. It was such a great time at the beginning of that friendship, before everything went wrong —it had been one of the only times I'd had a real guy friend. "There was nothing romantic between us. It was hard to keep up with Brian's love life. He's very handsome. Not as handsome as you, but you get the idea."

"You have to stop saying things like that. You'll give me a big head."

"I think you're entitled to your big head." I paused for a drink of water and Chris wrapped his hand around my arm when I turned back. It was tingly, but I could concentrate enough to talk.

"After senior year started, we went to see a band and I got really drunk. Brian walked me home to put me to bed. The last thing I remembered was taking off his clothes. We tried a boyfriend-girlfriend thing for a few months, but it was a disaster. I figured out I was pregnant three weeks after we broke up."

"Wow."

"He said he wanted to be there for me, but he wasn't in love with me. He was there when Sam was born and he sends her gifts on birthdays and Christmas, but that's about it. He moved to upstate New York, got married, and has three kids." There was a whole continuation of this story, about my mom getting sick and dying while I was pregnant with Sam, easily the darkest chapter of my life.

Chris stroked my forearm and took my hand. "That must've been hard. I can't fathom becoming a parent at that age. I was so self-absorbed."

"I think that's why Sam and I are so close. We had to grow

up together." I couldn't help but think about the child he'd lost and the sadness he had that would never go away. "I can't imagine what my life would be like without her."

I suddenly felt very cold and retreated further under the covers, twitchy, with goose bumps. Chris put his arm around me and moved closer, keeping me warm. He tenderly swept my hair behind my shoulder and rubbed my back. In the dark, I could've been with any man in the world, but I very gladly wasn't.

———

I SOMEHOW MANAGED to get cold in the middle of the night, which was crazy since Chris was such a hot-body, literally. He seemed to run at least five degrees warmer than me. He'd insisted on getting the extra blanket for me and I had to talk him through it since my bedroom was unfamiliar terrain in the dark. I felt terrible when he stubbed his toe, but I laughed as he unleashed a string of incredibly cute British profanity.

The quilt was one my mom had made, the only one she ever finished, although she'd had a closet full of ones she started. The squares and triangles were faded blues, seams intersecting in a mostly ordered way—everything about my mom had been a shade off-kilter. I couldn't escape the significance as I cozied up with him under it, that it was the blanket on my bed when I was seventeen, when I first dreamt of him.

He woke in his usual sunny mood with a smile and arms that reined me in; he didn't say anything, but kept to humming an odd tune in my ear. I would've paid anything to know what he was thinking. Maybe there was a chance he was sad about leaving. Maybe he was preoccupied with going back to New York and returning to work. He'd said that we had weekends ahead of us and I wanted specifics, but was terrified to ask. I would've been disappointed by any answer other than, "I've been eyeing that cute little house next door."

"When can I see you again?" I blurted, only partly shocked that the words in my head had erupted from my mouth.

He hesitated, which made my heart pound. "That depends on when you finish the story." He released his hold on me and rolled to his back. His eyes were such an unusual shade in the morning light—the color of old Coke bottles. "It's obvious you won't feel comfortable with this until you've turned in your article."

"It'll only take a few days to finish now that I have the CD." I propped myself up on my elbow.

"I'm mixing through Thursday. Sam told me yesterday that her spring break starts next weekend."

My shoulders dropped. I knew there had to be a bad part. I'd completely forgotten, so wrapped up in the story and my own head that the calendar was a foreign concept. "I guess that throws a wrench in things."

Chris laughed, which seemed like a mean-spirited response. "You're so quick to assume the worst. I was thinking that her spring break was an opportunity." He rolled back to his side and put his hand on my waist with a playful tug.

"I'm listening." I fought to hide the growing smile on my face.

"Good. I'd planned to take a break after mixing. Since I'm already on the east coast, I was going to go down to my place in the Caribbean for a few days, but I don't have anyone to join me. It'd be a lot more fun if you let me take you and Sam."

I was floored. I also couldn't imagine a proportional response. Was I supposed to hop out of bed and jump up and down and shriek like I'd just won a car on a game show? That never would've seemed believable coming from me, no matter how excited I was.

"Well, wow, thank you. That sounds amazing. It makes me nervous though, taking a trip together."

"I knew you'd say that. It'll be fine, I promise. We'll have total privacy. Just a few days to relax and get to know each other better."

I watched as a happy look took hold in his eyes and he ran his thumb along my lower lip, leaving me with only one answer. "You have to let me pay for our flights."

"Absolutely not. I'm not bringing you unless you let me pay for everything." He held a finger to my mouth when I tried to argue the point. "Don't say another word. You'll never win."

It wasn't in my nature to give in to a man, I usually had to put up a fight about something, but Chris wasn't like any other man, so I held my breath then said yes.

CHAPTER SIXTEEN

ANDREW AND SAM had a lengthy performance of "goodbye" the morning we left for our trip. At least it kept her occupied for a few minutes. Watching them hang on each other in the driveway tugged at my heartstrings, but in a "spare me" sort of way. His arms tightly wound around her neck and her hands deep in the back pockets of his skinny jeans, as if they were doing a slow dance in the school gym. I was happy they liked each other so much, but I also worried about her acting like me, jumping in with both feet, unconcerned with the ramifications if anything went wrong.

Sam and I had our first surprise of the day when we checked in at the airport and learned that Chris had booked us in First Class. She passed the time in the land of leather seats and legroom by requesting snacks and sodas as if they were her last meal, fully decked out in her island-hopping gear, white Capri jeans and flip-flops. I'd had the worst time deciding on an outfit, up late, trying things on and second-guessing. I settled on one of two new sundresses—navy blue with a quirky button detail down the front, an off-white cardigan to ward off airplane cold and a pair of strappy leather wedge sandals.

We arrived in Miami twenty minutes before Chris's flight was due to come in and I dashed to the bathroom to check my make-up. My hands trembled as I re-applied mascara. I didn't remember being quite so nervous when he came to visit me, but the anticipation was of a different scope now.

When the door opened at his gate, he was the third person off the plane. It was exactly like the morning in the lobby of The Rivington—everything turned dark and my focus was Chris, as if he was walking through a tunnel of light, in slow motion, of course.

He wore my favorite jeans and a black dress shirt, sleeves rolled up and an extra button undone. The ubiquitous sunglasses were swiped away once he saw me, causing me to hold my breath as his eyes lit up and worked their way into mine.

"Hello, beautiful," was all he said as he wrapped an arm around my waist and pulled me in for a kiss. He hesitated for a second, holding me close, and the heat between us was highly inappropriate given that there were old people and babies around.

"Hi, handsome," was my not-so-clever reply. Like a shot of good tequila, he killed off a bunch of my brain cells. My entire body felt like it was on fire.

Chris took my hand while we walked down the concourse. "I got your message last night. I'm glad everything went well when you turned in your story," he said.

I was so disoriented by being in his presence again that the article had slipped my mind, completely. "Oh, it went great. Patrick called me this morning before we left for the airport and it's definitely the cover. Did anyone talk to you about an exclusive?"

"Yes, I got a text about it before we left New York." He

glanced at me and smiled. "I assured them that I'd only spill my guts for you."

"Did you really say that?" I asked. "That's the kind of thing that got me in trouble in the first place."

"Don't worry," he said as we approached our gate. "I'm sure it's fine."

Waiting to board, I glimpsed a couple with two girls around Sam's age. The wife seemed to recognize Chris, directing her husband to take a picture with his phone. I turned away, fearing another surprise. Chris either didn't notice or didn't care.

Chris and I huddled in the last row of First Class with Sam in the seat in front of me. He stretched his legs into the aisle and held my hand. He eyed me once when he raised my fingers to his lips, driving a splendid shock through me. I thought about telling him to cut it out, but decided that part of giving in, a skill I was working like crazy to master, was to sit back and allow him as much influence as he wanted.

The flight attendant, with pert brown hair and crinkles around her eyes, offered airplane wine in her drawl. She watched us, resting her hand on the back of the seat in front of Chris, looking as if she might burst. "Let me guess. Honeymoon?" She wore the convinced grin of a professional.

Chris replied quickly, "Guilty, as charged." She giggled at his goofy response while he patted the back of my hand. "Although, to be honest, this is a second honeymoon. Fifteen years. It seems like yesterday. Right, honey?"

Sam overheard the exchange and glanced back, snickering at Chris. He muttered the continuation of his charade, nodding at Sam, "Our daughter. We adopted her from a Swiss orphanage. Her parents were killed in a tragic skiing accident. They both ran into a low-hanging branch." He made a slow slashing motion across his neck and I covered my mouth.

The flight attendant's eyes flew open and her face paled

before she stuck out her lower lip. "I'll be sure to bring her an extra cookie," she whispered.

"Swiss orphanage?" I asked under my breath, when she'd finally gone.

"I told you I'm unable to read or sleep on the plane. This is my only source of entertainment." He arched one eyebrow, driving me crazy.

"I can't wait to see your villa." With no previous experience, I had nothing by which to measure. I'd imagined a few things, all of which were probably ludicrous.

He gathered my hand again, rubbing his thumb over the tops of my fingernails. "This is my second place on the island. As I'm sure you know, since you were president of the Banks Forest fan club, the band used to spend a lot of time there."

"I was not president of the Banks Forest fan club."

"Please, Claire, I'm trying to talk." He smiled at me and softened my heart a bit further, with no real effort on his part. "After Elise and I got married, she made me get rid of the first house. She thought it would remind me of the other women who'd stayed there."

It was another example of Elise's paranoid manipulation, but there was a part of me that would've done the same thing. If he were mine, truly mine, I wouldn't want to imagine him with anyone else.

"It was a pain in the ass because the really good houses are hard to come by, but now I like this one better. It's up on a cliff. I can't wait for you to see the view from the shower in your room."

He'd made a point of giving me my own room, to be sensitive to how Sam might feel about it. Nearly every man I'd dated had viewed her as an inconvenience; never before had one considered her feelings above his own.

We switched planes in St. Maarten for our final leg to St. Barts, which Chris said would be short and "exciting". I thought nothing of it until we stepped onto the tarmac and identified the plane we were to board, which looked more like a rusty tuna can than an air-worthy means of transportation.

"You're kidding."

"Think of it as an adventure." Chris pulled me along while Sam was so excited she was like a shaken can of soda.

A scraggy man with dark greasy hair in an airline uniform stood at the bottom of the metal stairs leading to the airplane door. He puffed on a cigarette, squinting while he took tickets. His long sleeves were rolled up to reveal a topless tattoo and several gold bangle bracelets. As we passed him, Chris said, "That's our pilot."

"Very funny."

"If you say so."

Chris had to stoop to get through the door and make his way to our seats. I followed, with a glorious view of his backside in those jeans. There was room for about forty passengers, two on each side, but it wasn't a large plane—the seats were tiny and close, made for the miniature people of an era that pre-dated us all.

Next to a salt-streaked window, I tried to focus on what was waiting for us after we landed if we were all still living. Chris plucked my hand from my lap and settled it in his own.

"It'll be fine," he said again.

The final passengers boarded and as Chris predicted, greasy hair guy climbed aboard with another uniformed man, and they took the seats in the cramped cockpit. You could see them flipping switches and checking gauges, which wasn't reassuring in the least. The plane door squeaked and strained when the crew outside closed it.

Our pilot slid a tiny window open to flick his cigarette ashes. With it hanging from his mouth and smoke billowing about his head, the plane began to taxi. We sputtered down the runway and were ultimately airborne.

The plane dangled over the sprawling Caribbean Sea, swinging as if we are at the end of elastic, dipping and bouncing. Chris and Samantha were having a grand old time, chatting across the aisle while I focused on keeping my lunch down. Mere minutes later, we were over land again, but we were ascending, flying straight up the side of a mountain, precariously close to the tops of trees.

"This is the exciting part," Chris said.

As if I needed more excitement. The plane crested at the top of the rocky slope and abruptly pivoted, nose down, swooping over a twisted roadway with cars a scant ten feet below us. Ahead was a landing strip that looked like an abandoned parking lot—it was far too short for slowing down, let alone stopping. A brilliant white sand beach sat at the end of it, with ocean beyond.

I closed my eyes, I couldn't watch, but before I knew it, Chris patted my knee triumphantly and we bounced along, stopping shy of the beach. I opened my eyes, relief washing over me, and peeked out the window. A man sunbathing in the sand looked up from his book, took a drink of water from a plastic bottle and returned to his pages.

"We're here."

CHAPTER SEVENTEEN

DELIGHTED to be on terra firma, I relaxed now that the adrenaline had worked its way through me. We hurried to the tiny airport terminal, painted a chalky turquoise with a red tile roof. The air was warm and supple, yielding to sweep against my skin, like Chris's hand in mine.

We zipped through customs and wheeled our bags outside. An earnest young man approached us; Jean-Luc, I presumed. Chris had mentioned him when we planned the trip, saying that he was nineteen, the caretaker's son, and that he might hit it off with Sam. After meeting him, I was sure that would be the case, at least from Sam's side of things.

He was neither tall nor short, with a capable air and an extra dose of charisma—deep tan with sun-bleached light brown hair. His smile was as blindingly white as the shorts he wore while his icy blue eyes conveniently coordinated with his shirt.

Chris shook Jean-Luc's hand and clapped him on the back as he introduced us. I surveyed Sam's reaction to our new acquaintance. Jean-Luc was doing quite well for himself, enchanting her by heaving luggage into one of the waiting jeeps.

"I had a friend drive over the second car, Monsieur Penman. I thought we would need both vehicles."

"Please, call me Chris. I know your dad likes you to be formal, but Monsieur Penman makes it feel like I'm not on holiday."

"Of course, I forget. Chris."

We took the first jeep and Jean-Luc took Sam in the other. "I hope he's a good driver," I said, irked that I sounded like a mother hen.

"That's hilarious coming from you." Chris punched the gas and sped out of the parking area.

The salt air pulled my hair straight up in a twist that flopped over before spiraling again. We jerked over the bumpy road at what felt like record speed. I clung to the handgrip above the doorframe, if only to remain upright. Chris and the other drivers seemed unconcerned with speed limits. St. Barts might be the perfect place for a bad driver, if that was what I was.

We began zigzagging on a dirt road up a mountain, littered with rocks and boulders. The island was more arid than I'd imagined, more like Arizona than Hawaii. The sky was a gauzy blue-green and the sun beat down fiercely, even though it was quite late in the afternoon. I watched Chris, the smile on his face was crystal clear, and I felt thankful for the chance to dig my hand into the back of his hair with a minimum of hesitation. I glanced back at the other car to see Sam smiling so wide at Jean-Luc that I wondered if she was explaining that she'd once had braces.

We pulled into a narrow parking area with a tall white stucco wall and a red wood door at one end. There was no other sign of a house—the door was the only indication that there was anywhere to go. An unpredictable cacophony of wind swirled tropical, salty smells around us.

Beyond the door and down a massive stucco staircase, was a

large central courtyard with palm trees planted in circular voids in the tile-edged concrete. The villa was a series of small buildings, all with red tile roofs. Chris had said that each room was separate to make it easier to keep them cool.

The kitchen and living area were in one open building near the bottom of the stairs, with vast windows on the ocean side. When facing the courtyard, the window openings had only cobalt blue storm shutters. A shaded outdoor dining area sat beyond the kitchen, next to the pool. The breathtaking view Chris had mentioned was now apparent, through towering slabs of glass spanning the gaps between the buildings and one at the far end of the pool, to keep the wind at bay.

"Jean-Luc, will you show Samantha to her room, please?" Chris asked.

The pair scurried away, Jean-Luc carting everything she'd brought, at his insistence.

Chris led me across the courtyard to the farthest building. Beyond a knotty wood door was a quaint bedroom with terracotta tile floors. There was a carved wood bed, spread with an intricate white quilt. A picture window framed the vista and the stirring sea.

The hall led to a spacious bathroom decorated with blue and green hand-painted tile. The infamous shower was open to the room on two sides, sunken several steps down into the floor. At the far end was a floor-to-ceiling window and this part of the house was cantilevered over the cliff—you could see straight down to the rocks and water.

"Wow." I stepped into the shower and pressed my forehead to the glass to get the full effect of the view. "Not for the faint of heart."

"You'll love it. I promise." Chris's voice came from behind me.

"I don't want any strange men to see me naked." It was a

joke, but the heat was building again, especially now that we were alone. I turned to see in his eyes that I'd just stoked the fire.

He didn't bother with flirtation, folding me into his arms and kissing me with great intensity, raw and pleasantly unrefined. My hand grabbed the back of his neck, pulling his head toward mine to close the tiny gap between us. His hand nimbly slid from the back of my sweater to the top of my leg. I went limp when he walked his fingers, one by one, to gather up the side of my dress. Once he reached the bare skin of my thigh, I felt as if I might flare into a plume of smoke, wispy and blue. I was so swept away that my body was triumphing over my brain —for once.

He gave me a few hesitant kisses and stopped. "I'm sorry. I didn't mean to start that now." He shook his head. "I mean, with Sam here, in the middle of the day."

I leaned against his chest. "If it wasn't you, it would've been me." When I looked back up at him, my jaw stuck, caught by his eyes. He looked as if he was resisting every temporal instinct. "Tonight?"

"Right. No excuses. I don't care if there's an earthquake."

I kissed him and we both sighed at the same time, the only source of relief. Retreating to the picturesque courtyard was certainly better than my kitchen at home, but I couldn't help but feel the same defeat I had the first time it'd happened.

Chris fetched us each a beer and I vowed to no longer question my good fortune as I watched him—or at least, not as much. Sam bounded into the kitchen and immediately ran to sling her arms around his neck, pecking him on the cheek.

"Thank you, thank you, thank you! This is so amazing. Mom, you have to come and see my room."

Chris was smiling, but overwhelmed, unused to sudden bursts of teenage enthusiasm. "You're welcome." He blinked.

"Please, make yourself at home. Swim, sleep, eat, whatever you want."

Sam was all over it, eager to put on her bathing suit and drag me along to check out her new digs. Her room was much like mine, but with her stuff strewn all over the place.

I picked up the mess she'd already made while she changed, and checked out the book on her bedside table, a zombie version of *Pride and Prejudice*. When she emerged from the bathroom, I had to broach the subject. "So, Jean-Luc, huh?"

"Mom, he is so cute. I can barely look at him he's so cute."

I chewed on my thumbnail. "I'm sure he's a nice boy, but be careful. He's a few years older than you."

"I'm fine. I just want to have fun."

She skipped past me in her aqua and yellow tropical print bikini that seemed much skimpier in broad daylight than it had at the mall. The audience waiting downstairs had me second-guessing the choice.

I didn't even make it to the bottom of the stairs before Sam was in the pool. The seductive shake of her hair when she broke the surface was likely completely innocent, but I could've sworn I heard Jean-Luc swallow from across the courtyard. He fetched a floating pool lounger and slipped it into the water, nudging it over to her. She tilted her head and granted him an extra-sweet "thanks" and managed to gracefully climb on board.

Chris was in the kitchen, making himself a snack of French bread and cheese. "I was hungry. Want some?"

"Of course you're hungry. I'm good." I figured the beer would loosen my opinion of Jean-Luc faster on an empty stomach. "What are we doing for dinner?"

Chris held his finger in the air while he finished chewing, flashing goofy eyes at me. "We have a cook coming, somebody new, her name is Mary or Meredith or something like that. She'll come for breakfast every day, too." He inched next to me and drew my chin up with a single finger. "Does that work for you?" He kissed me on my nose and smiled. Despite my ready acceptance of every wonderful moment, my patience for our waiting game was wearing thin.

Chris and I lounged in the teak deck chairs poolside while Sam floated with eyes closed. A smile spread across her face, scooping her hand into the water and allowing it to spill out between her fingers.

The door upstairs clunked twice. Chris and I turned to see a pretty, young woman making her way down the stairs with bags of groceries. She had black pixie hair and a graceful, angular jaw, stepping with perfect posture. Jean-Luc rushed to help her with the bags and Chris returned to the kitchen, presumably to discuss the details of dinner.

One thing I found amazing about Chris, on a very long list, was that he was so calmly in control of everything. It was such a luxury and not because everything in his world was expensive. It gave me permission to do nothing. As a single parent, I'd spent years in charge of everything. There was nobody to swoop in and take over. I'd been so annoyed with him the first time I experienced this aspect of his behavior, but now I understood it was the way he did things.

Marisol made a perfect dinner that night, pan-roasted snapper, sautéed vegetables and basmati rice. A light breeze flickered the candles on the table and Chris, Sam, and I enjoyed each other's company, laughing at times more than I thought possible.

"So, Mom." Sam cleared her throat. "Jean-Luc invited me to go with him to the beach tomorrow and tour the island. Is that okay?"

I raised my eyebrows at Chris, as if it was somehow his fault. "Doesn't he have to work tomorrow?"

"I don't think so," she said.

"Not on Saturday," Chris interjected. "He usually comes by in the morning to check on things."

"Yeah, Mom, it's fine."

I rearranged a few grains of rice on the plate with my fork. "I guess it's all right."

We remained at the table, Sam and Chris enjoying a fruit tart for dessert while I dwelled on the topic of Sam and Jean-Luc. I looked up and had never seen the sky so dark; pin-dots of light the only sign that there was anything above us. It was remarkably quiet, with just the soft roll of waves, far out of reach.

Sam yawned and my heart hammered for a different reason as I realized the time had finally arrived for Chris and I to be alone.

"I'm going to bed." Sam stretched her arms above her head. "I didn't sleep last night. I was so excited." She smiled and dutifully came over to allow me a kiss on her forehead.

"Good night, honey. Sleep well."

Chris and I eyed each other as she walked away. Now that it was just the two of us, I was ready to tear his clothes off at the dining room table.

He leaned into me and whispered, "I wish I could say something really smooth, but I can't think of a single thing."

He slid his hand on top of mine and gave me the look, my cue to wrap my fingers around his hand before we raced to his room. Once inside, the boil returned, and we were finally operating at the same speed.

CHAPTER EIGHTEEN

"THESE BUTTONS ARE PISSING ME OFF," he complained.

They were all different sizes, preventing him from completing his task in a timely manner, but I had no problem with his shirt.

"You're doing great," I mumbled, standing on my toes to kiss his shoulder.

My dress dropped to the floor.

"Finally." He eyed me from head to toe and ran his warm hands around my waist, pulling me along, walking backward with a goofy smirk on his face.

The terracotta tile was cold, but the air was sticky and close despite the steady whir of the ceiling fan. We toppled down onto the blue and white quilt.

"Did you lock the door?" I asked.

He forged ahead with strong hands and his heavenly scent all over me. "I don't think the door even has a lock. Why?"

"Never mind," I replied, burrowing my face into his neck.

Our kisses were wet and sloppy, a frenzied scramble of lips and tongue. Chris began to skim his mouth along the base of my throat and my entire body shuddered in anticipation of everything we had delayed. My hands smoothed over the landscape of his strong back, feeling the muscles as I went, as if I was searching for the back of an earring that'd rolled under the dresser.

He kissed my neck, my jaw, and then my lips, being playful and loose, and then he finally, mercifully, reached behind me and unhooked my bra. He pulled the straps forward and we both welcomed the release, leaving us with a new and fragile familiarity.

He gently rolled me to my back and pushed my hands far up over my head, running his fingers down the tender underside of my arms. He made it clear, with words, that he wanted them to stay put. I arched my back to meet his lips, hurrying the surrender, and he descended, his kisses uncommonly stirring. He managed to rouse my every nerve ending with his astonishing mouth, velvety and perfect. He stopped for a moment and gave me a sly look, breaking me down a little further, before returning to my breasts with fire in his breath, using his tongue in a most staggering, specific way.

My eyelids fluttered as the sensation rushed through me. His touch was so charged that it was as if my brain ran ahead, racing to give in to the bliss. I wanted time to savor the pleasure postponed, so I took charge and changed our focus.

I pushed him to his back and kneeled on the edge of the bed, unbuttoning the shorts he'd changed into after our arrival. Worn and soft, I wondered if he'd owned them for a long time.

He shifted up on to his elbows, surveying the view of everything I was doing. "You're not a cheap date, Claire. I didn't know I was going to have to fly you to an island to get you into bed."

"You're so romantic," I quietly shot back as I unzipped and

removed his shorts, tossing them over my shoulder. "You get what you pay for."

I climbed on top of him, delaying the removal of the final items of clothing between us. I grazed my entire torso along his, rolling my spine like a cat stretching long in the sun. Pushing up on my arms, my hair hung down around us while I kissed him again, working to build the heat when I wasn't sure I could take it if it got any hotter. His determined grip rocked my hips, our bodies grinding against each other, frustrated in fits that clothing continued to intervene.

I sat back, walking my hands alongside his body as I studied him, taking two passes at his lovely patch of stomach. His eyes were closed, the lids edged with feathery brown lashes. Everything about him was so beautiful that my chest ached.

He peered out from beneath his eyelids then closed them again. "Please don't stop."

"Don't worry. I won't." I kneeled a second time and gently peeled back his light blue plaid boxer shorts, so very British of him.

There was no polite way to express how primed he was and how much it took the breath right out of me. He was different than I'd imagined, better, now that we were leaving my imagination and entering the real world. All I could think was that I never, not in a million years, thought I'd get to see it and yet here it was, eager for my full attention.

I stretched out next to him and broke the tension with a soft but deliberate brush of my fingertips. A resounding exhalation escaped his lips and I responded with a fervent, craving grip. I knew then that every time I'd been with a man, it had been nothing more than a dress rehearsal, vital practices to polish my technique for Chris. I continued, reveling in every sensation I could create. I slowed things, traced my fingers up and down as I kissed his chest, then I tightened my grip again.

He openly expressed his appreciation, so taut and unyielding that I feared he might be close to his own conclusion of our evening. I wasn't about to let that happen, so I rolled on the condom and brought my lips to his, giving him a long and sweaty kiss.

He sighed and hummed with quiet gratitude, his eyes closed. "That settles it. We're never leaving this room."

"I told you. You get what you pay for."

He kissed me with urgency and twisted me onto my back before stretching out his heartbreaking body next to mine. He caressed my breasts and watched, his dark eyes reflecting every shade of my reaction. His hand skimmed down my stomach and passed my waist, stripping away the final trappings between us.

The brush of his thumb against my hipbone sent my body into overdrive and he was a second ahead of me, expertly stationed with his fingers, in complete control. I closed my eyes and rolled my head into his arm in utter ecstasy.

As soon as he moved his hand, I took my chance and wrapped my arms and legs around him, greedily pulling him closer. A warm, glowing relief overcame me as we began to move, finally joined.

He felt the need to mark the moment. "Oh, Claire. You feel so good."

"Shhh. Be quiet."

"You're funny," he snickered against my neck.

"No, I'm not."

My hands spread out over his back, the muscles felt markedly different now that they were engaged in forceful motion. I opened my eyes long enough to appreciate him and was happily greeted by the mole on his cheek.

After weeks of build-up, there were only a few minutes before we shattered each other's thresholds in less than perfect unison. Breathless, he returned to his back, holding my hand while we watched the endless twirl of the ceiling fan.

He turned to me. "You're smiling."

I laughed. "Of course I'm smiling."

"I plan to smile for an entire week after that." He let our moment of quiet satisfaction pass, but then he insisted on saying more, "I mean, wow. You know, I'm not used to delaying things. This is usually the first date for me. I can see the advantages now. Was it just me or was that extra hot?"

"Will you please stop?" I rolled onto my stomach. "Do we have to analyze it? Can't we be happy without putting it into words?"

"So says the writer." He scratched my favorite spot on his belly. "You know, you have my full permission to do any of that to me whenever you want. Don't even ask. You can start and I'll set aside whatever I'm doing at the time, unless of course, I'm driving. In that case, you'll need to let me know in advance so I can find a safe place to pull over. Maybe we can devise a secret signal."

I closed my eyes and pressed my forehead into the pillow. "You're such a goof." I moved closer and kissed him. "You were amazing and wonderful, but you probably already know that." Someone so practiced had to be aware of his own ability, but I blessed him with my approval. "I'm not a big fan of the post-sex re-cap. If you want to tell me what you liked, you can show me next time. I don't need the words."

"Oh, I liked all of it, especially the part where you—" He stopped when he caught my expression.

"You can't help it, can you?"

A smile crept across his face. He moved closer and the come-hither look returned to his eyes. "I'm only expressing my enthusiasm for your talents." He kissed me. "Come on. There's ice cream in the freezer. I'm starving."

———

I AWOKE to the blazing sun, Chris at my side. He leaned over me with sloppy morning hair and kissed my collarbone, gently coaxing me from my sleepy state. The fact that he was naked was the perfect detail that made it so much better than I'd ever imagined.

"Claire, Sam will probably be up soon. I wasn't sure if you wanted her to see you leaving my room."

"Good point," I said once I'd had a minute to wake up. "I should talk to her before she sees me in yesterday's clothes."

The room looked as if we'd hosted a ticker tape parade with clothes. I tiptoed, picking up the litter as I went, clutching mine to my body and tossing Chris's on the bed.

"I could watch you do this all day," he said.

"I bet. Is it the picking up dirty clothes part or the bending over naked part?"

"Dirty clothes. I hate picking up."

I stepped to the bathroom to tame my hair before getting dressed. Chris groaned in the other room and noisily hoisted himself out of bed, joining me as I finished the last few buttons on my dress. He stood before me in his boxer shorts and it felt as if my hormones were going berserk, like I'd never get enough of him. He scratched that spot on his stomach, my spot, and it took everything in me to remain standing.

"Everything okay?" he asked, folding me into his bewitching bare chest and arms.

"Yes. I was noticing how beautiful you are." It was funny how the words came easier sometimes than others.

He raked his hand through my hair and kissed the top of my head. "I think we both know that I'm not the beauty in this relationship."

I took the compliment although he was delusional about his

appearance if that was what he truly thought. I set my hand on his chest and caught a flash of his green eyes.

He squeezed me and pecked the end of my nose. "You'd better get out of here before you get me worked up."

We smiled knowingly at each other. He swatted me on the butt when I walked away and I looked back for an instant, but kept going.

I grabbed a quick shower in my room, loving the view, as promised. I hadn't even thought to ask what we were doing for the day, but I figured we were on an island; it was hard to go wrong. I dressed in a white tank top, khaki shorts and bare feet after slathering on sunscreen. Tousling my freshly washed hair was the extent of styling, but I had to put on makeup. I felt naked without it.

The scent of coffee lured me out to the courtyard. The glare coming off the pool was immense, the surface silver and the bottom a deepest black. Marisol was busy in the kitchen and greeted me with a pretty singsong as I helped myself to a cup of coffee. She'd set out cream and sugar and three shiny spoons, all lined up on a napkin.

I stood at the butcher-block kitchen island and watched her arrange a rainbow of tropical fruits on a platter—mango, pineapple, papaya, kiwi and star fruit. We smiled at each other and she continued to work, like a mama bird feathering her nest.

I wandered to the other side of the room and sank down on the fluffy white couch in the seating area, marveling at a different version of the view, untamed and blue. The gentle rock of the sea consumed me so much that I didn't even notice Chris until he plopped down and made me pop up on the other end of the cushion.

"You shaved." I stroked the now silky skin of his face as he leaned in for a kiss. "Mmm, you smell good too." I nuzzled his neck for a second and remembered that Marisol was steps away.

"There's coffee," I started, but Marisol was already on her way with a tray. "What's on the agenda? Sam's running away with Jean-Luc so I think heavy drinking is in order."

"Don't worry. I'll talk to him." He was so casual about it, stirring his coffee.

The now familiar thud of the heavy wood door told us that Jean-Luc had arrived. On cue, he appeared, his blinding white smile leading the way. He was wearing too much cologne, which was no way to sway me—it brought back nightmarish memories of an old boyfriend.

"Bonjour, is Mademoiselle Samantha with you?" He inquired, scanning the room.

Chris answered. "No, she hasn't come down to breakfast yet." Jean-Luc excused himself but Chris called after him. "I want to speak with you privately before you two leave." He had a sip of coffee while I became fixed on the curve of his lips on the mug and then he asked the inevitable. "What's for breakfast?"

Marisol set the dining table with her masterpiece of a fruit platter along with fresh croissants, juice, and bacon. Chris dug in with his usual enthusiasm for food.

"I don't understand how you can eat so much and stay thin." I took a croissant, hoping I'd have the willpower to eat only half, and filled the rest of my plate with fruit.

He was shoveling. "I have no idea. Good metabolism, I guess. I don't really think about it." He smiled.

Lucky bastard.

Marisol brought more coffee and I noticed how stubby her fingernails were as she topped off my cup. She seemed like a sweet girl, somewhat timid, and I wondered if she had aspirations beyond cooking for the wealthy on a tiny island. I hated the thought of Sam in that position, stuck somewhere without options.

Samantha soon arrived, in a short yellow sundress with bathing suit ties looped at her neck, lugging a blue and white striped beach bag. Jean-Luc was testing the pool water, flicking his finger at vials, but watching her closely. She waved at him and he perked up and smiled wide. I couldn't help but worry about what he might be cooking up in his nineteen-year-old brain and how that might involve his penis.

"Jean-Luc, come on," Chris called out, and Jean-Luc obediently followed to the terrace outside Chris's room.

"Good morning, honey," I said to Sam, her sunny face well-rested. "Marisol made a big breakfast."

Sam helped herself to some of everything, shrugging off my suggestion to slow down. She glugged her juice and was nearly finished by the time Chris and Jean-Luc returned from their talk. Chris held his arm around Jean-Luc's shoulder, but Jean-Luc's face told a different story. I almost felt sorry for him.

Taking his seat next to me, Chris patted my knee and whispered, "We're good."

"Mademoiselle Samantha, we can leave whenever you like."

Her eyes sparkled. "I'm ready." The flirtation oozed out of her.

I cringed at the thought of what she'd said yesterday, that she wanted to have fun. "Do you have water with you? How about sunscreen?" I ran down the checklist and hoped like crazy it didn't need to include condoms.

"Yes. I put on a ton of sunscreen and I brought extra. Can we go now?" Jean-Luc was trying to lure her away, walking backwards and smiling his no-good schoolboy smile.

"Yes. Go." I shooed her away, but it felt more like ripping a bandage off my leg when I'd forgotten to shave.

"What did you say to him?" I mumbled. "He looked like he was going to be sick."

"Nothing, really. I told him that if he was anything less than a perfect gentleman, I might have to kill him. I thought it was best to lay down the law."

I admired Chris's protective side, especially the way he would've been if he'd had a daughter, if things in his life had been different.

"He's a good kid," he added. "He just has a fondness for Sam. I'm guessing the curls and the bathing suit have something to do with it." He pointed to the last half of my croissant. "Are you going to eat that?"

"Go for it."

He put it away in two bites, a beautiful bottomless pit. Finished, he rested his elbow on the arm of his chair and leaned over for a kiss.

"Mmm," I said. "You taste like bacon."

"Good," he laughed, holding his lips close to mine. "That's what I was going for."

I jumped at the sound of the refrigerator door closing. I'd forgotten again that Marisol was there.

CHAPTER NINETEEN

BY LATE MORNING, it was just the two of us. In Chris's room, I couldn't help but notice his pitiful attempt at making the bed and I tried to straighten it. "I don't know about this grueling schedule of yours, lounging by the pool, eating. Now you're making me get a massage." The sheets were completely twisted under the quilt. No wonder he'd given up.

"I enjoy barking orders." He tossed me a fluffy white robe from the closet, holding another. "Now I get to tell you to get naked."

Chris drew back the blue and white batik curtains across the expanse of glass doors overlooking his terrace. The sound of the sea rushed in as he opened the doors, folding and stacking them back against the wall, leaving the room open to the view and stretch of sky.

"I thought it'd be nice to have the breeze," he said.

"Of course you did."

"Is there a problem?"

"No. I'm wondering how you make everything so perfect. It's very discouraging for the rest of us." I finished smoothing out the quilt and yanked it taut.

I turned and he circled his arms around my waist. "Do you know how long I've waited to romance a woman? My whole life." He tilted his head to the side. "Well, that's not entirely true. Priscilla Faircloth let me give her a flower when I was nine, but she eventually spurned my advances."

I smiled. "Priscilla?"

"Look, I've never had the chance to do these things because I wanted to. Most of the time, it wasn't necessary and the rest of the time I was meeting a request. I meant it when I said that part of the reason I like you is because you don't expect things from me." He tightened his arms around me, making me woozy. "I'm not trying to be perfect. I want us to enjoy our time together."

"I'm sorry." I ran a finger along the neckline of his robe. "I promise to be a willing participant. But you have to let me say thank you."

"I can't wait for that."

We were immersed in a soft and simmering kiss when there were voices in the courtyard. Chris pried his lips from mine to greet our masseurs. I was excited when Tristan and Stephanie came in the room, and not the slightest bit suspicious that everyone on the island seemed to be absurdly beautiful. Stephanie was flawless, tall and lithe with long blonde hair pulled back in a ponytail. I would've been upset if Tristan hadn't been the smoking hot package that he was, with hair shaved close to his head and electric blue eyes, a steamy tower of muscle.

They both looked away while we removed our robes and we climbed onto the tables, starting face up. They didn't give us much to cover up with, Chris had a single towel and I had two. I'd been so relaxed with Chris that I hadn't taken the time to worry about a stranger looking at my bare belly, let alone putting his manly hands all over it.

Our massage put my every expectation to shame; gusts of ocean air and the rustle of the sea only magnified it. I stood as much chance as a stick of butter in the sun as Tristan smeared me with massage oil scented with lavender and orange. His firm hands kneaded away every shred of uneasiness festering in me, which was saying a lot. There was always something brewing.

I kept an eye on Stephanie for a minute as she worked her work her way into Chris's frame, feeling a strange fondness for her. Under any other circumstances, I would've felt a wrench of jealousy, watching such a witchy woman with her hands all over him.

By the time our ninety minutes were up, Chris and I were both so at ease that you would've thought we were dead, but it was a lovely kind of dead. We were slow to get up once they left us, both of us with creased foreheads from the table headrests. I slinked over to give Chris a kiss, but I was still naked and that was a mistake. That one brush of our bodies after all of the rubbing and massage oil put us both in the starting gate, Chris suffering from the outward evidence of the kiss. We both looked down, me feeling childish when I laughed.

"Great, thanks," he said. "You couldn't wait five minutes for them to leave?"

I giggled. "Sorry." I put my robe back on while Chris did the same, struggling to tie his and remain inconspicuous.

"This is all your fault. I could shelter small animals under here."

We both laughed.

"I'll stand in front of you."

"That won't bloody work. I'll go in the loo and wait. You can pay them. My wallet is on the top shelf of the closet. It was three hundred. Give them five and get them out of here."

"No problem. Got it." I fetched his billfold and jogged back to open the door.

Tristan and Stephanie brought us bottles of water and Stephanie said to be sure to drink plenty, to flush out the toxins. Chris's wallet was fat with hundred dollar bills, which made the math easy enough.

"The coast is clear," I whispered, traipsing into the bathroom. Chris was leaning against the counter, looking at his phone, which he promptly put down.

"You're in trouble," he said, while he pulled me closer and untied my robe, pushing it off my shoulders and on to the floor.

"That's not fair." I yanked at his tie, watching for a reaction, but he did nothing but stare at me, his startling eyes wide awake. "It was an innocent mistake." Once I'd brought his robe down, he made his move.

He drove his shoulder into my stomach, lifting me off the floor, my butt in the air. I pretended to struggle because I figured that was what a girl does in that situation.

"Stop squirming so much or I'll drop you."

I assumed we were going to bed, but he had other plans, boldly walking out into the courtyard. The sun was like a white hot flash and I squinted like crazy. "Where in the hell are you taking me?"

"It's a surprise." A few of his extra long strides and he stopped between the deck chairs.

"You wouldn't."

"Oh, I would."

The massage oil began beading up on my skin the instant my body hit the warm water. I came up for air, laughing, shaking drops from my face as he skimmed along the pool bottom. He reached for my legs and I shivered as he rose to the surface with a sober look on his face. He scooped me up in his arms and said nothing while I clutched his neck and wrapped my legs around his waist. I couldn't help but notice the matter that started our spat as it rubbed against my leg. Pool or not, that wasn't going away without some effort on my part.

I pushed his dripping hair from his forehead. He kissed me by only faintly touching his lips to mine, frustrating me. I couldn't reconcile my feelings about it—half of me craved one of his potent kisses and the other loved the tease of this approach. The lavender and orange of the massage oil perfumed the air, but it was different on him, more like bourbon than anything flowery.

He waded us deeper as we kissed. He took me by surprise when he pushed me up against the wall of the pool, the glassy cobalt tiles cool and slippery against my back.

"Don't let go," he said as he gripped my hips, my legs loosely wrapped around him.

I looked up at the whitish blue sky and then back down at the black and blue of the pool as he pulled me down to him. I gasped. "A condom."

"I'll pull out in time."

He was rougher with me from the start, bearing down against my pelvic bone, driving me closer to my peak with every crush of his body. The raw fervor on his face was a total turn-on —he was in charge, with no input needed from me.

He kept one hand at my back, jerking me closer, and the other kneaded my breast. He didn't even seem to want to kiss me as he pressed his forehead against the top of my head, and that was fine. Between the massage and my over-active brain, kissing was no longer necessary.

The tiles stung my back and it was nearly unbearable by the time I reached my release, an incredible contrast to the burn. We both recovered in the deep end, sucking in breaths, my arms draped over his shoulders.

He let me go, playfully splashing me in the face. "You know, that was strictly for Jean-Luc's benefit. I'm sure the pool chemistry is all dodgy now."

———

I'D STARTED to wonder if I would ever see the island. After the pool, we had lunch and collapsed in Chris's room having only the energy for a nap. He left the windows open and the curtains coiled in the wind as we slept enmeshed. It was pleasant and in no way sexual, which was a distinct change of pace. When we woke up, it was late in the afternoon. I didn't want to be the one person in paradise who cared what time it was, so I used Sam as my excuse.

Chris grabbed his phone from the bedside table. "It's half four. I'm sure they'll be back any minute." He propped himself up on the pillows wearing his old shorts and equally well loved gray t-shirt.

I scooted closer and set my chin and a hand on his chest while he fiddled with his phone. "Any naughty messages from strange women?"

Chris smiled, distracted, and held up his finger to signal me to wait, a habit of his that was really starting to perturb me. "I have a text from Graham. He and his wife are flying in, in the morning. We should have them for dinner tomorrow night."

"Graham as in Graham Whiting?"

"Yes. He's the only other member of the band who kept his place here."

Compared to the many other improbable things that'd happened since I'd met Chris, this was still remarkable. It had never crossed my mind that I'd meet any of his former band mates.

"It'll be fun. You'll get a kick out of Graham and I'm sure you and Angie will get along great." Chris turned on his trademark smirk. "I just don't want you to wear your Banks Forest tour shirt to dinner."

"Very funny. Don't worry, I'll try not to geek out," I said, mentally adding something to my post-island to-do list: hide Banks Forest t-shirt.

He pushed me over and kissed me. "They're going to love you." He sneaked his hand under my tank top just as the court-yard door made a heavy thud.

"Mom? Chris? We're back."

Sam and Jean-Luc were waiting for us outside, acting less friendly with each other than before they'd left. Sam's eyes were watery and Jean-Luc watched her like a frightened puppy dog.

Chris slung his arm around Sam's shoulder. "Everything okay with you lot? No jellyfish stings?" he asked, politely staring down Jean-Luc.

"We had fun," she said.

Jean-Luc quickly excused himself.

As soon as he was gone, she turned to me. "Mom, can we talk?"

"Sure, honey."

Up in her room, Sam flopped onto the bed, the teenage drama likely for my benefit. "Is there something wrong with me?"

"No, of course not." I sat on the mattress and rubbed her back. "Why would you ask that?"

"I tried to kiss Jean-Luc today and he kept stopping me. I don't get it. He acts like he likes me and he's always staring at me, but I tried to kiss him and he turned away."

I'd only imagined a scenario with Jean-Luc as the aggressor —I never suspected Sam would make the first move. I didn't dare tell her about Chris's talk with Jean-Luc. She'd be furious if she knew we'd interfered to such a degree.

"He's being a gentleman. He's French. They're much more polite," I added, making up everything as I went.

"I even went topless at the beach. That didn't work at all."

My heart sank. My plan had officially backfired. I searched for the right thing to say, but all that came to mind was the lies we tell our children to get them to do what we want them to do: Santa Claus and the magical dye that's released if you pee in the pool.

"Showing a guy your boobs is never the way to go." I knew the opposite to be true, that you could get almost anything you wanted if you were willing to take off your bra. That was a lesson she'd have to figure out on her own. "We're only here for a few days and then you won't see him again. I want you to be smart about this. You need to think about Andrew too." Although the idea made my brain swell, I knew I had to let her make her own mistakes.

"You're acting like Andrew's my boyfriend or something." She turned over and her baby-blues were ringed in pink.

"If Andrew's not your boyfriend, then what was with the long goodbye in the driveway? What about the late nights up in your room?"

"I like him, we've kissed and stuff, but he can't make up his mind. He's sweet when it's just the two of us but then he's kind of a jerk to me when we're at school. It's very confusing."

I sighed, so thankful to not be a teenager anymore. It had been fun to reminisce about it when I met Chris, but there had been plenty of rotten parts, too. "Boys can be like that sometimes. But, if he likes you, he needs to treat you nicely all of the time."

She picked at her fingernail. "I want to have fun while I'm here. I really like Jean-Luc."

That string of words was like a pillow smothering my mothering instinct and me along with it. Now I had to ask Chris to call off the dogs with Jean-Luc and hope Sam didn't turn around and do something stupid.

"Promise me you'll be careful."

She rolled her eyes. "Yes. I'll be careful."

We sat for a moment. "Um, I was hoping we could talk about Chris." When the words came out, it struck me that I sounded just as confused as the seventeen-year-old. "I'll probably sleep in his room while we're here. I thought it was best to tell you so you won't be surprised."

Her face came alive and she raised her hand. "Up top, Mom."

I laughed and gave her the high-five. "You're funny."

"That's so awesome. He's totally the first guy you've gone out with that I thought was good enough for you." She had the sweetest look on her face and then her eyes grew wide. "Oh, I forgot to tell you one thing. It's kind of embarrassing." She wrinkled her nose. "If you go topless at the beach, make sure you put sunscreen *everywhere*."

I headed downstairs after my talk with Sam. Chris was playing DJ in the living room and tried to dance with me, kissing my neck and goofing around. At any other time, I would have soaked up every minute of his charm.

"We have a problem."

"Mmm. I love it when you talk dirty." He moved me around the room, pressing his long body against mine and rooting around in my neck.

Marisol was busy with dinner and I had to whisper. "No, really. We need to talk."

He stopped, finally grasping that I was serious, and led me outside. The sky had darkened and the wind came in fierce gusts out on the terrace. Most of the time, it was so calm in the courtyard that I forgot we were on a cliff in the middle of an ocean.

"The Jean-Luc thing backfired."

"What do you mean?" Chris furrowed his brow. "Did he touch her?"

"No, and oddly enough, that's the problem." I blinked at how backward it was, explaining what had happened.

"She tried to kiss him. We didn't see that coming, did we? She obviously takes after her mother." He pulled me into a debilitating hug before I had a chance to hit him. "Claire, it'll be fine. On the bright side, nothing happened today. That counts for something, right? I'll talk to him again if you want me to. But, you'll have to decide what your new rules are."

I groaned. "I have no idea." I shuddered from the chill of the tropical winds, nervously peering over the short stucco wall protecting us from a gruesome death.

"She's your daughter. I can't tell you what to do. I'll tell you what I think, but you can't get mad at me."

"Fine."

"Well, I think we tell him that it's all right if he has physical contact with her as long as he takes it slow and it's consensual." I was ready to blast his stupid opinion, but he continued. "And I'd tell him that we still expect him to be a perfect gentleman and if Sam told us otherwise, we'd have problems. I mean, he's nineteen and she's seventeen. There's not a whole lot you can do. If they want to have sex, they'll find a way."

CHAPTER TWENTY

THAT NIGHT MARKED the third time we made love, and it was again different. Chris was still working on curbing his penchant for sex talk, but I let it slide. We all lapse into bad habits and his commentary was easy to take coming from his gorgeous mouth. I did not, however, allow my handsome wordsmith to busy himself with only his verbiage and he quite decisively rang my bell—four times, not that I was keeping score.

His rumbling stomach woke us both the next morning and I understood that Chris had no need of a clock or watch. I wondered if he'd been born hungry or if his appetite kicked in when he was older. Either way, his poor mother—she'd probably been at the grocery store every day.

Marisol had set out muffins and milk, berries and juice for breakfast. Sam was already up, lounging poolside in her bikini as any good teenage girl would do, and we chatted while I sipped my French Roast. Her expression changed when Jean-Luc arrived, a coy smile replacing quiet contentment.

Chris motioned to me from the kitchen, looking as if he was scheming and plotting again. He wrapped himself around me the instant I was within reach, regarding me with eyes that were especially vibrant in the morning light. "Jean-Luc wants to take Sam to the beach and lunch today. I told him I thought it'd be fine, but I want to make sure you're okay with it."

I'd dim-wittedly given Chris the green light to relax the rules on a Sunday when Jean-Luc had most of his day free. "I can't say no without making her hate me." I turned and watched the two of them talking by the pool. Samantha's giggles reverberated throughout the courtyard. From the back of my head, my mom urged me to put my most positive thoughts out into the universe, and hope for something good to come back.

Chris placed his hand on my cheek. "I want to take you somewhere special today."

"Outside of the compound?"

"I can't keep you locked up in the castle forever."

An hour later, Chris had us racing along a winding dirt road. "Why won't you tell me where we're going?" I yelled. The white noise in the swift moving jeep, with the top down, was deafening. "It's not like I've been here before."

He looked over, his hair flopping around in the wind and shoulders jumping with the motion of the car. "I want to see if you recognize it when we get there."

"That doesn't make any sense."

He pursed his lips. "Will you stop? We'll be there soon enough and if you don't recognize it, I'll tell you."

We drove for several more minutes, the car jostling us with every rock it ran over, sometimes coming treacherously close to the edge of the narrow roads.

Chris pulled to the side and parked, no beach in sight. In fact, we were still far up the mountain. I couldn't begin to estimate how far we'd driven.

"Ready?" His antsy boyish smile chiseled a fracture in me. I'd grown nearly immune to his aura, but every now and then, he caught me.

He'd advised me to wear my running shoes because we'd have to hike. At first, it was down a dusty path among low brush that scraped my ankles and the occasional brown lizard that would dart at the sight of us.

It was another ideal day with the sky and ocean composing a sweep of closely matched blue. I followed Chris and he held my hand behind his back when the pebbly path became skinny and harrowing. The mountain was blanketed in green, nowhere for us to go but forward or back, with a precipitous drop to the sea on the right, and on the left, the slope raced up at an illogical angle.

Once we began to descend and curve around the far side of the mountain, the ocean was finally visible ahead. Sweaty and overheated, I was relieved to see a discernable path to the water, but as soon as I saw the beach, I gasped.

Chris laughed. "See, I told you. I knew you'd recognize it."

Seeing the beach in person caused a thrill, a flash; another of my teenage daydreams coming true. The familiar, sprawling white sand wrapped around a tranquil inlet with a dozen boats anchored, bobbing and floating with flags from different countries. A handful of people swam and waded in the crystalline water. One jump off a high sand dune and Chris and I were down on the beach.

"This is so amazing." I looked in every direction, taking it all in. "Thank you for bringing me here."

"Tell me where we are."

"This is where you filmed the video for *Love, Destroyed*."

"You really were the president of the Banks Forest fan club." He put his arm around me, apparently pleased that his plan had worked.

Love, Destroyed had been far and away the biggest hit Banks Forest ever had, topping the charts in the U.S., England, and the rest of the world for months. Like many of their songs, Chris had written it, about whom I didn't know. He was stunning in the video, dreamy and tan and bare-chested, of course. Banks Forest was one of the first bands to shoot their videos with film, making them seem visionary and groundbreaking, but I suspected they'd done it because they were known as much for their good looks as their music.

I'd watched the *Love, Destroyed* video hundreds of times on the VCR in my dad's home office, so I had no problem recognizing the clusters of rock and the arc of the beach. Thinking about it forced me to take stock as we walked over every unbelievable grain of sand.

We found a private spot at the far end of the beach. It was hard to believe such a place existed, unspoiled, with no cars, no houses to be seen—as if the modern world didn't exist. My first impulse was to kick off my sweaty running shoes and push my feet into the soft ivory, unworried about the pumice ruining my pedicure. I gawked as Chris took off his t-shirt, especially enthralling in navy blue board shorts with white topstitching.

He pointed at my chest. "Can I help you with that?" One of his smiles spread across his face, making it hard to say "no". "It's okay, Claire. No one will think anything of it."

Feeling brave back at the house, I'd prepared ahead of time with sunscreen in the appropriate places although Chris had generously offered to tackle the job himself. Now I was feeling far less bold. A fleshy, wrinkled woman near the shore wasn't shy about it at all. She solicited conversation from the people on the beach, casually standing knee deep in the water, bending to swirl her hands.

I decided that if I was going to get over one of my hang-ups, I might as well do it with Chris in a completely idyllic spot. "I got it," I replied.

"Even better." He stretched his wiry legs out on his beach towel, watching through sunglasses, holding his hand at his brow and shielding his eyes. I took off my bikini top with little fanfare and tossed it in the beach bag.

"Can you turn to the side?" he asked. "I can't see anything with the glare."

"Very funny." I kneeled next to him and stretched out too, feeling better now that it was done. I rolled on to my back and bravely propped up on my elbows, exposing the ladies to the only natural light they'd seen since I was a little girl running through the sprinkler with my sister. My mom would've been so proud.

Chris removed his sunglasses and for the second time, I was in awe of the brilliance in his eyes today. His dazzling smile wore me down as he played with my hand in the sand, rubbing the tips of my fingers in tiny circles.

"Let's cool off," he said. He stood and tugged on my hand before he piloted me into the translucent sea, unmatched in its warmth, soft and pleasing. Comparing it to bathwater only would've cheapened the experience. It was a wonder, I felt as if I was immersed in a graceful, fluid extension of myself. Admiring the boats, some modest and others monstrous, I knew that if I ever had a life where I could flit around the world on a boat, I would always stop at this beach. I envied a young man on one of the decks, taking pictures from his unique vantage point.

We swam until it was over my head but Chris kept me afloat, holding me close. We kissed as if time meant nothing and I savored every subtle move of his lips while combing through his damp hair. Lightly drumming his fingers along my spine, Chris was quiet when we came up for air. I sensed something between us, making my heartbeat fitful.

"I want to tell you something," he said. "I'm bollocks at this, so you'll have to be patient." He gazed at me, his face casting a shadow across mine as I clung to his neck. "The last few weeks have been great. You're such an incredible woman. I'm so glad that we met."

My breaths grew shallower. "It's sweet of you to say that. The last few weeks have been amazing for me too." I looked down into the water, worried that whatever I said would be inferior. "Most of the time I can't believe this is happening."

He cleared his throat. "The other thing I wanted to say is, well, I wanted you to know that you're the first woman I've really wanted to spend any time with since my divorce."

His words were sweet at first listen, but I didn't want to take it the wrong way, nor did I want to think things that might later prove presumptuous.

"I, just," he continued. "I want you to know that you aren't just a hook-up."

"Oh..." It hit me then. I'd thought we were embarking on a fairytale romance. Maybe to him, at least at first, I was nothing more than another girl in line. And everyone knew there was always another girl after that. "That's good to know. I guess."

He shook his head. "I don't want you to misunderstand what I'm saying. It's a compliment."

I looked him in the eye, finding the color less enchanting than before. "It doesn't really feel like a compliment."

"We talked about this the day after the interview. In the cab on the way to the airport, about my spending all of my time with actresses and models. It's no secret that I've been with some stunning women since I left Elise. None of them can hold a candle to you."

I blinked, hoping this would somehow end up being a bad dream. "That doesn't make me feel any better."

"I was trying to tell you that you're important to me."

"By reminding me that you've had your pick of women since you left your wife but I'm the first one that means something?" I felt my face grow hot with frustration, and it wasn't all his fault. My reaction was partly born of an irrational wish to be the only woman he liked enough to be with.

"Yes, exactly." He cocked his head to the side. "Although it sounds awful when you say it."

"Am I supposed to feel good about that? I don't want to think about all of the women you've been with over the last year."

"It was just sex."

I groaned and shook my head. "No woman wants to hear that. Do you have any idea how insulting that is?"

"And do you have any idea how bloody insane you sound? You don't get to be angry for something that happened before I even met you." He looked me right in the eye. "If it makes you feel any better, I haven't had sex with anyone since we met. That wasn't easy."

I stared back. "Sorry to hear it was so hard for you to go without sex for a whole month." He'd done an excellent job of burying his expression of affection. "Can we talk about this on dry land? I'm starting to prune." I didn't wait for a reply, breaking free of him and swimming back to shore. I grabbed my towel when I reached the beach, clutching it to my chest, no longer in the mood for being a purveyor of free peeks.

Chris trudged through the sand and I felt the force of every deliberate step, not knowing how mad he was. He fell to his knees and flopped down to his stomach, onto the towel, dripping wet. I peered over my shoulder and the water on his back sucked the breath out of me; hundreds of defenseless droplets popping in the gradual fade of the sun.

I shook out an extra towel and sat with my knees pulled to my chest, resting my head, feeling empty and torn. He was silent, turned away.

I watched him for a long time, thinking that nothing about the situation was right. We had so much unfinished business.

My lungs ached with every breath. Sitting still, doing nothing, became uncomfortable. I found my top in the beach bag and put it on, just as he chose to turn back to me.

"Is that your way of getting even?" His annoyance had seemingly dissipated, but he certainly wasn't smiling.

The strap snapped against my back. "No. You'll know it if I'm trying to get even."

He softened his eyes, leaving me hopelessly vulnerable. "Claire, I'm sorry. I never wanted to hurt your feelings. I guess I didn't do a very good job of saying what I wanted to say. I feel like a bloody jerk."

I took a breath, making an unflattering sound like a hiccup. "I'm sorry too. You're right. I don't have the right to get mad at you about that stuff. But just so you know, no woman wants to hear those things. I don't want to think about all of the women who could take my place."

He groaned, quietly. "But that means nothing to me, seriously. You know, you don't realize that you're just as capable of breaking my heart as I am of breaking yours. We have to trust each other." He granted me a fraction of a smile. "I would say more, but I'm afraid of digging myself a deeper hole."

I had to cut loose everything swimming in my head if I was going to get back to where we'd been before. I stretched out next to him, fighting my feelings of unworthiness. "I don't know if you're capable of digging a hole with me."

CHAPTER TWENTY-ONE

"I'M STARVING," Chris muttered. He gnawed a hunk of day-old baguette and shook out the wet towels from the beach.

"Let me make you something. Eggs and toast?"

"Perfect. Can you make it four?"

"Sure." I smiled and felt as though things were getting better.

I bungled my way about the unfamiliar kitchen, digging in drawers for a whisk when I caught a glimpse of Sam and Jean-Luc through the kitchen window and across the courtyard, outside her bedroom door. They were a confusion of lips with Jean-Luc sending his hand up the front of her shirt, a vision I could've lived without.

I whipped around, slamming the utensil drawer shut with my butt. "They're outside her room, making out."

"Sam and what's-his-face?"

I loved Chris's new pet name for Jean-Luc, but I cringed at the thought of being the mom who barges in on her daughter. "What do we do?"

"I don't know." He shrugged and looked around the kitchen. "We could make some noise and hope they take the hint."

I clanged pots and dishes together. Chris, seeming at a loss, turned on the empty blender without its lid. A horrendous scraping rang out. We both jumped and had to cover our mouths when we laughed, but his plan worked and they were in the kitchen in no time.

"Oh, hi, honey. Did you just get back?" I asked.

"Yeah," Sam said, avoiding eye contact.

"Did you have a good day?"

"We had fun. We went to lunch and the beach."

"Great. I'm making eggs if you're hungry."

"No, thanks. I'm going to walk Jean-Luc out to his car." He remained silent, which was as much as I wanted to hear from him, anyway.

"Okey-doke," I said, sounding like I was Mrs. Cleaver while I finished Chris's eggs. The courtyard door clunked. "I'm timing them. How long should I give her?"

Chris stared and shook his head. "Claire, honey, you've got to let this go. What are you going to do? Impose time limits on snogging?"

"But I don't like the idea of those two together."

"They're teenagers. That's what they do." He came up behind me and placed his hand on my back. "I wouldn't let Jean-Luc within a mile of Sam if I thought he was a bad kid."

"Thank you." I pushed his eggs on to the plate. "You're right. I'm acting crazy."

"It's okay. I love your particular brand of crazy." He pecked me on the cheek and took his plate to the kitchen table. He dug in while I sat with him and drummed my fingers on the table at full tilt.

Chris flattened my hand. "Say this after me. I will stop acting like a lunatic."

I rolled my eyes. "I will. As soon as she's done locking lips with the French kid."

"You have to do everything your own way, don't you?"

"Pretty much." The door slammed upstairs and I let out my breath. "Okay, I'm better now."

With the threat of teenage sex thwarted, I sequestered myself in my room to clean up and shake off the remnants of the day, spending plenty of time in the shower. I made an extra effort, dressing in my new black linen sundress with ivory embroidery at the hem, still feeling badly about the confusion at the beach.

Chris came in without knocking. "Damn. You're already dressed."

"Sorry you missed the show."

He went to my neck as I put in an earring. "Mmm. You smell good, like waffles." He was wearing a rumpled white shirt and long khaki shorts. His feet were bare and tan and his scrubby hair smelled sweet. "Are we okay after the beach today?"

I'd already replayed the entire fight, if it qualified for that designation, in my head several times. On paper, he hadn't done a single thing he wasn't entitled to do.

"Yes, we're good. Other than the fact that you told me I smell like waffles."

His finger landed on my nose and he focused. "How did I miss your freckles?"

My hand flew to my face. "It's from the sun." I wrinkled my nose and rubbed it. "I hated them when I was a kid."

He pulled my hand away and smiled, his eyes glimmering. "I love them." He grazed my nose with his pinky. "I think they're the cutest thing I've ever seen."

I wrapped myself around him, pressing my hands into his back and settling the side of my head against his chest. He squeezed me and I felt warm and protected, like nothing could ever hurt me. One short kiss and I knew two things—we were back to a good place and we had to get out of my room before we had the chance to undress each other.

I curled into Chris on the couch once we got to the living room, and we watched Marisol, a blur of cutting and chopping.

"I'd tell you about Graham and Angie but you probably know more about them than I do," Chris said.

"Please don't say anything about that stuff at dinner."

"Got it. No embarrassing Banks Forest fan club comments."

An unfamiliar voice bellowed, "Hello? Everybody decent?"

I'd seen countless pictures of Graham but like Chris, he was of a much different magnitude in person. His tan skin set off his golden brown eyes and his sharply receding hair was cut so short that I couldn't tell what color it was anymore. He was dressed head to toe in wrinkly white linen, a pair of buttons fastened on his shirt. Angie had creamy flawless skin and a rolling shock of deep red hair, wearing an emerald green sundress and hefty diamond studs.

Chris's face lit up when he saw them and he gave them both big hugs. He introduced me and in a flash, Graham assaulted me with a suffocating embrace.

"I can see why you actually told me about this one," he said to Chris as he grabbed me by the shoulders, tilting me from side to side. He was a bit like my uncle, my aunt's second husband, without kids of his own or any sense of personal boundaries.

"Graham, will you please leave her alone?" Angie nudged him out of the way and took my hand. "Claire, it's so nice to meet you. Have you been enjoying your time on the island? I want to hear everything you lot have been up to." Her accent was so prim and lovely that I had a sudden urge to have tea and ring my mum.

Graham interjected, "We don't want to know about every-thing." He elbowed Chris in the stomach. It was hard to imagine

Chris putting up with Graham on a daily basis for all of the years the band was together.

Angie whispered, "I'm sorry. I swear, he's not always like this but I think he had a few nips while I took my shower. He'll seem perfectly normal once we all catch up with him."

In the kitchen, Marisol opened a bottle of wine and set out a plate of fruit and cheese. Angie and I sat while Chris and Graham stayed in the courtyard, talking with words flying.

"Claire, tell me how you and Christopher met."

My heart raced. It was the first time I'd been asked to tell the story. Aside from Sam, nobody in my life knew about Chris and it had to stay that way until the *Rolling Stone* issue was on newsstands.

"Oh, it's not much of a story really. I'm a music writer, and I interviewed him a few weeks ago. We hit it off and well, here I am."

She smiled at me sweetly. "Christopher is very good at pursuing a woman he's interested in."

Graham and Chris joined us, putting an end to that thread of the conversation, one that I would've liked to explore further.

Graham sat and squeezed me closer with his arm, leaving Angie at the opposite end of the couch. "The P-Man tells me that you wrote the *Rolling Stone* cover story about him. Lucky bastard."

So much for secrets.

"Graham suggested I play a small club in LA," Chris said. "To let the fans know I have a new record."

"Smart. Great idea," I said, wishing I were exchanging body heat with Chris instead of Graham.

"Smashing. Claire's on board," Graham quipped as he tightened his grip on my shoulder.

Using only my eyes, I pleaded with Chris for a rescue from Graham. Chris crossed his legs and bobbed his foot in the armchair next to us, openly amused by our every interaction. He didn't say a thing; he melted me down with his gaze instead.

The adults drank far too much during dinner, so much that I didn't recall eating a meal and my wine glass seemed to magically empty and refill. It was plain after a while that it was an uncomfortable situation for Sam and she excused herself from the table before dessert, saying she was going to bed early.

We foolishly kept drinking and at one point, some idiot suggested we start doing shots of tequila. I was sure it was Graham, but that was conjecture. For all I knew, it could've been me. Marisol ignored our obnoxious behavior while she tidied the kitchen, the four of us laughing hysterically at stories told by Graham and Chris.

"Okay, hold on a second," Chris said, slurring his words and raising his damn finger to get our attention. "I haven't told you that Claire was a huge Banks Forest fan when she was a teenager. Huge."

I glared at him. "Please don't say another word."

He winked at me.

"Aha!" Graham blurted, his eyes lighting up even though he could hardly keep them open. "Claire, you have to tell me which of us you had the hots for," he insisted. "Come on now, don't be shy. Just don't tell me it was the P-Man."

"Graham, darling, I'm sure it wasn't you." Angie had a comely smile on her face as she snickered.

"You two actually talk about this stuff?" I asked, irked that Chris had done what he swore he wouldn't. "That's completely pathetic."

Angie giggled and slugged down the last of her wine, turning the glass upside down in disappointment when it was gone.

Chris leaned over to me, permeated by liquor. "It's the best part of our story. She had it for me."

"Yes, honey," I responded, trying to disguise my own slur. "Me and a million other girls."

"Well, that doesn't make it sound romantic at all." Chris frowned—he was beyond the point of being drunk, still terribly handsome with that awful look painted on his face. He tried to kiss me and I pulled away. He persisted and I dodged to the side and back again before he stopped my game and grabbed my head. "Come here," he said, planting one on me, messy and with a bit too much tongue considering we had company.

It was obvious that Graham preferred the spotlight be on him, so he took our brief make-out session and a ten-second lull in the conversation as his opportunity to take off his pants. He then proceeded to show us exactly what kind of underwear he favored before he jumped in the pool, shouting at Angie to get in with him. I'd only known her for a few hours, but I was sure he would've had to be drowning for her to do that.

Chris erupted in laughter at the one-man act taking place in the pool, clapping his hands and doubling over. I then realized how he'd tolerated Graham all those years—he'd been wasted the entire time.

CHAPTER TWENTY-TWO

I HAD a dreamless sleep the first night back at home. When morning came, the bed seemed like it stretched out for miles, I its sole inhabitant. I ached to have Chris there, twisting his long legs in the covers and breathing on me.

Our last day on the island had been a somber affair; me with a horrendous hangover and the two of us growing more melancholy as our time together dwindled. The only bright spot, the carrot dangling before my face, was Chris's invitation to come to LA for the weekend since Graham had convinced him to book the acoustic show.

The sound of footsteps came from Sam's room as I headed downstairs for coffee. A few days of spring break remained, but her mood was so miserable that I couldn't imagine her enjoying a minute. It was a shame to think about the condition in which she and I'd left the island. We were both so happy when we got there.

My hand poised to knock, I wondered if today might be the day she decided to zip her lip and shut me out. I rapped gently, cracked the door, and she unraveled before I had the chance to say "good morning".

"I miss Jean-Luc. I miss him so much. I can't believe I'll probably never see him again." She slumped down on the bed, cascades of flattened flaxen curls hanging around her face. Her fingers worked at the hem of her faded t-shirt, pulling at a loose thread. She flopped onto her side, curling into a ball. "I close my eyes and he's the only thing I see."

I rubbed her back. "Honey, I'm sorry you feel so bad. I know it's hard, but you'll eventually get over him."

She stared at me like she'd never done before. "Why do you hate him?"

"I don't hate Jean-Luc. I didn't want you to have to go through what you're going through right now."

"I think you hate him. Did you even talk to him while we were there?" Before I could answer, she chimed in on my behalf. "No. You didn't. You let Chris do your dirty work for you."

"What do you mean by that?"

"I'm not stupid. I saw Chris pulling him aside, having their little secret meetings. It wasn't hard to figure out why one day he wouldn't touch me and the next day he was all over me."

I took in a deep breath and exhaled with puffed cheeks. "Don't blame Chris. He only did what I'd asked him to do. I didn't want Jean-Luc to take advantage of you."

Her response was lightning fast. "I knew it!" She sat back up and her face was scarlet. "Mom, you just can't butt out, can you? Just so you know, he treated me better than any other boy ever has. He was polite and held my hand and he wasn't afraid to tell me nice things. He told me I was pretty and funny and tons of other things that Andrew would never say." Her tears spilled and dotted her t-shirt. "If that's what you're protecting me from, I don't want to be protected."

Everything I'd misread was obvious now. "Honey, I'm sorry. It's just..." my voice wobbled. "I know I can't protect you forever and that I need to let you make your own decisions. But it's a lot easier to say those things than to actually do them. I saw Jean-Luc and he was so enthralled with you and it scared me. I was sure that all he wanted was sex."

She rubbed the hem of her t-shirt again before she tucked her knees under her chin. Her eyes cast down, avoiding mine. "I was the one who wanted it. I had to talk him into it. He was worried about me, my feelings, if we did it." She peered at me, eyes swollen with moisture. "Mom, don't you remember what it was like to be my age? Boys aren't the only ones who want sex. Girls want it just as bad."

I felt like the world's worst mom. I was trying to protect her from the mistakes I'd made when I was her age. In the process, I'd tainted her memory of a boy she'd probably remember forever.

"Yes, honey, I remember what it was like to be your age. I remember it very well." I remembered what it was like to be desperate to be rid of your virginity, like it was something you had to lug around that you didn't want to own anymore. I took her hand and pulled it into my lap, her skin pristine and smooth.

"If you really remember, then you need to start letting go of me. I'm going to college after next year and then you won't be able to protect me at all. You'll have to trust me. I can make my own decisions."

It felt as though the future was narrowing to a very lonely point. I knew what was coming in a year, I knew I was supposed to be excited for her, but I kept giving in to horribly selfish feelings. "Honey, I'm so sorry. It's been the two of us for so long and that's all going to change and—." The words were there, but they felt impossible to say. "It's going to be hard for me to watch you go. I won't lie to you about that." I reached for a tissue from her bedside table.

She looked at me with her clear blue eyes. "Mom, it's going

to be okay. I have to grow up some time. I can't be a little kid forever."

"I know, honey. I know. And I want you to grow up. I want you to have your own life and watch you do great things." I touched her hair and silence settled us while our tears subsided. "I might have to check into a mental hospital, but it's not a big deal."

Sam turned the corners of her mouth and it felt like the best gift anyone had ever given me.

"You don't have to say anything if you don't want to, but did you have a nice experience with Jean-Luc?"

"Um..." Pink bloomed on her cheeks and she went back to the hem of her t-shirt. "Yes, it was nice. He was very gentle. It hurt a little more than I thought it would, but it hardly hurt at all the second time."

I closed my eyes and gathered the strength to be calm about her admission. She deserved credit for confiding in me. "I take it you used protection?"

"Of course. You hammered that into my brain a million times."

I closed Sam's door quietly when I left, dazed by her revelation and in desperate need of coffee. After half a cup, I still couldn't stomach the thought of the avalanche of e-mail likely waiting for me when I started my computer. Even more daunting, I had several stories to finish if I was going to go to LA on Friday. When my cell phone rang and I saw Chris P. on the caller ID, I smiled and my shoulders relaxed, the best possible reason to put off responsibilities.

"Hi." I started sweetly, but my voice splintered at the thought of how much I already missed him. "Is everything okay? It's early your time."

"Everything's fine. I couldn't sleep and I was thinking about you."

"I miss you."

"I miss you too. I hated not having you in the same bed with me last night. Do you think you can come out on Friday? I'm already miserable without you."

My pulse fluttered. "I talked to my dad last night after we got home. He can get here Friday morning if that works."

He let out a breathy laugh. "You have no idea how happy that makes me. Let me take care of your flight."

"You don't have to do that. I can do it." A part of me still wanted to do something for myself, as nice as it was when he took care of everything.

"I tell you what, I'll have my travel agent call you and you can arrange everything with her. Will that make you feel better? Otherwise, you'll probably just put yourself in coach."

"I spent my entire life in coach. It's not that bad."

"I know, but I want you to have better."

Although I would have gladly spent the day on the phone with Chris, I could no longer ignore the pile of work on my desk. A voicemail was waiting when I got off the phone, and all at once, Kevin managed to sully my restored happiness. I dialed the number, facing the inevitable. Avoiding Kevin never worked.

"Claire Bear, I was starting to think you were avoiding me."

"I was on vacation. And I've asked you to stop calling me that."

"Oh, come on, you used to love it when I called you that. It brings back nice memories, doesn't it?"

"Not really."

"Whatever," he said, avoiding the topic of bad memories, of which he and I had a few whoppers. "Hey, you never called me after you finished your Chris Penman interview. I'd say I'm sorry, since he's such a train wreck, but it sounds like you hit the jackpot."

I closed my eyes. "How do you know I hit the jackpot? Patrick is keeping a lid on that story. He isn't even letting staffers see it."

"Is that what he told you?" He snickered. "Patrick and I are pretty tight these days. He hooked me up with the ghostwriting gig on Elise Penman's book."

I pinched the bridge of my nose and my brain clicked in my skull, cringing at the thought of Kevin and Patrick, tight. "Wait, Elise Penman is writing a book?"

"You don't know about that? Oh, shit. I just assumed Patrick mentioned it." He laughed. "You'll love it, a total piece of trash about being a Rock 'n' Roll wife. Turns out Mr. Pompous British Asshole screwed her over when they got divorced. She needs the money for that pesky drug habit of hers so she's going to drag him through the mud and cash in at the same time."

"That's awful. I can't believe she'd do that to him after everything she put him through."

"Jesus, Claire, did you actually fall for his sob story?" He paused and my stomach sank. "Oh my God. Tell me you didn't sleep with him to get him to talk. Is that why he spilled everything?"

"I'm not even going to acknowledge that." My heart raced at an unhealthy pace. If Kevin became the reason things came crashing down, I might have to kill him.

"I wish I could've taken a crack at Penman. I mean, I wasn't hired on Elise's book until a week after your interview, but damn. There are some nasty stories in this book. I could've nailed him to the wall."

"Nothing like skirting the whole journalistic ethics thing."

"Yeah, right. Good one." He snorted. "But seriously, this will be good for you. There's a great buzz on your story and Elise's book is just going to add to it once word gets out. Patrick told me he's already planning on offering you another feature, maybe another cover."

The mention of another big story made my heart race in a better way, but I struggled to wrap my head around the mess about to unfold. "What's in Elise's book?"

"Sorry, babe. Sworn to secrecy. They don't want anyone in Penman's camp finding out about it. I think they're hoping for a bit of an ambush."

"Lovely." *And here I am. Squarely in Penman's camp.*

"I'll be back in LA in a few days, do you want to come and visit? Maybe you could persuade me to tell some secrets. You know, I miss that thing you do with your tongue."

"Oh, gross. Cut it out. Will you at least tell me when the book is coming out?"

"Fine." He paused and I heard him swallow, which was beyond disgusting. "It comes out a few weeks before your story. It's called," he laughed, "you won't believe this, it's so genius. The title is *Love, Destroyed.*"

Just like that, the thing that was going to crush Chris got even worse.

CHAPTER TWENTY-THREE

CHRIS PICKED me up at the airport, waiting outside of the security checkpoint in his sunglasses and gorgeousness, leaning against the wall as if being beautiful took no effort at all. We hardly managed words before we were kissing, oblivious to the commotion of the airport swirling around us.

"I need to get you out of here," he whispered into my hair, "now."

We waited for the valet and I leaned on him as if I didn't have the strength to stand on my own, with my hands deep inside his jacket. The feeling of his arms around me was bristling and intense, having gone for days without it.

When they brought his car around, a glossy silver-gray Aston Martin, the men within sight of the curb turned their heads in perfect unison and watched with lustful eyes. Chris was predictably cool about it with his hand at my back as the valet opened my door. Knowing nothing about cars and caring only slightly more, I could say that even I found the car super sexy, making it a perfect match for its owner.

He zipped around like he owned the city, but I appreciated his likely motives. His show wouldn't have had the same effect in my Volvo station wagon in Chapel Hill or in a beat-up jeep on dusty roads. No, if he was going to impress me with a car and his skill, it had to be in that particular vehicle, on his home turf.

My skin prickled as it dawned on me that I had just been plunged into Chris's world. The island had given me a taste, but it was fantasyland. Today I would see where he spent his days, ordinary for him and something more for me. He glanced over and grinned as he made another risky maneuver with the car, leaving the heat to ripple over me in steady, persistent crests.

"I find it funny that the person who drives like a complete maniac loves to criticize my driving." I cracked a smile.

He slid me a handsome smirk, erasing days of lonely, and shifted in his seat. "But I'm in total control of the car. You're one distraction away from running off the road."

"That's not true," I insisted. Watching him, I noticed his hair was too perfect. I made a mental note to make it extra untidy as soon as we got to his house.

It was early evening and the sky was a gaudy shade of pink, a fitting backdrop for the endless sprawl of palm trees and donut shops. I'd been to LA many times, the last being when I ended things with Kevin. He was a great writer but would've made a better lawyer, quite practiced at wearing me down with his convoluted arguments until they almost made sense. Sure enough, his excuses for cheating had been well crafted, but I could only be a gullible idiot for so long.

This time was entirely different. It was more than the person I'd come for; it was what was already here between us. Things felt as though they were about to burst forth. I had optimism in my heart, not a head full of scorn and acrimony. If I hadn't been carrying around a secret about his ex-wife and her nasty book, everything would've been perfect.

The car climbed the hills, pivoting precisely at every turn, and just when I thought we couldn't go much higher, we stopped at 4521. We waited for a heavy black iron gate to roll across the driveway before the engine crept us up to the house. He parked the car exactly where he felt like it, askew, forgoing the three garage bays.

The house was modern; dark gray with black exposed metal framing in orderly rows of rectangles and a flat roof. Inside, the space opened dramatically, sweeping in all directions after a wide entryway and two steps down to the living room.

We'd entered on the second floor and my eyes were drawn to the million-dollar view of rolling California hills through the towering windows at the back of the house. The sun was setting, shifting into black and blue.

The polished concrete living room floor was covered with a white shag rug, the ideal setting for his enviable collection of vintage 60s furniture, Scandinavian blonde wood tables and low couches and armchairs in gray textured upholstery. I adored the fact that he'd skipped the standard issue wealthy bachelor furniture, black leather and chrome.

"Well?" he asked, breaking me down with the sound of his voice.

"It's beautiful. Incredible." I set my purse on the coffee table.

He smiled and took my hand. "Good, I'm glad you like it. I want you to be comfortable here." He pulled me close and wrapped me up in his arms, exploring my neck with buttery soft lips. I dug in and ruffled his hair just as I'd promised myself.

He pressed his lower body into mine and slid a hand under the back of my top, peeling it away in one seamless motion. "I vote that we postpone the house tour."

My breath caught in my throat. I closed my eyes halfway before I answered, overwhelmed by his smell and presence. I began to unbutton his shirt. "It would be nice to see where we'll be sleeping." I pushed the sleeves back over his broad shoulders and skimmed my hands across his chest, admiring one of my favorite parts of him.

"That's so far away." He moved his hands up my back, unhooked my bra and dropped it to the floor. "It'd take too long to get there." He took my hand and kneeled on the fluffy rug and I followed. He stretched his body out on the field of pure white.

"Well, see, I'm at a disadvantage." I kissed his chest between words while the carpet tickled the bare skin of my torso. "I've never been to your house before." I smoothed my hand across his stomach and whispered with hot breath against his neck, "I had no idea it was a trek."

He popped up on his elbow. "Claire, darling, you're killing me. Enough." He quickly unzipped my jeans and helped me wiggle out of them. He flattened his hand against the side of my face and looked me straight in the eye. "No more being clever. You're making me barmy. Please take my pants off."

"Uh, of course," I replied, blinking at the immediacy of his request. "I hope you have a condom."

"In my pocket."

"You're prepared."

"Yes, my dear, I am." He rolled me to my back without another word and everything became a frenzied blur. Minutes later, we both collapsed, breathless. I felt as though I'd been hit by a particularly handsome freight train.

"Tell me that isn't the usual version of the house tour," I said, still catching my breath.

"Uh, no. That was a first for the rug." He laughed. "It's your fault, you know. I thought I was going to pass out in the car. It's not good to have all of that blood flow diverted when you're trying to drive."

I shook my head. "My fault? I'm surprised I was able to walk out of the airport without falling down."

He rolled back to his side and smoothed his hand across my stomach. "I promise to take my time with you later tonight." He smiled half of a smile, his eyes smoldering, and I became peppered with goose bumps.

I shook my head again to break the spell he'd cast on me, at least long enough to speak. "Do we wear clothes for the rest of the tour?"

"Of course. We can't be completely uncivilized."

Both of us sporting the appropriate attire, Chris began the official tour where we'd started, in the living room. One wall housed an expanse of floor-to-ceiling bookcases, brimming with a collection of books that I was intent on exploring, curious about what new things I might discover. I'd entered our relationship knowing a lot about Chris. Learning anything new would be a novelty.

He put his arm around my shoulders, gently squeezing me toward him, and led me out to the second floor terrace. The view down to the pool was lovely—the lights, reaching from the depths, showed off the water's smooth glassy green. Palm trees cast exotic shadows against the tall walls surrounding the property.

The air was at a virtual standstill, but pleasing when it chose to turn and become a breeze. He put a hand to the railing and I felt as if the mole on his cheek was toying with me. I smoothed my hand across his back and leaned into him.

He pecked me on the cheek before pushing back from the railing. "You can see the kitchen later. I want to show you the music room." Inside and downstairs, at the end of a wide hall, sat a massive black metal door.

Once I stepped over the threshold, I knew that the volumes in his living room would only be a small part of learning more about Chris. The sheer size of the music room and the extent of its contents made it impossible to take it in at one time. My eyes pinged everywhere, drawn to one fascinating object after another. There were at least two-dozen guitars; some hanging in display on the dark felt walls while a few sat in stands near a glossy grand piano.

I ventured farther to the walls lined with gold and platinum records. They hung in neat rows to make room for all of them and there were many. It was surreal to stand there and look at the album covers, to think about a far-off time when his band was one of the most important things in my life.

"*Around the World*. I remember waiting in line to buy that the day it came out." I pointed at a picture of the band holding their gold records. "Who's that handsome guy?"

He smiled. "No idea."

I continued and he was clearly amused to watch me. "*Deadly Guest*. My dad hated that title. He thought it had some satanic meaning. Wow, *White and Gray*." I pointed again. "That was my favorite for a long time. You sold eight million copies of that one?"

"It appears so."

I wandered at a careful pace; the room was an impressive statement about the importance of music in his life. I could see how much it defined him. "You wrote all of the songs on the new record here?"

"This is where I escaped when things got really bad."

"It's unbelievable." I choked up, thinking about the way he must've felt then. He'd worked hard to move on with his life and much of it was going to come rushing back with Elise's book. I knew I should tell him, but I was petrified of what it would do to him, of what it would do to us. I caught his eyes and he returned the gaze. *Tomorrow. Let us keep tonight.*

He stirred me up with his smile. "Come on. We don't want to miss our dinner reservations. Let's get you settled in my room."

Back upstairs I poked my head in his lovely guestroom, twice as big as mine. Next down the hall was another bedroom he described as empty when we passed the closed door.

Chris's room was spacious and serene, painted a light cocoa brown. It was also minimalist in decoration, but that may have been his inner bachelor speaking. Earthy Asian inspired paintings were on one wall, and some edgier black and white art prints on another. His furniture was dark wood, modern and masculine.

I couldn't help but think about he and Elise in the room, together, for years. The four walls had likely seen many arguments and make-ups to follow. The bed had an icy blue coverlet and crisp white pillows that looked new. I could only presume he'd gone about the business of replacing things after he asked her to leave.

On our way out for dinner, we held hands and laughed, walking down the hall from his bedroom. We passed the closed door and I wondered if at one point in his life, he'd hoped that the room next to his, the one that was empty, would be the baby's room.

CHAPTER TWENTY-FOUR

WE WENT OUT FOR SUSHI, but of course, it had to be the sushi restaurant where reservations were impossible to get and everyone came to be seen. We still didn't want to be seen, by anyone, and Chris had made arrangements. The manager met us at the back door and we were ushered through the kitchen to a booth that shielded us from most of the restaurant. We sat on the same side and tortured each other with wandering hands.

I was glad I'd taken fifteen minutes at the house to doll myself up because the amount of silicone in the room was unsettling for someone with average endowments. I'd always liked my barely B-cups, but I stuck out like a sore thumb in my low-cut dress, as if I was bragging about nothing. Chris caught me staring at the astounding display from our waitress and then reflexively glancing down at my own. I knew better than to be truly envious. Her ladies looked as if they'd rolled off an assembly line. He tucked his arm around my waist and scooted me even closer.

The lights were dim, the candles on the table the only real illumination, casting his freshly shaven face with a flushed glow.

We shared a menu and I leaned into him, uninterested in food even though I was starving.

He muttered from the corner of his mouth, "Yours are better."

"Hmmm?" I turned toward him, our noses inches apart as I waited for his breath on my lips.

He glanced down at my chest. "Yours are better. They're a perfect handful." He smiled at me before he returned his attention to the menu. "Just like you."

I nestled my mouth against his ear. "You think you're funny, don't you?"

Our dinner conversation was effortless now that we had shared experiences. Many of the laughs about our trip were at Graham's expense, but I was sure that if he'd been with us, he would have been pleased to be a topic of conversation.

"So, I have to ask. Has Graham always been so loud and obnoxious?" It did occur to me that I was insulting his oldest and dearest friend.

Chris chuckled. "Since we were kids. He likes being the center of attention. That's what made him an amazing front man."

"I guess I just didn't think he'd be so...exuberant."

"I'm sure that was for your benefit. You were someone new to perform for. He loves that." He reached for another spicy tuna roll. "Did your lunch plans work out with Angie?"

"Yes, we're going out tomorrow. Is that okay?" I finished my seaweed salad, forgetting how it likes to stick in your teeth.

"I'd prefer not to share you with anyone, but I'll manage."

As we waited for the waitress to return with Chris's credit card, he took charge of my hand and my heart began beating like a moth against a light bulb, flapping to get inside the glass. I steadied my eyes on him and he was possibly the most handsome I'd ever seen him. I wondered if it was because he was becoming mine.

Just as we stood to leave, a woman, a walking flip of blonde, approached us with her orangey spray tan and insufferable perfume. She went in for a kiss on the cheek from Chris and I felt his body stiffen as he squeezed my hand.

"Hello...you." He looked at her and then at me, bugging out his eyes. "This is my girlfriend, Claire."

Our guest seemed disappointed that I wasn't introduced as his sister. It was also uncomfortably obvious that he couldn't remember her name.

"Hi, I'm Sharon." She shook my hand with a girly grip while confusion clouded her face, although she probably spent much of her life disoriented. She managed to smile at him while she stared at me, tilting her head to the side. "Christopher, I didn't know you had a girlfriend."

"It's a recent development." He hooked his arm around me and pulled me close.

She possessed enough brainpower to take that as her cue to leave and we ducked out the back of the restaurant.

"I'm sorry about that. I guess I blocked out her name. She was a bit of a loon," he said, peeling out onto the street.

"It's okay." I reached across to his leg. He could've told me he slept with her fifty times. It would have made no difference. He'd called me his girlfriend.

Back at the house, I followed him to the kitchen. It was ultra-modern with simple dark wood cabinets topped with white stone. The backsplash was glass tile and everything else stainless steel. I hopped up on the counter and kicked off my heels, feeling drunk and then regretful when I thought about the money I'd spent on my shoes and the way I'd treated them. Chris leaned with a hand on the counter and studied my every move. He smiled and pulled a bottle of Limoncello from the freezer. I shivered from the blast of wintry air as he poured a round.

"Are you cold?" He slid his hot hand down my back and handed me a glass.

I tossed back my shot in a single swallow. The lemony goodness crept down my throat, mild and summery at first. I licked a drip from the corner of my mouth, aware of how his face was tempting me.

"You're supposed to sip it," he quipped.

I gave him my glass. "I know. Hit me."

"You have to promise you aren't going to get so leathered that you pass out. That would be a disappointment."

"I promise."

He handed me the second drink and then brought out the big guns, relinquishing the look that never failed to trigger my least ladylike response. He hovered closer, our lips inches apart, electrical pulses crossing the imaginary dividing line between us —and I started to laugh.

"What's so funny?" He whispered, resting his hand on my leg.

"I can't help it." I continued to giggle, letting the Limoncello get the best of me. "I'm a little tipsy."

"No kidding." He finally kissed me, using his body to set my knees apart while his hand went from on top of my dress to under it. He made a clinging advance up my leg and grasped my hip.

I wrapped my arms around his neck and bent each leg behind him before I dug in my heels to muscle him closer. I could've kissed him for hours; our lips were a perfect match and tasted the same, but I doubted that was his plan and it didn't meet the extent of mine either.

"We've spent a lot of time kissing in kitchens," I mumbled,

when he'd stopped to brush my hair aside and float along my neck with his lips.

"Some day we'll try for more than kissing." He pulled my hips until I had no choice but to slip off the counter. "But we already christened the living room rug today."

I took his hand and left my shoes on the floor, stumbling to his bedroom, where things boiled over at a mercurial pace. I hurried him out of his shirt and pants. My dress was no match for him this time—one quick pull of the zipper was all it took. He slid his arms to my back, but I twisted my shoulders and broke away to turn off the light.

"I don't mind the light. You could've left it on."

"Of course you don't mind the light. You look good from every angle."

"We had all kinds of light earlier today."

I tiptoed back to where he stood. "That's different. I didn't have a chance to make you move to a dark room."

He went back to covering every square inch of me with his hands. "I love the way you look, from every angle." He unhooked my bra and smoothed his hand across my collarbone. "Your skin is gorgeous." He kissed my shoulder and then mumbled into my ear, "Don't get me started on your hair and your butt." He leaned down while he gripped my ribcage and kissed each breast. "And don't forget my two best friends, Penelope and Guinevere."

I flushed red. "Don't tell me you gave them names."

He laughed, breathlessly. "I didn't. I just made that up."

I pulled his face back to mine. "You're a very funny man." One knee at a time, I dropped to the floor, dragging my hands as I clutched his chest and stomach, before separating him from his boxer shorts.

He looked down at me with pure excitement on his face.

"This is like Christmas morning." He pushed his hands into my hair. "The anticipation is killing me."

"No talking. You're ruining the moment."

"But what if you aren't doing it right?" He laughed.

"You've got to be kidding."

Although there were no discernable words escaping his lips, Chris told me that indeed, I was doing it right. Being with him made me feel different, uninhibited, and I savored every minute of pleasing him. He surprised me when he tugged on my arms, interrupting one of my most elaborate efforts.

"Come here." He pulled me up and gave me a soft kiss. "As much as I was enjoying that, I need all of you." We walked sideways to the bed, never allowing our lips to part.

I dragged him down on top of me; the full force of his body weight was perfect, like he belonged there. "I missed you so much," I said. "I missed everything about you." I kissed his shoulder and his neck, dotting his skin with fading prints of my lips. "I missed the way you smell and the funny thing you do with your eyebrows and the way you're hungry all the time."

He tipped his head to the side in acknowledgement that I'd broken my own rule. "Aren't we chatty? I missed you too." He returned to my neck with his lips and lightly traced his fingers between my ribcage and my hip. "I don't like being apart from you either. At all." Then he got the look in his eyes again.

He put a hand on my stomach and made a slow descent before he glossed my entire chest with his luscious mouth. He remained unhurried in his motions, revisiting some extra sensitive spots a second or third time. He settled for a moment in the slip of skin between my breasts. Most men overlooked it, but the brush of his lips there was indescribable, a mysterious pleasure, and I felt a stitch of disappointment once he moved on—until I realized where he was headed.

He kissed my belly button and kept going with his lips, gently urging my thighs apart with his hands. As incredible as his mouth felt on every other part of my body, this was a different stratosphere. I sank further into the bed with every torrid flicker; gathering up the bedspread in bunches to have something to do with my hands.

More than talented, he was inventive, and before long, even the most insignificant parts of me were ignited, poised for release. I tried his trick and pulled on his arms, but he ignored me and forced me to use words. "Chris, come on. Get back up here. I need you. Now."

"I love this new talkative side of you." He pressed his lips against the base of my throat.

"Shhh. Get a condom. Quick."

"You're so bossy."

Emotion coursed through me when I felt his now familiar presence. It flooded my entire body with happy abundance. Our eyes connected and he drew me in, no words between us. I was sure I'd never felt better than I did at that moment, like I was exactly where the world wanted me. The pinnacle crept up on me and I became riddled with electricity as I gave way, succumbing to the moment much more noisily than usual. We continued with our pitch until he, too, collapsed in breathless, relieved contentment.

Without obligations, we reveled in the chance to be together for as long as we wanted. We tangled our limbs under only the sheet, as I was certainly no longer cold. We kissed and talked, lazing until his growling stomach let its needs be known.

"I have to eat something."

"Didn't we just have dinner?" I felt the smile spread across my face. "Of course, let's feed you."

I'd brought two nightgowns for the trip—the first was black, silky and short, but could still pass as legitimate sleeping attire. The other, wrapped in tissue paper, was dark blue with black lace, obscenely short and low-cut, with straps that made dental floss look like mariners' rope.

I stood over my suitcase, trying to decide which to wear. Certainly, my audience would be pleased either way, but something didn't feel right. At that moment, all I wanted was to be enveloped in Chris, to be as tipsy from him as I was from the Limoncello. His gray dress shirt sat puddled on the floor. As soon as I smelled it, I knew what to wear to bed.

He came out of the bathroom as I was rolling up the sleeves.

"That is the sexiest thing I've seen in a long time," he said, stepping closer, a sly grin across his face. "We don't want to get carried away with the buttons. That's far enough." He set his hand on mine and pecked me on the top of my head.

He dug through the refrigerator wearing only his gray plaid boxers, likely unaware of the effect on me when he did things like scratch his stomach while his hair flopped into his face or talk while stretching his arms above his head. He eventually decided on a turkey sandwich and I brewed myself a cup of decaf Earl Gray. At the kitchen table reveling in each quiet moment, I watched him as he made the sandwich disappear. I remained in awe of everything he possessed in his glorious body.

He reached for my hand after pushing his plate aside. "I have a surprise for you." He smoothed my hair back softly, looking at it, rather than me.

"Really?" My heart and mind fluttered.

He left the table and returned with a small box that made me freeze—it was the instantly identifiable Tiffany blue, tied with a white satin ribbon. I couldn't take the box from his hand without my throat feeling jumpy. I was so excited, from head to toe; I'd always hoped a man would give me a Tiffany blue box, preferably a small one. I'd never dreamed that the man would be Chris.

My hands quaked when I pulled at the ribbon. I told myself

to remember every moment, frame by frame. He wore a luminous smile, soaking up my reaction as he sat next to me.

I removed the top and held my breath. There was a bracelet —exquisite, heavy silver links with a heart shaped charm. It was engraved *Please return to Tiffany & Co., New York* on one side and on the other, a perfectly good reason to cry, *For Claire, with affection, Chris.*

"Oh my God, Chris, I love it. It's beautiful." I pulled the bracelet from the box, admiring his excellent taste.

"I had to pull a few strings to get them to engrave it with words. They usually only do monograms." He reached over to hook the clasp for me. "I just wanted to give you something. You know, I was thinking about it on my way to pick you up at the airport. I think you're my first girlfriend that I've been friends with."

That word—girlfriend, made for a flash of excitement inside me but I was bewildered by what he'd said. "That's sweet, but are you sure? You must've been friends with a lot of your girl-friends."

"No. I think you're the first." He held my hand, inching the bracelet along with his thumb. "I think it's because we didn't jump into bed right away. You know, the weeks we spent talking and getting to know each other before anything became physical, and even then it was just a bit of snogging since you shot me down." He smiled shyly, not at all like him. "That's never happened to me before, by the way. I didn't want to tell you that night." He continued to toy with the bracelet.

"Aren't you glad we waited?"

"I was glad when it was over."

I smiled. "You must've been friends with Elise. You were together for so long."

"Not really. I'm not even sure we liked each other. There was chemistry, we were drawn to each other, but we never had what I already have with you. We never talked for hours on the phone. We never wanted to be alone with each other doing nothing. She never understood my love of music, but you feel the same way. You get it. That's important to me."

The fact that he valued the friendship that accompanied our romance made it feel as though he was unfolding everything inside me. He was proceeding slowly, taking great care—like you would with an old letter in hopes of deciphering the black scrawl, praying that it wouldn't part at the creases. I knew then that I would never reside in the class of his disposable women.

I admired him with a brand new set of feelings when I'd been worried I already had too many. "That's the nicest thing a man has ever said to me."

"I'm not just being nice. It's true." He smiled, but it faded. "I could've saved myself a lot of heartache if I'd had you from the beginning."

CHAPTER TWENTY-FIVE

WE TALKED in the dark for hours. One time, we laughed so hard that the headboard banged against the wall and I couldn't catch my breath. Even the bittersweet subject of Sam and Jean-Luc was tolerable. Chris worried that he should've done more, but I'd already had time to resign myself to the facts. It'd gone exactly as he'd predicted—they wanted to have sex and found a way.

"You know, I've been wanting to ask about your mum." He put his arm under my head. "You don't talk about her a lot."

He was right. I rarely talked about her. She and I were always discussing everything in my head. Some days it almost felt as if she was still around.

"Oh, well, her name was Sara. She was a great mom. She passed away when I was pregnant, about three weeks before Sam was born, from..." I choked back what had long been stuck in my throat, "ovarian cancer."

"Claire, I'm so sorry. That's awful. Were you two close?"

"We were." My voice cracked. Seventeen years later, the pain was still tamped down inside me. My sister never wanted to talk about it and my dad simply wasn't able. Worst of all, Sam had never known her. "We were a lot alike, emotional, but inde-pendent. Creative, she liked to write poetry. She looked out for me with my dad, because we never got along. He didn't have a lot of patience for me when I was a kid. Especially when I was a teenager."

I cleared my throat. "My mom thought my Banks Forest obsession was great, even though it drove my dad up a wall. She remembered what it was like to be a teenage girl."

All I could think was that my mom would've adored Chris. She would've bragged about him to her sister and her friends and said something off-color about his butt after he left the room.

He caressed my arm. "It must've been hard losing her right before Sam was born."

"It was." I started to choke up again. "Things would get tough when Sam was a newborn and I'd reach for the phone and remember my mom wasn't there anymore. It just hadn't sunk in. I had no idea what I was doing and I was all by myself. I just remember being exhausted and frustrated all of the time. You add that when you're still grieving for someone and it wasn't pretty."

"How did you get through it?"

"Honestly? I have no idea. Sam was barely crawling when I moved to Chapel Hill and I only knew a few people—I had no girlfriends, my sister was wrapped up in her own kids and my dad was dealing with his own grief. I used to hold up the line at the grocery store to have a conversation with the cashier, so I could talk to a grown-up. Babies are cute, but they're incredibly draining." I heard the words come out of my mouth, not believing I could be so insensitive.

He cleared his throat. "Yes. I suppose so."

"Oh, no, no. I didn't mean that to sound the way it did. I'm sorry. That was an awful thing for me to say."

He waited before responding, which only made me feel worse. "No, it's okay. I understand what you're saying. At least I think I understand. I'm sure having a child is a lot of hard work. I don't doubt that it's a very tough job."

There was more silence and I felt a tug inside. "Chris, honey, I'm sorry. I was babbling. You know, seeing you with Sam and how you were so protective of her with Jean-Luc. I'm sure that you would've made an incredible dad." I brought my hand to his face and kissed him on the forehead. "I'm so sorry."

"It's okay." He kissed me lightly and that made me wonder how badly I'd hurt him. "I'm dead knackered. Can we say good-night now?"

———

WHEN I WOKE the next morning, the other side of the bed was empty. I'd had a hard time falling asleep, replaying my idiocy. I just couldn't pass up the chance to wallow in everything that had been hard at that time in my life. Good things had happened then, too.

I jumped out of bed to find Chris. He was nowhere in the house and didn't answer when I called his name. Finally, I went out on the terrace and was relieved to find him swimming.

I walked down to the pool deck on the massive metal and concrete stairs that were cold and scratchy on my bare feet. I watched as his body skimmed through the water. His back was particularly beautiful, shoulder blades moving precisely with each stroke.

I perched on the end of a chaise lounge and waited, hugging his shirt to my body to ward off the morning chill. He stopped when he spotted me, popping up from the water and squinting through buggy goggles.

"Four more laps."

"Sounds great. I'm just watching."

He swam over when he was finished and climbed out, dripping and stunning. "Good morning." He loomed over me and I couldn't have cared less that he was getting water all over me.

"I didn't know you were such a swimmer."

"I love it." He was still catching his breath, pushing his wet hair back and toweling his chest. "I get up early every morning. The pool at the house in St. Barts is too small for laps."

I'd discovered something new about him and it all came together as I eyed him from head to toe: broad shoulders, skinny hips, and ridiculously long legs—a swimmer's body.

"You must be starving," I said, tracing my finger down his thigh.

"Dying. Will you make me breakfast?"

"I'd love to."

After breakfast, we became sidetracked in the bedroom for most of the morning. It helped me work up an appetite for my lunch date, although I almost wished I'd taken more time to get ready. Angie was so put together; I wanted to look good.

Chris jingled the car keys when we walked out the front door. "Have you seen yourself in those jeans?"

"Uh, yes, I have," I answered. I craned at my butt in the driveway. "Why?"

"You're bloody killing me, that's why." He hooked his arm around my waist and we continued to the garage. "I can't believe you're going to put those on and then go somewhere without me."

We stepped into the narrow space between the garage wall and his Mercedes SUV. Every other car he owned was, in his opinion, much too advanced for me to drive. He nuzzled my neck and pressed himself into me. I could smell his clean, damp hair above the faint aroma of motor oil.

"Are you sure you can't be fifteen minutes late?" he asked.

"Aren't you tired?" I bit my lip when I saw the look on his face, so charged that I was sure he could start the engine without the key. "Sorry. I won't be gone long."

He opened the car door. "You know I'm not good with delayed gratification."

I slipped into the driver's seat. He reached across and pointed to the dash, unsubtly grazing my breast.

"Careful," I said.

He cleared his throat. "There's the GPS. Please use it. I don't want you getting lost." He gave me a piece of paper with a five-digit number. "This is for the security gate. The clicker is being temperamental. Call me if you need anything."

I felt like a teenager with permission to take the car out for the first time. "You're cute, but I'm going to be fine."

"No, you're cute." He leaned in and kissed me on the forehead. "Please be careful. I don't want anything to happen to you. And don't be long. It won't be any fun if I have to start without you."

I waited for the automatic seat to inch forward enough for me to reach the gas. I then consulted the GPS and decided I couldn't stand to get directions from the bitchy British chick. The hunky sounding Australian guy was more my speed. He could direct me to the nearest Outback Steakhouse if I got lost.

The thought of my lunch date with Angie was so exciting. In many ways, she was the best shot I had at a real girlfriend. It was impossible to make friends as a single mom in a town full of married people. The other moms most often greeted me with suspicion.

Inside the restaurant, Angie's red hair was immediately evident in the sea of blonde. We shared a chummy hug and audible kisses on opposite cheeks before sitting. The restaurant was your typical southern California bistro—white table-cloths, aspiring actors as waiters, and plenty of artificial sweeteners on the table. We each ordered an iced tea and read the menu.

I couldn't help but notice Angie's mood. She seemed on edge, even when she smiled at me. I tried not to over think it, like I always do. Her hair was pin-straight, not a strand out of place about her pristine face. I squinted at one point to see if she had any wrinkles and then realized I was only making the crease between my own eyes worse.

Angie set her menu to the side. "Claire, I've brought something to show you and I really hope it doesn't ruin our lunch." She reached across the table for my hand. "I wish I were bringing you a gift."

Her comment was so out of the blue. I couldn't begin to guess what she was talking about. "Okay."

She reached into her exquisite black leather bag and pulled out a magazine. "I saw this while I was getting my pedicure today." She held it to her chest. "This happens to a lot of people and you shouldn't let it get to you." She set a dog-eared magazine before me.

My heart stopped when I saw the two photos. One was large, half of a page—Chris and I on the beach the day we first argued, me with an editor's bar of jumbled pixels across my naked chest and Chris's hand on my stomach. The smaller inset picture was a close-up—the two of us at the breakfast table, kissing. I read the caption and felt my head spin.

"*Notorious rock bad boy Christopher Penman canoodles on a St. Barts beach with music journalist Claire Abby. The couple reportedly visited Penman's luxury villa last week with Abby's daughter. Ms. Abby wrote the upcoming Rolling Stone cover story about Penman, in which he is rumored to tell all about his rocky marriage to ex-wife, Elise Penman. The former Mrs. Penman has written a book containing her own account of their marriage due out next month.*"

Angie's expression was so awful that it was hard to imagine how bad mine must've been. "I'm so sorry. I know it's hard the first time this happens. I was horrified the first time it happened to me."

"Unfortunately, this is the second time." I squeezed the lemon wedge too hard into my tea and squinted.

"Oh. I didn't know." The concern on her face never wavered. "Well, the good news is that neither of these show you two in an unflattering light. You're kissing and talking, they're quite sweet."

Actually, under further inspection, the beach shot was highly unflattering—one of my thighs was spread out on the towel like a pancake.

"I am so screwed. My editor is going to find out and that will be it for me. He warned me twice about getting involved with Chris." Our waiter brought our salads but food was the last thing on my mind.

"I wondered if you were trying to keep your relationship quiet."

"You and Graham are the only people who know about us other than my daughter. Even my dad thinks I'm out here visiting a friend." I looked down at the pictures again, trying to deduce who could have taken them. Then I remembered the guy on the boat with a camera and the only other person who had spent so much time in the kitchen. *Marisol.* "Chris said we'd have privacy on the island."

Angie looked at me with pity, she the seasoned veteran and I the ditzy novice. "He did? Photographers love St. Barts because so many celebrities vacation there. I'm sure someone got a tip about where he would be and that he'd brought a new companion. I hate to say this, but I think he's going to have to call and have his cook fired. I'm sure she took the photo of you at the table."

Angie shared the story of her first go-around with this sort of public embarrassment. It'd been shortly before she and Graham were married; they were photographed picking out wedding bands, through the jewelry store window. It wasn't horrible, but it was the invasion of privacy, especially when they were sharing a pivotal romantic moment, that had bothered her so much.

It had been only the beginning for Angie and Graham. There had been photographers outside of the hospital when their daughter was born and that was nearly two decades ago. The paparazzi were much more aggressive and unscrupulous now, tracking them down when they went to visit their daughter at university and waiting for them outside their home.

"Please, let's talk about something else." I finally had enough appetite to start on my salad, but my hand trembled. "You're coming to Chris's show tomorrow night, right?"

"We wouldn't miss it. Graham is really excited for Christopher. It's so cute. We should have dinner beforehand; a double date." Her eyes sparkled and she eyed my wrist, for at least the second time. "That's an awfully pretty bracelet. Tiffany, right?"

I blushed. "Yes. Chris gave it to me last night."

"Interesting." She smiled at me and winked. She was so effortlessly beautiful and I had such a girl crush on her. I wished she could be my sister or my best friend. "Christopher isn't much for jewelry. He must like you quite a lot."

I set down my fork. "What do you mean?"

She dabbed at the corners of her mouth with the napkin. "Well, there were issues when he was with Elise..."

"Go on, please."

"Christopher used to buy jewelry for her all the time. Then they'd have a fight and she would leave for weeks. She'd sell whatever he'd given her to, um, support herself."

"Buy drugs?"

She looked at me with a note of surprise. "Yes. It happened many times before they got married. Graham was worried when Christopher bought her an engagement ring because he'd spent a fortune on it." She took a sip of her iced tea and we sat quietly while the waiter topped off our glasses. "Graham was right. Christopher and Elise had an argument a few weeks after the wedding and she left for a month. She eventually came back, but the ring was gone."

CHAPTER TWENTY-SIX

DESPITE CHRIS'S WORRIES, I made it back to the house in one piece. My lunch with Angie had been slightly traumatizing and not what I'd looked forward to but she was so sweet about it all, such a lovely person. Struggling for a bright spot, I felt like we'd shared something—something yucky, but it was still something.

There was no sign of Chris in the house, but I found a note on the kitchen table.

My dear Claire,

I know I told you to hurry back but I had to dash out to run an errand. Please don't go anywhere. I swear I'll be right back. Don't take off the jeans. That's my job.

XOXO Chris

I took a beer into the living room with my laptop. I re-read the note and smiled, hoping the tabloid photos wouldn't ruin our night. Checking email, I replied to Sam's complaints about her grandfather and his rules. I reminded her that it was only for a few days and that she should enjoy their time together. I knew I was full of it as soon as I hit send, expecting from her what I wasn't able to do myself.

A new message appeared in my inbox and I sensed that my worst fear was about to materialize when I saw that it was from Patrick. My head began to pound, my stomach filled with dread. Sure enough, a frustratingly non-specific note instructing me to call him first thing Monday morning. Of course, I would be flying home from LA on Monday morning.

I couldn't think about it with any seriousness, things were out of my control. I turned off my computer and tried to relax. I shut my eyes, but that only made my anxiety balloon. Being alone with my thoughts was a terrible idea. My eyelids fluttered open and the books served as my reminder. I was blowing my opportunity to check out Chris's library unsupervised.

There were so many books to look at, an array of colorful spines, an eclectic mix of authors and subjects. I browsed and came across some about art and photography. A few had dark and gritty stuff—black and white images of people in despair, living lives that were unimaginable, poverty and filth. But then there were books filled with bright and colorful pop art. More than a few focused on artful portraits of beautiful women, some with clothes and many without.

I opened a volume of sepia tone photographs of a grungy late Nineteenth Century London. The pages spread open to the middle, held by a photograph. There was a lanky boy with thick reddish-brown bowl-cut hair in a striped t-shirt and navy pants with rips at the knees. He leaned against a graying man in a wide maroon necktie and scuffed cordovan shoes.

The Tudor house behind them had a wobbly roof and a latticework of thick brown slats over the cream-colored exterior. The garden behind the fence was overgrown, blooms popping through the pickets. I turned over the photograph and the caption was written in what appeared to be a woman's hand, beautifully formed cursive letters: *Alistair and Christopher May,*

1973. I counted the years in my head. It had been taken the year before Christopher's father had died.

It made Chris so human, so ordinary, to see him like that—I'd never once thought of him that way, normal, a boy with his dad. It was heartbreaking to see the happiness in their eyes, neither aware of how little time they had left together. His anguish was likely as great as my own over my mom, simply different circumstances and times.

Chris came through the door as I wiped away a tear. My first reaction was to slam the book closed and dash back to put it on the shelf. I smudged my hand across my cheeks while he set his things down on the entryway table.

"Glad to see you're home safely," he said, entering the room.

"You weren't honestly that worried about me."

"I was." He kissed me and draped his arm over my shoulder. "I missed you."

"I missed you too."

"What's wrong?" He focused on me. "Something's wrong."

I took a deep breath, still dazed from the photo of Chris and his dad. For that one moment, I'd forgotten what had come to light at lunch. "Let me show you." I pulled the magazine from my bag. "Angie brought this to lunch." I handed it to him, standing to gauge his response as he plopped down on the couch.

The corner of his mouth went up as he started to read. "Canoodling? Is that what we were doing that day?" He held the magazine out at arm's length. "I'd love to have the X-rated version of this photo for my scrapbook."

"Doesn't this bother you?" I snatched the magazine from him. "Because I'm kind of freaking out. I have to go to PTA meetings and the grocery store when I get home. My dad might see this. You said we'd have privacy on our trip. I wouldn't call this privacy."

"Of course it bothers me, but do you have any idea how many times this has happened to me?" He stood and closed the distance I'd made, wrapping his arm around my shoulders, holding me immobile. "You're never going to have total privacy with me. There's always someone lurking around with a camera."

I rested my forehead on his chest. "I think Patrick knows. He wants to talk to me on Monday morning. What am I supposed to do about that?"

"You should come clean. Frankly, that will be a big relief. This whole business of keeping secrets is driving me bloody crazy." He rubbed my arm. "Don't worry, you can make me the bad guy if you want. I pursued you, after all." He took my chin and turned my head toward him. "Seriously, I think it'll be fine."

"He already warned me about this, twice, and I lied to him about where I was going on vacation. There's no reason for him to ever trust me again."

He looked at me as though I was a child. "You love to assume the worst, don't you? You need to relax. There are always other assignments."

My reaction spurted out of me. "Don't tell me to relax. I've spent years trying to land a cover story that could move me into feature writing." I broke his hold on me. "The *Rolling Stone* piece is everything I have to stand on."

Chris remained quiet and I couldn't help but notice how my bracelet clunked against my wrist when I shifted my arm. He clutched my hand. "I'm sorry. Of course, you're upset, but it will blow over."

I froze. He didn't understand what else was about to happen and how much it could hurt him. I wrestled with telling him, making a completely irrational wish for the news about his vengeful ex-wife to disappear.

"This isn't going to go away. None of this will blow over." I looked him in the eye and it hit me. He'd just read what I was terrified to tell him. "Wait. Elise's book." I felt as if the air had been forced from my lungs, like a flattened dog toy. "You knew about it."

"Elise's book? Yes, I knew. She threatened me with it a few weeks after I kicked her out. I never thought she'd go through with it. It's not like she's managed to accomplish anything at all over the last ten years."

My thoughts ran, struggling to keep up with everything. One look in his eyes and I knew I owed him the truth. "I knew about it too."

"Before today?" His cheeks flamed red. "When exactly were you planning to tell me? Why would you keep this from me?"

With the tables turned, I felt the full force of how hard it was to come clean. "I found out a few days ago. I didn't want to tell you over the phone and I didn't want to tell you yesterday. We were having such a nice night and I was afraid. I knew how much it would hurt you." I saw his face calm. "I found out from her ghostwriter. He's my ex-boyfriend."

He laughed under his breath, shaking his head. "Well, this is a bloody mess we've got now, isn't it?"

"I know." I slumped down on the couch with him and he rubbed my back. "I'm really sorry. I should've told you right away. I didn't want to be the one to break the bad news. Guess I was being a big chicken."

"It's okay. I don't want you to keep things from me, though. You can tell me everything. I can handle it." He cocked his head to the side and touched his thumb to my chin. "I'm sorry things are a wreck with your editor. Hopefully you'll be able to work it all out." He pushed my hair back over my ear. "Can we take this in the kitchen? I'm starving."

CHAPTER TWENTY-SEVEN

I WOKE that night with a new fear, a thought that came on a mission to rob me of a good night's sleep. If Chris knew about Elise's book before I did the interview with him, had he planned to tell me everything all along?

I tossed and turned, unable to get back to sleep and hoped that jostling the bed would wake him. I even nudged him in the back a few times. It didn't work and I eventually drifted off, but the worry was waiting for me when I woke up for real.

It was an extra smoggy day in Los Angeles, making it difficult to see anything beyond Chris's domain through the wall of glass in the living room. I walked outside and watched him from the terrace, his movements in the water a beautiful distraction even when I felt sick to my stomach, dreading the question I had to ask.

He climbed out of the pool and I felt his pull from fifty feet away. "Hey, Mark Spitz. Do you want breakfast?"

He grinned. "You know it. I'll be right up."

He arrived in the kitchen with the towel around his waist and kissed me on the cheek while I cracked eggs. "What are we having?"

"French toast and bacon. Did you know you have a ton of bacon in your freezer?

"I love bacon."

All through breakfast, I remained preoccupied with what was hanging over my head. I'd told myself I'd ask him, but then I would delay, and then I would gather my strength again. By the time we'd finished eating, I was still scared, but I had to come out with it. Being a chicken wasn't going to get me anywhere.

"I was thinking about something you said yesterday," I said, standing up from the table. I watched him finish off the carton of orange juice with the fridge door open. "You said that Elise told you about the book a few weeks after you split up. So, that means you knew about it before we met." He closed the fridge. I trembled. "Did you agree to the *Rolling Stone* story knowing that you were going to tell the interviewer everything about Elise?"

He waited before looking at me, which was terrifying. He was always so quick to talk if he was called out on something. "Do you really want to do this to yourself?" He turned and pleaded with his eyes, the very force that got me into this in the first place.

"So, that's my answer," I said, flatly.

He moved closer and I folded my arms across my body.

"Please, don't do this. It won't accomplish anything," he replied.

A swarm of thoughts buzzed in my head.

"Look, I had no idea that you were going to be the person I would meet that day," he continued. "If I had a crystal ball and knew that it was you and what would happen between us, I would've done things differently. But, I didn't."

Frozen, I still didn't say a thing—the supposed pinnacle of my career had been built on a house of cards and he'd known it all along.

He closed the inches between us and cupped my shoulders. "Say something."

"I don't know what to say." I felt as if I was on autopilot, words streaming from my mouth on their own. "I was proud of that piece. I put everything I had into writing it. You were there the whole time, in my head, talking to me and pushing all of my buttons. I wanted to do the right thing for you, because you'd put your trust in me." I scanned his face. He looked hurt, but I was hurt too. "Remember what you said that night? That it would kill you if I screwed you over?" I stepped away, needing the physical space if only to think. "Now I know that I wasn't so adept at my job that I convinced you it would be okay."

"Claire."

"No. Don't do that. Don't say my name. You knew that you were going to tell me everything. You just let me work for it. You even pretended to get angry with me. It was all an act, just like you do with strangers all the time." My voice cracked. "I was a stranger then, wasn't I? I was no different than a bellboy or a flight attendant, someone to play one of your jokes on."

"You weren't a stranger, but I didn't know you like I do now. That's my point. I'd never intentionally hurt you. You have every reason to be proud of the piece. You made it worthy of the cover. And it wasn't like I gave you everything easily. You had to convince me about a few things."

"We both know you were toying with me that night. You toyed with me that whole day."

"I swear I didn't plan to tell you everything I did." He leaned back against the kitchen counter, his long legs propping him up. He dug his hand into his hair and exhaled. "I wasn't going to say anything about the baby." He looked me in the eye. "I wasn't prepared to give up that secret. Graham was the only other person who knew. Not even my mum or my sisters knew about it. It wasn't an act at that point. I really wanted to tell you."

"Why, because I'm a woman? Because I'm a mom?" I cringed at my questions. They made me sound like a monster.

"I don't know the reason, all I know is that I wanted to do it." His voice turned sad. "I don't know if it was the chemistry between us, or what. I meant it when I said that something told me to trust you."

"How am I supposed to trust you? It's not like you haven't had plenty of chances to tell me this."

"When? I couldn't tell you over the phone and I wasn't about to ruin our first weekend together or our trip. You would have been out of there before it started."

"And you couldn't tell me before I'd finished the story, because that would have meant an end to your plan."

"Look, Elise is going to nail me to the wall with her book. I had to fight back, to tell my side before she had a chance to destroy what's left of me." He threw up his hands. "Honestly, what good is this doing? It's done. We need to move on."

My entire body shook. Something about him made the betrayal more potent. I wanted to escape, but I had nowhere to go and everything I could lose was standing in front of me.

He pushed off from the kitchen counter and reached for me.

"Please don't touch me. I need to be by myself."

"Whatever you want." The weight of his stare was unbearable. "I'll be downstairs." Just like that, he fell back to the place he went when things got bad.

I didn't know what to do with myself. There was no space I could occupy that wouldn't make me think of him. His presence was everywhere. I trudged back to his room and sifted through my suitcase until I found my running clothes. I put them on, scribbled a note, and was out the door.

I'D NEVER RUN SO FAR in my entire life, my body pushing to keep pace with my brain. Up and down the hills, I had no idea where I was, but something told me to keep going. He'd let me believe a lie and continued to let me live off that lie, all the while drawing me into his world. It had been easier to let the lie remain as it was. Otherwise, it would've ruined everything. I felt like it was ruining everything anyway.

It was purely by accident that I made it back to the house. I stumbled across it, exhausted—my thighs and calves throbbing, my back sore.

He was there when I opened the door, in khaki shorts without a shirt; yet another low blow. "Thank God, you're back. I was about to call the police. Seriously, Claire, a four-hour run? I was sure you were lost. Please don't scare me like that again."

My body was rigid but I swayed, like a tall building in the wind. He reached for me and I turned my shoulder and pushed past him, down the hallway to the bedroom.

"Please say something. Talk to me." He followed me and groaned in frustration. "I can't stand the silent treatment. I don't care if you want to scream at me. That would be better at this point."

I splashed cold water on my face in the bathroom and he looked at me expectantly, his eyes roving from left to right and back again. I pressed the towel to my forehead, strangely enjoying the roughness of the terry. "I'm afraid to say anything. You'll say something to win me over and it'll work because you always get what you want."

He plaintively held out both hands. "But I don't get everything I want because what I want right now is you. I can't stand to look at you, knowing you don't want me to touch you. It's killing me."

Everything seemed to creep along in slow motion, as if the universe wanted to make the most of the anguish. "That's what you do, isn't it? All you would need to do is touch me and everything would be back to the way it was." My voice was raw from hours of breathing through my mouth. I sat on the bed and took off my shoes, staring at him. I hunched, feeling as if I could collapse at any moment while my sweaty smell ripened.

"You know I don't mean that. I know I've hurt you and I want to make it better."

"There's no way to make it better. You can't take it back."

"Don't you think I would if I could?"

"You don't understand. I've spent years working twice as hard for half the money because I didn't want to raise Sam in New York or LA, so that I could be close to my dad if he needed me. I'm getting ready to put her through college and I barely have enough money saved for her first year. This was probably my final shot to make a better living as a writer because I've come up short with every other chance I had."

"If this is about money, I'll give you whatever you need."

I sighed and my shoulders dropped again. "This isn't just about money. It's nice of you to offer, but I don't want your money." I closed my eyes and exhaled. "I feel like such a loser. So much for my big accomplishment."

He sat next to me. "Don't say that. Nobody needs to know about this."

"I'll know. If anything good comes out of this, it'll be tainted." I crossed my arms. "I hate that feeling."

"It won't be tainted. You're an incredible writer. You turned my pathetic stories into something worthy of the cover of a magazine. They wouldn't have put your story on the cover if you weren't a great writer."

"That cover is all about what you said."

He scanned my face and moved closer. "I think it took both

of us for it to be anything. I don't want you to dismiss your role because it didn't happen the way you wanted it to." He moved closer still. "No other writer would've treated me as fairly as you did. I'm so lucky that I got you."

I looked at him. I couldn't push aside what had already made itself at home in my heart. We sat silent for minutes as I realized he was right, even though it was completely annoying to admit.

"You're still coming to the show tonight, right?" he asked.

I didn't hesitate, even though the contrary part of me wanted to leave him hanging, if only for a moment. "Of course. I wouldn't miss it." His eyes lit up and I smiled and shied away.

"You're so bloody beautiful when you smile like that." I looked back and his eyes struck up an entirely separate conversation with me, saying everything I wanted to hear. He leaned back against the headboard and held out his arms. "Come here."

"I'm sweaty and gross."

"I don't care. I'll take what I can get."

"No. Seriously. It's bad. I stink."

"And I said I don't care."

"Will you promise me one thing first?" I asked.

"Of course I will. Anything."

"No more secrets. We tell each other everything."

"No more secrets."

I inched over to him until we were unable to stay apart. He put his arm around me and I curled into him, setting my arm across his bare stomach and closing my eyes. My heart beat a heavy rhythm and we remained for minutes before he spoke.

"Please tell me I can kiss you."

"I told you I'm all gross."

"We've been over this. I don't care."

I kept my eyes closed and tilted my head to wait. I first felt his hand at my jaw and fingers reaching to the side of my neck.

Then I could smell him better, a combination of clean and his own smell floating somewhere underneath. My breaths moved my shoulders and I felt paralyzed by the anticipation.

The heat came as he crept closer and his nose brushed against mine, not once, but twice. Finally, he kissed me, a show of pure affection that melted away every pessimistic thought I had. I felt a tear roll down my cheek, silently and involuntarily, and my heart shuddered against my throat when I kissed him back. My feelings swelled inside me, full of life, and I turned to be closer to him.

CHAPTER TWENTY-EIGHT

CHRIS LOADED the SUV with several guitars and we left for the club late afternoon. It was a narrow escape—my mini marathon and the second act of our argument had left me with less than an hour to shower and get dressed.

The moment he turned the key, the GPS came to life and he turned to me with a smirk. "The Australian guy?"

"That British chick is a bitch. She thinks she's better than me." I was happy to smile at him again, without reservation. "Give Lee a chance. He's very good at his job. But don't be jealous. He's a hottie."

"Only you would be on a first name basis with the GPS." He leaned over the center console and gave me a slow and patient kiss. That one quiet moment assured me that everything was okay.

The club was small, with a capacity of only three hundred people—Chris wanted it intimate. Stale beer perfumed the close barroom air and the way my shoes stuck to the floor was oddly comforting.

Even though the tabloids had already let the cat out of the bag, Chris did everything in his power to keep our relationship from becoming a spectacle. He had the bar manager clear out everyone but the sound guy for sound check. He played one song, *Long Lost*, from the new record, and I stood on the side of the stage, excited to see him perform actual music. As much as I loved to watch him and hear his voice, I didn't think I could listen to the word "check" anymore without going batty.

Under the sparse stage lights, his profile was graceful but strong. I studied everything he did—the way his jaw moved when he sang and how that changed the structure of his neck. I watched the movement of his hands as he strummed the guitar and he pulled me in, making me tingly, bringing the lyrics to life. When the song was over, he turned to me and flashed his devastating smile while arching his eyebrows. I became so woozy that I had to reach for the wall.

After sound check and dinner, Graham and Angie hung out with us in the tiny backstage dressing room. They sat together, Graham's arm around Angie snuggly, kissing her on the cheek. He was on his best behavior, subdued and charming. Angie was being her usual lovely self, when she smiled at me it made me feel like I was a better person just for knowing her.

Chris made himself at home in a wide fuzzy green armchair that smelled like booze and smoke, rattling a handful of peanut M&Ms before he popped them in his mouth. He and Graham went back and forth about Chris's set list. Graham wasn't shy about making suggestions.

Chris scooted over in his chair and patted the sliver of space he'd left. "Sit with me," he said to me, his voice a distinctly softer tone than he'd taken with Graham.

I wrinkled my nose, opened another beer and tossed the bottle opener on top of the cooler. "Uh-uh. There's no way I'm putting my ass in that chair."

"Your ass will love it down here," he replied and he and Graham laughed.

"Then let me sit on your lap."

"There you go, P-Man," Graham muttered, grabbing his own beer. "Ass problem solved." He winked at Chris.

Chris patted his thigh in invitation and his eyes flickered. As soon as I sat down, he swung my legs over the arm of the chair, leaning me back and cradling me close. I squealed as quietly as possible when he burrowed his face into my neck and tickled me in places Graham and Angie couldn't see. It was another lifelong goal realized, becoming the ultimate Rock 'n' Roll cliché —the giggly girlfriend on the rock star's lap backstage. I only needed Graham to sign my chest with a Sharpie to complete my new persona.

After Graham and Angie stepped out into the hall, Chris gave me a deep, lingering kiss. Our eyes locked and he brushed the side of my face with the back of his hand. My heart beat with anticipation of later that night, when we could make-up completely.

We walked toward the stage hand in hand as the sounds from the crowd grew louder. I stood with Angie and Graham in our special viewing spot at the side of the stage and I peeked through the heavy curtains. The size of the audience seemed implausible, people crammed into the small space with shoulders shrugged and all semblance of personal space erased. The first several rows were all women, no longer adolescent girls in their Banks Forest tour shirts, almost all of them wielding cleavage and jockeying for the best spot to ogle my boyfriend.

I was under Chris's spell from the moment he strode to the barstool at center stage and the crowd erupted in cheers. He played everything from the new record and re-worked versions of two songs from his first record. It was nice to see he hadn't given up on those songs because they still had an essence of him, even if they hadn't turned out well the first time around. He worked in several Banks Forest songs to satisfy the audience, sharing clever stories with them. They responded with laughter and applause and soaked up every word.

The real apex of the show was the moment he called Graham out to sing with him. Everyone went crazy for the Banks Forest hits—the instant they started *Love, Destroyed*, it was as if they'd detonated a bomb in the room.

My heart swelled watching them on stage together; the pairing was electric, the crowd going nuts for every note. Graham made no effort to be the center of attention, it just happened, and he lapped it up as if no woman had ever looked at him twice. About halfway through the song, I felt a tap on my shoulder and turned to find the only thing that could ruin such an inspiring moment. Kevin.

I employed Chris's annoying habit of holding up a finger to tell him to wait. I wasn't willing to give up the last few bars of the song for Kevin. I did my best to focus on Chris, but I trembled. Kevin had to know something.

When the song was over, Kevin spoke into my ear, taking his mouth and hot breath uncomfortably close to my cheek. "Don't I get a hello?"

The crowd showed no sign of quieting down, screaming for more.

I turned and the sight of him the second time was worse than the first. "What are you doing here?"

He waited with his arms held out and an evil smile. "Don't I get a hug?"

"No."

He crinkled his lips. "Suit yourself." His eyes were all over me, putting me on edge. "You look great. Even more beautiful than the last time I saw you."

"We broke up the last time I saw you." *Idiot.* My shoulders drew together and my spine tightened.

"I thought it'd be harder for you to be such a bitch in

person." He looked at me with his murky brown eyes, the ones I'd once thought were warm. That felt like a lifetime ago.

"What can I say?" The crowd still roared and I gladly yelled in his face, "I'm a total bitch."

"Not the Claire I know. She's confused, but not a bitch." He moved closer again and touched my shoulder, producing a faint echo of the physical attraction that was once so strong.

I stepped back and crossed my arms. "Why are you here? And how did you even get back stage?"

He tossed his eyebrows back as if I'd just asked the most ridiculous question ever. "I know every bouncer in this town. And I'm here because I had a hunch you'd be here. I thought you weren't coming to LA any time soon." He wore a smug look that I was eager to knock off his cloyingly handsome face.

I returned my sights to the stage where Chris and Graham were starting an acoustic version of one of my favorite David Bowie songs, *Moonage Daydream*. Chris looked at me for a moment with questions in his eyes, undoubtedly about why my body language was now so agitated.

I turned back to deal with the unpleasantness, deciding it would be best if I could get rid of Kevin before Chris even had to meet him.

"Just tell me why you're here."

"Look, Claire, I saw the photos of you and Penman. You have no idea what you're getting yourself into with this guy." For an instant, the concern in his eyes seemed genuine. I'd forgotten how much he'd once cared for me and that the feelings had been mutual.

I sighed. "Is it too much to ask that you don't say anything to Patrick about it?" I asked, hoping there was a chance Patrick merely wanted to talk to me about a new assignment Monday morning.

"Too late. He already knows. He's not happy."

My stomach dropped. "Perfect."

"I can't believe you thought you wouldn't get caught." He hesitated for a moment, shaking his head and gnawing on his thumbnail. "I came tonight to warn you. You know I can't say anything specific. I know a lot about Penman after writing the book." He reached for me again, this time clutching my forearm. "Claire, if you think I'm a bad guy, he's ten times worse."

"I find that hard to believe." I leered at him, angry that he was trying to plant doubts in my head.

He pursed his lips. "You know, he's already messing things up for you. You're never going to get another word printed in *Rolling Stone*. Every editor on the planet is going to think you slept with him to get him to talk."

"Are you finished?"

"No, I'm not. When the book comes out, his life is going to be a joke. He's going to drag you down with him."

CHAPTER TWENTY-NINE

"I CAN'T BELIEVE that guy has the nerve to turn up at my show." Chris was obviously stewing, changing lanes without looking. "And then he tells you to stay away from me. He's never even met me before."

I'd told Chris everything, keeping my promise about no more secrets. "Don't let this ruin your night. You had such an amazing show." I reached over and caressed his leg.

"Do you think the crowd really liked the new stuff?"

"Of course they did. They loved it," I answered, hoping I could throw him off the topic. "They loved you."

He groaned and shook his head. "Bloody idiot. I'm twice his size. I'd kill him if I thought I could get away with it."

I kept my frustration to myself. "I don't want to spend my last night talking about Kevin. It's our make-up night." I sweetened my voice, wondering if the prospect of sex would finally get him to drop it.

We waited as the gate traveled across the driveway. "Your ex-boyfriend is an asshole." He pulled into the garage and turned off the ignition. "I need to get in the shower. I'm sweaty and pissed off." He opened his door and jumped when I grabbed his arm. "What?"

"Don't go in the house all grumpy." I unbuckled my seatbelt, turned and climbed over the center console before crawling into his lap.

"What are you doing?" He furrowed his brow.

"I am..." I said, reaching out and closing his car door, "improving your mood." I kissed him softly and combed my fingers deep into his hair before making a playful tug at his lower lip with my teeth. His shoulders stiffened as I tilted my hips closer to him.

"I'm too big for us to do this in here. It won't work."

"Won't it be fun to find out?" I asked, trailing a finger behind his ear and down the side of his neck.

"No, seriously, I've tried this before. I'm too tall."

"No, you're not, silly," I said, coming up with what seemed like a brilliant idea. I reached down and pulled the lever on the side of his seat, thinking it would only tilt back a few inches. I was wrong and he abruptly slammed back. Flat. His head bounced off the headrest.

"Oh my God—" I sprang forward and hovered over him. "Are you okay?"

He rubbed the back of his head, squinting. "Are you trying to kill me?"

"No." I cringed at my own ineptitude. "I was trying to be romantic."

"By giving me a concussion?"

"Of course not. I wasn't thinking."

He grasped my shoulder. "I'm all for exotic locations, but I don't want your last night here to be in the car. Can I please go inside and take a shower and clear my head? So, we can do this properly? Just you and me, no head injuries or steering wheels."

I dropped my forehead against his chest. "I'm sorry."

Back inside, as soon as I heard the shower door close, I rushed to my suitcase for my silk and lace nightgown, still wrapped in tissue paper. I hurried out of my clothes and slipped into it, stealing a passing glance in the full-length mirror and fussing with my hair.

The steady spray of the shower called and I crept to the door before peeking around the corner. His back was to me, arms raised, hands working the shampoo into lather as he gracefully knocked his head from side to side. The air in the bathroom turned warm and billowy as the steam advanced up the clear glass shower walls. I drank in my quiet moment alone with him, the weight of going home suddenly wedged in my chest.

Chris stepped from the shower oblivious, drying his face with a towel that was the only thing obscuring my view of his long body. My chest heaved, watching him with beads of water on his shoulders and a few stray, dripping twists of hair falling into his face.

He scrubbed his hair with the towel and I caught his gaze. He eyed me from head to toe, flattering me with every second he went without blinking. "I'm afraid I don't have anything to wear to bed that could possibly rival that."

"That's okay." I wanted to be sultry, but could only gleam at him. "I'll take you just the way you are."

He came to me with downy lips and a delicate touch, pushing the silk into my skin in circles. My hands caught on the clean skin of his chest, slightly sticky from soap and hot water. His smell was clear, it was his alone, and I wished I could capture the essence and take it with me. Then I could cover myself in it every morning and feel better, less lonely.

He walked me to the bed and took charge, pulling me to the center and softly touching my stomach and then my breasts through the smooth silk. His hand went to the strap closest to him and he looped it around his finger, slipping it off my shoulder. He grazed the back of his hand against my throat and down to my chest, dragging his index finger behind. He made me unravel inside, my heart floating and every bit of me hot and tingling. I felt brave enough to keep my eyes open and watched in awe as he studied his effect on me.

Continuing along my midline, never losing touch, he stopped at my hem. His hand turned over to palm my thigh and he rubbed his thumb along the ridge of my hipbone as he pushed the nightgown up and away.

With the full measure of skin pressed to skin, we rolled back and forth taking turns pinning each other down. He was more successful at it than I was, but I loved giving in to his advantage. Back on top, I sat back and raked my fingers up his chest to his collarbone, feeling the structure beneath his skin, the dips and ridges. My breaths grew shorter. He was still able to surprise me with his handsome, perfect being.

"You're being quiet tonight," I murmured. "No commentary." My fingers worked across his chest and I lowered myself. Shifting to his side, I rolled my hand over his shoulder and became lost in his face.

He looked back at me, a bent smile of amusement. "I've spent enough time in trouble today. I'm trying to keep you happy." He moved across my back with the tips of his fingers.

I felt bad about quashing his bedroom talk—the prudish part of me had been embarrassed, but now I missed it. "It's okay if you want to talk." My finger marked a line down the center of his chest.

He laughed and teased my hair behind my ear. "What, exactly, would you like me to say?" He furrowed his brow. "Oh, baby, you make me so hot?"

"No, not that." I hid my face, the heat radiating from my cheeks. "I shouldn't have said anything."

He lifted my chin and kissed me, his tender lips hot against mine. "If anything comes to mind, I'll be sure to share." He pushed my hair from my face, refusing to let me hide, and he gazed at me without a word. Smoothing a hand around each of my hips, he tempted me toward him and then back to settle my body down on his. As we began moving together, I pushed away to sit back, but he stopped me, pulling me forward. "Stay here. I want to keep you close."

CHAPTER THIRTY

THE SUN WAS DECIDEDLY un-sunny the next morning. I'd watched it come up, completely failing to herald a new day the way it should have. Instead, it forced the pain deeper inside me. Chris was finally stirring, rolling to drop his arm around my waist. I stared out the massive bedroom windows with my back to him, wanting to shrink away from everything I had to do once I got out of bed.

There was no getting around it; we needed to find a different way to continue. The ebbs of joy and sadness involved with coming and going were too much.

"If I pin you to the bed, you can't go to the airport," he said into the back of my neck, prodding my hair away with his nose. He inched closer and pressed himself against me. Even though we hadn't parted, the desperate longing for him had already taken root in my body.

"I wish that were true." My voice cracked and I had no strength to fight it.

He rubbed my shoulders like a trainer does to encourage his fighter after he's been punched in the face so many times he can't see straight. "Don't be sad. I'll come and see you this weekend."

I turned back to look at his incredible face, full of life in the morning light. "Then what? I can't fly to LA every other week. It's not fair to Sam."

He seemed deep in thought, concentrating on my face. "You're right." He pushed the hair off my forehead with his thumb. "Don't worry, we'll come up with something."

The goodbye at the airport was more of the same, sad and arduous. I couldn't help it—I instinctively took survey of everything and where it was going. Perhaps it was something women were wired to do, survival of the fittest, but I didn't want the words "Let's talk about our relationship and where it's going" to ever pass my lips. I didn't want things to happen like that.

Chris gave me countless kisses and many long, reassuring embraces; every loving gesture only underscored how painful it was to do what we were doing. I couldn't even pucker long enough to return a real kiss. My mouth was busy turning down with sadness, my lower lip a quivering mess. He rocked me back and forth in his arms and pressed his lips to the top of my head until it was time to go through security and walk away.

My highlight today, seeing Sam, was still ahead, but with that would come the unavoidable back and forth with my dad. I was an overflowing vessel of emotion when his preference is pleasantly even and well tempered. Whenever I had problems beyond a dishwasher on the blink, I was being difficult.

The lights were on when I got home, but I didn't see anyone downstairs. "Hello? Anybody home?" I set my keys and bag on the counter, noticing that the kitchen was immaculate. I'd never realized the counter was that particular shade of gray.

Sam came thundering down the stairs. "You're back." She gave me an enthusiastic hug, an unusual teenage greeting. "I saw the magazine today. Leah brought it to school. Are you totally freaking out? Don't worry, I didn't show Grandpa."

"Hi, honey." I held her arm, realizing how much I'd missed her and the way she loved to launch a glut of information at you at one time. "Leah brought it to school?" I rubbed my temple. "Seriously?"

"Yeah, her mom bought an extra copy. We were careful not to let any of the boys see it, but I think some of them already had." She winced as though she was waiting for my reaction.

I shook my head. "Where's your grandfather?"

"At the store. He's been driving me crazy." She made a choking sound and crossed her eyes. "He was a total grump when Andrew came over last night. He wouldn't let us go upstairs so we had to watch TV in the living room and he kept checking on us." She smiled at me, shyly. "We still kissed without getting caught."

The girl who'd been devastated by Jean-Luc seemed to be fading away.

"That's my girl. But we're still keeping Andrew on probation, right? He needs to prove he can be a good boyfriend."

"Right." She held a look of quiet assurance. "Oh, and you got a giant thing of flowers. I didn't read the card, but Grandpa did and said they were from someone named Chris." She snickered. "They're in your office."

Chris had sent tulips again, my favorite, deep pink this time. There had to be seven or eight-dozen—an enormous arrangement in a modern glass cylinder with a matching wide satin bow. The envelope was tucked back in the plastic florist's fork, as if I wouldn't notice that the flap was torn. The message was simple: *Miss you madly, Chris.*

The back door slammed shut and I took a few quick breaths as I reminded myself to be a good daughter. "Dad, hi." I drew out the "hi" in an attempt to sweeten it and gave him a kiss on the cheek as he set the grocery bags on the counter. He leaned in, without warming to the kiss at all.

The reliability of his wardrobe never faltered. He was wearing the same flat-front khakis, brown belt and neatly pressed light blue button-down shirt he'd worn every day of his life for the last forty years. The gray Members Only jacket was his attempt at being cool and I wasn't about to tell him he was thirty years too late.

"I went to the store to buy all of that fancy stuff you like. Soy milk, baby carrots, wheat bread." He was already making small talk.

"Thanks. That was nice of you." I let the grocery comment slide, undoubtedly the first of many things I would let go over the next thirty-six hours.

"I want to take care of my little girl." He smiled, my father's one-sided grin, and folded the paper grocery bag neatly while Sam sauntered back from the pantry with a package of Oreos. "Sammy, bring Grandpa some of those good cookies."

She smiled at him warmly, making me struggle with the "Grandpa's driving me crazy" comment. "Grandpa buys all the junk food you never let me have."

"I do," he said. He winked at her before downing a cookie as Sam poured them each a glass of milk.

"I buy junk food," I said, defensively. "But it's easier to resist if it isn't in the house." I took a cookie and my shoulders dropped at the first bite. "Believe me, I love Oreos," I said, through a mouthful of chocolate crumbs.

The two of them at the kitchen counter scarfing cookies were fascinating. He had such adoration in his eyes when he looked at her; I had to ask myself if he'd ever felt that way about me for one day, other than the day I was born.

Sam excused herself to go upstairs and finish homework, leaving me alone to face the inevitable inquisition.

"Thanks, Dad, for keeping an eye on Sam. I hope it wasn't too much work."

He washed and dried his glass. He used the towel to wipe away the droplets of water left in the sink and polish the faucet. "I love my time with my granddaughter. We're two peas in a pod." There was an uncomfortable moment of eye contact that he put to a quick end. "I finished everything on your to-do list. The hot water in your shower is fixed and I caulked everything in there too. You need to keep an eye on that or you'll end up with water damage."

"Great. Thanks. That's a big help. I'll try to be better about the caulk." I was such a bad daughter; I was already formulating my plan of escape, lining up my excuses in the event that one or two of them failed.

"Flowers came for you. I was on my back working on that clogged drain trap in the bathroom when the deliveryman came. Hit my head on the darn vanity." It couldn't be that I'd simply received flowers; it had to be that he was inconvenienced and injured while slaving away in an uncomfortable position on my neglected plumbing.

"Sorry about that. I hope your head's okay."

"Are they from someone special?"

He couldn't even look at me when he asked such questions, pretending to scan the headlines of the paper he'd surely read. "Yes, they're from someone special." I took a deep breath. "The friend I went to see in Los Angeles. His name is Christopher."

He looked up from the paper, but not at me, addressing the doorway into the living room. "I see. I'm disappointed you didn't tell me from the get-go. You know we can talk about anything, Ladybug."

"I know." I made my own lie, in response to his. "I'm sorry. I haven't told anyone about him." My eyes were suddenly so dry that my lids were sticking to my eyeballs.

"Must have a lot of money, sending flowers like that. What does he do for a living?"

Here it comes. "He's a professional musician." I crossed my fingers that the word professional would throw him off the trail.

"Not again." He groaned. "It never works out with these guys. When are you going to learn that?"

I sighed and crossed my arms, jostling my bracelet.

"Is that from him?" he asked, reaching for it.

"Yes."

He studied the charm, peering through his thick, rimless glasses. "Tiffany? This guy certainly likes to throw his money around." He turned the charm to the other side before releasing my arm. "Is this serious? Does Samantha know?"

"Yes, she knows. She's met him, and it's a little serious, I guess. Not super serious."

The reaction in his eyes suggested what was coming. "Excuse my language, but what in hell are you doing? You're thirty-nine years old and you're flying across the country to see some man, another one of your musicians." The word tumbled out of his mouth as he began pacing, looking everywhere except at me. "He sends fancy flowers and buys you an expensive Tiffany bracelet and you don't know if it's serious?"

As annoying as it was, he hadn't pointed out anything that wasn't true. "I appreciate your concern, but I know what I'm doing." I struggled to keep my cool.

"You're a smart girl. You're pretty." He started to walk away, shaking his head. "I don't understand why it's so hard for you to settle down with a regular guy like your sister. She's very happy."

My dad adored my sister Julie, the golden child, straight-A student, driven to succeed. She'd married the first reliable man who wanted her virginity. I'd been the one with a B average and a lack of focus who dumped the good-looking guy who got me pregnant.

"I'd love to settle down with a nice guy like Julie, but I haven't been as lucky." I followed him, determined to keep the conversation from ending on this point. "I'm happy too."

"Your sister isn't lucky, she's sensible. She knew a good thing when she met Matt. You always had to chase every guy you couldn't hold on to. And Ladybug, I'm sorry, but you're not happy. You're all alone. What are you going to do next year when Samantha goes off to college? Get a house full of cats?"

"No," I huffed. "And what's wrong with cats? I love cats."

He crossed his arms and looked at the floor. "You know, my granddaughter has missed out, not having a father figure. She was stuck to me like glue all weekend. It's obvious she needs more attention."

The tears welled in my eyes. I didn't want him to have the satisfaction of making me cry. My jaw tightened and I lowered my voice. "Your granddaughter has not missed out. Yes, she has seen me struggle, but I've taught her a lot about self-reliance. She knows she doesn't have to depend on a man for happiness."

He shook his head in slow motion. "I'm glad your mother didn't have to witness this. She'd have been very disappointed that you never found a husband."

That broke the dam in my eyes. "That's not fair. You don't know how she would have felt about it." It was a horrible thought, but at that moment, I wished it'd been my dad who was gone and not my mom. She would've found a way to love me and be happy for me because that what was what she did. She always found a way.

"I guess we'll have to agree to disagree."

It felt as if he'd dug extra deep for the most dismissive way to end his side of the argument. "I can't talk to you. I'm going to bed."

CHAPTER THIRTY-ONE

I WELCOMED the alarm at six the next morning the same way I might regard a red-hot poker in my ear. Mustering every ounce of energy and determination I had, I rolled out of bed. It would've been so easy to hit the snooze and bury my head in the pillow, but I wanted Sam to have a hot breakfast before school.

I rapped on her door, mom as the back-up wake-up call, and cringed with disappointment when I reached the end of the hall and smelled coffee. My dad was already up. Knowing him, he was probably shaved and dressed, even wearing shoes. Sam and I were always walking around the house in bare feet; a practice he saw as another sign that our society was crumbling.

"Morning, Jellybean. Coffee's on," he said.

I poured myself a cup and joined him at the kitchen table, still emerging from the stubborn effects of a sleeping pill and jet lag. He offered a section of the paper but I passed, knowing he would tell me what was in it anyway.

"Boy, people sure are upset about the library expansion. It says here that the town wants to delay it again."

The heat from the mug spread through my hands and I

tightened my grip. "Fascinating." I stared off into space, doing my best to still listen.

"Looks like we're going to have a good day today, almost sixty degrees. There's a thirty percent chance of rain tonight. Hopefully that won't interfere with Sam's science fair."

"Let's hope it doesn't rain."

Sam stormed down the stairs with a head of wet hair and her enormous backpack.

"What can I make you for breakfast this morning?" I asked, grinning at today's wardrobe choices, the highlight of which were red and pink argyle knee socks.

"I'm totally late, I forgot we have study group for Spanish this morning. Andrew's picking me up in a minute. I'll just take a banana."

"Okay, honey, whatever works." I got a kiss on the forehead, she was out the door, and just like that, I was back where I'd started, stuck in the house with Dad.

"Dad, what do you want to do today? I have a lot of work to do."

"Don't worry about me. I was thinking I should replace the screen in that back door today. I'll go to the hardware store and get that puppy fixed for you." He smiled. Manual labor was his way of apologizing. If it weren't for the one-inch rip in the screen, he would've found something else that was wrong or invented a project, all to keep the balance of power straight.

The phone rang and I jumped, hurrying to my office. The name on the caller ID was unfamiliar and I answered nervously, thinking it was never good news when someone called so early.

"Hello. May I speak with Claire Abby?" a woman asked.

"This is Claire." My mind scrambled as her voice failed to register.

"Hello. My name is Nicole Fowler. I'm a writer for *Star*

Magazine. Can you tell me the nature of your relationship with Christopher Penman?"

My hands went cold. This was an unimagined scenario. I'd certainly never taken the time to mull over possible answers to this question. I'd done such a horrible job explaining it to my own father; there was no way I'd fare better with a stranger.

"Uh, he's a friend." *Wait. Was I supposed to say 'no comment'?*

"And can you tell me the nature of your recent trip together to St. Barts?"

Crap. My heart sank. Every word out of my mouth would only keep her on the phone longer. I was digging myself a hole and it wasn't like I could afford to tell her the truth. "I'm sorry, I know you're just trying to do your job, but I can't discuss this right now. I have to say no comment. Goodbye." I felt terrible, knowing what it was like to be on the other side of that conversation.

My father, the snooper, was all over the situation. I'd watched him sneak closer the instant I answered the phone. "Everything all right?"

"Fine." I answered, dazed.

"Who was that on the phone? Why would you need to say "no comment" to someone?"

I should've known he would never accept my non-answer. "It was another reporter calling about a story I wrote."

"But what about the first thing you said? He's a friend?"

"Dad. Please." A headache with an uncanny resemblance to my father began growing between my eyes. "It was nothing."

He watched me, narrowly. "All right, Ladybug. I suppose you know what you're doing."

To escape further scrutiny, I took my chance to call Chris while my dad was at the hardware store. It was still early on the

West Coast but I called him anyway, deciding that being a girl-friend got me a free pass on calling at odd hours.

"There you are," he answered, with gravel in his voice. "What happened last night?"

"I'm sorry, I collapsed when I got home. Did I wake you?"

"No, I'm awake but I'm still in bed. I'm too tired to get up and get in the pool. I couldn't sleep last night. All of my pillows smell like you."

If I closed my eyes, I could still feel what it was like to wake up in his bed tucked under rumpled sheets with the ultimate view of him and his messy morning hair. "Thank you for my flowers. They're beautiful. It's a humungous arrangement. You didn't need to do that."

"Sure I did. I tried to send more, but that was everything they had."

I smiled and cradled the phone closer while the tingles branched out across my chest and over my shoulders.

"How are things with your dad?" he asked.

"I'm surviving, but we butted heads last night. He was asking questions about you and the flowers and the bracelet."

"I hope I'm not in the dog house with Richard." He snickered. "May I call him Dick when I finally meet him?"

I laughed, a bit sad. "Not if you want him to like you, although I'd love to witness that exchange." I sighed. "He said some things about you that pissed me off, but it's okay, he goes home tomorrow."

"Ooh, I want to hear what he said about me." He seemed to find the idea of my dad humorous. It would be interesting to see how that opinion lived up to the real thing if they ever met.

"It was stupid. He said you must like to throw your money around."

"I wouldn't call tulips and a three-hundred-dollar piece of jewelry throwing my money around."

"Like I said, it was stupid," I replied, eager to end the analysis of my father and his opinions. "Um, I got a phone call from a magazine, a tabloid, this morning. They were asking about you." I winced, unsure of his reaction.

He groaned. "Just tell them 'no comment' and hang up. You may want to stop answering the phone."

"Is that what you do?"

"Yes. You can't give them anything. I'm serious. Don't say a thing." He paused for a second. "Did you get things straightened out with Patrick yet?"

I switched the phone to my other ear; the side of my face becoming hot and feeling stuffy. "I didn't have to get it straightened out. He sent me a second email some time yesterday. I think he must've talked to Kevin." My stomach soured at the thought of the way things had unraveled. "He said that I'd broken his trust and he'd prefer it if I didn't come to him for any future assignments." If I hadn't been flat-out exhausted and torn up about missing Chris, I would've let the email ruin the next several months.

He blew out a long breath. "I was being an idiot when I thought this wouldn't be a big deal, wasn't I? Does this put you in a jam financially?"

"No. I'm fine."

"You need to tell me if it does. Seriously. Whatever you need."

"That's very generous, but I wasn't counting on anything. I've learned from that mistake in the past."

"Claire, I'm worried about you. I've made a mess of your professional life."

"I've got enough work to get by."

"But I don't want you getting by. I hate that idea. Let me send you some money, so you have a cushion."

"I'm fine, I swear." I fought the tears that were coming. "Can we please talk about something else?"

———

MY DAD SPENT the entire day rapping on the back door with a mallet. No matter how many times he tried, he was never quite satisfied with the way the screen had gone into the frame. I'd spent the day sequestered in my office, counting down the minutes we had left together, compulsively checking my watch, tapping on the crystal because at one point I was convinced it was moving backwards.

That night, as I pulled into the parking space at school that my father found satisfactory, Sam's phone beeped. She giggled and I glanced in the rearview mirror to see her smiling. "Mom, it's Chris wishing me luck for the science fair."

"Oh, is Chris one of your girlfriends?" my dad asked.

"No—"

Sam interrupted me, "It's Mom's boyfriend."

He shook his head. "Is that what we're calling him? Your boyfriend?"

I closed my eyes and pinched the bridge of my nose. "Yes, Dad. That's what we're calling him."

My dad and I left Sam to man the table for her project, titled "Polar Caps and Global Warming". We made the rounds through the gym as he formed a running commentary, words dribbling from his mouth to fill some imaginary space. It brewed an awkward undercurrent for everything else taking place as the curious eyes of other moms filled the room, many who'd usually stop to chat. Some I'd thought were friends. Some women openly whispered about me, mouthing words behind hands, making a pit in my stomach. Then there were the ones who sought me out, all of them exactly like the popular girls in school, tittering and plastic. I was okay to invite to coffee now that I had a famous boyfriend and had been in a magazine, but never before today.

A few exhibits away, I spotted my single-dad crush, Jeremy. He nodded at me and smiled, a beacon of normalcy. Sam and his daughter, Bailey, used to hang out; it must've been three years since that friendship had fizzled, but he and I kept our innocent flirtation.

Dad and I ran into Jeremy at Sam's table. My face felt flushed when he smiled at me. I'd forgotten what a gorgeous set of teeth he had, surely expected of an orthodontist.

"Is Beth with you tonight?" I asked, glancing around the gym for his girlfriend.

He stuffed his hands in the pockets of his khakis. "We broke up."

"I'm sorry. I didn't know." I could tell my father was listening in on our conversation while he made small talk with Sam and Andrew.

"It had been coming for a while. She didn't want to get serious." He made contact with his warm hazel eyes. "I was hoping I'd run into you tonight. I wanted to ask if you'd like to have dinner with me."

I blanched at the invitation—I would have cut off my arm to go to dinner with him six months ago. "I'm actually seeing someone right now." He must've been the one person in the gymnasium who hadn't seen the magazine photos of Chris and me.

"Of course you are. I've always had really bad timing." He laughed, but retained every confidence; much like the way Chris brushed things off with ease.

The attraction between us bounced back and forth and I was annoyed by it. *Why are the good ones single when you aren't?* "Maybe we can have coffee some time." I added, but regretted it, unsure why I could never just say "no".

"You know, I'm going to take you up on that invitation."

It was after nine when we got home, which meant Dad was close to turning in for the night—the end, in sight. He, Sam and Andrew threw a cookie party in the kitchen in celebration of Sam's showing at the science fair. I congratulated her with a hug and made a graceful exit to my office, listening to their voices in the distance.

My visit with Jeremy pedaled through my thoughts—I felt sick to my stomach, disgusted with myself, to think about the way I'd still felt attracted to him. I'd rationalized the flirtation at the time because it seemed wasteful to refuse the attention of a good-looking man. Replaying it in my head made it so much worse, thinking about who considered me his girlfriend and what he would've thought if he'd seen the exchange for himself.

I took my phone to my room, telling everyone I had a headache, only half of a lie. Chris didn't answer and I left a pathetic message, feeling more torn and regretful with every passing syllable. I must've said, "I miss you" twenty times.

The hole in me, the one that would never close, burned. These were the moments when I missed my mom the most; she was an expert at stepping back from a situation and distilling it, figuring out what was truly bothering me. She could always see everything that I couldn't.

I closed my eyes and focused, calling up every memory of her voice and physical being, every mannerism I could remember. I saw her, a shadow of strawberry blonde with a constellation of faded freckles across her nose and perfectly penciled auburn eyebrows. I struggled with words as I soaked up her pale blue eyes and welcomed the sting in my own. She listened with a mother's patience, never judging, understanding how much Chris was changing everything inside me.

CHAPTER THIRTY-TWO

WE CHECKED under the guest bed for stray socks and then we checked again. "Dad, it's not a big deal. If you leave something, I'll mail it to you."

"Then you're just giving money away to those fat cats down at the post office."

I faked my way through the final survey on my hands and knees, still sweaty from my run early that morning. "It's the post office," I mumbled.

My mood lightened once he was finally packed and at the door. "Thank you for everything, Dad. Love you."

He gave me what he'd call a hug, a shoulder to my neck and a double slap on the back. "You're welcome, Ladybug. I want you to think about everything we talked about. You should go out to dinner with that Jeremy. He's a looker. I know that's important to you."

I was prepared to say anything to make him get in his car. "I'll think about it." When the phone rang, I had an excuse to shoo him into his midnight blue Le Baron. "Gotta run. Call me when you get home."

The caller ID said it was my sister, Julie, and I had the sinking suspicion that Dad was waging a campaign.

"Hi, Jules. What's up?"

"How's my baby sister?"

"I'm fine. Dad just left to go back to Asheville."

"Dad was there?"

I groaned quietly. "Let me guess. He called you yesterday and asked you to talk to me. I haven't heard from you in months."

"The phone works both ways, Claire." She cleared her throat. "Fine. Dad put me up to it. He's worried about you and he doesn't like your new boyfriend. He told me about the photos. I had to look it up online because I didn't believe him. I don't read those magazines."

I never should've underestimated the snooper. That was a rookie mistake. Of course, he would ultimately find out about the magazine. He'd probably dug through Samantha's backpack. If he disliked the idea of Chris before, he loathed him now. "Dad's just mad because I didn't tell him everything from the beginning."

"Then why don't you tell me what's really going on?"

I obliged her with the abbreviated version of the story, hitting the high points and leaving out the more tawdry details.

"So, Christopher Penman is the guy from Banks Forest, the band you were obsessed with in high school?" Julie always liked the geeky bands that the boys were into like Styx and Rush. Those guys were old when we were in high school. "How weird is that?" She seemed to be edging toward girly delight of the story, which was much more fun.

"I was dying when I found out I was going to get to interview him so there were some very surreal moments when the other stuff happened."

"Have you had sex with him?" She whispered, funny because her kids were at school and she works from home.

"Julie. He's handsome and charming and took me on vacation to a secluded island." I waited for the right words. "Think about it. The man was my ultimate teenage crush."

She squealed on the other end of the phone. "Oh my God. Is it rude if I ask what he's like, you know, in bed? He must know stuff that other guys don't know."

The blood rushed to my face—my sister and I did not discuss such things when we lived in the same house. "No, it's not rude, you're my sister. But, that doesn't mean I'm going to tell you. Let's just say that I'm extremely satisfied." I was glad she couldn't bust me on the enormous smile plastered to my face.

"Oh, come on. Tell me one thing. I've been having sex with the same man for the last eighteen years."

"Jules, I really care about him. It's too private."

"Okay, I get it. Be careful though. I don't want you to get your heart broken."

"Yeah, thanks, I'm working on it. I've got to hop in the shower, but let's try to not be strangers."

Halfway up the stairs, the doorbell rang and I felt like re-enacting the temper tantrum Sam threw when she was three and I'd taken her shoe shopping. I stomped down the stairs, opened the door, and my stomach crumpled into a knot. There stood Jeremy while my stringy runner hair clung to the side of my face.

"Claire, hi." His eyes began to dart; down at the front step, at the threshold, before he seemed to become comfortable with the sight of me. "I didn't want to drop in unannounced, but I don't have your cell number and then I remembered where you live from the time the girls had a sleepover. I was running an errand before lunch and I was just a few blocks away, and...I'm sorry if this is a bad time."

I wasn't sure if it was better to apologize for my appearance or ignore it, but the latter seemed like less work. "No, it's fine," I said, waving it off. "Here." I invited him in and jogged to my office, snapping up a business card and handing it to him as we met halfway, in the living room. "This has all my numbers." I folded my arms across my body, masking my grubby t-shirt.

"I was hoping to take you up on your offer to have coffee."

"You know, I shouldn't have offered. I don't think my boyfriend would like it."

He grinned and all I could think about was how salty and gross my face was. My pores were probably visible from space.

"It's only coffee." His eyes were warm and earnest and different in the mid-day light. Damn him and his timing.

"I know, but he's kind of the jealous type," I said, now trying anything.

He cocked his head. "You'd think a guy like that wouldn't need to be jealous." He smiled again, a handsome set of teeth nestled between very inviting lips.

"Oh." I cast my eyes down. "I didn't think you knew." I tightened the wrap of my arms around me.

"I'd have to be living under a rock. It was all people were talking about last night. Nice picture, by the way, the one on the beach. One of the moms showed me."

My shoulders rose and stubbornly stayed. "I'm sorry. Maybe some other time."

"Call me if you change your mind." He started to leave, but stopped and when he turned back, I knew exactly how good he smelled. "I'm serious about that. Call me if things don't work out. Then I can take you on a real date."

CHAPTER THIRTY-THREE

THE PHONE WASN'T CUTTING it, at all. Ten days had passed without seeing Chris and I felt more on edge as every hour came and went. He had tried to find a time to come to Chapel Hill, but something always managed to push things back for a few days. I'd hoped to convince my dad to come and stay with Sam for the coming weekend, but he was having none of that, his thinly veiled attempt at keeping me away from Chris.

When Chris called that afternoon, I had an intense desire to cry. I only felt lonelier every time I said goodbye and the last talk had ended awkwardly, with a failed attempt at phone sex. He had said he needed to feel closer to me and I just couldn't say the words without feeling like an idiot.

"Hi, honey," I said, trying to sound happy.

"Claire. Hi." His voice was uncertain, tentative. "Do you have a minute? I need to talk to you about something."

"Of course. What's wrong?" I sat on the edge of my bed and pushed back to lean against the headboard.

He sighed. "Elise did an interview with the *LA Times* about her book. It came out this morning. There are bloody photographers staked out at the end of my driveway. The phone's been ringing off the hook."

"Crap. That's awful. I'm sorry."

"I knew this was going to happen but I forget what a circus it is. It's going to get worse with her book coming next week." His voice trailed off and it hurt to imagine what the strain was doing to his perfect face.

"Come here," I blurted out. "Get on a plane and come here. No more letting other stuff get in the way." My heart pounded at the thought of seeing him again.

"Are you sure? I'm just springing this on you."

"Yes, I'm sure. Get on a plane."

"I probably can't catch anything before the redeye. I wouldn't get in until tomorrow morning."

"Just get on the plane."

———

THE HOLLOWS beneath his eyes told me how much everything weighed on him. Still, life surged when Chris smiled and I was plunged right back into his familiar hypnotic presence. Our greeting was entirely different than when I'd gone to visit him. We embraced without a kiss, clinging to each other. I turned my face into his chest and took in his superhuman scent, closing my eyes, intensely grateful to have him back. Relentless bursts of cold morning air forced us to part and we rushed to get in the car while he reminded me to relinquish my car keys.

"Are you sure you want to drive? You look exhausted." I couldn't keep my hands to myself, slipping one underneath the collar of his distressed leather jacket as he moved the seat back.

"Yes, I'm sure. It'll keep me awake." He leaned in for the kiss I was still waiting for, long, but sweet. The traffic guy ruined the romance with an obnoxious blow of his whistle and a gesture to move us along. Chris muttered, "bugger off," as he sped away.

When we got to the house, he dropped his heavy black suitcase to the floor as if he was home. Seeing him have that inclination at my house brought a smile to my face, even if he likely had no idea what he'd done.

"Will you come upstairs and talk to me until I fall asleep?" He loomed over me with his tired green eyes, working his fingers through my hair. The redeye flight wasn't meant for people who weren't able to sleep or read on the plane.

"Of course."

I loved seeing Chris's tall frame at the sink in my bathroom splashing water on his face. He changed into pajama pants while I lowered the roman shades. It was overcast and blustery outside, the wind whipped against the windowpanes, but it was all for the best. He needed sleep.

He pulled back the fluffy white comforter and climbed in on what was now his side of the bed. He kicked out the flat sheet from the tuck at the bottom of the mattress. I'd forgotten that he didn't like the way it would squish his feet.

"Much better." He secured my hand beneath his as I leaned against the headboard, propped up on pillows. "I don't know if I could be any happier right now."

"But this must be bothering you, at least a little. Do you want to tell me what was in the article?" We'd mutually skirted anything of consequence in the car, to enjoy being together again.

He took a deep breath and tilted his head toward me. "She said that I cheated her out of money in the divorce." There was an unfamiliar pain in his eyes. "Technically, she didn't say anything that was untrue, it just sounds worse coming out of her mouth."

"Like what?"

"She said that I hid assets because the St. Barts house is in my mum's name and I have some accounts that her lawyers suspected I had, but never found. Stuff like that. She's right about both things, but I'd never admit that to anyone but you. I only did what the accountant told me to do."

"But she still got what she deserved, right?"

"I guess. I didn't think she deserved anything by the end, but I suppose she was entitled to something." He worked his thumb under my bracelet. "Can we talk about this later?" His voice softened with every word as he gave in to sleep. "Being here makes this much easier."

I pushed back an unruly tuft of his hair, noticing one or two grays, and kissed him on the forehead. His warmth made my mouth want to stay. "Get some sleep."

He quickly drifted off once he closed his eyes and I couldn't give up the opportunity to study him in the soft light. I'd never noticed that one of his forearms was hairier than the other. Nor had I seen the tiny scar at his temple. I smoothed his hair, which caused him to mumble and smack his lips. Once he was back in a deeper sleep, I set my head down on the bed and closed my eyes.

It was hard to imagine my life a few months ago, when Sam and I had a perfectly good and quiet existence. Now everything was the opposite of quiet, crazy and inexplicable. Yet, I'd never felt like my life was more full, especially when he was with me.

I managed a few hours at my desk, but it was distracting to think about Chris asleep upstairs. I wondered how long he could stay, when he'd have to leave, and then I worried about feeding him. I was woefully unprepared for the beautiful bottomless pit. He would need food and lots of it.

There were footsteps soon after I returned from the grocery store and I waited at the kitchen counter, a smile plastered across my face. Chris bowled me over with the appeal of his lopsided hair, as if there was a neon sign flashing "Put Your Hands Here" above his head. I was ready to turn him around and steer him upstairs, but Sam was due home any minute and as fast as we could be, I didn't want to rush.

"How was your nap?" I asked. He didn't answer. Instead, he brushed his lips along the side of my neck and hummed. "Sam will be home from school any minute." That prompted him to switch to the other side. I closed my arms around him and inhaled his smell.

"I can tell time, you know," he said.

"So, don't start something we can't finish."

His mouth grazed my ear. "It can wait until tonight, but I promise you that we'll finish." He pulled me even closer as Sam came through the door, but he didn't let go until she screamed.

"Chris!" She launched her backpack at Andrew and bounded across the room, throwing her arms around Chris's shoulders.

Andrew's eyes bugged out like a Muppet when he saw Chris. He stood in a delayed state of shock, holding Sam's backpack. Sam had mentioned that Andrew hadn't realized who Chris was the first time they'd met.

Chris was gracious, deflating the star-struck moment. "Andrew. Hey."

Andrew didn't set down his armload, making his reach quite short when he extended his hand out from under the backpacks. "Oh, wow, Chris. Hey."

Chris smiled. "How are you? How's your band?"

Poor Andrew, his face was turning a deep crimson. "Really? I mean, great. It's cool."

Sam and I leaned against the kitchen counter, smiling at our guys, watching the exchange as if they were lobbing tennis balls at each other.

"I brought a guitar with me. Maybe we can jam while I'm here." Chris said, and winked at me.

Andrew's eyes went unimaginably larger. "Seriously?" Then he seemed to sense that he needed to be a little smoother. "That'd be cool. I'll be around."

Chris grabbed me as soon as Sam and Andrew ran upstairs. "Where were we?"

"I was reminding you that we don't have complete privacy here like we do at your house."

"Oh, right." He loosened his grip on me, but kept his fingers laced behind my back.

I studied his face. "Are you okay? You can talk about Elise. It doesn't bother me."

The sun peeked out from behind the clouds through the kitchen window, rebounding off the sill and across his face, showing him in a fragile golden light. "I'm trying to ignore it. We'll see how long I can keep that up." He kissed me on the forehead and his stomach growled.

"I'm being the worst host ever. Let me get you something to eat." I poured an iced tea and brought it along with cheese and crackers to the kitchen table.

He smiled at me, with soft eyes, while his snack disappeared.

"I don't think I could be as calm as you are right now," I said.

"It's only because I can hide out here with you. It doesn't seem real when I'm here. Everything's so quiet, no drama." He came into my world for quiet and calm and the opposite happened when I entered his. "I'd be miserable if I was at home by myself. I wouldn't be able to get away from it. That usually makes me feel sorry for myself and I get depressed. It's a vicious cycle."

I didn't know exactly what to say, the things he said sometimes didn't have a simple response. "I'm glad if I'm helping." Still, I was sure he was exaggerating.

He slipped his hand under mine, on the table. "I've got something I want to play for you. It's the new song I've been working on." He grabbed the guitar from the corner where he'd propped it up in its case. "Let's go in the living room."

My heart was pounding wildly—I was so excited to have him play for me. I perched on the edge of the couch, not feeling like I should sit all the way back. That would be treating it as if it wasn't a big deal and it was a huge deal to me.

He sat next to me and I watched intently as he tuned the glossy black guitar, smiling to myself, feeling so proud of my talented boyfriend. His hair still looked goofy and his clothes were rumpled, perfect.

He smiled. "It isn't finished, but you'll get the idea. It's called 'Tell Me'." He played a few notes and stopped. "Oh right, I forgot the important part. It's about you."

> Tell me if this works for you, I take your one and
>   make it two
> There's light and dark, you only see everything
>   you find in me
> Tell me how then tell me why, every low now
>   skims the sky
> Tell me what then tell me when, I'm meant to
>   break, you only bend
> I thought by now you'd surely go, my faulted
>   heart would have to know
> The mystery that has come to be, everything
>   you see in me
> Tell me how then tell me why, every low now
>   skims the sky

Tell me what then tell me when, I'm meant to
    break, you only bend
Show me secrets for tonight, I'll never tell, I'll
    hold them tight
A miracle if you learn to need, everything you
    find in me

I remained motionless when he made the final strum on his guitar, soaking up the artistry, the poetry of the words he'd written for me. Holding the side of his face, I rested the bridge of my nose against his cheek. I was afraid to move and have his eyes sweep me closer to everything that waxed inside me.

"Thank you. It's beautiful," I whispered, the tears starting on cue. "I can't believe you wrote a song for me."

He set his guitar down and gathered me up in his arms, rocking me from side to side. "I'm glad you like it. I figured it was the least you deserved."

CHAPTER THIRTY-FOUR

CHRIS and I took joy in discovering the random things that we both liked, as all new couples do. On his first night back, we added a mutual love of Chevy Chase movies to the list.

We snuggled while watching *Fletch* on cable, Chris splayed out at his full length and me tucked in between him and the back of the couch. My head rested in the crook of his arm with my hand on his stomach. I bent my leg around one of his, quite content.

"If this is what it's like to live at your house, I might not ever leave," he said when the movie ended.

"Fine by me." I made an innocent pass with my hand across his stomach. My pinky brushed a sliver of his stomach where his t-shirt had hitched up a quarter-inch.

He bolted upright, "Time for bed."

His urgency was so overt that I couldn't resist the chance to mess with him. I stretched and yawned. "Oh, you're right. I'm probably going to fall asleep before my head hits the pillow."

"Then let's keep you away from the pillows." He hopped up from the couch and yanked on my arm. "I need to get you into bed."

"You can't possibly be tired."

"I'm not. That's the point. Claire, come on. Stop mucking about."

"I'll get up." I remained on the couch, still warm from his body heat.

"When, exactly?" He stared at me with brilliant green, impatient.

"Soon," I whispered, swishing my hand across the seat cushion. "Will you do something for me?"

"Yes. Anything. What?"

I bit my lip. "When we get upstairs, will you talk to me without hiding your accent and say some of those cute British things you say?"

"I don't hide my accent." He bent an eyebrow. "And what do you mean by cute British things?"

"You know," I muttered, dropping my head shyly. "Tell me I'm sixes and sevens. But sex stuff."

"It's at sixes and sevens. You forgot the at."

I gnawed on my lower lip when a smile rolled across his face. He pulled on my arm and I followed him upstairs.

I closed the door quietly, since Sam's light was still on, and tiptoed toward him. "We have to be quiet."

"How am I supposed to talk and be quiet?" He asked, stepping out of his track pants.

"Whisper."

He talked in my ear as he inched us along the creaking wood floor toward the bed. "Let's see." He snickered, which only made me giggle like a twit. "Do I give you the fanny gallops, Claire?" He kissed my mouth, then my cheek. "Hmm? Are you arching for it?" He laughed. "I can't do this. I sound like a dirty old man."

I pulled at the back of his head and pressed his lips against mine. "Not to me you don't. I have no idea what you just said."

The bed was still unmade from his morning nap and we collapsed onto it.

"Don't you dare get up and turn off the light," he said, rolling me over to my back.

"It's my house." I slipped my hands underneath his t-shirt and removed it, admiring the shoulders I hadn't seen in days with the tips of my fingers.

"It's your house, but we're playing by my rules tonight." He began unbuttoning my blouse, bestowing a kiss where each button was once fastened.

"What does that mean?" My hands dug into his delightfully unkempt hair.

"Well, I have a list somewhere, I suppose I should have brought it with me, laminated it perhaps." I smirked as he went ahead with his attempt at making fun of my rules. "Mostly it means that your rules are null and void." He smiled deviously and once he was finished with the blouse he intently reached behind me for the hook of my bra.

I giggled as he patted. "It's in the front."

Despite the new location, he had no problem making quick work of the clasp. "This is so like you, creating problems. When we're playing by my rules, the hook always goes in the back."

"Shh...Sam will hear us." I tittered. "Sorry. I didn't get my laminated rules sheet." I mumbled into his hot and stubbly neck, his balmy smell a bit more potent than usual. "There seems to be a lot of discourse involved with your rules."

"Very observant, my dear." The button on my jeans was the next to go. "There will be a lot of talking, discussion really, about a variety of topics." He kissed my shoulder as he unzipped me. "First, I'd like to hear exactly what you want to do to me. After that, you can tell me what you want me to do to you."

"You know I'm not good at that. It's too embarrassing." The thought of all that inhibition made me want to hold back—I had no problem *doing* the things he wanted to do, the narrative he expected was the problem. "I can't do that and have the lights on. My brain will implode."

He separated me from my pants and caressed my stomach with a delicate touch, grinning. "You're a clever woman. You'll figure it out."

"But all of that talking seems pointless." I sat up and helped him out of his boxers.

"Is it that difficult for you to follow someone else's rules?"

I kissed his chest, moving down his stomach. "I'm just saying my mouth can only do so many things at one time."

He lifted his head and his eyes lit up when they met mine. "Right. Excellent point."

———

THE FOLLOWING AFTERNOON, Chris slammed the back door after picking up Sam at school. "There's a bloody idiot with a camera outside." He tossed my car keys on to the kitchen counter. "He followed us the whole way home."

Although he was upset, I smirked at the adorable image of him in the pick-up lane at school.

"Mom, isn't it cool?" Sam asked, embarking on her afternoon forage through the refrigerator. "I might be in a magazine or something."

Chris shook his head. "Sam, these guys are scavengers. They have no respect for a person's privacy." He looked out the kitchen window again. "I tried to lose him on the way home, but it's not easy when there's a speed lump every twenty feet."

"Hump," I said.

"What?"

"They're called speed humps. Sometimes bumps, but definitely not lumps." I snickered.

"Bloody nuisance is what they should call them."

I rubbed his back and glanced out the window. "That guy's a photographer?" My hand froze mid-rub. "He was out there in his car yesterday when you were taking your nap."

He pressed his lips together, eyes wide. "You should've said something. I'm going to go see if I can get him to clear out." Out the door he went, with extra long, determined strides.

Sam and I watched, looking for clues in Chris's body language as to what was happening. Much of what we saw was the view of Chris, from behind, as he leaned down to talk. I couldn't imagine a more picturesque scene.

After a few minutes, he headed back to the front door when out of nowhere Rosie from next door entered the frame. She made a slow but steady beeline across the yard toward him, white leather grandma shoes shuffling through the newly green grass.

"Oh, crap." I made a break for the front door.

Chris was already talking to her by the time I made it outside. The normally pleasant Rosie, all five feet of her, was crossly pointing a finger at him, causing him to recoil—an old lady in elastic-waist pants with lips coated in coral-pink lipstick, could be shockingly scary.

"Is that man in the car your friend? He's been out here since yesterday and every time I tell him to leave, he ignores me," she said.

"Oh, Rosie, no," I assured her. "He's not a friend of ours." I placed my hand on her shoulder. "Please, I want to introduce you to my boyfriend, Christopher." I focused on him, sending a secret signal that it was an excellent time to turn on his copious woman taming skills.

"Boyfriend? Dear, you should have said something." She straightened from her hunch. "It's nice to meet you."

"Rosie, the pleasure is all mine." He gave her the shiniest version of his trademark smile.

You go to it, honey.

He took her hand with both of his. "I am quite sorry about this chap. I've spoken to him and it seems he is unwilling to go. I'm going to recommend that we ring the police and have them ask him to move." His overly polite speech and thickening of his accent worked like a charm. She was already smitten.

She came inside with us and I made her a cup of tea while Chris called the police. "He's a handsome one, Claire," Rosie offered, leaning precariously out of her chair to get a better view of him in the other room.

"I'm a lucky woman." I was ready to grab her by her seer-sucker pants if she leaned too far. The last thing I needed was an old lady with a broken hip in my kitchen. I finished my tea just as the handsome one joined us.

"They're going to come by and talk to him," Chris said. "The local ordinance says that he's free to park on the street as long as he isn't bothering anyone. Hopefully they'll be able to scare him off."

The police did their job, but he was back an hour later. It was strange to know there was someone outside, watching the house, waiting to take pictures. Chris suspected that he wasn't even real paparazzi; perhaps a student who'd answered an ad for a cut if he caught anything good. It was scary the lengths people would go to now that the world cared about the details of Chris's private life again.

Chris would check on the guy periodically, wave at him as if they were neighbors while he said unsavory things. "We've only got a few days until Elise's book comes out and then it's probably going to get worse. I thought I'd be safe from this here." He joined me in my office, where I was finishing up a story. He rubbed my shoulders and I closed my eyes and let him do his magic. "I'll go home if this is worrying you. I'm sure he'll leave when I'm gone."

I tilted my head back to look at him. "Don't be silly. It's not like he's peeking in the windows." He worked on my neck with deep folds in his forehead. I studied his face, attractive in a different way, upside down.

"What are the chances your ex, what's-his-name, hired this guy?"

"Kevin? You think he hired the photographer?" My stomach churned. It wasn't that difficult to imagine.

"Just a theory. He seems hell-bent on keeping me away from you and I'm sure he knows about everything that Elise is doing, the interviews and such."

I closed my eyes and shook my head. "I don't even want to think about that. I really hope that isn't what's going on."

"At least the tabloids haven't been calling you."

I winced. "Actually, I turned the ringer off. Everything's going straight to voicemail. I had four messages from reporters the last time I checked."

His eyes narrowed. "Of course." He spun my chair around. "I noticed the same number on your cell phone several times from yesterday and today. Did someone get that number?"

"My cell phone?"

"I wanted to make sure there wasn't anyone bothering you."

I calmed myself, to let him have his macho moment. "It's a friend of mine."

"Male or female?"

"Why does that matter?"

"I'm curious." He leaned against the edge of my desk and crossed his arms over his chest.

"His name is Jeremy. He's a dad from school. Sam used to be friends with his daughter. It's nothing."

CHAPTER THIRTY-FIVE

THE PHOTOGRAPHER PROBLEM got worse when the rest of the neighbors started complaining. They weren't as swayed by Chris as Rosie was—especially Mr. Henderson across the street, who had no right to say a thing about being a bad neighbor as far as I was concerned. His satanic Pomeranian, Cupcake, took off after me every morning when I jogged past their house. Mr. Henderson seemed to enjoy watching, often wearing his too-short bathrobe and slippers.

Chris called the police repeatedly; the photographer would leave for an hour or so, but he always came back. The guy was making himself at home—once we'd seen him have a pizza delivered.

The photographer's presence made everything complicated. Both Chris and I wanted to read Elise's book the day it was released, but the image of one of us buying it would've meant big headaches down the road. I was kicking myself for not pre-ordering it online, but Kevin unexpectedly came to the rescue. He'd left a message on Monday saying he was sending it overnight—two copies, in case I wanted to "share" with anyone.

I was thankful, although I was sure he'd only done it to be an arrogant prick.

Chris seemed on edge all morning, drumming his fingers on the table while he did the crossword, and downing cups of coffee. I tried to help him relax, massaged his shoulders, but nothing seemed to help. The doorbell rang around lunchtime and he was off to the door in a flash. I heard muffled voices from my office and then they came closer. My throat closed when I turned and saw who was there.

"Jeremy." I coughed. "I take it you met Chris." I blinked and shook my head, trying to gauge Chris's reaction.

"We've met," Chris said.

"Sorry for dropping in. Sam left this at our house the last time she stayed over. I wanted to return it." Jeremy handed me a spiral bound notebook. "I didn't know if it was important, for school or something."

It'd been years since Sam had had a sleepover with Bailey and I was positive it'd been at our house. I opened the notebook and the pages were blank. I glanced at Jeremy, he winked and I felt sick. "Okay, well, great. Thanks for bringing this by."

"So, Chris, how long are you in town?" he asked.

My shoulders felt as though they'd been lashed together.

Chris stepped closer and wrapped his arm around me. "I'm not sure. I believe I have an open invitation." His lips grazed my temple. He and Jeremy were now having a staring contest and I couldn't help but feel that I was the prize.

"Yep, uh huh. Okay." I clapped my hands. "Thanks for coming." I wriggled out of Chris's iron grip to lunge for the front door in an attempt to get Jeremy the hell out of the house. "Thanks again."

Jeremy took one last look at Chris before setting his hand on my shoulder and squeezing. "No problem, Claire. Anything for you." He kissed me on the cheek. "Don't forget we need to plan our coffee date."

I groaned inside while I held on to the door. "We'll see."

He winked at me again before strolling down the front walk to his BMW, just as the Fed Ex guy pulled up to the curb and our photographer friend opted for a few shots of everything transpiring in the front yard. My shoulders rolled and I slumped forward. Today had already been exhausting and it wasn't even one o'clock.

Chris's reaction was swift once he'd signed for the Fed Ex delivery. "What the hell was that? Is Jeremy another one of your old boyfriends?"

I kneaded my forehead and followed him into the kitchen. "You've only been around one of my ex-boyfriends so don't make it sound like there's a lot of them. He's not an old boyfriend."

"You should've seen the way he was looking at you. I know that look. It only means one thing. He couldn't have cared less that I was here." He tore open the padded mailer.

I desperately wanted to calm him down. Our day was only going to get worse. "Honey, it's okay." I rubbed his arm. "I couldn't care less about Jeremy. He's an idiot."

Chris pulled the books from the envelope and our heads dropped to the sight of the cover—colored in a scheme of yellow and black like crime scene caution tape, the jarring image of Elise and Chris in their infamous fight outside the restaurant. All life drained from his face. The title, *Love, Destroyed: What It's Really Like to Be a Rock 'n' Roll Wife*, was nothing more than a knife in Chris's back.

IT WAS TOO painful and awkward to remain in the same room,

so Chris and I read our copies apart. The book was a load of innuendo, artfully crammed into scant one hundred-fifty pages. Even I had to admit that Kevin had done an excellent job capturing the voice of a strung-out and jilted ex-wife.

The laundry list of Chris's supposed transgressions while married to Elise read as this: he was controlling and jealous, verbally abusive, and openly flirted with other women. She said his mood swings were extreme and unpredictable and that he once refused to come out of his music room for a week. He sometimes insisted the house be kept in total darkness.

Then came the gut-wrenching allegations. She said her addiction and her numerous infidelities were all due to Chris. Drugs were her only escape from the pain of being married to him. Because she'd felt so lonely and afraid, he drove her to cheat on him. There were three different men she was involved with over the course of their marriage, one of them a Banks Forest roadie, the second an old friend of Chris's and the third was Chris's guitar tech of eleven years.

The most painful of her stories, certainly for Chris, was saved for the final chapter. Elise claimed that she'd always wanted a baby, not him, and that when she got pregnant, he told her to have an abortion. She said she'd refused because in her heart she was sure of one thing. The baby did not belong to Chris.

When I finished reading, I had no earthly idea what I was supposed to do with the avalanche of information. *How much of this is true? How do I ask him without it sounding like an interrogation?*

Some things she'd said were plausible; I could understand why she found him controlling and jealous. I could see him flirting with other women because I'd witnessed it myself. I didn't want to believe the rest of it, but it cast doubt in my head.

I had very little time to think about it. Chris came to my

room minutes after I finished, the fury visible in his eyes. His shoulders were rigid. He sat next to me on the bed and I pulled my knees under my chin.

Ultimately, the silence became too much for me. "Say something, please."

He cleared his throat and crossed his arms. Closing his eyes for a moment, I saw the translucent skin of his lids, reminding me of every time I'd watched him in peaceful slumber. "I'm not surprised that she would sink so low for money. It's smart if you think about it. Nearly everything in the book is unverifiable. It's all stuff that happened between the two of us, so now it's about who people want to believe." He stared straight ahead, almost as if I wasn't there, holding his lips in a thin line. "Are you going to ask me anything? You must have a lot of questions."

I swallowed. "Uh, I guess, but I know that most of it is a lie and that's all that matters."

His eyes darkened. "She's such a bitch. I knew she was cheating on me, but I didn't know it was with three guys and that I knew all of them. And I don't understand how she could say that the baby wasn't mine, because she had no way of knowing that. And the idea that she was the one who wanted a child in the first place, that's the bloody worst." He became deathly quiet and the blood rose in his cheeks, his skin shifting to scarlet.

I wondered if he would tell me anything else. Instead, he did the last thing I expected—he leaned over and pinned my arms against the bed. He kissed me roughly, forcing his mouth against mine. He weighed me down and pulled up my shirt, his hands aggressive, as if they weren't his own.

I pursed my lips and jerked my face from his. "Don't, Chris. Don't do this."

He tore into my neck, his stubble scratching at my skin. "Come on, Claire. You like it when I'm a little rough."

"Not like this. Stop it." I pushed against his chest with both hands but he was an unmovable weight. "Get off of me." He groaned and relented and I rolled out from under him. I scrambled off the bed, into the bathroom, and locked the door while I gasped for breath.

There were only seconds before he was there pounding. "Don't be so fucking dramatic. Open the door."

I stood paralyzed but my eyes darted back and forth as I became frantic to make sense of what had just happened. "No way. Not until you calm down."

He made a frustrated grumble. "Please come out of there. I need you." The agony in his voice was palpable. I could feel it through the door.

"Not until you swear that you're never going to touch me like that again."

"I've touched you like that tons of times. What's your problem?"

"It's not the same. You're angry with Elise and you're taking it out on me." I felt like I might cry, but I couldn't. "You're scaring me."

That garnered no response. I put my ear to the door after a few minutes but heard nothing. With my courage gathered, I clicked the lock and cracked the door. He was on the bed.

"Can we talk now?" I asked. "Are you okay?"

His face was blank, in utter defeat, but he pleaded with his eyes. "Claire, I'm so sorry. I don't know what happened." His tears came in a silent stream. "You're right. I'm angry. All I could think about was how much I need you. I want things to be the way they were before this happened."

The flood of adrenaline had made its way through my system. My fear was gone. I put my arms around his head, holding the side of his face to my chest as I stroked his hair. "It's okay. I understand. At least I think I understand. She said awful things."

He wrapped his arms around my waist. "It's not just the book. That guy Jeremy, I was ready to pound him after seeing him look at you like that."

"Don't think twice about Jeremy. I only want you."

"I don't want you to think that this is what it's like to be with me," he said, his voice cracking.

"I don't think that. I don't care about the book or the photographer or any of that stuff. It'll get back to normal soon."

He pulled his head back and peered up at me. "But none of this is going away soon. The *Rolling Stone* issue comes out in less than a month, but I can't say a thing in the meantime."

My heart stopped. "Right. The exclusive." The thing I'd hoped for after the interview, a guarantee that he'd be on the cover, required his complete and utter silence.

"Even if the story dies down, that'll bring it back into the headlines and it'll start all over again."

"What now?"

"I have to let people call me a monster and try to ignore it."

I thought about his predicament, our predicament. "Don't go home. Stay here. I know there are people watching you here too, but it's better than if you were at home." I combed my fingers through his hair. "Just stay. At least until things blow over."

He gazed at me, a tinge of hope in his eyes. "Claire, I would never, ever, hurt you." His voice became shaky again. "I don't want you to doubt how much I care about you."

I couldn't sleep for a minute that night, unable to shake the idea that some things in the book could be true. I didn't want to imagine the version of Chris that was in the book—verbally abusive, moody, volatile and dark. The stories worked their way through my head and my stomach lurched every time I doubted him.

How would I have felt if the roles had been reversed? If someone had written a book about me, I wouldn't want to sit down with Chris and explain myself point by point. I would expect unwavering trust and faith from him and if I was sure about anything, it was that he would need that from me.

CHAPTER THIRTY-SIX

I COUNTED the days on my fingers, but quickly grew frustrated with the numbers. The day Elise's book had come out was Tuesday, that was three days, which meant that today, Friday, was six. Six days. I'd been four. I'd even been five, but never six. I steadied my hands on the white porcelain pedestal sink noticing the rust stain from the drip my dad must've missed.

I glanced in the mirror of my old medicine cabinet with the silver turning black at the edges. The wrinkles that didn't seem so bad last year were deeper. I was less than two months away from forty. The entire concept was crazy, the idea of being—having a—I couldn't bring myself to think the words. Pregnant. Baby.

Chris was working on a song in the living room. Now that he was staying for a while, we'd settled into a comfortable routine at home. I'd cleared out some drawers for him that morning.

I told him I needed to run a few errands and luckily, he didn't invite himself along. That would've meant telling him what was going on and dealing with the photographer. Standing in line at the drug store, my brain took on thoughts like a leaky rowboat takes water. I bailed and bailed, but the boat continued to fill from the hole at the bottom until eventually, it gave in to the weight and dipped beneath the surface.

As soon as I got home, I hurried upstairs, closed my bathroom door and tore open the packages. I'd bought three different tests, passing on the one with the smiley face. After a cursory scan of the directions, I did what I needed to do and placed the white plastic sticks on the edge of the sink.

The memory of the same moment seventeen years before was far off and fuzzy. I'd been so numb when I got the news the first time that I ignored it for days.

Knowing I was needlessly drawing out the drama, I glanced at the tests, as if I was picking out polish at the nail salon. The first had a pair of pink lines, the second had a steadily darkening blue plus sign, and the third one, the newfangled digital one, presumed to speak for the other tests: Pregnant, with a capital "P" no less. *Fuck.*

Sam would be home from school in an hour and the news wasn't going to get better. I felt queasy. I had no idea what it would do to us. I tiptoed downstairs to tell him, but part of me hoped he wouldn't even hear me.

"There's my baby," he said, when I found him in the living room.

Seriously? He'd never called me baby, one of my most hated pet names, right behind lover. "Hi, honey. What's going on?"

"Not much. Working on a song."

"That's great. I'm glad you're writing. I know it makes you happy." My words came with a choppy mix of inflections.

"What's wrong?"

"What?"

"Something's wrong."

"Well, um, I need to tell you something." I focused on my hands as they clenched each other and my bracelet dangled back and forth. "It's surprising, and, uh, maybe it's more unexpected than surprising."

"Claire. What is it?" His eyes narrowed and he stood, setting his guitar on the couch.

I took a breath, as much air as could fit in my lungs, and then some more. "I'm pregnant."

There was silence, without question the sound of nothing. He wrinkled his brow. "You're what?"

"Pregnant. I took three tests and they're all positive."

"Oh, wow." He stared, the smile creeping across his face. "This is...wow. Pregnant? A baby? This is, wow." His enthusiasm gained momentum with every word and his eyes grew wider. "I mean, it's a little out of nowhere, but it's fantastic. It's bloody brilliant is what it is." Every elated word was a new blow. He bounded over and scooped me up in his arms and then held me out at arm's length. "Is that what you were doing when you ran your errands? You should've said something. I could've been with you." He brushed my cheek with the back of his hand. "Are you okay? How do you feel?"

"I realized I was six days late this morning, but I didn't want you to worry."

"Can I see the tests?" He grinned like I'd never seen him grin. "Claire, really, this is so exciting."

He made it sound like a fanciful adventure. "They're upstairs in my bathroom. I'm going to stay down here. I need some time to think."

"I don't understand. I know this is a surprise, but isn't it a happy surprise?"

"It's not that I'm not happy. It's just that..."

"It's just that what?"

"This isn't what I planned on doing for the next twenty years. This changes everything, our whole lives. How are we even going to make this work? You live on the other side of the country, for God's sake."

"You sound upset." He directed me to the couch and sat me down next to him. "We're going to have a baby. A baby. That's an amazing, miraculous thing. Don't over-think it like you do everything else." He pushed my hair back behind my ear and dragged my hand into his lap. "Claire, I love you."

His words had me stuck, immobile. I hung my head, feeling dizzy. "Please don't say you love me because of this. That's not what I want."

"I'm not saying it because of the baby." He broke into me with his gorgeous green, a look of all sincerity. "I really love you."

"I love you too," I replied, and he smiled. "But this is a lousy time to tell me. What took you so long?"

"I don't know. I guess it felt too soon, before. But that doesn't mean the feelings weren't there, just because I didn't say it." He twisted his lips. "And you could have said it too, you know."

"What, are we ten years old? Are we playing chicken with 'I love you'? If you think it's too soon, then we have no business having a baby."

"Claire, come on. I know you're freaked out, but this is great news. We'll make it work."

My frustration was getting the best of me. He didn't understand the ramifications of what was happening, he'd never had to function for days at a time on minutes of sleep. He'd never had magic boobs that transform into rock-hard squirting footballs. He'd never played Barbie for so many hours that he began to have unforgivable thoughts about a certain doe-eyed doll and her closeted boyfriend, Ken.

"I just need some time."

CHAPTER THIRTY-SEVEN

LESS THAN TWELVE hours into Operation Baby, Chris was already enjoying the hell out of it. By the time I came to bed, he was waiting for me with the goofiest look on his face, deliriously happy.

"Come here. Let me see you."

I blushed. Even in my shell-shocked state, that was always my reaction when he extended an invitation to come to bed. "What? There's nothing to see." I climbed in and scooted closer to him while he put his arm around me, parking his other hand on my stomach. "I'm serious," I pleaded. "There's nothing to see."

Pushing up on his elbow, he gazed into my eyes. "I know. I just want you close."

This scenario was never part of my original teenage fantasy. Birth control was unnecessary when we went on our endless sex benders. I simply didn't get pregnant. He swallowed me whole with the look on his face, his hold on me exponentially stronger now.

"I'm tired."

"Of course you are," he answered, his voice turning buttery.

I folded into a ball and turned my back to him—freezing, as usual. He bundled me up with his arms, curling his long body around mine and I sank into the heat radiating from his bare chest.

It was hard to believe that his faultless gene pool, beautiful and talented, had decided to make a baby with mine. Knowing him, he probably had exceptionally good-looking sperm, charming and smooth, mixing cocktails and making sexy, witty comments. I was sure my pushover eggs fell for the very first pick-up line, keenly aware that since they were a bit beyond their freshness date, they were damn lucky to have the attention.

I reached over and turned off the bedside lamp. "We have a lot to talk about."

"We do." His voice was quiet and calm. "But we don't need to figure everything out right now. I know this isn't what either of us planned, but I've always wanted to be a dad and you're such an amazing mom. I feel great about us doing this."

I rolled back to flatten my face against his shoulder, to smell him and feel his skin against mine.

He raked his hand through the tangles in my hair. "I really do love you." He stirred me up, speaking softly in my ear. "I knew I was falling in love with you when we were on the island. I didn't say the words because I didn't want to scare you off."

Whenever he spoke about scaring me off, or holding on to me, it felt odd, as if he had things turned around. Considering him and all he had to offer, it still felt unlikely that he'd ever choose me for real.

"I love you too. I do." I pushed his floppy hair away from his face. "I'm scared though. It feels strange to be doing this when Sam's nearly finished with school. I never saw myself starting over and having another child." He rubbed my arm and I let my legs unfurl.

"When do you want to tell Sam?" he asked.

"Not for a while. Anything could happen in the next month or two, including a miscarriage."

His body tensed.

I'd thought the night we told each other "I love you" would be all about passion, not babies and cold feet. Even so, there was no denying that when it was just the two of us, I felt like things were right.

————

He was still wearing his excited new daddy grin the next morning. I was relieved that Sam was using her Saturday morning wisely, sleeping in; she would've sensed that something was going on.

"I'm going for a run," I said, finishing the morning dishes.

He held up his finger while he finished jotting his answer in the crossword puzzle. "Is that safe?"

"Yes, the baby's the size of a peanut," I whispered, not wanting Sam to overhear us.

"Okay, if you say so." He eyed me with trepidation. "Can I take you to lunch today? I'm tired of being cooped up in the house."

"What about our friend outside?"

"It's lunch with my girlfriend. What's he going to do?" He let out half a laugh. "Take a picture of me with my elbows on the table?"

"I'm glad you can have a sense of humor about this."

Lunch was at a modern re-make of a diner that afternoon, with a young tattooed chef and waitresses with lots of piercings.

Chris insisted on eating outside on the patio even though it made us easy prey for the photographer. He sat right next to me, with his arm slung over the back of my chair. Our shadow watched from his car across the street. I tried to ignore it. Chris was much better at it than me.

"What are we in the mood for today?" he asked, leaning closer and nuzzling my hair.

"I was thinking the bacon cheeseburger. The fries are insanely good here. I might need to save room for dessert though. They had strawberry shortcake on the specials board."

He dropped his menu on the table. "No grilled chicken and salad? No tofu veggie scramble with a side of fat-free packing peanuts?"

"Hey, smart guy, I need to take advantage of my condition. It's not every day I can pig out without the guilt." I closed my menu, settled on the burger. "What about you?"

"I don't know. Do you think I can get away with saying I'm eating for two?" He pooched out his flat belly and rubbed it. "Because I'm starving."

The weather was temperamental, like it couldn't decide what kind of day it should be. The sun would come out for a few moments and it felt amazing, my face drawn to the glow. Then it would retreat behind gray and purple clouds and the wind would start. I huddled and pressed myself into Chris when it became too cold to bear.

I was finishing my strawberry shortcake when he sent the waitress off with the check. He'd already made short work of an enormous piece of chocolate cake on top of a steak sandwich and chili cheese fries. He seemed fascinated by watching me eat.

"Can I help you with something?" I asked, licking whipped cream from the spoon. "Didn't anyone ever tell you it's not polite to stare?"

He smiled and said nothing, but rather leaned over and totally laid one on me—soft and steamy. He hummed and grinned afterward, plucking his sunglasses up from the table.

"You know that's going to end up on some trashy celebrity website," I said.

"I don't really care anymore."

I looked into his face, seeing my own silhouette in the reflection of his silver aviators, marveling at how easily he plunged me into sensory overload—his sweet and musky smell, the sound of his voice, the sensation of his skin against mine. Sometimes it felt as if I could disappear into him and it wouldn't matter. I would still be happy.

"Ready?" he asked.

"I need to pick up a few things from the drug store across the street."

"If you want your privacy, I can duck into the coffee shop. Our friend will most likely follow me."

Luckily, I didn't see anyone I knew in line while I discreetly held my folic acid tablets, Tums, and copy of *Fit Pregnancy* magazine. I did, however, recognize someone in the magazine rack. Chris was one of the sidebar images in *People*. The photo looked to be a few years old, his hair was longer. The headline promised an exciting bonus: an excerpt from the now bestselling book, *Love, Destroyed*.

Chris had lectured me about reading the tabloids, but I was curious after Elise's book had come out and I'd looked online. Bloggers posted crazy and inaccurate details about what was supposedly in the *Rolling Stone* article. I felt like screaming at the screen since I knew exactly what was in that story. The online gossip hounds voiced their opinions of Chris as if it all was fact, when it was entirely based in rumors. To my astonishment, people had no sense of boundaries when it came to the baby. There were countless theories about what really happened when they lost the pregnancy, none of it sympathetic to either Chris or Elise.

I sent him a text from the checkout and met him at the car.

On the way home, Chris stole the trick I use on Sam, where I bring up potentially uncomfortable subjects while driving. "I'm thinking we need to get you a new car."

"By we, you mean you." I shifted in my seat. "Nice try. I don't want a new car."

He was quiet, but I sensed he wasn't going to give up so easily. When we turned into my neighborhood, photographer guy splintered off, probably for a late lunch and a pee break.

Chris pulled into the driveway and turned off the ignition. "Don't you think this car's a bit past its prime? I'm sure the airbags are completely insufficient." He took my shopping bag from me.

I huffed as we walked inside. "I don't care. I love my car. End of discussion."

"End of discussion? I'm not twelve years old."

"You're not buying me a new car and you know I can't afford one."

"What if it's to keep our baby safe?"

I let out a very distinct but nearly silent hiss. "Sam's upstairs." I pulled his hand and tugged him to the living room. "Don't you think we should figure out some other things before we talk about a car?"

"Like what?"

"Uh, like where we're going to live. Let's start with that."

"Well, I assumed we'd move everyone to LA. My house is much bigger and we can make the room next to the master bedroom into the nursery. We can redo the guest room for Sam. It's twice as big as the room she has now." He pulled a small red and white tin out of his pocket. "Mint?"

"Uh, no." I shook my head, flabbergasted. "Please, continue."

"We'll need to send Sam to a private school but I'm sure I can pull some strings. I thought we'd put your office downstairs, across the hall from my music room and then we'll see each other during the day. We'll get a nanny so we can both work. It'll be perfect."

Wow. I blinked erratically. He'd already planned everything, without me. "Okay, well, that's the exact opposite of what I was thinking. I don't want to make Sam change schools for her senior year. And your house is the least baby-friendly place I can think of. There's all of that glass and the pool."

"Hey, Mom?" Sam called from the other room. "Where are you guys?"

I grabbed Chris's arm. "In here, honey," I yelled.

"There you are." Sam was in jeans and a t-shirt, looking untidy and like she hadn't tended to her curls. "The house was empty when I got up and I didn't see a note."

"Hey, Ms. Abby," Andrew said, as he unexpectedly trailed Sam, eating out of a box of Wheat Thins and smiling like he'd just found out that looking at boobs makes you smarter. "Hey, Chris. What's up man?"

"Not much, Andrew," Chris replied, clearing his throat and hitting my leg with the back of his hand.

I didn't say a word, hoping silence combined with my practiced mom-stare might make one of them crack. Sam and Andrew had had plenty of time alone in the house if Andrew had come over right after we left. There was a preponderance of messy hair and rumpled clothes between them, which was the norm for Andrew, but certainly not for Sam. Andrew's permanent grin was beyond bothersome—he was a happy kid, but not *that* happy.

"What've you two been up to?" I asked, my eyebrows arching.

"Homework," Sam blurted.

Andrew added, "Big calculus test on Monday."

Chris couldn't leave an ideal set-up alone. "Sounds like you lot have been hitting it pretty hard."

CHAPTER THIRTY-EIGHT

CHRIS WAS BEING INSANELY CUTE about the baby thing, reading and looking up terms online with endless curiosity. It almost made me feel good about what we were doing.

"Are you learning a lot?" I asked, sneaking up behind him at my desk.

"I am. It's amazing what your body's going to do. I can't believe there's a part of you that can stretch this big." He held his arms out in front of him and made a circle the size of a hubcap with his thumbs and index fingers.

I gulped, having forgotten about what was waiting for me after forty weeks of fat ankles and sore boobs. "That's not right. Your hands are too big. It's more like this." I molded his fingers to make the circle less scary.

"Are you sure?" He returned to the computer. "I bookmarked a diagram that shows how big it gets."

"That's okay. I don't need to see a picture."

"I found a message board for first-time dads. I thought that'd be good for me. I want to make sure I do a good job."

He turned and looked up at me before circling his arms around my hips. His adoration, seeming to grow by the minute, made me feel as if I'd eaten an entire tub of chocolate frosting—on a high from the sugar, but also like I'd completely overdone it.

With morning came my first real bout of nausea, but it wasn't terrible, just enough to wake me. It was early, a few minutes after five, and Chris was dead asleep, breathing heavily into my face and conspiring with my brain to keep me awake.

The question of living arrangements weighed down my every thought. It was hard to see how we'd never agree. Then there was the commitment talk. We hadn't gone there at all, not even close. Perhaps he felt that with a baby, the commitment was implied. It wasn't like I wanted to get married; I only wanted to know his intentions, but that made me sound like my dad.

I crept into Sam's room to wake her, beating her alarm clock by several minutes. I perched on her bed and studied her sweet face as she slept. She'd probably never thought she'd have a little brother or sister, our "little nipper" as Chris had already dubbed him or her.

When Sam was born, I was on autopilot, having been in the trenches for weeks over losing my mom. Labor and delivery just happened. I'd never felt as though I was participating. After she'd arrived, I longed to look at her like the moms did in the pregnancy books, but at the time, I felt as though I'd made the most irreversible choice ever. There was no way I could be responsible for another human being for the rest of my life.

That first night in the hospital had been awful. Sam couldn't latch on to breastfeed. She fussed. I panicked. I was completely spent, no gas left in the tank. I rang the nurse, but they were short-staffed and must have forgotten me. All I'd wanted at that moment was my mom, to tell me what to do, to cradle Sam, to tell me everything would be okay. But she was gone, forever, and I'd never felt more alone.

Sam flailed her skinny newborn arms that night and I watched as her hand went to her face and she rooted around, squawking like a baby bird. Eventually, she found her three middle fingers and sucked them into her mouth.

She slept for the rest of the night comforting herself with her hand and I woke up to a lecture from the nurse about sleeping with her in my arms. I looked into Sam's tiny red face, edged with the pink and white hospital stocking cap, and felt so scared, so horribly inadequate that I hadn't been able to feed my own child. That was when I first knew that I needed Samantha much more than she needed me.

"Sam, honey, time to get up." I gently rustled her arm.

She opened one eye and closed it, turning over on her side. "I hate Mondays."

I waited before attempting to raise the dead again. "Time to hop in the shower."

"I'm trying," she whined. She pulled the covers over her head.

"Sam, honey, I have a question." I chewed on my fingernail. "Were you and Andrew having sex in your room on Saturday afternoon?"

The lump under the covers didn't move. "I'm awake now, if you're wondering."

"Good."

The lump moved her hand and pushed the blanket away from her face. "What happens if I say yes?"

"I don't want you to worry about what happens. I want you to worry about the truth."

She scrunched back in bed, straightening the t-shirt that had twisted around her torso. "Yes."

"Did you use a condom?"

"Of course. I'm not dumb."

"Good, because not using one would be really dumb." *Lord*

knows you wouldn't want to be knocked up, like your mother. "Is this the first time this has happened?"

She eyed me uncertainly. "It's the first time at our house. We did it once in his car." She sat up further in bed. "I think I messed up though."

My breath caught in my chest. "Messed up?"

"Yeah." She looked down again. "Andrew thinks I was a virgin. I couldn't tell him the truth because he'd be mad. Especially if he found out when it happened."

I sighed. "I can't tell you what to do about Andrew. I think you know it's not right to lie to him. Especially if you want your relationship to go anywhere."

"Am I in trouble?" she asked. "I mean, for the sex in my room thing?"

I studied her face—her cheeks were an enviable shade of pink in the morning. "I don't know yet. It's better if you do it in the safety of our house but I don't want you to think I'm giving you free rein to have sex whenever you want." I groaned quietly. "Just don't do it in his car again. It's dangerous. Now get ready for school."

Chris came downstairs soon after Sam left, shuffling his feet and rubbing his eyes. He looked irresistible, even with a pillow crease across his forehead.

"Can I convince you to come back to bed?" he asked, with an enticing rumble to his voice.

I peered up at him from behind my oh-so-sexy reading glasses, the latest sign that I was giving in to the nonsense of turning forty. "I don't think I need any convincing, but I need to brush my teeth."

"You're killing the romance, you know."

We brushed our teeth at the sink, smiling at each other through foamy mouths. The moment passed in slow motion, and it struck me how much we liked being with each other. It made me think for the very first time that we were doing the right thing. It wasn't the way we would've chosen for it to happen, but we could find a way to still be happy.

"Taste test." He pulled me close and brushed his lips against mine.

My hands washed over his back and his slid under my blue and white pajama top to ease it over my head. I arched into him as he worked his way across my back—usually his hands were so warm, but they were arctic. "Oh, ouch." I separated myself from him by a few inches and looked down at my chest. I prodded my breast with a fingertip and flinched.

He seemed fascinated. "This is new. I like it."

"I'm not trying to turn you on." Another poke and I winced. "It'd be better if you didn't touch my boobs."

"Huh?" He lowered his head in complete befuddlement.

"They're a lot more tender than they were yesterday. Try not to touch them."

His shoulders drooped with disappointment. "But that's like taking someone to Disneyland and telling them they can't go on the rides."

"I'm not thrilled about this either." I took his hand and walked to the bed.

"But they're starting to get bigger," he said, just like a child. "When can I have a proper go at them?" He sat on the bed next to me and I popped up on to my elbows.

"What happened to liking a handful?"

"I never said I wouldn't take more if I could get it." He touched my stomach tentatively. "I don't want to hurt you."

"Just go easy around my boobs."

"And you're sure this is okay for the baby?"

"The little nipper has no idea what's going on. I swear."

THE DAYS BEGAN to run together once we were in our new routine, Chris and I adjusting to the idea of what was coming, on our own schedules. We both wrote all day long—he worked on new songs and I had a steady stream of assignments. At night, Chris would help me with dinner or more specifically, he would distract me with kisses and wandering hands while I attempted to make dinner. He and Sam would watch TV and goof around. We functioned like a family. We still didn't have a plan, but we were only a few weeks into our new situation. Keeping things stable and normal seemed to be enough.

"Chris, I'm running to the grocery store to pick up a few things."

He was catching up on email, mostly with his record label. It was only six weeks until the CD release and a few days until the *Rolling Stone* issue was out. He already had a handful of phone interviews scheduled the day the magazine would be released, when he could finally fight back.

"Hold on a minute and I'll drive you." He was hunting and pecking his way through the keyboard; it took him forever to compose a message.

"Don't be silly, you have work to do. The coast is clear outside and it's a quick trip. I'll be fine."

He looked up from the computer. "Are you sure?"

"Of course, I'm sure."

Stuck at the light around the corner from the grocery store, I flipped on my blinker and I remembered. *Paper towels.* I stretched across the seat for the grocery list in my purse. The handles flopped away and I wagged my fingers, straining to grab it. I almost had it—a few more inches—and then my foot slipped off the brake. The car lurched then began to inch ahead. I bolted upright as a white delivery truck ballooned in my window. I stomped the brake and missed. Stupid. The driver swerved but it was far too late.

CHAPTER THIRTY-NINE

MY BRAIN WOKE UP, but my body remained in a muddy detached state. My eyes were closed against my wishes and my muscles immobile. Still, I could hear noises and sense people around me. I could smell, too—the chalky antiseptic aroma of a hospital, and weaving in and out of the unpleasantness, Chris's heady scent. My mouth tasted sour and metallic. My lips were frozen rubber, stuck.

I willed my leaden arms to move and my struggle brought a whimper that set off a chain reaction, telling me Chris had been holding my hand. I hadn't felt it until he jerked suddenly.

"She said something," he said, with his heavenly blue voice.

Wow. I love your voice. Keep talking, honey. I'm listening.

"Sam, she said something. Get your grandfather."

Shit. Seriously? Who invited Richard?

"Claire, honey, I'm right here."

That's better. Just keep talking or maybe you could sing to me. I love it when you sing.

"You're going to be okay. Sam's here and she called your dad and he drove down this morning. We're all here."

That's nice. My skin tingles when you touch my face like that. Your hand feels so warm, like you just took off your mittens.

"Is that a smile?" His voice trembled.

Don't worry. I'm okay. I just feel a little funny.

He touched the side of my face again and my head turned to his hand as if he was the magnet and I was the metal.

"Oh, no, no, no." His voice became panicked. "Don't cry, honey. It's okay."

Am I crying? I don't feel it at all. I can feel your fingers on my cheeks though. They're soft, like a rabbit's foot. Oh, wait. Hold on a minute. I'm sorry. My mom's calling for me. I guess it's time for me to go back to sleep now.

And then everything went away.

———

IT WAS hard to know how long I was out, but at some point, my brain turned on the lights. I felt more connected to my body and that brought a monumental difference—the pain. It wasn't that I couldn't move. I didn't want to. It hurt like hell.

One at a time, I forced my eyes open, the fluorescent light buzzed at me and I closed them before I realized that I'd seen what I was hoping for.

When I opened them the second time, Chris was floating above me with indelible green set within the framework of that face, covered in days of facial hair. Now I felt the tears bursting out of me with their full force. He did the same and that only made me cry more, but it was wonderful and cathartic, my lungs readily filled with air—it made me feel alive.

He kissed me on the cheek with salty tears mixing from his face into mine. Finally able to part, my lips quivered, overcome with how badly I'd missed him.

"You're awake." He touched my face with the tips of his

fingers and I hoped that I was still alive, that this wasn't the other side of my original dream, happening because I was dead. "I love you so much, Claire. I was so scared, you have no idea, but you're going to be fine. Sam and I have been here the whole time. Your dad came yesterday."

I wanted to speak, but it came out like a quiet cough, a precarious sputter. "The baby." The tears burst again when I saw the answer in his eyes.

CHAPTER FORTY

"I'M NOT EATING JELL-O." I coughed. "Nothing that color is good for you."

"Mom, Chris told me I have to make you eat something. What about the broth?"

I made a face. "It tastes like salty dog water. Why can't I have real food?"

"Dog water? Grandpa, can you help me out here?"

He peered through his glasses, over the newspaper, from his spot in the corner. "Just make an old man happy and eat something. You'll feel better."

"Fine. I'll have the broth." I took a sip of the tepid yellow liquid and the salt stung the cuts around my lips.

That morning had been the first time I'd seen myself in the mirror since the accident. The doctor described it as multiple lacerations, but that made it sound so insignificant, as if there were only four or five when it looked as though there were forty or fifty. None of the ones on my face were huge, just big enough to bother me.

Bruises—purple, blue, and a most sickening shade of yellow —were everywhere, especially on the left side of my body. The worst one was nearly black, in the perfect shape of a seatbelt, across my chest and stomach. Otherwise, the doctor said I got off easy considering my car had been totaled, a few cracked ribs and a concussion. The miscarriage was likely a result of the accident, but there was no way to know for sure and I didn't want to dwell on it because it was too sad, for both of us.

"When is Chris coming back?" I asked. "It seems like he's been gone forever." The broth went down, but my stomach wanted more, now that it had sustenance beyond ice chips and flat store-brand ginger ale.

"Soon," my dad replied, without looking up. "He had to do something."

A knock at the door postponed the litany of questions I had for my dad about where Chris was and what he was doing.

"Hello?" Jeremy peeked around the door anxiously, like he was worried about walking into the wrong room. "There she is." His voice was drawn out and he smiled, seeming relieved. "How are you?"

I watched the way his eyes were immediately drawn to the toll the accident had taken on my face. "This is a surprise." I fussed to straighten the sheet and cover my one exposed leg. "Dad, you remember Jeremy."

They shook hands and Sam waved to me silently, on her way out into the hall.

Jeremy asked, "Did Chris mention I came by twice yesterday?"

My dad seemed to relish this turn of events. "Let me take these flowers. Aren't these beautiful, Ladybug?" My dad had never cared about flowers in his life, ever. Now it was like he was a wedding planner.

"Yes, Dad, they're beautiful." He took the pale pink lilies from Jeremy and set them on the cart next to my bed being so prissy about it that I thought he was going to bust out a doily. "I guess Chris forgot to tell me. Thank you for the flowers. They're great." They were pretty, but lilies were the perfect reminder of funerals, not a pleasant subject considering I'd just narrowly avoided my own.

"I'm so glad you're awake." He smiled and my dad offered him the chair at my bedside where Sam had been sitting. "Chris told me you're lucky to be in one piece."

"That's what they tell me." I rubbed my wrist. My bracelet had been damaged in the accident. Chris was sending it in to have it repaired and the charm replaced, but I missed it.

"When do you go home?" Jeremy asked.

The snooper was making things awkward, hanging on every word between us. It was so obvious that he liked Jeremy and didn't like Chris. He was like a senile old caveman: orthodontist good, rock star bad.

"Tomorrow, hopefully."

Jeremy grinned at me again. "That's good news. I hope you know I'm going to call you this week about our coffee date. I can bring it to you if you're too tired."

"We'll see."

He hesitated and his eyes tried to break into mine, creepy with my dad in the room. He had to know that I wasn't on the same page. "I know you need to get your rest, so I'll get going."

Jeremy reached across to put his hand on top of mine, just as Chris walked into the room with a smile that disintegrated when he saw the placement of hands. "Hello, everyone. Jeremy." He set down some brown paper bags.

I jerked my hand away from Jeremy, but that made me look guilty for something I hadn't enjoyed. Chris shook hands with his adversary before stepping to the head of my bed to tend to me, fluffing pillows and smoothing my hair back. "How's my girl?" he asked and rested his thumb on my chin.

"Get better, Claire. I'll call you about our coffee date."

I willed my dad from the room after Jeremy was gone, but he kept reading the paper.

"I brought you some real food," Chris muttered. Like a dead-sexy magician, he produced a chicken Caesar salad and a mango smoothie. "I had them put protein powder in the smoothie."

I smiled at him and warmth rolled over me. It felt like he was the one person on the planet who really got me, who could anticipate my every want and need. "Thank you for doing that." I slurped the smoothie and looked at him with my lips pursed around the straw, only thinking about how eager I was to get home, feel better, and be alone with him.

"Anything for my beautiful patient." He promptly moved Jeremy's flowers to the other side of the room, in the corner.

That seemed to miff my dad and he rumpled the newspaper in dramatic fashion. "I'm going to get some lunch," he announced. He opened the door, but came to a halt before exiting. "Did you take care of the problem downstairs?" he asked Chris.

"Yes. It's done," Chris answered.

"Good," my dad said brusquely. "I don't want that guy within a mile of my daughter and granddaughter."

"I don't either," Chris said, his voice short. "It's taken care of."

"What problem?" I asked, after my dad left.

Chris sat on the edge of the bed. "The photographer was hanging out in the parking lot and asking the nurses questions. I paid him to go away, for good. I should've done that in the first place." He smoothed my hair back again. "You know, your dad hates me."

"He's like that with everybody, don't take it personally." I took a big bite of salad and my stomach growled in contentment. "I'm pretty sure he hates me too."

"Claire, come on. Don't kid around about this. He hates me. You heard what he said. He thinks I'm trouble." He looked out the window and folded his arms across his body, totally unlike him. He never shut himself off from me, not like that. "I should go home. He really doesn't want me here. I don't want to create problems."

I choked on my salad and took a slurp of the smoothie. "No, you can't leave. We need to get him to leave. I need you here. I want you here."

"But I don't like feeling like I'm interfering in my own girl-friend's life."

"Don't say that. I want you interfering in my life. If you hadn't been here, he never would've known about this."

"But, he's your father. He should be here. I had to tell him what happened."

"I know, and you were right to call him. You're a much nicer person than I am. I'm an insensitive brat who would've bribed Sam to keep it quiet."

———

THE NEXT MORNING, I found out exactly why my dad was so pissed at Chris the minute the car pulled up to the curb outside the hospital. Chris was driving a brand new white Volvo station wagon—this year's model and probably loaded, another example of him throwing his money around if you were to ask my dad.

The smile on Chris's face when he got out of the car was priceless, pure and proud. He bounded over to me and swiped off his sunglasses. "What do you think?" He helped me out of the wheelchair.

"I think you're in trouble." It'd likely taken him a lifetime of restraint to not buy something fancier.

He whispered in my ear as he walked me to the car, holding

me up and being careful to avoid my sore ribs. "Good trouble?"

"Definitely good." He leaned down and kissed me on the forehead after he eased me into the front seat.

My dad grumbled. "I told him to buy a used one. These new cars are a waste of money. They lose half of their value when you drive them off the lot." He and Sam sat in the back; she thumbed through the keyboard on her phone, oblivious to the hostility, all of it coming from her grandfather.

Chris smiled politely at my dad's attempt to spoil his fun. "But this model has the best airbags yet. It has a GPS, keyless drive and a blind spot detector." He looked in the rear view mirror, to address Richard. "I don't care about the value if she's safe and happy."

I couldn't keep the smile from my face. "I love it. It's beautiful. Thank you."

At home, the only break we could get from my dad was by sneaking upstairs and locking the bedroom door. I needed to cool off anyway. My dad had had the nerve to tell me that he was uncomfortable with the idea of Chris and me sleeping in the same room since we weren't married. I had no idea what he thought we'd been doing up until that point. Maybe he thought his mouthy daughter had managed an immaculate conception, not that my dad would even acknowledge that Chris had gotten me pregnant in the first place.

Chris propped me up with pillows, behind my back and under my knees, before he mercifully stretched out next to me and took my hand. I loved those moments with him the most; it was enough to make me forget my aches and pains.

"I mailed off your bracelet this morning. It'll be ready in a few weeks." He looked at my hand as he played with it. The cuts and the burns from the airbag were starting to fade.

"What are you thinking about?" I asked. He seemed preoccupied.

"Everything. There's a lot to think about. I hate to say this, but I think I have to go back home tomorrow or the next day. I have some interviews to do and I need to get caught up on bills and things at the house."

The thought of him leaving drove a pain through my chest, an awful burning. We'd been together for weeks and had just been through an insane amount of trauma—Elise's book, the baby, the accident.

"I don't want you to go, but I understand." I hung my head, depressed because my dad planned to stay for at least a week and maybe longer, depending on how I was doing.

"It won't be forever. You can fly out to see me, maybe bring Sam for a weekend after you feel well enough to travel."

"That sounds great, but—" I didn't want to bring up the dreaded subject, again.

"But what?"

"All we do is come back to the same problem. I'm just wondering how long we can sustain this. It's really hard for me to be away from you."

"Believe me, I know, but what do you want to do about it? You don't want to move and neither do I."

"I didn't say I didn't want to move, I said I didn't want to do it before Sam graduates from high school."

"And I have to be in LA. My record comes out in a few weeks and the label wants me to do a tour. That's more time apart unless you can drop everything and come on the road with me."

"You know I can't do that."

"There you go. We're back to the beginning."

We sat in silence, both of us realizing that if we wanted to be together, it would have to be at a distance. The phone would have to make up for being together and I already knew that it didn't come close.

CHAPTER FORTY-ONE

CHRIS STAYED for less than forty-eight hours. We were able to celebrate the release of the *Rolling Stone* cover story with a beer, but then he had to go the next day. There'd been so much build-up to the magazine story and it felt like the most insignificant thing in my life now.

I worked to keep a happy face while he packed up the last of his things, but it was a chore when my body felt like the life was being drained from it, again.

"I called a cab. I don't want you driving." He zipped up his second suitcase and hoisted it off the bed.

"No." My voice rang out with panic. "I'll be fine. I can drive back from the airport. I want to be with you every minute I can."

"Claire, you're being silly."

"No, I'm—"

"Shhh. It's okay." He wrapped his arm around my head and kissed my forehead. "You can come with me and I'll have the driver bring you home."

Chris took his bags downstairs while I struggled to put on my running shoes. I'd stubbornly insisted I could do it myself, but bending over was torture to my tender ribs. Just like a Kindergartener who'd finally figured it out, it took me forever to tie the laces.

When I went downstairs, the front door was wide open and I was surprised to see my dad and Chris talking by the driveway while the cabbie waited. Chris had his sunglasses on and he glanced at me when I stepped outside, his lips held in a thin line. There were no words between them when I reached the car, but the uneasiness left hanging in the air was intense—a cloud, dark enough to plunge me into the deepest parts of sadness.

We spent the first ten minutes of the car ride in silence, holding hands in the back seat. It felt so awkward to have someone in the car with us, when I just wanted to hold on to Chris and never let go. "What did my dad say?"

"He wanted to make sure I didn't change my mind about leaving."

"Don't say that. I know you think he doesn't like you, but he'll get better about it. I don't care what he thinks anyway."

"Well, I care. It's hard to imagine him ever changing his mind."

"You won't have to see him for a while. I'm hoping the same thing for myself." I smiled and leaned forward, trying to catch his eye, maybe make him happy for an instant.

"You're probably right, I won't see him any time soon."

I hated my dad for turning a hard day into a horrible one. "I'm sorry. If I could change it, I would."

We stood on the sidewalk outside the terminal without saying a thing, clinging to each other. I soaked the front of his shirt, wanting to climb inside his jacket and disappear, my tears a deluge.

"Claire, I have to go."

"I know." I could barely convince the words to leave my lips.

He placed his hands on either side of my face. "Don't be sad. You need to get better and it'll be easier if you can find a way to be happy." He placed his lips against mine, the slightest brush of his tender skin. He knew I still couldn't take a real kiss; it hurt my pudgy purple lips. "I love you."

I looked up at him, his face burning an image in my mind, to take with me. "I love you too."

"I'm serious, Claire. I really love you."

———

I LINGERED in bed the next morning, avoiding my dad and the rest of the world. Chris hadn't called last night and I'd gone to bed early, yearning for the escape of sleep.

I reached over and dragged my cell phone across the bedside table.

"Fuck!" Chris had, in fact, called, but I'd left my ringer off. I was furious with myself when I pushed the voicemail button.

"Claire, hey it's me. I just got home. Hopefully you're sleeping right now. You really need to get your rest. I, well, I didn't want to leave this on your voicemail, but maybe this is better for both of us, easier. I spent a lot of time thinking on the flight, about us. I don't see us making it through a whole year of this long-distance. It's hard on both of us and we both have so much going on in our lives."

He took a deep breath and his voice quaked. "We, um, there are so many things standing between us and you deserve better than that. We both know Jeremy wants to be with you so maybe you should try and see if you're happy with somebody who's a little more stable."

There was another pause, this one longer, and I heard him

sigh. "I don't want you to call me for a while. We need to make a clean break. I think that's best for both of us and hopefully we can still be friends after some time. That would be nice. Take care of yourself and Sam and please be careful. Okay, um, bye."

CHAPTER FORTY-TWO

THE DARK BECAME EVERYTHING, the familiar embodiment of my new life. There was hope in the dark. It meant there was still a chance that the dark would weigh me down and smother me, be the heavy hands mercifully holding the pillow to my face.

I begged my mom to come and sit with me in the dark. I needed her, I pleaded with her, but she never answered. It felt as if I was reaching for her at the bottom of a well, our fingertips would brush, but I couldn't see her. I couldn't find her voice.

Days after Chris's message, I was still in bed. I'd saved his voicemail and listened to it at least a dozen times, secretly hoping that at some point it would hurt so much that it would numb the pain. Luckily, my injuries were a good excuse to stay holed up and I had my dad to take care of Sam—feed her, stuff like that. I was too busy wishing I'd had enough sense to die in the accident.

On day four, my dad had had enough. He barged into my room and threw open the shades. "Up and at 'em, Claire. Today's the day you get out of that bed. You're never going to feel better if you sleep all day."

No wonder Sam found me so annoying on school mornings. "Dad, go away. I'm tired. I need to sleep."

"No, you don't. You're feeling sorry for yourself and I'm not going to allow it. Jeremy has called for you twice today and I think you should call him back." I hadn't planned to tell my dad that Chris and I broke up, but Sam had dragged it out of me and he'd dragged it out of her.

"Fine. I'll get up." I sat up in bed and pulled the comforter to my chin.

"No, I'm not talking about sitting up. I'm talking about getting out of bed, taking a shower, eating something, and calling Jeremy. He's going to think I don't give you your messages." He stared at me, determined. It nearly made me feel like he cared.

I started to cry again; I couldn't be awake for more than five minutes without starting again. I'd tried. I watched him as he busied himself, unable to stay still. Thirty-nine years on earth with him and I still had no idea what he was thinking or feeling.

"Dad, why do you love me?" I watched him turn as if I'd asked him to explain Quantum Physics. "I mean, other than the fact that I'm your daughter. What is it that makes you love me?" It was a trick question. I wasn't certain he loved me for any reason beyond his genetic obligation.

"Where is this coming from? Is this because of Chris? Because I don't want you to think you aren't worthy of someone's love because you got mixed up with the wrong guy." He stepped forward and sat on the bed, something he'd never done before.

"No, it's not because of Chris. This is about you and me. I don't want our relationship to be like this. It feels like a war half of the time and I'm tired of it. We should be able to get along, for real."

He crossed his legs and arms and stared off into space. Face-to-face time was difficult for my dad. I gave him credit for trying. "Well, I don't agree that we don't get along, but I'll answer your question if it'll help." He took a deep breath. "Other than the fact that you're my daughter, I love you because you're a good person and you're a great mom. I also love you because I see your mother in you. You're your own person too, but I see my Sara in there." He looked me in the eye, something he usually avoided. "There are things you do that are just like her, like the way you cluck your tongue on the roof of your mouth. It used to drive me crazy when she was alive, but I miss it." He swallowed and stared at the ceiling. "But here's the thing. I don't ever see myself when I look at you. I never have." He cleared his throat and adjusted his glasses. "I've never told anyone that, not even your mother. I know you're my daughter, but we're so different. That makes it hard for me to understand you."

My breaths became shallow. I was flabbergasted that he would share this with me. "What about Julie? Is that why you like her better?" I was so desperate to get rid of the bullshit between us that I had to keep going. Complete honesty from him might never come again.

He furrowed his brow. "I don't like her better Ladybug, it's just different. I don't have to try very hard to understand her. You're more of a challenge." He flattened a wrinkle in the quilt. "I don't want you to think that's a bad thing. Sometimes I worry about your sister. She doesn't get as much out of life as you do. Your mom got a lot out of life. She was never afraid to laugh or cry. I always admired that about her." He looked up at the ceiling again.

I watched him, thinking about my mom, part of me always wondered what drew her to him. "Do you miss her?" My tears ran freely.

"Every minute of every day. I think about her all the time." He was staring off, wistful. "Sometimes I talk to her, when I'm by myself, around the house. I'm sure I'd be sent off to the funny farm if anyone heard me." He laughed then; he usually only did that with Sam. "Look, Jellybean, I know you've had a hard time with the accident and now this Chris thing, but I really think you should give Jeremy a chance. Let him take you out for coffee. He's a nice man with a lot to offer and he's crazy about you."

He handed me a tissue, but I needed the whole box. The sadness about everything in the world that I wished I could change filled me to the brim. It was no surprise I was a human spigot.

CHAPTER FORTY-THREE

A WEEK after the dreaded coffee date, I agreed, reluctantly, to a proper date with Jeremy. Sam was waiting for me when I got out of the shower, sitting on my bed in a lime green beaded skirt with her ankles crossed, her nose in a romance.

"Are you going to help me pick out something to wear?" I asked.

"Grandpa told me to hang out while you took your shower. In case you fell or something."

It was like I was a geriatric patient. "Thanks, honey. That's nice of you." I sat next to her, tightening the tie on my mom's pink terrycloth robe that I'd dug out of my closet. "What's up tonight?"

"We're trying to get Leah together with one of Andrew's friends."

"Sounds like fun." I poked my finger through the hole in the robe pocket.

"Are you okay, Mom?" She closed her book and sat forward. She touched my arm gently.

I shut my eyes, conjuring the strength to speak without tears. "Um, well, honey, it's complicated."

"You can tell me you're sad. It's okay. I'm sad too."

I laughed, but the ache deep inside me roared. "I wish I could say I'm sad. That would be better." I swallowed and gave in to the drag I felt when I talked or thought about Chris. "I still love him and I don't understand what happened. I miss him. I miss talking to him. I feel like I lost my boyfriend and my best friend at the same time." I focused on the ceiling to keep the moisture at bay, but it was futile.

"I'm mad at him. I can't believe he would do this to you. I can't believe he would do this to us."

I realized then that I wasn't the only one hurting. "It's okay, honey. I know it doesn't make sense, but we'll get through it." I brushed her curls from the side of her face.

"What about the baby? Are you sad about that?"

I didn't know how to respond. I hadn't dealt with it, at all. It was so awful that I muffled it inside me like everything else I didn't want to think about. I took a deep breath and blew it out. "That's a hard one, much harder than I ever imagined." I took her hand. "I hope you know we weren't trying to keep a secret from you. We didn't want to say anything until we knew everything was okay with the pregnancy."

"I know. I might've freaked out a little bit, anyway. I never thought about having a little brother or sister." She managed a diminutive smile. "What about Jeremy?" Her smile faded and she wrinkled her nose.

"He's a nice guy. He's, well, it's hard to imagine anyone ever measuring up to Chris."

Jeremy was a textbook dream date at the restaurant, making a valiant attempt at romance by opening my car door and ordering for me. In the delicate light of the dining room, there was no denying that he was what my dad had called him, a looker. The dark gray suit and deep blue tie he wore made him even more so, setting off his eyes in an appealing way. I couldn't remember the last time I'd been on a date with a guy in a tie.

He was sweet enough, had a decent laugh, and was very obviously smitten with me. That had always been difficult for me to resist. We had some things in common; TV shows and books, not a lot, but enough to help when the conversation dragged. I was probably a fool for not falling madly in love with him.

Dad considered Jeremy a catch, but my mom weighed in after nearly two weeks of silence. She felt he was wrong for me; he was too buttoned up, too predictable, which I found hilarious since she'd married the King of Predictable.

After dinner, we sat in Jeremy's car in front of my house. Knowing my dad was inside made it feel so strange, a teenage déjà vu, except that I wasn't to come inside until we'd fogged up the windows.

"Thank you for dinner. It was nice to get out of the house." I said, folding my hands in my lap, unsure of what to do with myself.

"I'm glad I was finally able to take you on a real date." He turned up the radio, a very middle-of-the-road station, a song that Chris had once called bollocks. "Seeing you in that dress made the wait worthwhile."

I blushed, even though it was uncomfortable to have the attention. "Thanks."

I knew it was coming, but I still jumped when Jeremy reached over and took my hand, rubbing it softly with his thumb. Things shifted into a lower gear and I looked up to see his hazel eyes focus on me in the darkness. There was endless chatter in my head—my mom, my dad, Sam, and regrettably, Chris's voice was the loudest. It felt like he was sitting on my shoulder, whispering in my ear, his breath soft against my skin. He wasn't telling me anything he hadn't already said. I should be happy. I should take care of myself. I had no idea what those things meant anymore.

I closed my eyes when I sensed Jeremy's advance. I was too polite and defeated to do anything but play along. I turned and waited, even tilting my chin upward to make it more believable.

It wasn't at all what I expected when his lips touched mine. I was so sad, I was sure I didn't want it, but once it started, I didn't want to stop. Technically, he was a good kisser; he had all the moves down pat and put his hands in the right places. He was overzealous with his tongue, but I ignored it and the fact that there was no passion, no real warmth or tingle. It simply felt better than anything else, so I went with it to erase the pain of losing Chris, if only for a few moments.

The interrogation from my dad began the minute I came through the door. "So? How was it? Did he make his move?"

"Dad, that's none of your business." I set my bag and keys on the kitchen counter.

He studied my face. "I don't know, Ladybug. It looks like you might have been kissing him out in that car. Your face is red around your mouth."

"Isn't it past your bedtime?"

He consulted his watch, tapping the face. "So it is." He smiled, his mission sewn up for the day. "Well, I'm off to hit the hay, kiddo. Good night." He walked away, happily. I half expected him to start whistling a merry tune, perhaps befriend some butterflies and other creatures from the glen.

I went to get ready for bed, sliding the laundry basket from the bottom of my closet and crouching down to fish out some pajamas. Behind the basket, in the corner of my closet, sat a skeleton from my not-so-distant past.

A sound leaked out of me when I touched Chris's gray t-shirt, a sound so bizarre that I couldn't imagine ever claiming it as my own. I pressed the shirt against my face, the worn cotton against my cheeks, took in his still present smell. My shoulders drooped and my chest heaved. With my eyes closed, it was almost as if he was in the room with me.

I took off my dress and pulled the shirt over my head, deciding it couldn't make me any more miserable than I already was. It was too big, the hem fell to the middle of my thighs and the sleeves to my elbows. The way it pleasantly skimmed my bare skin was almost intolerable.

I climbed into bed and curled into a ball, burying my face in the t-shirt. I wished I had someone warm and tall and British and musically inclined to mold himself around me.

My body craved sleep, but my mind sought reflection and it drifted back to Chris whenever I dropped my guard. It showed a slideshow of our time together, played out of order; times when we were happy, times when we weren't, times when nothing else in the world existed but each other. The vision of his glorious face, the one engraved in my mind, stayed with me whether my eyes were open or closed. My chest burned with the pain, at odds with my heart which had frozen up to protect itself from my foolish choices.

I couldn't stand it any longer. I sat up in bed and reached for my cell phone, pressing the speed dial. He didn't answer, but I never expected him to. I only wanted to leave Chris a message like he'd left for me.

My eyes clamped shut when I heard his voice—like the undertow, it pulled me down, deep, all the way to the murky bottom. I told myself to go with it, float. Never fight the current.

"It's me. Claire. I know you said to wait a while before I called you, but I decided that you don't get to be in charge anymore." I knew for certain there was nothing left to lose. "I was calling to say that what you did really sucks. I can't believe that you'd take everything between us and throw it away. You said you loved me. We were going to have a baby. You told me that was what you wanted, more than anything."

I sucked in my breath with a pathetic gasp. "I guess I was kidding myself. Of course you'd eventually get tired of me. You're probably out with one of your little friends right now, somebody new to play with. What flavor are we going for tonight? Brunette? Redhead? A blonde would probably remind you of me. I wonder if you'll remember her name tomorrow. My guess is you won't. Anyway, I wish you'd call me back so I could call you a jerk for real, not just on your voicemail."

I felt so much better when I hung up—broken clean in two.

CHAPTER FORTY-FOUR

THERE WAS no longer any question. I was being haunted. My ghost liked to visit at night, probably because he was an opportunistic asshole and that was when I was most vulnerable. Some nights my ghost made swirling diaphanous dreams for me, full of fog and smoke and wind. They were enough to make me groan and roll my eyes, overly dramatic reenactments of events culled from a romance I would only read on vacation. Sometimes my ghost dug up the moments that had seemed insignificant at the time, void of drama and fog. Those never failed to wake me—to a wet face and soaked pillow, gasping for air.

It didn't help that the physical evidence of my ghost was everywhere. Dealing with the things he left behind in my brain was hard enough. I avoided driving my new car at all costs. It was a totem of my misery, complete with leather interior and a killer stereo system. It never would have wound up in my driveway if there'd been no accident. I wouldn't have lost the baby. I wouldn't have lost Chris. I couldn't bear to be in the car at all so I walked or rode my bike everywhere. Sometimes I didn't go anywhere.

Then there was the *Rolling Stone* story, which I spent hours a day touting to editors, to dig up new work so I could move forward. It meant thinking of him every time I talked about it. It meant looking at his face on the cover every time I sent someone a copy. It meant remembering what led up to it, which was everything that had happened between us.

My dad was still staying with us and it'd been nearly a month. Every day, I'd drop several hints about how he must be missing his own bed. It wasn't like he was being difficult. Since we'd had our talk, he'd been much better and as long as I pretended to like Jeremy, he was pleasant. I was simply ready for things to get back to normal—Sam and me.

Jeremy was another matter. My feelings for him were tepid at best. He was my chocolate Easter bunny—glossy and mouth-watering on the outside, the shell collapsing when I took a bite, and not even very good chocolate in the first place.

He came over every night unless he had his daughter, which wasn't often. We did everything on a schedule and the night he forced the issue was the same. Dinner was at six, we watched a movie around seven, and he was all over me by nine-thirty, right after my dad went to bed.

"Your hair smells awesome," he said. "New shampoo?" He flipped it to the side and kissed my neck, eager but without finesse. I stared at the ceiling to avoid the cloud of his cologne. His hands clamored under the back of my top and to the clasp of my bra. The instant that was undone, he moved to the front and moaned, loudly.

"Shhh. My dad will hear us," I pleaded. I kissed him back to get him to shut up, never seeking any part of him other than his lips.

"Your dad's dead asleep. I can already hear him snoring." He began to lift up my top and I pushed it down.

"Don't. Sam might come home." I kept my eyes closed.

He returned to my neck, lapping at my skin. "Then let me

take you upstairs and we can finally do this." He reached under my top again. His hands were doughy for someone who was in such good shape.

I stopped kissing him. "I don't feel like it. I'm tired."

He rolled his eyes and released his grip on me. "Come on, Claire. I feel like a damn teenager. You never let me get past second base."

"I'm sorry. I'm not ready."

"You're driving me crazy. I want you." He took my hand and kissed the back of it. He circled his tongue, batting his dark eyelashes. "Let me take you upstairs and take off your clothes." He flipped over my hand and pressed his lips to my palm. He licked it from the heel to the base of my fingers. "Let me make you feel good."

I tried to contain it, but I couldn't help it. I burst out laughing. It felt like a golden retriever was trying to get me into bed.

"What's so damn funny?"

"Nothing," I tittered. "I'm sorry." I pursed my lips, forcing a serious expression on my face.

"This is ridiculous." He dropped my hand. "Fucking British asshole. He breaks your heart and I get to pick up the pieces."

I moved back and reached behind to re-hook my bra. "It's not about Chris," I lied. "I'm tired."

"You know what? I didn't want to have to say this, but somebody has to. What you had with the rock star wasn't reality. It wasn't real. You know what's real? Me. I'm real. We could be real. But you have to let me in."

My eyelids became heavy and thoughts raced in my head before crashing into each other. *No, you're wrong, Chris was real. He really did love me, at least for a while. I really loved him. I still love him, even though it's killing me.*

"I think you should leave," I muttered.

"If you tell me to leave, I might not come back."

"I know."

Seconds later, car keys jingled and the door slammed.

———

THE PACKAGE that arrived in the mail the next day came as a complete surprise. When I saw the small box and the outline of unmistakable blue on the mailing label, my heart plunged to my stomach. Rosie waved from her front yard as the sky rumbled and threatened to open up and I waved back, distracted, praying that she wouldn't want to come over and talk.

I paced in the kitchen while the box sat on the counter like a neatly packaged bomb. I was terrified to touch it, but I couldn't leave it there or someone would get hurt.

I thought about forwarding it to him, unopened. That would've been a good way to call him an asshole. I could've written "You're an asshole" on the outside of the box if I was worried it was too ambiguous. I considered putting it in a closet and waiting until I felt ready to look at it or stumbled across it when searching for extra towels.

I chose a third option: open it, look at it, feel sad, and send it back to him—the best of all worlds. I carefully cut through the clear packing tape, opened the flaps and the Tiffany blue teased me. The memory of the night he gave it to me flooded my brain. I tried to focus on what a lovely color it was rather than the fact that I had spent my entire existence as a girl wishing for a box in that particular shade.

I held in my tears, trying to be a brave soldier, like that would ever work. I lifted the lid and slowly removed the white cotton fluff and it took my breath away, like the first time. My hand covered my gaping mouth and it was too beautiful to not pick up, to hold one last time.

Its weight surprised me again, the cool, smooth links against my fingers. I felt my insides cave at the thought of what it all meant. The bracelet was mine. I could keep it. I could think of it as a piece of jewelry and nothing more. But that would mean giving up on what it once symbolized and my heart wasn't there yet. There was an excellent chance that it would never be there.

The charm flipped over when I moved it in my hand, and it caught my eye—the inscription was different, longer. I looked away before I read it, thinking that someone had made a mistake, they'd sent the wrong bracelet. When I turned back, I knew the shipping department at Tiffany & Co., New York, NY still had their act together. *For Claire, with my undying love, Chris.*

CHAPTER FORTY-FIVE

THE PHOTOS and magnets went everywhere. It was the strangest feeling—my legs had never given out from under me before, but the tonnage that accompanied the inscription was too much for my body to bear. I sagged against the pebbly white surface of the fridge and swept it clean on the way down, landing in a messy heap on the kitchen floor.

Clutching the bracelet, my head between shaking knees, I wept for what felt like the one-millionth time. No wonder I was so tired. My misery was about more than losing him; I missed the parts of me that he took with him, everything I'd never get back. Things like the tiny new sliver of me that was capable of being carefree. That was something that only he'd been able to cultivate. That would be missed.

My shoulders twitched, forward and back, as I struggled with the air and my lips buckled. It was hard to fathom a moment in time, years from now, when I would be okay with all of it, able to accept that sometimes things don't work out.

The sound of the doorknob sent me into a panic. I scrambled to my knees, picking up photos, old grocery lists, and magnets from the places Sam and I had been together. She and

Dad were deep in conversation with arms full of rustling brown grocery bags.

The scene was far too chaotic for me to hide. The boxes and packaging littered the kitchen counter, I'd only managed to put up a handful of the things from the front of the fridge, and then there was me—a sniffling, blubbering disaster.

Sam rushed to me, nearly throwing her bags to the floor, but Dad stood back, frozen.

"Oh my God, Mom. Are you okay?" She grabbed paper towels and handed them to me, to sop up the tears. She pulled me into a hug and I dropped my forehead against her shoulder and clung to her—the person in the world I loved most, who also loved me back. "Mom, it's okay. We're here. Take a deep breath." She gave me another minute. "Tell me what's wrong."

My dad moved closer, but he still kept his distance. My shoulders calmed and my heartbeat returned to its static rhythm until I lifted my head and looked at Sam, her head tilting to the side in pity.

"Um, my bracelet came today, from Tiffany." I sniffled. "Chris had, he, he changed the inscription on the charm."

Sam pried it from my grasp. She read it and looked back at my dad. "Grandpa, here. You should see this."

He was hesitant to take it. I was thinking his reaction to all of this was only half normal. The other half was something else. He flipped over the charm and looked away. Tears swelled when he turned back.

"Jellybean, I may have made a mistake." He trembled.

My focus narrowed. "I don't understand."

He didn't answer at first. He folded his hands in front of him, as if he was standing before the judge, and a heavy sigh left his lips. "Christopher and I had some problems while he was here. We, uh, we got into several heated talks." He swallowed. "I want to say in my defense, that I was only doing what I thought was best for you. I couldn't watch you make the same mistakes you always make, especially after the accident. You choose these men. Why are they always musicians?"

"Dad. They aren't always musicians."

"Well, you know the type. It's painful to watch. It was so obvious it wasn't going to work. Just like every other guy you've dated." The room was dead quiet other than his voice. "When he left to go home, I told him that I wanted him to stay away from you, to cut things off completely. If he really loved you, he would stay away and let you have a normal life."

My brain began to churn this revelation and how it played into everything that happened.

"Grandpa, that totally sucks. Mom loves Chris. *I* love Chris." She started to tear up and I felt her shake. "How could you do this? Can't you see how miserable she is?" Sam held me, by the shoulders. "Mom, say something. Tell him how miserable you are."

"I don't even know what to say." I held the mascara smeared paper towels in my iron grip.

"I'm sorry, Ladybug. I was trying to protect you."

"From what? I love him." My whole body quaked. "I thought you wanted me to fall in love and be happy and give Sam a father figure. I thought you didn't want me to turn into a cat lady. Why would you do this?" I felt my face become hotter with every word. "What kind of person does this to their own daughter?"

His eyes were huge, his mouth agape.

"Mom?" Sam cleared her throat and wiped the tears away from her cheek. "Don't get mad, but this is kind of the same thing you and Chris did to me with Jean-Luc." I watched her as she spoke and it was all a frame or two behind. I saw the expression in her eyes, the one my mom always had when she knew she was right. "I mean, you should still be totally mad at Grandpa, but I think I get why he did it."

"I also—" Now he wouldn't look at me, his eyes darting around the room. "I happened to overhear you two talking about your long-distance situation and well, I need you nearby and I don't want to miss out on my last year with Sam before she goes off to college."

"Dad, the only way you could've heard that was if you were listening at my bedroom door."

"The heat register in the hallway was stuck and I was trying to fix it."

I rolled my eyes and threw my hands up in the air. "Oh, my God. Dad, you're so full of it. You have to stop with the snooping."

"I really am sorry. Is there any way I can make it up to you? Do you want me to put up the shelves we talked about in the laundry room?"

"No, I don't want you to put up shelves in the laundry room. I want you to start making it up to me by staying here with Sam."

Her eyes lit up.

"Are you going somewhere?" he asked.

Sam clapped her hands silently and smiled at me. "She's going to LA, Grandpa."

"But, your birthday," he said.

"That's the last thing I care about right now."

"I see." He seemed both resigned and annoyed.

Upstairs, I packed by throwing anything clean in the suitcase. There was a soft knock and my dad peered around the door, pushing it open.

"I can't talk to you right now. I'm packing." I stormed into my bathroom and grabbed toothpaste and shampoo, stuffing them into my toiletry bag.

"Ladybug, I can't let you go until we talk."

"I really don't feel like dealing with this. We can talk when I get back."

"No." He cleared his throat. "We have to talk. Now."

I stopped dead in my tracks. My dad was the guy who avoided confrontation at all costs. "I understand why you did what you did, okay? I'm still furious with you." I turned to him.

"I know." His voice cracked and I could see the pain in his eyes. "But, I didn't say everything. There's something else." He took a deep breath. "When I watched you in that hospital bed, well, I'm not afraid to admit it, I panicked. I saw your mother. I was so thankful when you woke up and the doctors said you'd be fine. But then Christopher was there and I couldn't bear the thought of losing you to him."

I shut my eyes. "Dad, it's not like you would've lost me to him. I'm always going to be your daughter."

"I know that, Jellybean. But sometimes I feel like you and Sam are all I have left on this earth. Your sister keeps her distance because I drive her crazy. I know I drive you crazy too, but you find a way to put up with it. Don't think that I don't know the sacrifice you made by coming to North Carolina to be closer to me. Your sister wasn't willing to do that." His voice began to waver again. "That's the sort of thing your mother would've done."

I swallowed, his words working into me. I'd always thought of myself as a disappointment because I'd screwed up so many times in my life. I got pregnant in college and never got married, but I had managed to give him a granddaughter he loved more than anything. I was cranky with him most of the time, but he still wanted to visit, he didn't want me to go. He loved me. He just wasn't very good at showing it. I loved him too and I wasn't doing much better.

"Thank you, Daddy. That means a lot."

He stepped closer and wiped a tear from my cheek. "So you really love him?"

I blew out a breath. "More than you can imagine."

He gave me a hug and held on to me. "I just want you to be happy. That's all I've ever wanted."

CHAPTER FORTY-SIX

WITH THE EXCEPTION of my high school locker combination, I've always had an awesome memory for numbers—phone numbers, prices, and hopefully, security codes.

"5-3-7-2-6," I mumbled to myself and closed my eyes when I pushed the pound key. The gate creaked when it started to roll across the driveway. My heart hammered against my chest. *This is crazy.*

It felt as though I stood there forever after I rang the bell and I worried about what Chris was doing or with whom he might be as I kicked a stray pebble from the entryway. I rang the bell a second time and it occurred to me that anyone who got to the front door had to know the number for the gate. If the system worked the way it was supposed to, Chris didn't have to contend with Girl Scouts. Maybe he wouldn't answer the door at all. Maybe he'd just call the police.

I began re-thinking my plan, but then I heard the door latch and my heart resumed its frantic pace, forcing adrenaline through my veins. The door opened and we both stood there, staring at each other. All I could hear was my own heartbeat, throbbing in my ears. He looked surprised to see me, but I was in shock. Chris had shaved off his incredible head of hair.

I scanned his face and settled on the green, flat and dead. I felt as if my legs could collapse and each breath came with a piercing sensation through my chest. He stepped aside and held the door open, without a word.

"Thanks." I parked my suitcase right inside the entry, now worried that it looked like I'd presumed where I might be staying for the night.

My horror at the sight of his naked head was pushed aside by a new image, much like the path of destruction left by a tornado. There was a heap of mail on the foyer table, magazines and bills spilling onto the floor. Rows of books were splayed out on the white shag below empty shelves. Someone had apparently taken their hand and relocated them in several fell swoops. Dust bunnies congregated on the concrete floor, the throw pillows were everywhere, and there were a dozen or more empty beer bottles on the coffee table.

He'd taken down all of his favorite pieces of art and propped them against the wall, facing away. The room was depressing and dark, the massive windows hidden behind heavy black curtains. I never even knew he had curtains.

"This is a surprise. What are you doing here?" His voice was weak and gloomy.

"You didn't return my phone calls and I needed to talk to you."

He looked down again, at the filthy floor, and crossed his arms across his stomach, pointy elbows jutting. "I forgot to charge my cell phone. Don't take it personally." He made eye contact and it felt as though someone with big fat hands was choking me. "I would've called you back eventually."

He was a shadow of the man I knew; ghastly with somber half-moons under his eyes and a greenish-gray cast to all of him.

His cheekbones, normally the crowning touch of his ideal face, were so pronounced that it looked as if they might rub holes through his skin. I desperately missed his hair and his scraggly attempt at a beard was no substitute.

I was beyond uncomfortable, my mind racing and fighting to make sense of it all. *This isn't how this is supposed to go.* I wanted to jump into his arms and fix everything. Instead, it felt as though he didn't want me anywhere near him.

"I don't want to intrude." I choked at the thought.

"No. It's fine. Can I get you something?"

"Um." I swallowed. "Water?"

He shuffled off to the kitchen and I followed.

The sink held a dozen dirty glasses but no plates or silverware and there was no sign that anyone had cooked recently.

"Did you have a party?" I asked, feeling muzzy headed.

He handed me a bottle of water and I saw that except for many beers, there was nothing but a dried-up orange in the fridge. "No."

"When is Helena coming?" I set my hand on the counter, not that I was relaxed at all, but jerked it back when it landed in something sticky.

"I fired her. She's so bloody nosy. I don't need her anyway. The house practically cleans itself."

"Um, I think you need to get her back. The house could use some help." I shook my head and washed my hands at the sink, wiping them dry on my jeans. The lone kitchen towel emitted a foul stench.

"Maybe." He slumped at the kitchen table and brushed crumbs to the floor. "Why are you here?"

The question was seemingly innocent, but enough to bring a sting to my eyes. I trembled, willing myself to hold back the tears. "I'm here because my dad told me what he said to you and I couldn't stand the thought of you thinking any of it was true." I sat at the table and reached across for his hand, which he promptly pulled away before staring into his lap. His t-shirt was hanging on him and all I could think was that he was going to fade away if he didn't eat something. "When was the last time you ate?"

This time his eyes bore into me. "I don't know. I lose track of time."

I decided that we were never going to be able to discuss anything important with him in this state. "Let me make you something to eat." I was going to cook whether or not he wanted it; at least it would mask some of the stale smell in the house. I walked to the freezer and dug past bacon to find frozen chicken breasts and a bag of stir-fry veggies. "Brown rice will take forty minutes. Why don't you take a shower and put on some clean clothes?"

"I don't need you to be my mother."

I'd never heard him sound more annoyed and his bizarre show of stubbornness was already getting old. *Why can't he see that I'm trying to help him?* "Good, because I didn't come here to be your mother. Now go take a shower. You stink."

After starting dinner, I took a few minutes to clean the kitchen table and counter, but the rest of it could wait. Drawing back every curtain, I opened the massive doors out to the terrace. The breeze was light and I stepped outside for a much needed dose of smoggy LA air. I was completely lost, no idea what I was doing, where I was going to sleep, or what was going to happen. *Why is he being such a jerk?*

Chris came out on the balcony, showered, and wearing shorts and a t-shirt that looked clean although they were very wrinkly, like they'd been stuffed in a drawer. "Better?" he asked grumpily.

"Yes, better." I smiled. "Dinner will be ready in a few minutes."

We sat at the kitchen table and although he started tentatively, he was soon shoveling. I relished that moment of normalcy and felt a wave a relief. Unfortunately, that left me unable to stomach the thought of launching back into everything that needed to be said.

Ease into it. "What have you been doing for the past few weeks? How did your interviews go?" I asked, as if nothing was wrong.

He took a drink of water, but didn't look at me. "I cancelled everything. If anyone wants to know something, they can read your story."

My shoulders dropped. "What about taking your chance to get back at Elise? And you should be plugging the new record. It comes out next week."

"I had to let the Elise thing go. The more I participate, the more I'm just prolonging it," he said, easily the smartest thing out of his mouth since my arrival. "I have no confidence in the new record. I'd rather not talk about it."

"But that's giving up on something you worked so hard on. I can't believe you'd do that."

He took his last bite of food. "It's not a priority anymore." He pushed his plate away. "How long are you in town?"

"As long as it takes to fix things between us."

He looked right through me. "That's a long time."

My hands shook and I hid them under the table. "Why would you say that? This has been a big misunderstanding." I stopped when I saw his expression, stony and cold. *It's like he isn't even listening to me.* I knew I should tell him everything about my dad, but my head felt like it was bursting at the seams.

"Where are you staying?" He seemed annoyed, again.

"I was hoping I could stay here. I didn't book anything. I just went to the airport and got on a plane." My voice grew softer, now unsure of everything I did or said. When he did things like hop on a plane, he was being bold. When I did it, I was being desperate.

He tossed his napkin on his plate and stretched his arms above his head, a habit of his that I'd always adored. "You could stay in the guest room. I suppose I owe you that much."

I watched as he set his hands on his stomach. I felt exhausted and like I might say something worth regretting. "Why are you being like this?"

"Being like what, exactly?"

"You're so grumpy. And you aren't even listening to me."

"I'm a grumpy guy. You never knew the real me."

"That's not true. We were happy. Together."

"Happiness is temporary. It never lasts."

My eyes stung. "Don't say that. How are we supposed to work things out if you're like this?"

His eyes darted in my direction and then he laughed, under his breath. "Give it a rest, Claire. You're a smart girl. There's nothing to work out."

CHAPTER FORTY-SEVEN

IT TOOK me hours to fall asleep that night and not merely because of everything weighing down my mind. I knew how wonderful it was to sleep in Chris's bed with him—one of the best experiences I'd ever had sat waiting in the other room and yet there I was, down the hall, alone and missing him.

Day one hadn't gone down as planned. I'd foolishly thought everything would be simple—waltz in and tell Chris what my dad had said and everything would be back to the way it used to be. Now, bringing us back together felt hopelessly complicated, like a puzzle that had too many pieces. After all, even if that were straightened out, we would still have our old obstacles, baby and location at the top of that list.

I went for a run first thing to clear the clutter in my brain. Chris was still in his room when I left the house. It killed me to stand in that hallway and look at his closed bedroom door knowing that I was no longer entitled to enter without knocking.

He was up when I returned, sitting at the kitchen table.

"You found the coffee," I said, noticing that he'd closed the curtains while I was gone.

He didn't turn. "Yes. Thank you."

"Of course." I chugged a second glass of water. *Let's see how this goes over today.* "Can I make you something to eat?"

He turned, his eyes showing a trace of life, but only a fraction of their former brilliance. "You don't have to take care of me. You're not my girlfriend anymore."

It hurt like someone was crumpling me into a ball. "I want to take care of you. You used to like it when I made you breakfast." After some frustratingly awkward eye contact, a sliver of me felt like telling him to fuck off, but I kept it together.

"Let's see," I mumbled, digging deep in the freezer for anything suitable. That was a bust so I retreated to the pantry and returned victorious with pancake mix. "Pancakes and bacon?" I asked.

"Fine."

"I'm surprised I didn't find you in the pool this morning." I thawed the bacon in the microwave and measured the mix into a bowl, making small talk to fill the leaky chasm between us.

"I haven't been swimming."

I closed the box of pancake mix and shook my head. "But that's your thing. I thought you'd want to get back to it after spending weeks without a pool."

"I haven't felt like it."

"You should go get in." I took the butter from the refrigerator. "Go. I'll have breakfast ready when you're done. You'll feel better."

"I don't want to."

"Humor me. Try a few laps." I felt his eyes on me when I pulled out the griddle pan, but had no clue what he was thinking.

"Fine. I'll humor you for pancakes." He left and I resisted the urge to call him a good boy for listening.

I opened the curtains as soon as he was gone. Minutes

later, there was a splash. I crept out onto the terrace, but stood right outside the glass door. I didn't dare move closer to the railing.

He was beautiful skimming through the water, heartbreakingly perfect. I was still getting used to him without hair and it bothered me to see him so skinny, but he was otherwise as he used to be, at least on the outside. I remembered the way I'd felt the first time I'd watched him in the pool, when it felt too good to be true and love was taking hold, before everything came crashing down around us.

On my way back to the kitchen, I grabbed the stale smelling beer bottles in the living room. With my arms full, I poked my finger into the neck of the last bottle and noticed a paper square with familiar handwriting, stuck to the bottom. I peeled it off once I'd slipped the bottles into the recycling bin in the utility room off the kitchen. Seeing the photo of Chris and his father was different the second time, perhaps because it was accompanied by the image of Chris downing bottle after bottle of beer. I couldn't be sure that was how it had happened, but it wasn't hard to imagine.

I heard the slide of the terrace door and took the photo to the kitchen, setting it on the counter. Chris walked in with droplets of water on his collarbone and a towel around his waist. His pull on me was commanding, but the barrier between us, the force field he used to protect himself from me, felt impenetrable.

"Do I have time to shower before we eat?" The flush in his cheeks had returned.

"Sure. I still need to make the pancakes." It was torture to watch him walk away. I wanted so desperately to sneak up behind him, take his hand, and have him walk me down the hall to his room. I longed for it to be like it used to be.

He downed a huge breakfast when he returned, much more

like the old Chris, and had a hint of a grin on his face when he finished. "Thank you. I feel better."

"Good. That makes me happy." I cracked a smile and raised my eyebrows, hoping he would take that as an invitation to talk. *Do I really have to be the one to start this conversation again?*

He looked at me seeming puzzled, and then abruptly got up and put his plate in the sink. "I'm working on something in my music room." He walked away, not even glancing at me.

I set my fingertips to my lips, as if I could keep all of the questions and unhappiness inside me. It didn't seem possible that he could be so oblivious to my feelings.

I took my shower in complete confusion, feeling like a coward. *Why can't I ask him what in the hell is going on in that head of his? Why can't I just say everything I need to say? It's not like things could get any worse.*

My wardrobe was its own hurdle. I wanted to look good, to remind him of what he was missing. I dug through my suitcase and at the bottom was the Tiffany box. I shoved the clothes back on top of it. The bracelet was the least of my worries.

I walked out of the guestroom and saw that Chris's bedroom door was open. Curiosity had me in its clutches. I wanted to see if he'd done to his bedroom what he'd done to the rest of the house. I called out his name and when there was no answer, I crept ahead, but stopped after only a few steps. The extra bedroom was right there, the door closed, as always.

My heart thundered in my chest as I turned the knob and crossed the threshold. I'd never looked inside before. There was no furniture, no lamp in the corner of the room; it was even quieter than the rest of the house if that was possible. I turned and the pale green walls were a slow blur as it dawned on me whose room it was.

We can make the room next to the master bedroom into the nursery.

Everything he'd said the day we talked about where to live, the day he was so excited about everything ahead of us, was there in my head. This was our baby's room. *Our baby*. If my foot hadn't slipped off the brake, my belly would be swollen and full of life right now. We'd be together, talking about cribs and rocking chairs, having the discussions I never had when I was pregnant with Sam because I'd been alone.

I continued to turn but I listed, and caught sight of something through the cracked closet door. There were three worn hardcover books on the shelf. I opened the cover of *Horseshoes and Handlebars* by M.E. Atkinson and inside it read: *For Christopher on his 8th birthday*, in the same lovely script from the back of the photograph of Chris and his dad. At the bottom of the page, written in pencil, was: *Property of Christopher Penman* in a young boy's imperfect handwriting, with an adorable mix of capitals and lower case. The tears I'd been fighting for minutes rolled down my cheeks. I closed the book and held it to my forehead. I couldn't bear to look at the others.

I needed a project, something to keep my mind occupied. Otherwise, I was on the brink of collapsing into an all-too familiar heap of misery. My mom popped into my head and gave me the perfect idea—food. Chris was actually nice to me for five minutes after I'd cooked for him. I brought my purse into the kitchen and found a piece of paper to make a list.

The photograph of Chris and his dad was waiting on the counter and I propped it up against the gray and white glass tile backsplash. I felt like Chris's dad and I were getting to know each other. He had deep soulful eyes and the same smirk as Chris. Perhaps he and my mom could become acquainted some day.

Logically, I went to the fridge to take inventory, but closed the door when I remembered that the only thing he had was beer. I tapped the pen against my temple, recalling his favorites:

meat, potatoes, and cheese. Some veggies would have to sneak in somewhere, for my own sanity and digestion.

A muffled version of an unknown song rang from the depths of my bag and I jumped. Sam was constantly changing my ring tone so I was often surprised by the sound of my own phone.

"Hello?"

"Claire, it's me."

"Hey, what's up?" I'd relaxed my attitude toward Kevin since he'd stopped calling me by his asinine pet names. He must've found a new girlfriend or even better, a therapist.

"Hey, I'm glad I caught you. I just spoke to Laura Simmons at *Vanity Fair*. She asked me about you. She loved the Penman piece and she wants to meet you. Call her. She's in LA right now but I think she was hoping you'd fly up to New York next week."

I bit my lip and my heart plucked an erratic rhythm. "*Vanity Fair*? Seriously?"

"Yes, seriously. I would not kid about this."

"I'm actually in LA right now."

He laughed. I was glad there was a man somewhere that still found me amusing. "Of course you are. Thanks for calling, by the way. Seeing your boy toy?" Kevin always had the perfect way of putting things, annoying or not. That was what made him such a good writer.

"Something like that."

When I finished talking to Kevin, I called Laura right away. When I got off the phone with her, it took everything in me to keep from screaming.

"Holy shit."

CHAPTER FORTY-EIGHT

"HAVE you lost your bloody mind, Claire? You take my car, the Nine-eleven no less, without asking?"

I switched the phone to my other ear and dropped some green beans in one of those grocery store produce bags that take some secret talent to open. "I left you a note."

"You're the last person I want driving that car."

I realized I was blocking the aisle and the woman behind me wasn't happy so I waved her around me. She stormed past with her cart as if I'd told her she could stand to lose a few. "I'm doing your grocery shopping," I said quietly, through my teeth, stopping short of tacking "asshole" on at the end. "I'll be back soon. You can hold me personally responsible if anything happens to your precious car."

"But, Claire—"

"I'm hanging up now."

He was waiting when I got back to the house, looming in the open doorway before he came out to the garage. "Let me help you with the bags."

"That's very generous of you," I snipped.

"Don't be such a bitch. I can't believe you took my car, this car. Why didn't you take the SUV? At least you know how to drive that. You could've hurt someone or yourself."

It'd been nothing more than a bratty impulse that made me take the Porsche to the grocery store. I knew it would drive him crazy. "I couldn't find the keys for the Mercedes."

"They were hanging with the other keys." He huffed. "Hand me that other bag."

I was ready to whack him in the head with that other bag. "I had to do the grocery shopping. You have no food in your house. You're practically wasting away."

"Now you sound like my bloody mum again."

I stared at him and ran meditative thoughts through my head. *Breathe. Bite your tongue. It's time to be a grown up. Go to your happy place, Claire.* "And you sound like a bloody jerk."

We unpacked and put the groceries away, coated in silence.

"Look, I need to stay in LA for two more nights, I'm meeting with a *Vanity Fair* editor tomorrow."

"About an assignment?"

"Yes, they liked the *Rolling Stone* piece." Inside, I was thrilled by the idea. Unfortunately, it meant two more days of beating my head against a wall and tomorrow was a big day—my fortieth birthday.

"That's great. For you."

I squinted at his way of putting things. "I need you to tell me if you want me to check into a hotel. I can't be around you unless we talk."

He waited. "Fine then, let's talk." He shoved his hands in his pockets and looked at me with eyes that could only be described as hurt. "What exactly do you want to talk about, Claire? Do you want to talk about the car accident first or should we start with the baby?"

I stared, feeling frozen by his tone.

"Let's start with the baby, since that's such a special part of our tragic story," he choked on his bitter words and sat at the kitchen table, looking tired. "I was so excited when we found out you were pregnant." He rubbed his forehead and his voice became painfully quiet. "I felt like everything was perfect. I had you and we were going to do this amazing thing together. I honestly felt like I had everything I ever wanted. It was such a nightmare when the police came to the door that afternoon. All I could think was that it was my fault, that I should have driven you."

He drew in a deep harrowing breath and continued. "I was devastated when I got to the hospital and found out we'd lost the baby, but I couldn't even be sad because I was so worried about you. It didn't matter. I was such a git to get excited about it in the first place. It was so obvious you didn't want to have a baby with me. That really hurt a lot, Claire. I don't think you know how hurtful you can be sometimes." His voice trailed off and the damage I'd done sat staring me in the face.

He went on, "Blooming Jeremy was everywhere. The guy would not go away. I figured that I should let you two be together and go back to being a bachelor. There's no reason to be with someone else if I'm never going to be a dad. It's easier."

I stood, my hands at my side, part of me felt destroyed and the rest was confused. "So you want things to be easier? Is that what this is about?"

"In a way, yes. And not just for me, I was making your life much more complicated than it should be."

I closed my eyes and tried to suck in the tears. "But, I love you. I don't care about things being complicated. I don't care about stupid Jeremy. Nothing else matters."

"You don't understand," he said, his voice still hushed. "It's never going to work if we aren't willing to give the other person what they need. I learned that with Elise." He crossed his arms over his chest, writing volumes with body language. "You're so stubborn about everything. We were never going to work things out. It was an exercise in futility."

"Stubborn?" I asked. "You're just as stubborn as I am, but you think you aren't, which is even worse. You want to control everything and then things happen that you can't control and it's too much for you to take." I gripped the back of my neck, the tension exploding in my body. "Losing the baby hurt me too and you're a jerk if you think that isn't the truth. I admit it. I wasn't happy about the pregnancy at first, but that's only because I know what it takes to raise a child. I had no idea if you planned to stick around. You hadn't even told me you loved me yet."

"Why are you always reminding me that you're a parent and I'm not? Like I'm stupid for wanting to be a dad because I don't know how much work it is? And even if you were sad about the miscarriage, you wouldn't even talk about it with me."

"Why should I have a baby with you when you aren't willing to budge on where we live? I had no idea if you were going to be around in a month or six months, or a year."

"Why didn't you ask me if I planned to be around?" His stare was intense, but then he let it drop. "Because I did."

The word "did" made part of me evaporate. "What was I supposed to do? Ask you if you wanted to get married?" I whispered, sadness invading like an incurable virus. "You know I'm not that girl. I didn't want things to happen like that."

I studied his face and my heart crumbled to dust. That was all it could do. It had already shattered.

CHAPTER FORTY-NINE

I SOUGHT SOLACE IN SAM, someone to listen to me feel sorry for myself. Plus, I missed her, desperately. I only wanted to go home.

"Mom, I can't believe you aren't coming home for your birthday."

"I'd be getting on the next plane if it wasn't for this lunch appointment tomorrow."

"I still don't understand what's going on. Are you and Chris going to make up?" Her voice was unsettled.

I was determined to ward off the waterworks. It'd been forever since I'd gone for a whole day without blubbering, but I had to try. "I don't think so, honey."

"Did you tell him that Grandpa's sorry he said those things?"

"I tried to, but he didn't listen," I said, choking on air. "He kept changing the subject."

"That's not fair. He should listen to you."

"Yeah, well, it doesn't work like that." The sun was beginning to set outside the guestroom window, the sky blushing in brilliance. "I should let you go, honey. I'll call you tomorrow."

"No way, Mom. We aren't finished. I don't get why you're being like this. You're giving up."

"What do you mean? I've tried. It's Chris who's giving up."

"Well, I don't get to say this to Chris, so I'm saying it to you. I think you need to try harder." Every pep talk I'd ever given was being dished right back to me.

"I'm not sure there's anything left to do."

"Promise you'll try. There must be something." She sniffled on the other end of the line. "Love you."

"I love you too, honey."

It was nearly dinnertime and my stomach rumbled, without a thing to eat since bacon and pancakes. I thought the smell of food would lure him upstairs, but I was wrong and was forced to look for him when dinner was ready.

"Hi," he said, answering the door to the music room as if things were the way they used to be.

"I made dinner. Come and eat."

"I'll be up in a minute."

Back upstairs, I filled my wine glass and took a healthy slug so it looked less like I was hell-bent on getting drunk. I then set the table, anxious about the potentially miserable act of sharing a meal with him.

Two plates of pasta and salad sat on the table while I waited.

"You should've started without me," he said, finally showing up. "I was finishing something downstairs."

"I thought we should eat together." I wanted to follow Sam's directive, although I doubted my ability.

He picked up his fork and looked at me. "Good. Can we be civilized? For one meal?"

"I can do that," I replied, disintegrating inside.

He lifted his glass. "Cheers."

I reciprocated with the niceties and downed more of my

wine, embracing the burn that followed the swallow. I sneaked a look at him when I set my glass down. Now that he was eating and exercising, the color in his face had returned.

"Tell me about you and Jeremy."

My mouth opened, but not to eat. A bite of pasta sat on my fork in mid-air. "There's nothing to tell," I answered, returning the food to my plate. "He asked me out and he's a nice guy, but there's nothing there. Zip."

He studied me before returning to his dinner. "That's too bad."

The number of times I'd bit my tongue today was in the dozens—it was like spending the day with my dad. "Not really. He knows that I'm in love with someone else."

"Did you sleep with him?" He wiped his mouth with the napkin.

My eyes jerked wide. "Excuse me? I don't think you get to ask me that."

"Calm down. I'm just curious."

I stared at him, angry on the outside and happy on the inside. At least he cared enough to ask. "No, I didn't, but he wanted to," I answered, taking my inner brat out for a spin. "He practically begged me."

He frowned and a collapse was triggered. The whole world faded away and the memory rolled in like fog. The night in St. Barts with Graham and Angie seeped into my mind, when he frowned at me when he was drunk.

I lost control, everything becoming inky with pain. "I can't do this." I watched as he became transfixed. "I love you, more than I've loved anybody, and the guy who's in second place isn't even close." I wiped my tears with the back of both hands and my mom came to mind, how she was never afraid to show the parts of her that were raw. "I thought I knew you. I thought we had something real." I finished my wine in a reckless gulp. "I think you're a big idiot for wanting things to be perfect and for thinking that we can't compromise, but mostly for not loving me anymore."

I set my head in my hands, wishing for a fragment of my dignity, weeping quietly over the remnants of my dinner.

"Claire, I never said I didn't love you anymore." His words sounded as if they were floating out of him. "What we had was real, but it didn't work out, okay? You're torturing both of us by rehashing everything."

I lifted my head from my hands, mascara smudged on the heels. "And you're torturing me by letting every dumb thing stand in our way."

CHAPTER FIFTY

THE ALARM SCREECHED. Bolting upright, I scrambled to make sense of why the clock was so absurdly loud. My hand slapped around the bedside table to silence it, I felt the button under my fingers, but the cycling squeal persisted. I fumbled and turned the switch on the lamp just as the sound stopped.

I clutched the covers to my chest and sank back in bed as my heart began to slow to its normal pace. My eyes blinked, straining to adjust to the light from the lamp. A single tap came at my door and my heart picked up again.

"Claire?" Chris asked, softly. He ducked into the room, squinting at the light. "Are you okay? The bloody alarm went off. Sorry about that."

I shook my head. "I'm fine. What happened?"

"No idea. Go back to sleep." He turned and pulled the door.

"What if someone was trying to break in? What if they're in the house?"

He stopped. "I'm sure it was nothing."

"Why would the alarm go off for no reason?" I cringed, knowing I was a word or two away from pissing him off again.

"I'll check the house. See you in the morning."

"No. Don't go." I immediately regretted what I'd said, wishing it hadn't sounded like desperation. "I'm scared. I want to go with you."

He hesitated before stepping back into the room, leaning against the wall. "So we can both get hacked up by the axe wielding maniac in the living room?" He held a menacing expression that morphed into a smile.

"Will you stop?" I climbed out of bed and twisted my tank top back into place.

"Your hair looks lovely."

I flattened my hand on top of my head. "At least I have hair."

"Ouch." He peered at me with eyes that had regained their clarity. We stepped into the hallway and he flipped on several switches, illuminating the living room and foyer. "No maniacs in here. Let's try the kitchen." He walked ahead of me and I was mesmerized by the bare skin of his back and his navy blue boxers circling his hips. "I'll go first. Run for it if you hear me scream."

"Very funny."

He flipped on more lights and again, nothing. "I think we're safe." He went straight for the fridge and began rummaging, sliding drawers and clanging glass together. "Hungry?"

"Not really."

"Too much healthy stuff in there." He shut the refrigerator and walked into the pantry. "Ooh. What if I told you I have hot fudge?" He slumped against the doorframe and enticed me with a shake of the jar. "Come on. You know you want some."

"You're lucky I bought ice cream." I opened the freezer and plucked the carton from the drawer, turning back to hand it to him.

He nodded at me. "You should probably put a sweater on if

you're that cold." He pointed at my chest. "So that's what they mean when they say it's nippy outside."

My face flushed. "Grow up."

Chris smirked and pursed his lips. His eyes opened wide, as if he couldn't contain whatever was brewing in that head of his. His eyebrows twitched, his forehead wrinkled, and he could no longer hold back his snicker. "That was a good one."

"Oh yeah. A real knee-slapper." I wanted to be annoyed, but I couldn't watch him be happy without feeling it myself. I grinned, but shied away and opened the drawer for some spoons.

He let out a final breathy laugh as he reached up into the cabinet for the bowls. I gawked at him, at his chest and stomach, and felt frozen. *Am I still asleep?*

He removed the top of the carton and began scooping ice cream. "Are you nervous about tomorrow?" he asked. "I don't want you to be nervous."

I snapped out of my daze and put the hot fudge in the microwave. "I can't even think about it."

"You'll do great. She'll love you."

I closed my eyes. "Thanks for the vote of confidence." My hand began to tremble and I steadied it on the counter.

"Too bad it isn't a guy, then you'd have no problem."

I wrapped a kitchen towel around the hot jar and took it to the table. "What does that mean?"

Chris followed with the bowls and sat next to me, brushing my leg with his. He glanced down where our legs had touched, before pretending to ignore it. Taking the jar, he stirred it slowly. "How much do you want?"

"Not too much." My heart thumped in my chest when I thought about our proximity, both of us dressed for bed.

He shook his head. "Talk about a Claire answer." He dug an enormous spoonful of hot fudge and plopped it down on top of the ice cream before sliding the bowl across the table to me. "You know what I mean when I say you'd do better with a guy."

I took a bite of ice cream and the creamy fudge filled my mouth. "Oh, wow. This is good." I sucked the sticky chocolate from my thumb just as I felt his eyes on me. "I want to hear you say it."

He scooped a spoonful from his bowl and it was my turn to ogle him—to study the curve of his lips around the spoon. "Of course you do." He rested his elbow on the table and made a loop in the air with his spoon. "Let's just say that men like you. A lot."

I peered into my bowl. "Some more than others," I muttered.

I looked back and there was a moment of eye contact. His eyes were searching; I thought I saw questions, I even thought I saw the old Chris, but there was no way to know. After last night at dinner, after he'd indirectly told me he still loved me, I still felt as though I was clueless. *Do you still love me?* He was so damn confusing—charming and irresistible one minute, a total dickhead the next. I felt like I was on the crappiest rollercoaster ever. It was torture to sit there and be almost like we used to be —up in the middle of the night, together.

He shook his head and returned to his ice cream. "Let me drive you to your lunch tomorrow."

"Why? Because you don't want me driving your car?"

He sighed. "Just when I thought we were finally getting along." He shook his head. "Don't be so bloody paranoid. I need to pick up an amp at the guitar shop. It's literally around the corner from the restaurant you're going to."

"Oh. Fine."

"Good."

We finished our ice cream without another word. I rinsed our bowls in the sink and he waited for me before he turned off the light. I followed him through the living room and stopped at the guest room door—I half expected him to keep going, but he turned. I wondered if he would say something and my chest heaved while the quiet pounded in my ears; every inch of me ached for him.

"Good night, Claire."

"Good night."

And then I watched him walk away.

———

An uncomfortably hot shower the next morning seemed like a fitting start to my last full day in LA. I rolled my neck and heard the crackling and popping that reminded me that even though I'd tried to get out of it, my fortieth birthday had arrived. Special attention went to my hair and make-up, as I knew would be needed every day from now on. I wanted to show the rest of the world, show Chris, that I could still look good. In black pants and a sleeveless white blouse, I turned in the full-length mirror and knew I'd accomplished that for the day.

When I came out of my room, Chris was sprawled out on the living room couch, reading a book. He lowered it and looked up at me, smiling—again, a bizarre sight and not because he resembled a skinny Fidel Castro in his stupid beard. "You look great." He stared. "Ready to conquer *Vanity Fair*?"

Where in the hell were you for the last two days?

"I'll get the keys," he added. "We'll take the Mercedes."

I climbed into the passenger seat, feeling more anxious than I'd felt since I arrived, which was saying a lot. He turned the key in the ignition, and the GPS began to talk.

"You kept Lee," I said.

He turned. "What is your obsession with the GPS guy?"

"I'm not obsessed."

He shook his head and closed his eyes for a moment. When he opened them again, the jolt of green pulled on me. "I think I know you pretty well by now. You're obsessed." He smirked and put on his sunglasses before pulling out of the garage.

I leaned on the center armrest, but sat back up when I realized how close we were. "Thanks for driving."

He cleared his throat. "My pleasure." He glanced over at me and rolled his neck as if he was working out a kink.

I dug around in my bag to distract myself from the way his presence made me crazy. I fiddled with the air vents until I remembered how he felt about it. "Sorry, I know that bugs you." I sat back in my seat.

"It's okay."

I sighed. It was impossible to keep from feeling my immense attraction to him, the way he made me tingle.

He pulled over beyond the valet stand when we arrived at the restaurant. "Send me a text when you get the check. I can be here in ten minutes." He took off his sunglasses and gave me another shot of his now bristling eyes. "Good luck. You'll do great. I'm proud of you," he muttered sweetly before patting me on the hand.

CHAPTER FIFTY-ONE

"I'M glad we had the chance to meet. This was very productive." Laura signed the receipt and set the folio aside as the waiter re-filled our water glasses.

"Thank you for everything, for lunch." I tried to contain my excitement at things turning around. My trip hadn't been a complete waste of time and now I had something to look forward to, new purpose, from the ashes of the other disasters in my life.

Laura leaned across the table and her spirals of black hair shielded her face while she looked about the restaurant as if eavesdroppers were everywhere. "I have to ask, are you still seeing Chris Penman?" She had an unrepentant gossipy look in her eye, like your best friend in ninth grade, dying for the dirt on your trip behind the bleachers with the cute boy from biology class. "I was so in love with him when I was in high school." She set her hand to her chest and closed her eyes, drawing up her shoulders.

I smiled, thinking twice. "Not exactly, but we're friends."

"I'm sure you had fun." She winked. "A guy like that is hard to pin down."

"You might meet him in a minute. He's picking me up."

Her eyes grew wide. "You're kidding." She clapped her hands and I caught a glimpse of Laura at seventeen. We would've been great friends.

We stood outside the restaurant, she waiting for the valet and me for Chris, another hot and hazy day in LA. When the Aston-Martin zipped up to the curb, my throat abruptly closed and I found it impossible to focus on anything else when the driver's door opened and his stubbly head emerged. He closed his door and turned as if he was in charge, of everything, with one feature starkly improved. The wretched beard was gone.

Laura leaned over and whispered out of the side of her mouth. "What happened to his hair?"

"Long story."

His purposeful strides brought him right to me. He was finally dressed in something more grown-up than a grubby t-shirt and shorts—jeans that hung loose and an unwrinkled white shirt, an extra button undone.

I thought Laura might pass out when he greeted us with the return of his white-hot smile. I was certainly light-headed.

"Claire, ready?" I remained frozen as he lingered with his eyes on me before he turned to my editor friend. "Hello. You must be Laura. I'm Chris." He shook her hand and she obviously wrestled with when to close her mouth all the way, like a fish flopping around on the dock—she was lucky, he'd kept his sunglasses on.

"It's very nice to meet you, Chris." She managed to say each word at a different pitch and I smiled to myself, knowing how hard it was the first time you were in his presence. She shook it off, slowly, before saying goodbye.

When we walked to the car, he stepped ahead of me and opened my door but it wasn't with a lot of fanfare. I couldn't help but wonder what his game was, and I planned to ask him eventually, but for the moment, I was happy we weren't at each other's throats.

"How'd it go?" he asked, as the car purred and he pulled away from the curb.

He smelled insanely good, like chocolate chip cookies and Coppertone with a musky blend of him and his cologne. I closed my eyes when he down-shifted, imagining that he was driving me back to his palatial home, in the car that cost more than my house, so he could have his way with me.

"It was great. We hit it off right away. We're going to talk about a feature next week."

He smiled. "That's fantastic. Really. You deserve it." He playfully slapped me on the thigh and I stared at my own leg, dumbfounded.

When we pulled past the gate, I recognized the car in the driveway, a faded burgundy Delta 88 Royale—the same car my dad had driven when I was in junior high, except his had been yellow. "Is Helena here?" I asked, again astounded.

"Yes," he turned off the ignition and looked down at his lap. "You were right. The house was a mess. I rang her this morning and apologized."

I was curious about what he'd said or done that required an apology, and wondered if I should say something too; to make sure she stayed. He was lucky to have Helena—a sturdy Croatian woman who smoked like a house on fire and never took crap from anyone. I was sure she'd put up with about five minutes of his bullshit.

I went to the guestroom and tossed my bag on the bed, sitting to take off my shoes, but he followed me.

"What do you want to do this afternoon?"

I looked around the room, searching for hidden cameras and one-way mirrors. "Together?" I felt as though I'd made an embarrassing mistake when I said it, waiting for him to reply that he would never suggest we do something together.

"Yes, together. Do you want to go for a swim?"

I sat still, unable to arrive at a reason why one plus one equaled two again.

"It's not a difficult question, Claire. Yes? No?" He arched his eyebrows. It didn't have the same effect without his hair, but I still loved it when he did that. "Remember, you left your suit the last time you were here." He walked away before I could decide, yelling back to me. "It's in my closet. I'll get it." Sure enough, he brought me my swimsuit, the one I'd bought for our St. Barts trip, and a towel. "Do you need anything else?"

"Um, no." I shook my head. "I'm good."

"Meet you outside."

After some strategic shaving, I changed into my bathing suit and walked through the living room toward the terrace doors. A heavenly smell and the sound of busy humming drew me into the kitchen.

I poked my head in and went to Helena. She wasn't a warm woman, which made the hugs she chose to give out even better. "Helena, I'm so glad you're back. He needs you." Something about her rosy cheeks set in her tired face made me want to squeeze them.

"Yes. The house was so dirty." She took my hand. Her gravelly smoker's voice was sweet and her eyes went soft, the way my mom's did when she felt sorry for me. "He was so sad when he came back from North Carolina. I've never seen him like that before."

My throat felt tight. I saw from the corner of my eye that Chris was skimming leaves from the pool. "What happened when he let you go?" I asked.

"When he fired me?" She planted her hands on her padded

hips, as if she were reprimanding Chris in her mind. Her eyebrows drew close as she told me everything.

"I'm happy it worked out. For both of you." At least his relationship with one woman had been salvaged. I glanced at the kitchen counter and noticed that the photo of Chris and his dad was no longer there. "Did you see a picture on the counter?"

"Christopher took it. He was very happy to see it."

"Oh, good." I tapped the kitchen counter and grinned. "Will you come and say goodbye to me before you leave?"

She twinkled at me, smiling sideways. "I'll be here until tonight. Christopher asked me to make a special dinner for your birthday."

CHAPTER FIFTY-TWO

I SPREAD out my towel on the chaise well aware that he was watching me. Chris was in dark green board shorts, hanging low around his hips, his chest and stomach calling to me from across the pool while he fished for leaves.

His objectives were a complete mystery, although I sensed he had an agenda after I'd spoken with Helena. I didn't recall a time we'd ever talked about my birthday, but maybe we had.

He came over and perched on the edge of the chaise next to mine. "Can I get you a beer? Water?"

"Can I ask what you're doing?"

The enthusiasm drained from his face. "I'm offering to get you something to drink."

I stared at him, wondering if he truly thought I was that dense. "No, I mean, what are you doing? Why are you being nice to me?"

He closed his eyes and dropped his head. "I did a lot of thinking last night. I don't want you to go home thinking of me the way I've been since you got here."

"And?"

"What? I thought we could enjoy an afternoon together. Is that so horrible?"

Again, he had me questioning everything. "That sounds nice, but you just spent the last two days making me cry. You know how I feel. It would make this a lot easier if you told me what you're thinking."

He removed his sunglasses. "Can we see if we can get along for a few hours? I'm not convinced that we can be nice to each other any more."

I had at least ten more questions, all about the conditions under which we would be conducting his social experiment, but I decided that I had nothing to lose. "Okay. I already know we can be nice to each other. You can start by getting me a beer."

He quickly returned with two bottles and a bag of pretzels. It was nice to see him snacking, the return of the perpetual eating machine. I spread SPF fifty on my legs and knew he was watching as soon as I heard him clear his throat. I slowed my hands, thoroughly covering every inch with plenty of lotion—to torture him the way he still tortured me.

"Your bruises are gone," he said, confirming that he had, indeed, been looking. "Do you want me to put sunscreen on your back?" he asked, with a tremor in his voice.

I took a long swig of my beer and flipped over. "That'd be great." I set my head down, watching him squeeze the lotion into his hands. He rubbed them together, making that squishy sound, and I closed my eyes and inhaled the smells that circled —coconut, beer, and him.

His fingers swept my hair out of the way. "Hold on a second," I said and reached behind to unhook the strap across my back. "Don't want any tan lines." He caught himself in mid-action, and I grinned and closed my eyes again, wiggling my hips back and forth to settle in.

His hands on my shoulders were persuasive, turning me to putty, the way he used to. He hadn't touched me like that since before the accident, I'd been in too much pain afterward. We hadn't even had farewell sex before he left, something I'd dwelled on many times.

He progressed to my lower back with kneading fingers and pressing palms and my body responded silently to the pulses his created. He became more at ease with every pass, extending his reach beyond the flat plane of my back. I sank into the towel, allowing myself to enjoy something, and I tried like hell not to assign meaning to any of it. My only regret was that I hadn't left the back of my thighs for him.

"Mmm..." I hummed, when he finished. "Thank you."

"Of course," he said in his softest voice.

"Do you need sunscreen?" I asked, almost hoping that he didn't, so I could stay in my perfect spot.

"Even if I didn't, you know I'd say that I did."

I opened my eyes to an electric smile across his face—he was already on his stomach.

I reached behind me and re-hooked my top before I sat up and flipped the lid of the bottle. He closed his eyes and I thought twice before putting any sunscreen in my hands. I raised the bottle high above my head and took aim. I squeezed, hard. The squirt of lotion came out with more force that I'd planned, splattering wide across his back.

He jerked up onto his elbows. "Hey!" He looked at me and shook his head before he laughed and spread out again. "I was nice when I did your back. You could do the same, you know."

"I have my own methods." I sighed, knowing that was likely the extent of my revenge.

My fingers worked into his unforgettable back, with those deadly dimples above his butt—it was criminal for him to deny me the chance to see them every day.

His shoulders were next and they were beyond familiar; I knew every knobby part of him. I took in a deep breath when the tears began to collect, telling myself to let things go, that it was our last time together, the two of us.

He made a fake snoring sound when I finished and I forced a laugh, tossing the sunscreen on the concrete and lying on my side. I took the last few drinks of my beer and he opened his eyes again. They were becoming more vibrant every time he looked at me.

"You shaved," I said.

He propped himself up on his elbows and brought his hand to his exceptional, angular jaw. "I figured it was time for a change."

"You look a lot better." We connected for a moment and I shuddered on the inside.

"Did I look bad?"

I hesitated, knowing I should try to be nice. "You look better without it." The connection happened again and I had to say something to make it go away. I didn't want to be crushed by something as foolish as hope. "I'm glad Helena's back."

"I think I've gained five pounds since she got here this morning. She made chocolate chip cookies. I probably ate three dozen." He turned to me and rubbed his tempting stomach.

I chewed on my lip. "She said she's making dinner for us tonight. For my birthday."

"That was supposed to be a surprise."

"I didn't even think you knew when my birthday was."

"I didn't. Sam called me last night and told me."

My heart began to gallop as I went over the long list of things she was brave enough to say to him on my behalf. "That was clever of her."

"She's a smart girl. I think she might be smarter than both of us put together." He smiled and shook his head.

"Probably." I agreed, thinking of my dear Sam. "What else did she say?"

"Uh, well, how do I put this?" He rubbed his forehead. "She told me to stop being an ass."

"I need to give her a raise in her allowance."

"I should give her a whole pile of money." He swished his beer and drained it. "We talked for a long time. Hours." He glanced down and stole my breath when he looked back at me. "She loves her mom. Very much."

I ached at the thought of Sam trying to save me, knowing she understood just how miserable I was. Life was going to be so empty without her around the house every day, making everything sweeter with her dour morning moods and irreplaceable observations. "Did she talk to you about my dad?"

He caught my eyes with his gaze, dreamy and thoughtful. "She did. But let's take this one step at a time."

CHAPTER FIFTY-THREE

MY ONLY INSTRUCTIONS were to dress for dinner. I sorted through the oddball mix of clothing in my suitcase, choosing the black skirt that Chris had once described as a second skin and another of my sleeveless tops, in dark purple. It flaunted my limited assets as well as possible.

He was sitting on the couch when I came out of my room. "Wow." He stood and his eyes were all over me, the way they used to be. "I always loved you in that color."

My eyes met his and I wanted to move closer, but I froze. He inched toward me, smiling. Every step closer made my heart pump with anticipation. He grasped my elbow and kissed me softly on the cheek. It was only a peck but it reverberated through my entire body. "Happy birthday," he muttered.

"Thank you," I whispered, looking at the floor to distract myself. I eyed him on the way back—devastating in impeccable black trousers and a dress shirt in deep French blue, worn the way he liked to wear them.

"I noticed you aren't wearing your bracelet. It should've come back by now."

I found it hard to get past my throat. "I brought it with me, in case you wanted it back."

His brows pinched together, but I still wasn't sure what he was thinking, what he wanted to do about things, if anything. "The bracelet is yours, Claire." His voice became eerily soft. "You should wear it tonight, for your birthday."

I didn't want to be rude, and I crossed my fingers that politeness wouldn't make my heartache worse, although it was hard to imagine that there was a lower place to go. I walked to the guestroom to retrieve the bracelet from my suitcase and felt him behind me.

"Let me do the clasp." He reached around me and lifted it from the blue box. His unforgettable smell washed over me.

I focused on his warm fingers against my wrist. He spun the bracelet in a circle and the weight of the charm dropped and dangled. I swayed, my wrist hovering in mid-air. "You changed the inscription."

It sounded as though he held his breath. "I did."

"I can't do this if you don't mean it," I blurted. "I'm serious. It will literally kill me. You'll have a dead woman in your house."

He scanned my face, seemingly with deep consideration. "I swear I don't want to hurt you. I'm trying as hard as I can."

I took the stairs down to the pool where Helena had set the outdoor dining table for two, with wine glasses and white tulips. Chris had said he'd be right down. The sun was beginning to set, as if he'd choreographed every unbelievably romantic detail of the scene, which he'd undoubtedly done.

Everything he did or said pulled at my heart. I only hoped that he wasn't about to lead me into another circular argument, our road to nowhere. Music came drifting from the outdoor speakers and Chris turned up a moment later with cocktails.

"Mojitos. My favorite. Thank you."

"For your birthday."

I peered up at him, driving myself crazy trying to read every movement in his face. "Wow." I sputtered after I took a sip. "The Croatians pour a strong drink." I nearly sprayed him with what tasted like straight rum.

"Really? Sorry." He plucked a spoon from the table and took my drink, stirring it. "Try that. Sorry, I'm not the best bartender."

I drank, the sugar on the rim sticking to the corner of my mouth and the mint still swirling with the ice. "Better, but it still tastes like you're trying to get me drunk."

"I am trying to get you drunk." His cheeks flushed. "That'll make things much easier."

"What, exactly?"

The air stayed in place, unmoving. "Explanations. Apologies."

Helena came down the stairs with white dinner plates. She had a motherly smile for me when she reached the table, but gave Chris half a smirk. Chris pulled my chair out for me and I looked up to see him and Helena having a lengthy back and forth with their eyes.

"Helena, this looks and smells amazing. Thank you."

She described the meal of braised pork and roasted vegetables without flowery words, even though I knew she put a lot of love into everything she cooked. I wished I was able to savor every bite, but my brain wouldn't allow that, not when there was so much other meaty material to obsess over.

After Helena brought wine and left again, things became awkward, the lull in the conversation was hefty, especially after he'd promised explanations and apologies. We ate while watching the way the sky changes when the sun leaves for the day.

"So..." He cleared his throat.

BRING ME BACK   343

"Yes?"

He swallowed. "Sam isn't the only person I spoke to last night. She asked Graham and Angie to call me. Graham was a complete wanker about it. I never told him that we broke up. Angie was much nicer, but she isn't happy with me either." He took a long drink of water.

"Wow. I wonder how Sam got Angie's phone number."

"She told me she hacked into your email account. She put your dad on the phone with me, too. He's a talker once you get him going."

"What'd he say?" I squeezed my napkin in my lap and dug into my own hands with my nails.

"We talked about everything that happened. It's hard to know with your dad, but I feel like we understand each other now."

"Did he explain himself?"

He took another sip of water and his voice cleared. "He did. I know you think that he doesn't care, but he really does." He looked at me with an intensity I hadn't seen in a long time and his voice began to shake. "It's hard for him, the emotions, and that was where he was coming from when he told me to stay away from you. He was—" He looked away, composing himself again. "After the accident, he was scared. He didn't want you to get hurt. I don't blame him. I was scared too."

"But I still don't understand why you took him seriously, especially when you know how I feel about his opinions."

His voice became softer. "Because if I was going to be in your life, I wanted us to have everything. I didn't want you to have to schedule birthdays or Christmas around the fact that your dad and I couldn't get along. That he didn't want me around. I didn't want that for you."

"But—"

"Hold on." He held up his finger, his annoying and insulting finger, but now I could appreciate it. "You need to understand something. I felt so unsure of myself when you were in the hospital. Your dad wanted me gone and Jeremy was mucking about and I don't know, I suppose I felt like I wasn't good enough for you."

I took a deep breath, held in place by everything he said.

"Then I bought the car and that opened up a whole new can of worms, but I was so angry with your dad at that point that I had to follow through. After he asked me to break it off, I was worried that the car had been an empty gesture, that maybe I wasn't capable of giving you what you need, of truly loving you. I honestly thought your dad was right about everything. I've never been so confused in my entire life, and I'm not used to being confused. I'm the guy who always has everything under control."

Now that we were finally getting somewhere, Helena appeared to take our plates and pour the remaining wine. "Birthday cake?" she asked.

Chris and I looked at each other—I wanted to be alone, to continue on the still undetermined path.

"I don't know about you, Chris, but I'm stuffed. Maybe later?" I glanced up at Helena, but she and Chris were exchanging looks, this time she smiled wide at him.

"Of course. It'll be in the kitchen. I hope you have a wonderful birthday, Claire. I'm very glad you came back." She leaned down to give me a hug and whispered, "I'm not the only one."

CHAPTER FIFTY-FOUR

"I'M GOING to change the music," Chris said. "I'll be right back."

Moments later, I heard the opening strains of my favorite Stevie Wonder song, *Golden Lady*, a song dripping with sex and romanticism, for me at least.

He seemed so pleased with himself when he emerged from the house, exactly like he was up to no good. "I was hoping to dance with the birthday girl." He wiggled his fingers at me. His smile, his hand, even his damn eyebrows—he was using every unfair advantage he had.

"Dancing?"

"It's your birthday. We should dance." He pursed his lips. "Come on."

I stood. I wanted to be close to him, but it felt as though I was stepping foot into the lion's den. My body quivered as we were drawn to each other and his hand slid to my back. Of the many times he'd put his hand there, including the day after we met, it had never felt like that, never so tortuous. He tightened his embrace and I swallowed, hard. We swayed from side to side and I followed his lead, lulled into a false sense of security as he eased the side of his face against my hair.

"You aren't being fair." I sighed and closed my eyes, over-whelmed by his presence—the feel of his strong and bony shoulder coupled with his seductive smell, the way he once made me feel protected, his undeniable pull on me.

"I don't know what you're talking about." He spun us around.

"Yes, you do. You know I can't resist you when you're like this." I willed my shoulders to relax, but they would only go so far. My body craved his more than I thought possible. "It isn't fair."

Our dance slowed to nothing more than the shifting of weight from foot to foot. We went without speaking for minutes and his breath became uneven. "Claire, none of this is fair," he said, lightly touching the back of my head. "It isn't fair that I'm desperate for a baby and you're not sure. It isn't fair that we live three thousand miles apart." His hand moved between my shoulder blades and he pressed us so close that I felt his chest rise and fall with each breath. "It isn't fair that I can't get over you, that I wake up in the middle of the night and feel you next to me even when I know you're not there."

The sensation spread from my shoulders inward and into my throat; a mix of the way I felt every time he gave me the look and the way I felt the day he'd left. "I thought you didn't want to talk about those things anymore," I mumbled, the words strug-gling to make their way out of me.

He stopped moving, but he didn't let go and we stood, frozen in time. He sighed before turning his nose and lips into my hair. He whispered, "I don't want to talk about it, but I can't stand to leave things the way they are, like this. It isn't right." He combed his fingers through a few strands of my hair. "What made you come back? I was sure you were gone forever."

I allowed myself the luxury of his face. The color in his eyes had resurfaced as if the lights had been turned back on, incredible green lights. "I wasn't gone. You were." I watched as he listened and I felt his breath on my lips. "And I tried to, but I couldn't convince myself that you didn't love me anymore."

Tears welled in his eyes and he waited, possibly for the right words to say. "I was a bloody git to ever hurt you. I'm so sorry. I'll say I'm sorry every day for the rest of my life if that's what it takes for you to forgive me." He sighed again, as if he was shedding weight, and pushed my hair behind my ear. "I mean it. I'm truly sorry for everything I did wrong."

"Please don't do that," I muttered. "You know I hate it when my hair's behind my ear."

"You're so funny." A smile slowly spreading across his face.

"But, I'm not funny. I'm just me." I took in a deep breath, desperate to reclaim what was rightfully mine. "Listen, I love you, you...big British jerk. I can't be away from you because it's killing me. We have to figure this out or else, I don't know...or else I'm going to have to kick your ass." Now I could laugh, a tear making its way down my cheek.

Chris started to laugh too and everything that had once held us together grew again, standing up and coming back to life. It felt as if the whole world was splitting open, making way for everything between us. "I certainly don't want that. I don't know that my ego would ever recover."

"I'm sorry, too." I drew in a breath slowly. "I know I hurt you. I never wanted to do that."

We focused on each other for a heartbeat or two, his tingly hands gripping my shoulders, and I hoped like I'd never done before. I hoped it all was really happening, that it wasn't just a dream. It was like watching a movie at half speed, the film clicking and creeping through the projector, pops of black and light.

He set his lips against mine with gentle hesitation, resting a few unsteady fingers on my cheek. We didn't move—we resisted. The only sound was breathing; I couldn't even hear the music anymore. Then he leaned in, his lips parted slightly and it jolted me, unleashing my impatience for him. I smashed my body into his and grabbed the back of his head. I told him exactly how I felt without words. Like a little girl hungry for cinnamon rolls on Christmas morning with a box of kittens under the tree, I wanted everything I could squeeze from that moment.

"Okay. Wow," he said breathlessly, resting his forehead on the top of my head. "After that, I'll give you whatever you want. You can drive my Porsche to the grocery store. Actually, just take the blooming car." He laughed like the old Chris, *my* Chris.

The laugh, the look on his face, the last five minutes—everything I'd longed for was right there, mine for the taking. I kissed him quickly. "I couldn't care less about cars." I grabbed his hand and marched to the stairs.

He lagged behind me. "Where are we going?"

We continued up the stairs and I tugged on his arm. "Come on."

He laughed. "Am I in trouble already? I just finished saying I was sorry."

I yanked on the sliding door handle and we stepped inside before I turned and kicked off my shoes. "Hurry up." I walked backwards, pulling him along, my heart pumping against my chest.

A handsome smirk spread across his face. "Where are you taking me?"

"We're making the trek."

I came to a halt in his bedroom doorway and watched his lips form a devilish smile. I unbuttoned his shirt in seconds flat and pushed it off his shoulders. My hand smoothed over his chest and I swallowed a breath as he caught me with a look I'd never seen before—like a new version of his trademark look, but better, tickled and intoxicating.

He set a finger against the skin of my throat and traced along my neckline. My heart began beating even more forcefully than when he'd kissed me. It was the oddest sensation, beating more slowly, but growing stronger.

"I love you, Claire," he whispered. He pressed his lips to my cheek as he began to unbutton my blouse.

I had to close my eyes to get my bearings. His words and face were too powerful a combination. "I love you, too. I do. I never want to be apart from you again."

He wrapped his hand around the back of my neck and rubbed his thumb along my jaw. "I'll come to stay with you until Sam goes to college. Then we'll make another plan."

I unbuckled his belt before he shot me a flicker of his green eyes and unhooked my bra. I dropped his pants to the floor and he peeled away my black skirt.

"Will that make you happy?" he asked.

"Sounds perfect."

His eyes became smoky. "Good. No more talking." He led me to the bed, where he tossed aside the pillows and threw back the covers. He sat, stretched out his long body and I followed.

I kissed him, eagerly, and slid my hand down his stomach and under the waistband of his boxer shorts. A relieved moan came from him, escaping between our lips. "Does that feel good?" I asked as I pushed away his boxers.

He cleared his throat. "Of course it does, but I'm serious. No talking." He propped himself up on his elbow and gently set his hand on my hip. "I never thought this would happen. Let me make love to you." He pushed me to my back and skimmed my neck, and then my chest, with his lips.

He chipped away at my heart with each kiss, his nimble

fingers working their way over every part of me. He'd stop now and then to look at me, telling me how he felt with his eyes.

We took our time, moving in our own rhythm, and my heart swelled, knowing that Chris and I, together, was exactly what love felt like.

CHAPTER FIFTY-FIVE

IT WAS dark when I opened my eyes. I shut them slowly, asking myself if it was real. Then I heard him breathing, followed by a mumble—something about me, although the words were mostly indecipherable. The bed rocked as he flopped over and dropped his gangly arm across my stomach. He nuzzled his face into my neck and I settled my head against his.

I'd only been dozing, I couldn't fall asleep for real—there was too much to think about, an abundance of happy things. Chris didn't share my problem. He'd fallen asleep soon after we made love. I would've relished one of our all-night talks, but it didn't bother me that he was sleeping. I hoped it meant he was content and relaxed; something neither of us had been in a long time.

He stirred again and rubbed my stomach. "Are you awake?" He mumbled against my collarbone. "Get some sleep. Stop obsessing."

I laughed quietly. "How do you know I'm obsessing?"

"You're Claire. If you're awake, you're obsessing."

"There's a lot to think about." I turned on to my side and put my arm around his waist.

"Uh, huh. That's what morning's for." His voice trailed off.

He was right. I *was* obsessing. I'd thought about it non-stop since I'd found the books in the baby's room. I couldn't stop thinking about a baby—the baby we'd lost, what it would be like if we tried again.

My memories of those days with Sam came back as they often did, except now I found myself drawn to the good ones— the look in my dad's eyes when he first held her, the way she got delightfully hyper when she had chocolate, and the many nights she'd climbed into bed with me. I'd been scared for most of those years, unsure of how I would pay the bills or doubting my ability to be a good mom. I didn't have to be scared the second time if I got the chance. I wouldn't have to be alone.

I'd imagined the child we might have, hopefully as beautiful as Chris with my mom's freckles and natural musical talent. Maybe even a writer. I pictured Sam as the super cool big sister, reading bedtime stories while home during college breaks. And my dear old grumpy father would be jubilant to have another grandchild on which to dote.

I knew that Chris would miss a lot if he never experienced parenthood. He'd never know it was like putting on a pair of glasses when you'd always thought you had perfect vision. Everything in the world, beautiful or horrible, became painted in a completely different palette, in the most vivid colors and painstaking detail.

I also knew that Chris would make an incredible dad, but his desire to become one was more than an unfulfilled wish, it was part of what made me love him so much. He'd be an amazing husband too, if I decided to nudge him in that direction. It was hard to believe that Claire Louise Penman might become my real name one day.

"Chris? Are you awake?"

"Not really," he grumbled, in the cutest way possible. "Are you okay?"

"I want to have a baby." I didn't believe the words at first, but they felt so right once they were out of my mouth.

He coughed. "I'm up." He rolled away and turned on the bedside lamp before flipping back and squinting at me with heavy eyelids. "Really? Seriously?"

"Yes, really. I wouldn't say it if I didn't mean it."

He scooted closer and scanned my face, the green sweeping back and forth. "You want to have a baby, with me?"

"I'm certainly not planning on having a baby with someone else."

He watched me as a grin crept across his face. "You aren't just giving in. You really want a baby."

"I really want a baby. With you."

He laughed quietly and rubbed his thumb along my lower lip. It made me a bit woozy. "Do you have any idea how happy that makes me?"

"I have a pretty good idea."

"You do realize we forgot a condom earlier."

"Uh, yeah, I was there. Remember?" I nodded. "I guess I wasn't thinking straight." He drew me in with his eyes and that made the tears start in my own. "Either that or I already knew I wanted to do this."

"This is amazing. I mean, wow." He shook his head and smiled. "Bloody unbelievable."

"You have to promise you'll help me in the middle of the night when the baby's crying. We have to do all of it together. The laundry and making school lunches and all of the other things I wished I had help with when Sam was little."

"Of course." He circled his arms around me, smoothly

sliding a hand over my hip to my butt. "I can't wait to do those things."

My heart puffed up inside my chest, feeling a bit spoiled. "And I want one more thing from you."

"Why am I not surprised?" He nibbled at my neck, driving me completely nuts.

"Please tell me you'll grow your hair back."

"You don't like the bald is beautiful look?" He scrubbed the top of his head and bent his eyebrows.

"I prefer your hair." I bit my lip. "I need something to dig my hands into."

His eyes flashed. "Sold. I'm definitely growing it back." He kissed me tenderly, his tongue sweeping along my lip as his hands worked their way down my back. He stopped and rolled back to switch off the light, granting me a glimpse of his butt and those incredible dimples.

"Well, then," I said. "I guess everything's decided. That was easy. See? We can make decisions together." I fluffed my pillow. "You and I are officially trying to get pregnant."

He pulled me close with urgency, sending tingles through my entire body. He rubbed his nose against mine before he mumbled into my neck. "Officially trying to get pregnant, right now."

THE END

Want more Chris and Claire?
Download the sequel, Back Forever, today!

"Poignant, bittersweet and satisfying, "Back Forever" sustains the plausible fantasy-to-reality charm of "Bring Me Back".”-Book Crush

EXCERPT: BACK FOREVER, THE SEQUEL TO BRING ME BACK

Back together, Christopher is determined to have everything he ever wanted with Claire. But a ring and a baby on the way can't prepare them for the test they never saw coming.

Chapter One

Claire's sideways "What are you up to Penman?" grin was always at the ready. "Looking for something?" She rolled to her stomach, draping an arm across the pillow.

Her bottomless blue eyes stopped me in my tracks. They captivated me in a way that I'd tried like hell to put into words, but I always fell short. As well as I'd done in my music career, turning tales of women and love into song lyrics, attempting to distill anything about Claire into a few lines of poetry only reminded me that I had a lot to learn.

Still in boxer shorts after unearthing my trousers from the clothes slung over a chair, I traipsed across the aging hardwoods of her bedroom. At some point, she'd need to admit that her house was no longer quaint—it was bursting at the seams. It had been nearly four months of cohabitation and I was still living out of two sticky, stubborn drawers she'd emptied in her bureau.

"I'm sorry I woke you." I plopped down on the mattress, scratching my head. My hair was thankfully returning after I'd had the not-so-brilliant idea of shaving it. "I was trying to be quiet."

"You're sweet, but you're not quiet." She eased back to her side and stretched. "What time is it anyway?"

"Nearly six. Your dad wanted to run some supplies to the recording studio before I take you to the airport."

"Why am I not surprised?"

I circled my finger on the creamy bare skin of her arm. Without fail, it thrilled me to see that my touch gave her goose bumps. "How are you feeling this morning? Still no sign of your monthly visitor?"

"My monthly visitor? You sound like my grandmother."

"Come on. I'm just excited." I smiled and peeled the covers back. "Scoot over."

"Isn't my dad waiting for you?" She slid to the middle of the bed and I cozied up next to her. She giggled as I nosed around in her neck, a musical sound that produced welcome tremors in my body.

"Your father can wait fifteen minutes."

"Is that all I get?"

"Unfortunately, my dear, I doubt I can give you the full business this morning. Richard is far too punctual for that to happen." I propped myself up on my elbow and combed my fingers through her tangled, flaxen hair. "I was just hoping for a bit of a morning snog."

"I'm sure I have the worst breath." She quickly clasped her fingers over her lips.

"I'll take my chances." I pried her hand away and pressed

my mouth against hers. Even the subtlest sense of surrender had me eager to take her. *Damn her father and his schedule.* I reluctantly put on the brakes and kissed her forehead. "How many days late are we?"

"We?" She grinned, as sunlight filtered into the room and cast her in an unearthly, angelic light.

"Yes. We."

"Only two."

"Two days is better than none."

"I could take a test when I get back from New York tomorrow if you want."

"I don't want to wait that long. Let's do it now."

"It's pretty soon. It might be a waste of a pregnancy test."

"Do you honestly think I care about that?" Delayed gratification had never been my strong suit, and my impatience was much worse with this matter. A lifetime was a terribly long time to wait.

Claire tugged on my earlobe with her fingers, a seemingly innocent move that zipped electricity along my spine. "No. I don't suppose you care about that." Her forehead crinkled as she studied my face. "If we're going to do it, it has to be now. It's more accurate right when you wake up, when your pee is concentrated."

"Mmm. I love it when you talk about things like tests and urine."

"You have to promise not to get too excited. The test could very easily be negative and then you'll only be disappointed."

I skimmed my finger along the contours of her collarbone. "I don't think it's possible for me to be too excited. And of course, I'll be disappointed. I'd be lying if I said I wouldn't be, but we just keep on trying. I like that part."

"I know. I do too. I just don't want you to get your hopes up."

"We've been trying for four months. It's got to happen soon." I caught uncertainty in her eyes. "You aren't worried that something's wrong, are you?"

"No, not really." She shook her head. "But you're going to be forty-five this year and I'm already forty. It could take some time."

"It's not going to take me long to get you pregnant. I was bloody accurate the first time."

She twisted her plump, raspberry-pink lips. "I'm not a carnival game. You aren't swinging a mallet to ring the bell. Maybe the first time was a fluke. A lot of women have fertility issues at my age."

"As far as I'm concerned, we're a couple of kids." I gently lifted her tank top and kissed her stomach. "Hopefully there's a little nipper already in the oven, and if not, we try again." I circled my finger on her belly. "I vote that we take the test." I rolled out of the bed and pulled the covers back. "M'lady."

Claire scooted across the mattress. "Here goes nothing." She ran her hands through her messy blonde bedhead, shuffling into the bathroom. The cabinet door creaked when she opened it and took one of the pregnancy tests from our small stockpile.

"Do you really want to be in here for this?" She broke the seal on the box and unwrapped the test stick.

My brow furrowed. "Of course. I've been in the loo while you peed, darling. This is hardly new territory."

"Okay. If you say so."

I searched in the medicine cabinet for a distraction. Claire already felt enough pressure. I didn't want to make it any worse. *Band-aids? No. Pain reliever? I don't have a headache. Ah, yes, dental floss.*

She placed the cap on the test stick and set it on the side of the sink. "Get your watch. It takes five minutes."

I stumbled into the bedroom. Much like the rest of the

house, the top of the bureau was a mess of her things and mine, co-mingling. Under a few t-shirts, I found my watch. "Do we do four minutes since it took me a minute to find it?"

"No, just do five," she called back above the sound of rushing water in the sink. "It's the same difference."

I returned to the bathroom and tried not to steal a peek at the dreaded stick. She lowered the toilet lid and sat, so I took a spot on the edge of the tub.

My mind was a torrent of nervous anticipation. Something felt different, but perhaps that was wishful thinking. *Is she? She really could be. Our baby could be inside her right now.*

Claire crossed her legs and ran her hand along the bare skin of her calf. "I need to shave."

"I didn't want to say anything last night, but you are getting to be a bit scratchy."

She frowned in an entirely adorable way. "Gee. Thanks."

"Honestly? I hadn't noticed at all." I glanced at the watch. Only two minutes into this exercise in mental torture. *Bloody hell.* "You're perfect just the way you are."

Her chin dropped. "That's very sweet."

There it was—the look on her face, the early morning sun streaming through the bathroom window, seconds ticking away at a snail's pace—a moment captured in my consciousness. Something monumental was about to happen. It made the hair on my arms stand on end.

My vision dropped to the watch again. "One more minute. Can we look?"

She shook her head vehemently. "No. Just wait."

"But I don't like to wait."

She smiled. "I know you don't. It's adorable. And a little annoying."

I consulted my nemesis, the watch, again. "Ten seconds."

"Hold my hand." She reached for me, her fingers wagging. "We close our eyes and open them on three."

"Deal." I stood as she did, enveloping her hand with mine. My eyes clamped shut as ordered, she began to count.

"One...Two...Two and a half..."

"Very funny."

She giggled. "Three. Open."

I blinked. I focused.

There it was.

One blue line.

Bugger.

I caught the sigh before it left my throat. Sharing my disappointment would only make her feel worse. I tugged her into an embrace, pressing my cheek to the side of her head. My fingers trailed through her silky hair. "Weren't we just saying how much we like trying?"

She managed a quiet laugh, but trembled beneath my touch. "I didn't want to say anything, but I actually thought I was pregnant."

The admission only made me hold on tighter, never wanting to let her go. She wanted this as badly as I did and I'd talked her into taking the test. "It's okay, darling. Really. And it's still early, right? We could do another test in a few days if you're still late." I choked back intruding tears. "I love you so much, Claire. That's all that matters."

"I love you too. I'm just ready for this to happen. I don't like feeling like our life is on hold."

"Do you really feel that way?" *You know she's right. Our life is on hold.*

"Yes. I hate seeing that look of disappointment on your face. I want to give this to you and it hasn't happened."

"I don't want it to be more important than us." *You're all that matters.*

"You can't deny that you want this very, very badly."

"I don't want it as much as I want you." *Am I the most daft man on the face of the planet?* Without another moment wasted, I dropped to my knee, which hurt like hell when it thudded against the tile floor. "Ow."

"Chris, what are you..." She looked down at me with genuine puzzlement, certainly warranted as she was in her pajamas, me in my boxer shorts, both of us in the bloody bathroom for God's sake. *Not the most glamorous of settings, but I think it works.* Her lips were lovely and pouty. *Get on with it so you can kiss her.*

I took one of her hands, but failed to catch the other before it flew to her mouth. Her deep blue eyes were wide with wonder.

I cleared my throat and took a deep breath. I had one shot at getting this perfect. "Claire Abby, I love you more than I have ever loved another human being." The words left me feeling as though my heart might burst out of my chest. "You are the most extraordinary and wonderful and frustrating woman I have ever met and I want you to be mine forever."

She gasped. A giggle leaked out of her.

"Did you squeak, darling?"

"Maybe." Her shoulders shook, her eyes watered. "Please, go on."

"I want you to be mine. Forever. Even if we never get to have a child together, I'm never letting you go. That is, if you'll have me. Claire, will you marry me?"

Her other hand dropped and she smiled in a way that left her cheeks as full as ripe peaches on a summer day, mine for the picking. Her face was such a distraction that for a heartbeat or two, I didn't realize she hadn't yet answered the question. I wagged an eyebrow, hoping she had no defense for that.

"Well?" I asked.

"Shhh." Her smile returned as soon as she relaxed her lips.

"Shhh?"

"I'm savoring the moment."

"Why don't we savor the moment after you give me an answer?"

Download Back Forever today!

"I fell even more in love with Claire, Chris and Sam in "Back Forever" than I thought was possible."- Book Crush

ACKNOWLEDGMENTS

I'd like to thank the following people for making Bring Me Back possible.

Steve, my husband, who bites his tongue when I'm acting crazy, smiles when I'm happy, listens when I'm sad and loves me always.

Sara, my cheerleader, who believed in Christopher and Claire from the first word and begged me to keep going.

Karen Stivali, my critique partner, who pushes me to get better and is available when needed to yank me back from the brink.

Celia Rivenbark, Margaret Ethridge, and Piper Trace, who are always generous with authorial expertise, friendship, and off-color jokes.

The dedicated and talented women of my original publisher, Turquoise Morning Press, especially Kim Jacobs, Shelley Stevens, and my amazing editor, Suzanne Barrett.

The legion of early readers: Karrie Adamany, Angie Mack, Lisa Kaylie, Evette Horton, Christie Oppliger, Mairead Maloney, Laurie Cochenour, Amy Barefoot, Smudge Spooner, Jill Mango, Sarah Austin, Jennifer Resnick, Ashley Mattison,

Monica Meyers-Shelton, Annette Pratts, Diane Badzinski, Kelley Amrein, Maura Partrick, Shannon Murley, Jenn Prenda, Tema Larter, Jennifer McCafferty, Jane Greathouse, Susie Lektorich, Rita Robbins, and Diane Tameecha.

The superhuman women of Daily Duranie, Rhonda Rivera and Amanda Pustz. You helped me find an entire community of kick-ass readers.

Thanks also to Dad, Mom, Judy, and Margaret for parental avoidance of the sex scenes.

Other folks who helped along the way with advice and encouragement: John Strohm, Sarah Dessen, Heather Ross, Jay Faires, Pat Cudahy, Jared Resnick, Sam Stephenson, Nic Brown, Django Haskins, Tom Maxwell, David Dunton, Andrea Somberg, Regina Joskow, and Billy Maupin.

Special thanks to Bobbi Ruggiero for believing in Bring Me Back and telling Patience Bloom to read it. Special thanks to Patience Bloom for bringing me aboard at Harlequin as a result. Special thanks to Melissa Jeglinski and the Knight Agency for representing me as a result of that. (It's all connected, people.)

Extra special thanks to Peter Case for the irreplaceable and perfect lyric that inspired the title Bring Me Back.

ABOUT THE AUTHOR

Karen Booth is a midwestern girl transplanted in the South, raised on '80s music and too many readings of "Forever" by Judy Blume. An early preoccupation with rock 'n' roll led her to spend her twenties working her way from intern to executive in the music industry. Now she's a married mom of two and instead of staying up late in rock clubs, she gets up before dawn to write sexy contemporary romance and women's fiction.

Thank you for reading! If you enjoyed this book, please leave a review with your favorite online retailer or on Goodreads. Even if it's only a few words, it means so much!

Stay in touch!
karenbooth.net
karen@karenbooth.net

ALSO BY KAREN BOOTH

Back Forever

Save a Prayer - a prequel to Bring Me Back

Claire's Diary - a prequel to Bring Me Back

Hiding in the Spotlight

Rock Starred

The KISS Principle

Love Plus One

The Langford Family series:

That Night with the CEO

Pregnant by the Rival CEO

The Ten-Day Baby Takeover

The Locke Legacy series:

Pregnant by the Billionaire

Holiday Baby Bombshell

Between Marriage and Merger

The Eden Empire series:

A Christmas Temptation

A Cinderella Seduction

A Bet with Benefits

Made in the USA
Monee, IL
25 April 2024

57506831R00207